THE SEA OF ZEMIRA

A Fantasy Pirate Romance

D. L. Blade

To Tammy, the Enjoy the adventure!

D. L. Blade

Website: dlbladebooks.com
Instagram: instagram.com/booksbydlblade

Editing by Laura M. Morales
Book design by Laura M. Morales
Proofreading by Courtney Caccavallo
Formatting by Affordable Formatting
Illustrations by Larissa Wolf
Sea shanty: *Sam's Cursed Rhyme*, composed by Rich Maschner, exclusively for *The Sea of Zemira*

Printed and bound in the United States of America.
Second printing edition, June 2021
ISBN: 9781734415254
Published by Fifth Element Publishing. Author, D.L. Blade

ALSO BY D.L. BLADE

The Chosen Coven Trilogy

The Dark Awakening (The Chosen Coven Book 1)

The Dark Underworld (The Chosen Coven Book 2)

The Dark Deliverance (The Chosen Coven Book 3)

This book is dedicated to my neighborhood besties: Nicole, Samantha, Nichole, and Kala.
Many nights of drinks, shenanigans, and late-night bonfires in the middle of the cul-de-sac kept me sane as I created this story.

Now, let us drink rum and sing sea shanties together.
Cheers!

Zemira
Marsh Wetlands
Portland Sea
Eastland Forest
Brecken Terrace
Crotona
Westin

ONCE UPON A TIME

The Kingdom of Zemira
One year before the war

King Matthias looked down upon Argon, who knelt on the marble floor of the Grand Royal Hall, hands tied behind his back.

Matthias scowled at the captured Fae, whose tangled hair, as pale as porcelain, framed his beaten face. Argon was revered as one of the folk's most courageous, but the king would be sure to put an end to that.

He would break him.

King Matthias cocked his head to the right; all the hateful things he could do to him swirled in his mind.

"Do you defy my law?" the king spat. Distaste fell on his tongue.

Argon's eyes glared with a brazenness King Matthias was quite used to. "Your laws are not ours."

Matthias's lips curled into a smile as the fairy clenched his jaw when a guard's blow landed at the nape of his neck. A simple punishment would certainly not be enough for that Fae—for any Fae—something much more permanent would be required.

"I see," King Matthias said as he ran his fingers through his wavy, long, thick beard. "If punishment does not suffice; if you are convinced our laws are not your own, then only one option remains. Banishment. For you and all—"

Gasps from onlookers—including an audience of guards, servants, and his own two sons—echoed in the hall.

Queen Serena jolted to her feet from her wooden throne behind him. "Matthias! You can't—"

"I make the laws here, Serena! And they have chosen to disobey it!" he shouted at his wife, watching the look of dread pass across her pale features.

Slowly, Matthias turned back to Argon. "May no man, fairy, elf, or troll deem themselves greater than I!"

The queen sat back down.

Matthias knew how desperately she would want to intervene, as she always did. He would make sure she was suitably punished for her outburst later.

The king cleared his throat. "I, hereby, banish all creatures in this land who hold magic," he ordered. "My word is the law."

The crowd buzzed, and Argon squinted.

"Where—but where will we go?" he asked, his voice trembling from the shock.

A cruel smile crept its way onto the king's lips. He

loomed over his prisoner and, after a moment's pause, bent down until his lips were nearly brushing the fairy's ear.

"Into extinction," the king whispered so no one else could hear. "Into *absolute* nothingness."

Footsteps resounded through the room, bouncing off the high ceilings, and Matthias snapped back to attention, satisfied with the defeated look on Argon's face. Queen Serena, again arisen from her throne, crept cautiously to his side.

"I know—if I may suggest—a place, Matthias?" her voice stammered. "Please, my love. *Not* the Marsh Wetlands. They would die there."

The king's mouth came to a flat line but nodded for her to continue. Whatever place she suggested was irrelevant.

Zemira was, in Matthias's eyes, the jewel of his kingdom. They were teeming with life and abundant with food. From the mountain ranges to the evergreen woods, nowhere else would compare.

Magic ought to die no matter where it went. Bringing the Fae's demise was all King Matthias cared for.

"There's a place," she started, as she tugged at her dress, "The Eastland Forest. It is a seven-day journey by ship. The fruit is sometimes ripe, and the water is mostly clean. Though it is not as wonderous as Zemira, you may survive there, Argon. If your people can brave the wilderness, you can make your own laws, be your own ruler."

As much as the king wanted to punish the Fae for their defiance, as much as he wished for their complete annihilation, forcing them to the Marsh Wetlands would yield nothing but war.

The creatures had too many beastly allies who would fight alongside them. War was certainly not something Matthias had the upper hand on.

So, he resolved to go along with his wife's suggestion. The chances of them perishing were still high; it would keep him and his people protected from an uproar.

But the annihilation would come. Sooner or later.

The king stepped back, his arms out, and bowed to Serena, though his eyes never left the defeated Fae on the floor. "I accept. Will you do the honors?"

Serena extended out her hand. Mason, the head of the king's guard, rushed over from his perch and handed the queen a sword.

The king placed a hand on the small of her back to steady her.

"By order of the King and Queen of Zemira, I, hereby, banish you, Argon, along with all fairies, elves, trolls, pixies, dragons, and other magical beings, from these lands on which we rule," Serena said.

The king's chest swelled with pride until he noticed a single tear trickling down his wife's cheek as she sucked in an audible breath and placed the shiny blade lightly on Argon's shoulder. Then, she moved the sword over his head, landing on his other shoulder, and said, "I grant you the title of King of the Eastland Forest."

She withdrew the sword from the newly appointed Fae king and placed it by her side. "Once you and your kind leave our land, you will no longer be under King Matthias's rule. But if you are to ever declare war—"

"I understand," Argon said softly. "It's okay."

Serena gave Argon a brief nod, but their eyes seemed to linger for just a moment too long—so long, King Matthias grabbed her by the wrist and pulled her back to his side.

The king stepped forward and knelt to Argon's level. "Tomorrow at dawn, three ships will await you in the harbor. Then, you will depart our kingdom; should you fail to leave, the blood of your people and those alike will be on your hands."

The king pulled a small knife from his leather boot. Argon flinched.

"Do not fret, Argon; this blade is not for you." King Matthias chuckled as he walked around the fairy to cut loose the rope that held his hands tied. "Not today."

As the ropes fell to the floor, Argon stood. He massaged his raw wrists, and without another word, marched out of the Grand Royal Hall.

King Matthias took his throne, drumming his fingers on the intricately carved, golden armrest. He turned to look towards his wife and two sons, who stood nervously in the corner, along with a handful of servants and guards.

"Mason," the king said, with a nonchalant wave, as he sank back into his chair. "Draw up a letter. Send it to every hellish creature on this land who uses magic. Use your men to deliver this message, if need be. By tomorrow morning, I want magic out of my kingdom."

Queen Serena stood at the edge of the dock, watching the

people she had grown to love, filing in line with their families and boarding onto the ships. The sun lay at the ocean's horizon, spilling hopeful arrays of color into the sky above.

Her cognac-colored eyes flickered from the painted sky to Argon standing in front of her. He smiled weakly. A stabbing pain pierced her heart as she stared into his soulful gaze.

"All will be well, Queen Serena," Argon said, placing a gentle hand upon her cheek. The queen allowed herself to melt into the warmth of his palm. "Do not cry—"

"How can I not?" she choked, her words catching on the lump in her throat. Argon wiped her tears with a soft brush of his thumb. "Magic has a place here. Magic has always had a place here."

She lowered her head. Argon's finger caught her chin and lifted her delicate face back up. He stopped, then pulled his hand back.

"What is it? We have been friends for decades, Argon. I know you," she said, her brows knitting together.

"What if—" He bit his lip. "What if not all of us left?"

Serena shook her head. "He'll kill you. All of you. Here or otherwise, should anyone stay."

Argon smirked. "You underestimate the Elven race, my queen. Their elders raised them from birth to fight injustice. They are quiet, yes, but also strong. Hidden. Discreet. Undetectable."

"Are you suggesting some of them stay?" She arched an eyebrow and took a step closer in case the king's guard across the dock had taken an interest in their conversation.

"And what are you hoping the elves do exactly? Spy on the kingdom?"

Argon nodded.

"To what end?"

Now Argon stepped forward. They were but a breath apart. "I do not question for a moment that the king will declare war on us the moment we show any sign of weakness, regardless of whether we are here or in the Eastland Forest. At least with spies, we will know how soon before he attacks."

Serena rubbed her hands together, attempting to settle the soft tremor. The elves would undoubtedly perish at the hands of Zemiran forces, and magic remaining on crown lands would only antagonize her husband further. But the confidence on Argon's face told another story, one of hope and victory.

She sighed. "And you're certain this plan will work?"

"Yes," he whispered. The touch of his breath upon the queen's neck sent a chill down her spine.

"Okay, Argon," she conceded. "On one condition."

"Anything."

"I oversee their operations; where they hide, what they do, all runs through me. I know Matthias's daily routine. I command the guards. Without me, you're doomed to fail."

Argon nodded and leaned forward, kissing her gently on the cheek with his soft lips. Serena jerked away, barely allowing for a moment of touch between them. His brow furrowed in confusion, and he opened his mouth to speak. She cut him off quickly, nodding curtly in the direction of the guards, who had gotten even closer. Argon's face relaxed, and, with disappointed eyes, took a small step back.

They could not be seen so close.

"Let them believe we've left, and in ten days, I will send my finest warriors to hide amongst your people," he whispered.

A clattering noise from the end of the docks drew their attention. They both glanced up. One of the ships—the largest—was pulling in their gangplank. The few Fae and Elven folk that remained on the docks lined up to board the other two ships.

Argon bowed longer than he should have and then took Serena's hand in his own, laying a gentle kiss upon it.

"It is time for me to leave," he said. "Goodbye, my dear friend."

When Argon looked into her eyes, she wanted to protest, to beg him to stay, but by the time she found the words, her hand had slipped from his, and her life-long friend was marching down the dock to set sail to his new kingdom.

Around every bend, villagers yelled at Queen Serena's carriage and the accompanying guard as they journeyed back to the palace from the docks. The people shook their fists and yelled their outrage at the magical ban as the royal entourage went by.

The guards had to intervene on several occasions, and all the queen could do was hope that the Zemirans, who were only trying to be heard, did not end up in a cell . . . or worse, dead.

Serena breathed loudly as she was escorted to the peace of her chamber, walked across the black hardwood floor, and plopped down face-first on the plush, four-poster bed. She needed an afternoon to herself; she had just agreed to aid foreign spies, after all.

"Serena."

She jolted upright. Hidden in the corner's shadows, her husband stood from the leather chair in which he sat. He strode forward.

"Matthias."

He hovered above her; a crystal glass filled with tea lingered in his hand. "Whispers have reached my ears that you were a little too friendly with the magic folk—"

"I was just saying goodbye," she said a little too quickly, avoiding his gaze.

"Hmm," the king hummed, then took a sip of his tea. "Goodbye indeed."

Serena hesitated for a moment. Perhaps she could sway him to change his mind, to reconsider. She inched forward to the edge of the bed. "The Kingdom is in an uproar, Matthias. Perhaps—"

"Perhaps, nothing," he scowled, turning towards the window. The venom in his voice stung like a thousand needles. "The people only call for magic because the Fae and Elven folk have corrupted them. They'll all thank me eventually."

The king turned back towards her, with a fierceness radiating from his entire being. Serena recoiled.

"What I didn't expect was that you'd been corrupted too." Matthias walked to a safe casket hiding behind a painting of his father. Then he unlocked the box with a key hung from a wide ring tied at his hip. "But it is clear no one is safe from their vile ways."

"What are you doing?" Serena asked, scrambling to her feet.

The king pulled out a satchel, and from within it, a dazzling emerald crystal.

"No! No, Matthias, you cannot do this! It was not intended for them." Serena lunged across the room and latched herself onto his arm, clinging to the fur on his robe. With a jerk of his elbow, he knocked her aside, and her body slammed hard against the floor.

She stared up at her husband. He was nothing but an evil shadow of the man he once was.

Serena sighed. "Please Matthias . . . it was meant for—"

"I know who it's for, but I cannot allow this defiance. And I certainly cannot allow *my* queen to empathize with those who challenge my rule." He pulled off his crown, removed the center crystal, and placed the emerald inside.

"Please, Matthias," Serena pleaded. "If you ever loved me, even just a little, do not do this."

"Do not worry, my wife," the king said as he placed the crown with the glowing emerald on his head. "I will not allow it to touch our family or guards."

The queen's beautiful eyes watched as the king walked to the window, each step pleading with him desperately to change his mind. But he would not listen. He turned his back on her and peered out. Distant voices of protest from the villagers beyond the castle walls blended in with her own cries for leniency.

In a moment of complete silence, when Serena, and the entire world it seemed, had taken a pause from their cries, he pressed his hand against the emerald. An intense ray of light illuminated the sky, and then it went dark.

The world remained quiet.

"Oh, to the ancient Gods, what have you done?" Serena whispered as she pulled herself onto her knees. Her stomach wound in a tight knot.

Matthias turned back to her; a wicked smile flitted across his lips. For a brief moment, Serena could have sworn she had seen a flicker of emerald behind his dark eyes.

"They are now blind," he said proudly, "May the sight of magic never be seen again."

Chapter 1

The Eastland Forest
One year later

Steady wind solemnly blew King Argon's long, alabaster hair. He carefully loosened the knotted rope, allowing him to slide off the linen binding the muddy bronze artifact. Within, the antique compass started to reveal itself, sticking out through the sides. Dried mud crumbled with the slightest touch of his fingertips and dropped to the shimmering sand. He used the top of his velvet cloak to wipe off enough coarse dirt to read the ancient inscription.

"Kroneon," the Fae king read aloud, then turned towards his sister, Princess Cassia. Her azure-silver eyes would not leave the sea.

Argon brought his gaze back to the compass, which he delicately held in the palm of his hand, and cocked his head to the right as if admiring the rustic ore.

Maydean, Queen of the Undersea, reached out, running her fingers over the weapon. She felt its cold, stalwart, and vibrating aura against her skin.

The weapon held ancient power, capable of destroying entire kingdoms—a relic that could start thousands of wars. They finally had the Kroneon in their hands.

"Maydean," Argon called, gesturing to a large rock table standing by the edge of the cliff, and said, "hand me that goblet, if you may. We need to rinse it clean."

The siren queen gently placed a silk bundle on what looked like an algae cradle and then walked towards the goblet. After retrieving the cup, she hurried to a crystalline stream of water pouring into the ocean. Her knees dug painfully into the sharp grains of sand as she filled the cup with water. Maydean quickly stood to her feet and rushed to Argon, pouring the salty seawater carefully over the top of the ancient weapon.

She looked up into the king's moonlit eyes thoughtfully, exchanging a look of understanding, which went unnoticed by Cassia.

The Portland Sea was mostly silent that night. The only noise was the light breeze from the west, pulling in the trickle of waves crashing into the limestone cliffs.

"How much longer, Maydean?" Argon asked her, looking up to meet the queen's eyes, which seemed to have every color of the deep, blue sea in them.

"The ships were but a few miles west of the reef before we arrived at the Eastland Forest," Maydean said.

She lifted her wailing child, Seraphina, from the intricately knitted algae and clutched her close to her chest. She looked down, burying her face in her daughter's hair.

Queen Maydean's stomach churned as she looked up again. "We don't have much time before King Matthias's army arrives!" Her voice quivered as she tugged at the swaddle wrapped around her child to keep her secure. "What do you need me to do?"

Argon ran his thumb gingerly over the compass, his eyes transfixed as if power was summoning him. The gleam in the king's eye made Maydean's muscles tremble. She knew that look well; he was succumbing to its magic.

She placed her hand on the king's forearm, drawing his attention back to her, away from the enchanted device.

"Argon, do not look upon it for too long," she urged. A look of concern flashed over her face. She squeezed her fingers, digging her nails into his skin. The king's eyes narrowed, and then he blinked.

"Right," he said suddenly, back to his senses, "we must remove the key."

A breath of relief left Maydean's lips as she released the firm grip on his arm. Argon placed his hand at the compass's center and pulled out the key as gently as possible.

"Here," he said to Maydean, "wrap it in coral. We must keep the compass and the key separated."

Princess Cassia stepped forward in her silky crimson dress, clearing her throat to speak, but Argon held his hand up. "I know what you want, Sister. It doesn't belong on our land," he said.

Her expression hardened. "We have searched for the Kroneon since our banishment, Brother," Cassia hissed. "There is no safer place than here."

He fiercely shook his head. "We may as well plan for our kingdom to meet its demise tonight if we do not hide it," he explained. "Please understand my decision; it is an order."

Cassia's lips portrayed a sardonic smile. "Argon, I do not trust the merfolk—"

"Sirens," the queen corrected, "we are called sirens!"

The princess smirked at Maydean's remark, but her eyes were hardened with disapproval.

"Listen," Cassia said, modulating her tone, "our tree will protect it."

Maydean ignored the princess. Instead, she shifted her eyes to check on her precious baby girl. Despite being near the ocean, the air felt thick. She turned from the king, the child cradled in her arms, and began to make her way down the cliff into the water. Argon and Cassia followed them down and watched her stride amidst the cold, nocturnal waves as they stood on the narrow beach.

The sea queen was right to assume Cassia would be a problem, but Argon insisted she ought to be there.

"I will hide the key where no man will find it!" Maydean shouted towards the shore. She spoke bravely, trying to mask how terrified she was. "We must leave now, Argon. We have been here for too long."

Seraphina let out a loud wail as the sea bathed her tiny body. Maydean bounced on her heels to settle her cries and blinked back her tears.

Argon walked towards her, the water rising to his knees.

"Be safe, Maydean," he begged, stepping so close his words touched her skin. "Protect the key."

King Argon looked down at Seraphina, whose eyes met his for a moment before she cried out again. Then he reached for a strand of seaweed hanging from her child's swaddle and laced it around the key. He looked up at the skies as if pleading for strength, then wrapped it tightly around Maydean's wrist with his eyes beaming into hers.

Suddenly, a faint sound of cannons came from the horizon, alerting Maydean and Argon that their enemy was upon them. He turned to look up at his Elven army and nodded.

The Elven warriors were ever loyal, ever strong, and stood ready at the edge of the rock. They wielded their magical weapons in one hand and shields in the other.

It was magic itself that had fueled the conflict between the kingdoms; it was also magic that could save them all.

The Elven admiral trotted down the cliff to meet Argon. His height towered over the king; his long, metallic-colored hair was pulled into a braid against his back. The moonlight bounced off the elf's niveous skin, which was as fair as the shore's white sand. He reached out to the king, and Argon placed the compass in the warrior's hands, who then secured it in a leather pouch.

"Hide the weapon on Crotona Island," Argon requested, reaching into his cloak, and pulling out a map. "Hide it here," the king said quietly, pointing to a sketch of the caves. "Be wary of what lies on that island, Hagmar; you are the only one who has ever made it out of that land alive. Protect the Kroneon as if your life depended on it."

Maydean watched Hagmar stand straight as he gave Argon an agreeable nod.

"Aiden!" Hagmar summoned his son, who waited with the rest of the battalion. The boy hurried to the brave admiral and looked up. He was no more than the age of ten, and Hagmar set his hand on his son's thin, yet strong, shoulder, giving it a tight squeeze.

The young boy stood taller to try and meet his father's eyes; his lips shook as he said, "Yes, Father?"

Hagmar knelt next to his son, running a hand over the child's jet-black hair.

"I'll be back before sunrise, Aiden. You must step in my place and care for your mother. Protect her, as the enemy ships will be upon us soon," Hagmar said. His son sniffled, wiping his nose with the back of his hand.

"Where, Father? Where do we go?" asked the Elven child.

"The Eastland Caves," King Argon answered for him.

"Yes," Hagmar affirmed. "Take your mother and the other women and children to the caves, both elves and fairies." He dropped a fatherly kiss on Aiden's forehead. When he pulled back, he said, "You are next to lead the army. Show the king you can lead, Aiden. With or without me."

The boy stood back; tears welled up in his eyes as he nodded to his father. Hagmar secured his sword in his sheath and ran towards their ship, his battalion following closely behind.

Maydean looked up to find Dergis and Anaru, the Fae's dragons, flying overhead. She listened intently as they roared above—a warning. The ships were getting closer.

"Not much longer, Argon," Maydean cried.

Argon leaned forward, placing his hand on her crying child's forehead to soothe her. Maydean watched as something flickered in his eyes as he looked into Seraphina's.

"Go, Maydean, now," he rushed her, staring at the horizon. "Hide the key."

Princess Cassia unsheathed her sword, placing it in front of her. "I see their ships! Brother, I will fight with you!"

All Maydean had left was hope they would survive. She gave Argon one last glance before diving into the sea with her child, disappearing among the silver-crested waves.

Chapter 2

Zemira; Inside the palace

Zemira had once been the beauty of the world, from the mountain ranges to the evergreen woods. The lands were like none other yet explored, that was until King Matthias banished all creatures who held magic—the power that brought life to the soil.

Once magic left Zemira, the land began to die. All that was left were dozens of scintillating green trees that lined the main street from the Southland willow tree to the palace walls.

A strong gust of wind drifted into king's bedroom, creating a cold chill over his already dry and brittle skin.

King Matthias shifted his attention behind him, focusing on the small silver rays of moonlight shining down on his bed, right where Serena once slept. A pang of guilt pulled at his heart suddenly; he clutched his hand to his chest again.

A light tap at the door pulled King Matthias's eyes from the bed.

"Come in," he called.

Mason crept in slowly but stayed near the doorway.

"We found another Elven spy in Baylin. However, she refuses to speak to us and give up the location of the others," he explained. "What would you like us to do?"

The king cleared his throat, stood up straight, and then looked back through his window onto his kingdom.

"Do it inside the palace gates," he ordered. "We still do not know who has the sight and who does not. This will send a message to the other Elven spies. If someone asks, tell them it was simply the execution of a thief."

He laid a shaking hand on the windowsill while the other twisted into a tight grip.

The king continued, "My ships should have reached the Eastland Forest several days ago. Which means King Argon is dead." Matthias turned away from the window to face Mason. "Now the spies they've sent here will have no one to turn to but me. They must either surrender their sword or die by one."

"And what of your wife and Tristan?" the guard asked softly, almost to a near whisper.

The king flinched. "Serena does not have much longer. The Whale's Tongue poison will take her any moment now. And Tristan—" He stopped himself from giving any orders and placed both hands against the ledge. He let out a long sigh, and as he leaned forward, he said, "Please, Mason, go deal with the spy at once."

Mason saluted the king out of respect before leaving his bedchamber. Matthias turned from him when he heard a loud scream coming from the courtyard. He watched as they dragged the Elven spy to the fountain. She knelt, looked up, then begged for her life.

Moments later, one of the new guards, Thomath, raised his sword high. When Mason gave the order, he brought the blade down with one swing, slicing off the elf's head, watching it roll down the curb until it hit the grass—another death on his hands that did not have to be.

The king ran his hand over the enchanted emerald he wore proudly upon his crown, recounting the memory from the year before. He had doomed his people to become blind to what he hated—magic. Thus, in Zemira, magic became a mere fairy tale. No one remembered the dragons soaring the skies and the sirens that governed the seas. Even though it had only been a year since he ousted magic from the kingdom, those were not the stories parents told their children anymore. Instead, they put together fables and came up with not-so-happily-ever-afters. They told grim tales of giants as tall as the palace walls with legs as thick as trunks, crushing their victims with one single blow.

The stories that followed were those of sirens who would drag young sailors down into the depths of the dark waters. Or the ones about the monsters who haunted desolate islands, just waiting for someone to become marooned. They were as bizarre as they could be, but it made the king happy that none of them were good enough to be credible.

Tired of watching the chaos, King Matthias turned away from the window and sat on his extravagant velvet chair to ponder. The week before was a mere blur. His own child, Tristan, had been caught at the edge of the docks intending to deliver a letter to a sailor on board a trading vessel heading east.

Serena's letter not only warned King Argon that her husband had sent ships to kill him as an act of revenge; there was a more troubling piece to it.

The queen had discovered not everyone succumbed to the crystal's power—and Argon had to know. Many were immune, and several of those not affected by it formed a resistance against King Matthias, in alliance with the Elven spies protecting their cause.

Matthias glanced at the mirror on the wall and stared back at his reflection. A grin, not precisely of joy, pulled at his lips while he ran his hand down his thin, black beard. Power aside, his looks made him twice as intimidating. His towering height and barrel-chested figure alone drew men to their knees, and his fierce eyes were as black as his soul. The king ruled the land in a way that created fear in people's hearts. That was the only way to achieve utter control.

King Matthias stood and walked back to the window, gazing with his dark eyes out into the ocean lining the east palace walls—the scent of the salty sea loomed in the air.

Matthias rubbed his hands over his face right before he heard a quiet click at his door. The king searched the room for ghostly reflections hidden in the shadows. His children emerged into the light. Elijah and Tristan, seven and eight, shuffled their feet across the tile floor. They stood in front of him, their innocent eyes looking back at their father's.

"Father," Tristan's voice shook while his shoulders stayed tense, "we want to say goodbye to Mother, but—"

The boy swallowed and pressed his lips together as if contemplating his question.

Elijah smacked his brother over the shoulder and stepped forward to say boldly, "We want to say goodbye, except the guards won't let us in the room."

The king's face twitched, clenching his jaw as he dismissed his boys with a wave of his hand.

"Go now, children. Leave me alone. I want to be by myself." Matthias noticed a glimmer of tears in Tristan's eyes.

Tristan rubbed the back of his neck.

He is so weak, the king thought.

Matthias gave both his children a reassuring smile and regarded their words thoughtfully. He stepped closer to them, leaning in.

"You may say goodbye to your mother," he said, knowing it would be the last time they would see her, and he did believe himself to have some compassion left in him. He placed his hand on Tristan's shoulder. "Tell Mason I permit you to bid your farewells. However, do not hover. Go in, say your goodbye, and then return to me."

Tristan's expression fell after hearing his father's words. Under his breath, he muttered, "Thank you, Father—"

"Not like she'll want to see you," Elijah remarked. "You are the reason she's going to die."

"Enough!" the king shouted, clenching his jaw. His eyes narrowed at his boys while the air in the room began to feel heavy. The boys staggered back, tripping over their own feet. Matthias realized how young they still were, so he said, "Tristan, you acted carelessly when you tried to deliver that letter. But it is your mother who now lies in her bed, foaming at the mouth like a rabid beast." The corner of his eyes shuddered, but he contained the anger. "She betrayed you," he added. "She betrayed me." His voice hardened, cutting through the room once more. "And she betrayed her crown!"

He looked away, struggling to meet his children's eyes, his own self-guilt gnawing at him. "Now, be gone from my sight before the two of you join her." He cringed at the words that fell thoughtlessly on his tongue—no matter what truth lay behind them.

Tristan gripped Elijah's arm. "Let's go, Brother," he said wearily, "before he changes his mind."

Elijah's eyes narrowed at his father in an accusatory way before the two of them left him alone to wallow in his guilt.

The boys hurried out of the king's chambers, and Matthias glowered their way as Elijah slammed the door behind them. The contemptuous look painted over Elijah's face flashed over the king's mind, causing his scowl to shift to amusement. He acknowledged what a fine ruler Elijah would be someday, now that he would be his only heir. For his first-born, little Tristan, would be joining his mother that night.

Matthias drummed his fingers against the hilt of his sword until he gripped around it, feeling his knuckles crack. He flexed out his fingers, placing his hand back at his side.

"Harrowing sacrifices must be made to pave the way for the greater good," he said to himself.

The king acted quickly because if he had not, he knew he would change his mind. Matthias rushed to the courtyard and waved a hand in the air, signaling to his royal guard's captain.

"Mason!"

"Sir?" He stammered when he spoke.

The king laid out his orders and watched the blood drain from Mason's cheeks.

"King Matthias—" Mason began, showing a look of disdain, though he held his tongue when the king raised his brow.

Matthias puffed out his chest, raising his chin high. "You have your orders, Mason," the king fumed, assuming a fierce glower upon his face. "You'll take Tristan out to the middle of the Portland Sea, where he'll join the rest of those slaughtered tonight. I'll not raise a traitor."

Matthias watched closely as Mason's eyes grew wide, his shoulders slumping as he gave the king a hesitant nod.

"Make it quick and painless," the king added. "Then toss his body into the sea." As the order left his mouth, he felt the hateful, sour taste in his words—maybe that was what venom tasted like.

Mason bowed his head, signaled to the remaining royal guard, and then headed towards the chamber where they laid the queen to die.

Matthias's legs went unsteady once he heard Tristan's guttural cries echo through the castle walls. The king eyed Mason as he dragged the boy's small frame through the courtyard, wailing and screaming for his father to help him. Still, the king stood with his head held high with a forced, icy glare.

Elijah came out of the room into the courtyard,

following the guards. He shot his father a venomous look as his brother was taken away outside the palace's gates. The king stumbled back, catching himself on the corner of the wall.

And this is just the beginning, the king thought, trying to remain still.

He had to take back Zemira and bring order to his people. Matthias would put a stop to the nonsense, even if it meant executing his child.

In the small village of Baylin, outside the central city of Zemira, they could still hear the palace bells chime loudly throughout the night. It had been several days since the king set out his guard to track down the Elven spies.

Val Lardbrak sat on her couch with her knees up to her chest, wondering if, at any moment, the royal guard would knock down their door—not that they would find spies hiding within their home. However, the guards never played fair. So far, she had survived another day.

Earlier that morning, Val watched the king's men rummage through their village, asking questions she knew very well how to answer.

"An elf?" she had said, trying to mask the stammer in her voice. "What's a bloody elf?"

For more than a year, Val and her husband, Duncan, pretended to be oblivious to magic because it was the only way to survive. They had the sight, but most of their neighbors around them did not.

She pretended not to know any of the Elven spies hidden in their neighbors' homes or the fact that mystical fairies and mighty dragons existed. But she and her husband also knew the risks of keeping such secrets. Someday, the king would come looking for those who had deceived him—the resistance. Or whatever they called themselves. Val and Duncan wanted nothing to do with it because staying alive was more important than getting mingled with the king's affairs.

The soldiers barged through her door that morning, tossing everything in sight. She kept herself poised, looking out the window, hoping her husband would be home soon, but she knew he would not be. He was out in the sea, catching fish for the upcoming winter, and he was not expected until later that night.

She looked up as she heard laughter coming from her neighbor's window, two doors down.

"Elves?" the neighbor called out through her opened window, followed by another uproar of laughter. "Like those pointy-eared creatures in fairy tales?"

She will get 'erself killed wit' a tongue like that, Val thought.

Regardless of how many times she and her husband planned what they would say when the guards came looking for Elven spies, nothing had prepared her for when armed guards knocked on the door. Five of them stood in her doorway and pointed their pistols at her forehead, eyeing over her shoulder. Nausea gripped the muscles in her stomach, and when she felt faint, she told them she had not eaten that day to explain her reaction away. No elf was in their home, of course, but with five armed guards before her, she second-guessed.

Val took several steady breaths as she tucked her crimson curls behind her ear, not to alarm the guards. She nodded, smiling, knowing full well no spy hid behind their walls. Yet, not until the guards left did her fear simmer down inside her thin chest, burning like a hot stove.

Most of the resistance had given up overthrowing King Matthias. They no longer cared that their land had been dying for the last three hundred and sixty-eight days. They did not want war. At least Val and her husband did not. To her, it was better to stay blind to the deception and be alive than fight against it and die trying.

"Come 'ome, Duncan," she said aloud, "Please come 'ome."

Val assumed the worst, that they had found him, questioned what he knew, and saw the truth in his dark eyes. She was pacing the kitchen when she heard a click at the front door.

"Duncan! Where 'ave ye been?" she cried, running to meet him before landing a kiss on his well-groomed beard. Val noticed his soppy clothes as he lurched in the doorway, but her big eyes immediately drew to what he held in his arms—the blanket they kept on their fishing boat wrapped around a bulky thing he held close to his muscular chest.

"Wha' is goin' on?" she asked, not addressing the bundle in his arms. "Why do ye look like ye 'ave gone for a swim, Duncan?"

"Something happened, Val," he said, almost to a near

whisper. He looked over his shoulder at the window, then back to meet her eyes. "Something terrible has happened."

"I'm quite aware of wha' 'as 'appened, m'love. I 'ave locked me self in the house all day while the king's men roamed our village, rummaged through our things, looked under our beds, even inside the cupboards! I've 'eard shots today, right outside the village," she explained. "One of the guards dared to point a pistol at me 'ead." Her eyes went back to the blanket.

Duncan blinked.

"Wha' do ye 'ave there, Duncan?" Her eyes went wide, looking down at the blanket. "Duncan, what's wrong?" She rubbed her knuckles nervously when he did not respond. "Wha' the bleedin' 'ell did ye do?"

"The sirens were attacked today out in the sea," he said quietly, finding his voice. "I saw it with me own eyes. The ships were sailing from the east. The bloodshed wasn't in Zemira alone, Val. The guards attacked everyone," Duncan's voice pitched.

He retracted his hand from the blanket as a soft whimper muffled under the cloth.

Val's slim, reddish brows knitted together. "Is tha' a baby?" she asked and reached her hand out, lifting the blanket, staring down at two tiny eyes, the size of buttons, looking back at her.

"I had no choice, Val," Duncan said, running his hand down his face. "The king had at least ten of their ships out there, shooting their harpoons into the sea. I kept moving though, back to shore, but then—" The child let out a loud cry, and Val covered her mouth with her hand. "I couldn't leave her out there to die," he confessed. "They would have killed her. She looked as if she had been floating in the sea for days."

He looked down and pulled the thin blanket back to reveal the rest of the child's body.

Val's breath caught. "Aah, dear. Is tha'—?"

He nodded. "A siren. Yah." Duncan placed the child securely against his broad chest and gently bounced on his feet to soothe her. "We can't have children, Val. So maybe this is the answer we've been waiting for?" Duncan said. He reached his hands out, handing over the child to Val. "Here, take her."

She gave him a curt nod and wrapped her arms around the child, rocking her back and forth.

Duncan rushed to lock the door, then pulled the drapes over the window.

There was an empty feeling in the pit of Val's stomach as she watched her husband pace the room with his hands placed loosely in his pockets.

"We ain't keepin' it," she pleaded. "Duncan, we ain't—"

"Her," he corrected, stopping at the sofa. "The child is a her, my love."

Val pressed her lips together into a thin line, then sighed heavily. Her shoulders slumped, but she kept her eyes on her husband's.

"Duncan, 'ow do we 'ide a child from the king? They'll know she is not 'uman. They'll know she does not belong to us." She gestured to her husband. "Look at us." She threw a hand up. "Yer as dark as a crow, and I'm a pale-faced redhead. Ye crazy?"

She looked down at the light olive-skinned child with dark-brown eyes, like the color of pine honey. Her hair was a shade of dark brown to match her eyes, but with traces of purple and silver streaks down the sides. Not the physical traits that came naturally to humans.

"Tha' li'l tail of 'ers may be blinded to most of the people in our village, but the king 'ill know." She ran her hand through her tight curls. "He 'ill know what she is."

Duncan nodded, but a slight chuckle came from his lips.

Val scowled. "Not a laughin' matter, Duncan," she said. "They 'ill kill us."

His smile faded as he placed a hand on Val's arm, trailing his fingers down to her elbow.

"No, they won't," he assured. "We were prepared for the day the king found out 'bout the spies," he continued, "and we will do what we've been doing for the last year. Keep our heads down, stay out of the king's affairs, and now protect this child." He stopped and bit his bottom lip. "We'll say we adopted her from the Green Valley Orphanage." He gestured to the baby's tail. "From what I understand, once she fully dries, her legs will form, and them fins don't come back unless they're soaked in water."

Val rolled her eyes. "Well, look at ye. Aren't ye the expert on the siren race!"

He inched closer to the child and placed his hand on her head, brushing her strange-colored hair away from her eyes. A small smile grew on the child's chubby face.

"Will you look at that," he said, staring down at Val. "She likes us."

The baby's smile widened, revealing two little dimples on the side of her cheeks, and Val and Duncan grinned back at her. A quiet giggle escaped the child's lips, and she reached out her fingers at them and batted her eyelashes.

"We'll have to give her a name," he whispered to Val's ear, then kissed her pale cheek.

She stared at him, unblinking. "Yer serious 'bout this, aren't ye?"

He shrugged. "I don't believe we have a choice, my love." He placed his arm slowly around Val, bringing all three of them closer together. "I've never been more serious about anything in me life. We've never been able to have children. She came to us for a reason. We are to protect her with our lives."

Val's eyes drew to a bright, red object wrapped in coral and seaweed around the child's wrist. "Wha' is tha'?" she asked.

"Oh, right, that. I dunno; it was on her already when I found the little one floating on top of a wooden board. We'll need to remove it; the coral is burning her skin, see?"

Gently, Duncan began to untie the seaweed holding the little charm in place. Then, as he touched the algae, it crumbled open, revealing a dazzling, crimson ruby. Val and Duncan both widened their eyes at the beautiful sight.

They placed the jewel on the counter and wiped away the rest of the seaweed. "I'll make 'er somethin' more comfortable to dangle the jewel from when she gets older," Val said. "Obviously, 'er birth folks intended for 'er to 'ave it." She frowned. "Assumin' the king killed 'em, perhaps it was somethin' they wanted their child to remember them by."

"Are you saying we can keep her?" he asked, with a hopeful smile on his face.

She nodded slowly. "If we 'ear of a siren mommy lookin' for 'er child, 'en we must be willin' to 'and 'er back."

Duncan placed his hand on Val's back and pulled her close to him.

She stared down at the siren baby for a long beat before sucking in a heavy, defeated breath. "How's Finola sound for a name?" Val asked. "After me mother."

Duncan grinned and ran his pinky over the child's cheek. "That'd be beautiful, Val," he said. "We can call her Nola."

Chapter 3

The Portland Sea
Present Day
Twenty years later

Captain Lincoln, 'The Dragon,' gripped to the helm of the Sybil Curse to keep her steady. He watched the heavy rain pour down upon his ship as the storm rolled through.

Lincoln glanced over to one of his shipmates, Hill 'Tipsy' Penny, who tilted back on his heel, pressing the toe of his shoe against the ship's towering mast.

Hill rocked back to secure the mainsail with his fist locked tightly around the gritty rope. He winced as each heave burned his dry skin against the rough line, which resisted each pull between his long, bony fingers. The buccaneer's other hand held firmly to a bottle of rum, which he tossed back and chugged while he watched the waves rise tall.

There was a particular thing about the Sybil Curse's crew. Once their gaze locked in on the Portland Sea during a storm, it was difficult, nearly impossible, for them to avert their eyes from her captivating beauty. The wind pulled in fierce waves against the ship—each as strong and dauntless as the next.

Hill seemed to struggle to taste those last drops of rum dripping on his tongue. Most likely settling for the salty, savory taste of the ocean breeze pulling in from the eastern slope.

He wiped his one good eye with the back of his hand as a stream of mist sprayed against his face. The pirate cleared his hair from his forehead, exposing the scars left by every brawl he had gotten himself into.

Hill was an odd-looking, lanky buccaneer and somewhat of a lubber, who had been with the crew for almost two years. The captain rescued him before he was thrown into jail for trying to steal his neighbor's horse. They were hard to come by those days, horses, and Hill was desperate. The exchange was better than he had expected. Why worry about needing a horse to travel out of the town he loathed when he could board a ship out into the sea and become a stone-hearted pirate? At least as a pirate, he could drink as much rum as he pleased.

The rest of the crew bustled about the ship, getting rocked and tossed from bow to stern. The storm was fierce, but it was not the first time that ship had taken a beating, and they all knew it would not be her last.

It was an old vessel, medium in size, with a flushed deck to make it easier to work. The ship was strong, made with fine wood paneling the crew fixed up when the captain had purchased her—well, stole her.

Hill blundered across the deck as movement was spotted in the waters ahead.

Mazie 'Raven' Knight shouted from across the deck, "Captain!" Her hands flailed frantically in the air. "There's at least five of those creatures on the ocean's surface, staring at us with those creepy-looking eyes." A frown creased on Mazie's forehead as she placed a hand loosely on her hip. "They won't trust us, you know?"

Kitten 'Golden-Eye' Fox looked back towards the sea, shouting over the storm's boisterous squalls. "Right, but if we don't 'elp 'em, the one who's injured is goin' to die. They lookin' desperate, Captain," she said, "Should we lower the net?"

Mazie had her arms crossed stubbornly over her chest, biting her lower lip. A flicker of irritation shone in her eyes, but she nodded agreeably.

"Kitten's right," Mazie said. "We can't be responsible for a dead fish on our boat." She rolled her eyes at her own comment. "Half-fish."

Captain Lincoln narrowed his eyes out into the plunging waves and said reluctantly, "Pull her up."

There was an ample amount of mayhem on the ship, and he barely held on to his sanity. He was not about to let die a creature he could have saved.

Kitten replied with a swift nod as thunder cracked through the air. "Aye, aye, Captain," she bellowed, carrying her voice across the ship.

Lincoln looked past Mazie's shoulder at Dyson 'No Leg' Boots, who was already lowering the net overboard into the sea.

"Dammit," Lincoln cursed to himself and hustled towards the stern of the ship. "Keep lowering that net, Boots."

Lincoln and Mazie tied off the rope to rig up the net. They planted their feet at the edge of the ship to keep themselves from being flung overboard. He then wrapped the rope around his hand twice and waited for the tug. After a second, a sharp yank followed, and Lincoln yelled, "Steady, mates! Heave ho!"

The crew leaned back, gripping the net steady to pull a white-haired mermaid gently over the railing.

Lincoln looked over his shoulder at Mazie. "Get below deck and grab the medical kit," he ordered.

"Aye, aye, Captain," she said eagerly, then turned on her heel and hurried below deck.

Ardley 'Big Red' Fredrick, well-known for his scarlet red hair and wooly beard to match, held the net still until a beautiful bronze-skinned woman went under the ship's main deck. His mustache twisted up like a crescent moon, and his eyes shined blue as sapphire. He stood in a cloud of smoke curling around his lips and puffed heavily through his pipe—the breeze blew the smoke back into his face.

Ardley inched forward, clearing his throat. "Looks like her tail has been ripped deep, Captain." He brushed the tips of his fingers against the scales near the bloodied wound. The oozing drips of sparkling rich red reflected off the lightning crashing down over the water. "She'll be needing stitches, or she'll lose it." Ardley showed the captain. "And if she loses it—"

"Pirate," the mermaid breathed, her voice sounding

weak and shallow. Lincoln brought his palm to her cheek, cupping her face with one of his hands.

He shifted from her gaze as Ardley cleared his throat. Still, he pulled the mermaid's trembling body up against his chest, securing her in his arms. Lincoln knew they had three, maybe four hours to tend to the wound before she would need to get back into the sea.

"Easy. Try not to move, love," Lincoln said, brushing her long strands of hair between his fingers. "Tell me what happened?" His voice was calm, trying to ease her pain. Pirates were not the most trusted folk in the sea, and the last thing he wanted was to terrify the girl.

"Harpoon," she answered sluggishly. Her feeble, tortured voice tore at his chest. "They attacked three hours before the storm hit."

Lincoln gingerly touched her delicate fingers and rubbed his thumb against her wrist in a circular manner, which he had hoped would help calm her. Her shoulders throbbed against his chest and tears trickled down her rosy cheeks.

"Was it pirates who did this?" Lincoln asked, a sudden note of fury in his voice.

She shook her head but stopped short to bite her bottom lip, seemingly holding back from screaming from the pain.

"King—" she started but choked on a small amount of blood coming up through her mouth. As the coppery liquid dripped down the side of her chin, she swallowed and answered, "King Matthias's men."

Lincoln grouched, "Savages!"

Her eyes seemed hazed and heavy while she struggled to keep them open. "We thought it was the Sybil Curse," she added.

Lincoln raised an eyebrow questionably. "You know about the Sybil Curse?"

Her smile was small. "Of course. Everyone has heard of the Sybil Curse," she answered. "And I dare say, the rumors of the legendary Captain Lincoln are quite true—you are stunningly handsome." He cocked another eyebrow as she lifted her hand and gently brushed a stray hair away from his eyes. Smiling weakly, she asked, "Should I be afraid of you, pirate?"

Lincoln's mouth curved in a playful grin. He had done quite well with his reputation as the bloodthirsty buccaneer, and any man who had dared cross him and his crew would not make it back to their ship alive. At least, the tales he told painted that fate.

Boots leaned forward before Lincoln could tell her nay.

"Don't forget the Dragon part to his name. He—" Boots stepped back swiftly after Lincoln sneered at his poor taste in a joke.

The peg-legged pirate ran his fingers nervously down his bushy brown beard and looked over to Kitten, who met his gaze with a wink.

"I'll just, um, stand over here," Boots said. He hurried over to the side and did not dare make eye contact with his captain again, not until Lincoln had a moment to get his bearings. Boots was a smart lad, merry, and full of wit, but that moment was not the time.

Not paying much more attention to his crew, he glanced

down at the mermaid's exposed bosom and ran his fingers through her hair, covering her chest.

"Please, do not fear us," Lincoln said.

The king had been trying to wipe out the sea folk for two decades, and given their depleted numbers, he was succeeding with his plan. He intimidated and sometimes murdered the magical race to control the humans in his kingdom. Every creature King Matthias banished from Zemira had no reason to trust a human, especially a pirate.

Boots rhythmically tapped his peg leg when Lincoln pointed across the deck. Another mermaid's finger laced over the edge of the ship, lifting herself until she leveled her belly against the railing. Her hair was a slight greenish-blue, like the color cyan, which draped over her shoulders as she flipped her body onto the ship. Lincoln's eyes narrowed in on the shiny jewels wrapped around her throat despite her perfectly sculpted breasts. She slammed hard against the deck, flopping onto her stomach.

"A little help, please," she grunted, reaching her hand out for Kitten, who was already by her side, kneeling to help flip her on her backside.

She squirmed and wiggled about the deck before her tail split into two, and her scales smoothed out into long and slender human legs. The blue-haired lady stood to her feet, hurried towards the other mermaid Lincoln had cradled in his arms, and knelt beside them.

"Can you save Sydney's tail, Lincoln? If she loses it, she will die," she pleaded—her voice quivering as she spoke. "Please. She is my sister."

Her accent was thick, so Lincoln assumed she was from

the southern Kingdom of the Undersea, ancestors to the merfolk.

Captain Lincoln's eyebrows drew together, and he nervously rubbed his hand over the light scruff on his chin. "I don't know the first thing about saving a life, miss, but I can assure you that we will do everything we can. My first mate just went to get our medical bag."

"Miss?" She snickered under her breath. "You don't sound like any pirate I've ever encountered," she teased.

Lincoln found it odd how light-hearted she acted under the circumstances.

"Call me Ara," she added, then placed her hands under Sydney's back, lifting her slightly, pulling her away from Lincoln's chest and onto her lap.

As Ara leaned forward, the captain scanned her body and spotted the shark eye symbol above her navel, similar to a birthmark, confirming his suspicions. Mermaids were an evolved race, where many had lost the unique powers of their original anatomy. Many sirens became what humans referred to as the merfolk. Still, few held the ability to lure weak-willed men into the sea; she was a siren. Extraordinarily stunning, yet extremely deadly.

"I guess the question is, are we safe?" Lincoln asked, raising a brow.

The siren smirked. "No need to worry, pirate," she said, a subtle warning in her tone, "I won't draw you into the ocean with my voice and devour your flesh," she whispered. Then she giggled and shot him a wink. "I've already eaten."

The muscles in Lincoln's chest twitched. He did not fear much out in the sea, except for sirens. It would not be the first time those creatures had used their powers against him.

Lincoln closed his eyes, recounting his last encounter with her kind. The creature lured him deep into the sea, then nearly dragged his body to the bottom of the water before—

His vivid memory was abruptly interrupted by Sydney's loud, throaty cry. He wished he knew how to stop the agony, other than with a bottle of rum, which was all they ever used to numb the pain.

Lincoln looked up as Mazie dropped their medical supplies next to Ardley, who immediately zipped it open and retrieved a few items from the bag. He was the only one on the ship with some first aid experience, so he quickly tended to her injury. Ardley cleansed and sutured the wound as gently and delicately as he could, then looked up at the captain with a perturbed expression crossing his face. They both glanced down at the rags he had used to dig out the poison, to reveal a crusted, green substance.

Infection, Lincoln assumed.

Judging by the look on Ardley's face, he knew her fate.

"Son of a bitch," Lincoln cursed silently under his breath, running his hand down his face.

"Captain, may I speak with you in private for a moment?" Ardley asked, closing the bag.

Lincoln stood and walked towards the forecastle deck. At the same time, Ardley got up and followed him closely until they were out of earshot from the sirens.

"How much longer does she have?" Lincoln asked, turning to face the foremast where Ardley leaned.

He shrugged. "Whale's Tongue can be quick for a human, but I've never seen the poison on a sea creature. But, given her inability to keep her eyes open for longer than a few minutes—" He ran his hand through his mustache and said, "An hour, give or take."

Whale's Tongue was not what it sounded like. It was a deadly poison created by Matthias's men after the magic ban to rid the kingdom of everyone who did not pay their tax or contributed to the war. It was their way of executing those who stood in their way—a waste to society, they would say.

"If we are to send her back to the sea now," Ardley noted, "it will give her just enough time to swim down to their kingdom and say goodbye to her family. Or we can keep her comfortable here until she passes."

Lincoln cursed under his breath before patting Ardley on the back. "Aye. Thanks for giving everything you had back there. You did your best, mate."

Ardley pressed his lips into a flat line and sucked in a heavy breath. "You want me to tell Ara?"

Lincoln shook his head. "Nay, just blow the horn."

"Aye, Captain."

As soon as Ardley's hands rested on the foghorn, pulling it out towards the sea, Ara's eyes went wide, and her body, rigid. She fanned out her hand and placed it against her chest, and let out a thunderous cry so loud the crew had to muffle their ears to drown out the sound.

The sonic scream from a siren, who mourned the loss of someone they loved, sounded like a dragon's roar. It could shake the world around them as if a violent tornado was destroying everything in its path. It appeared as though the waves had picked up and slammed against the ship, but the storm had already passed.

Lincoln leaned down next to the sirens and placed his hand gently on Ara's arm, but she pulled back from his touch.

Ara looked up. "Thank you, Lincoln," she said, wiping a tear falling down her cheek, "for everything you've done for us tonight."

"What else do you need?" he asked sincerely.

The siren stared at him for a long beat as if she were considering his words, but instead, she looked back down at her dying sister. Sydney looked alarmingly worse than she had moments before.

"There are only a handful of us left," Ara explained. "Matthias has won. My aunt, Maydean, died years ago trying to protect our people. But not everyone has survived since that day. I swore an oath to continue her legacy when no one else could." She tilted her head, her eyes softening as she met Lincoln's gaze. "It was my responsibility, and I failed her. I failed my kind."

Lincoln wanted to tell her that she had not. He ached to convince her that nothing she could have done would have prevented that fate or changed the outcome of that brutal, murderous attack—or the anguish she felt.

"Where will you go?" His voice was low and somber.

"Anywhere is safer than here," she replied. "The sea has become a dark and dreadful ruin for my people. And the humans cannot protect us, not anymore. They do not know we even exist. And if they did, their fear would be clouded with mistrust and disgust. The seas have not been safe since Matthias took over what was once only pirate-infested waters. Pirates, we know how to handle them," Ara explained, then shut her eyes, and Lincoln watched a shiny tear plop down her cheek. "We don't kill pirates anymore—those days are in the past, Lincoln. Because you are not like them. You *see* us. You see us for what we truly are, and I can never repay you for what you have done for us this day."

Ara cradled Sydney in her arms, raced towards the back of the deck, and dove overboard into the sea. They were gone, quicker than they all could blink.

The foghorn's continuous noise sounded for five minutes before the crew gave the sirens a moment of silence for their fallen. Boots removed his hat and placed it against his chest.

Lincoln whirled around to his crew, who stood on the deck, looking at him intently, waiting for orders.

"We sail southwest tonight," Lincoln said.

"To Zemira?" Kitten asked. "Shiver me timbers, Captain! We can't go back there, not after this."

"Oh, bloody hell, Captain," Mazie cursed. "We be staying out of their affairs."

"This is not about retaliation, hearties," he corrected. "We do, however, need more medical supplies and water before our voyage to the Eastland Forest." He turned to Ardley, who gave him a curt nod. "We'll be in and out before anyone notices us."

Lincoln turned to Boots—their most amiable mate on the ship.

"Aye, aye, Captain." Boots raised his eyebrows and

nodded once, then hurried to the mast and shimmied up the post to crawl back inside the crow's nest. Lincoln watched him pull out his spyglass, pointing straight ahead, and shouted. "Ahoy, mates. Weigh anchor and hoist the mizzen! Full speed ahead and ten hours until sunlight."

Lincoln felt Hill's finger tap him on the shoulder.

"Can we stay for a cup of rum, Captain?" Hill proposed shyly.

A small smile flitted across Lincoln's lips. "As long as we're outside the main city, you're damn straight we will," he said. "But we be buying several bottles of rum before we head out. This will be our last journey to Zemira."

Chapter 4

The village of Baylin

Nola positioned the bow, drove her arm backward until her hand touched her cheek. She paused. Her hand shook slightly as the weight of the bow burned her arms.

"Straighten your pose, Nola; you're too low," her father said coolly.

Nola took a deep, steadying breath, but the bow staggered. "Father, you have shown me how to do this at least a thousand times." She looked over her shoulder as her father rested his hand to balance the arrow, keeping it level and still.

Nola wrinkled her nose but turned her eyes back to the target, spreading her feet shoulder-length apart. Her eyes centered on the giant tree with the painted red circle. She lightly closed her eyes, focusing on the calming sound of the sea. She felt her lungs expand with each soothing breath.

Breathe in. Breathe out, Nola said in her mind. *Show him you can do it.*

"Like this?" She opened her eyes, sneaking a glance at her father. "Right?"

Duncan cocked a brow as a playful grin shone on his face. "I thought you had done this a thousand times," he said teasingly, and then shifted his weight on his heel, released the grip he had on the bow, and stepped back. Raising his hands in defeat, he added, "Alright, Nola. You need to relax your shoulders; you're too stiff."

"I'm trying, Father," she said quietly as if her target was a deer and was afraid she would scare it away.

He folded his arms, resting his rear on a fallen tree next to him. "You're doing just fine," he answered as she took the perfect stance.

"Duncan, hurry yer lesson; breakfast is ready," Nola's mother called from inside their home. The two stayed firm until they heard her yell again; that time, she shouted so loudly it was deafening. "Duncan!"

"Alright, Val! Just give us five more minutes, will you?" He flapped his fingers in the air as if to shoo her off like she was a fly.

Nola remained focused on her target and sucked in another heavy breath. She did not want to cheat, but her powers had a mind of their own. Her eyesight moved swiftly in her target's direction to plan a more precise hit. She was sure her father knew what she had done. However, she told herself it still took tremendous skill to release the bow for the perfect shot, regardless of her abilities helping with precision.

Duncan pointed to the tip of the arrow. "This one is a little heavier than the ones I've made before. I might've you try one of the others."

But not caring much about her father's comment, her eyes narrowed on the target and released. "Just. Like. This," she whispered.

The arrow flew swiftly towards the tree and landed dead center of the red circle. "Bullseye." She smiled and patted herself on the shoulder.

"Honestly, Nola, what do you need me for?" he asked, a smile creasing his round cheeks.

She playfully punched her father in the shoulder and looked back at their cottage.

"We better get back before she locks us out again," Nola said jokingly.

He let out an intentional chuckle.

"Very well." Duncan picked up the arrows spread out over the field and handed Nola the bunch. Then he said, "Listen, Nola. I would love for you to join me at the marketplace today, but you understand I am still uncertain 'bout it all, right?"

She placed the arrows in her quiver strapped over her shoulder and gripped her bow. Then all expressions of happiness wiped from her face, and she nodded. "I know. But I cannot stay hidden in our village forever. I don't have many friends—no life outside this place. Besides, most won't even know what I am. And those who do won't say anything if they want to stay alive."

He forced a smile. "In our village, they love you, Nola. And those with the sight would protect you, yes. But this is the king's palace we are speaking of. Though the marketplace is not inside the palace, the king's guard alone will not hesitate to kill you on the spot if they discover what you are. So, if you come, keep that head of yours down."

She gave him one agreeable nod. "I'll do what I've always done when the king's men come near our land. I'll wrap my hair and not make eye contact with anyone. Besides, you told me before that the king holds no interest in the marketplace. Please, Father, I can't keep hiding like this."

Nola hated the idea of putting herself in the situation of others discovering she was a siren living amongst humans. There was slight ease in knowing they would know she was at least half-human. Leastwise, she looked nothing like the sea creatures her father had seen in the past. Sirens did not have smooth, porcelain skin, such as herself. The fact that she could keep her human legs at will was proof enough she was not fully siren. Nola somehow blended in with the people, well, despite her hair and eyes, which were quite odd for those around them.

"I understand, Nola," her father's voice pulled her away from her thoughts as they sauntered to their house. "Just keep your head down, will you? When you show them our merchandise, do not make eye contact with anyone. Do you understand?"

She did understand. Her eyes' color was not what was strange; it was what they did when her powers ignited. They swirled in a circular motion that beamed bright white when she focused on a target. It was not human-like.

"I do, Father," she said agreeably. Nola looked up at the

dark, ominous clouds forming overhead and said, "Though it might be canceled anyway; it looks like another storm is rolling in."

She turned towards the sea, fixing her gold-brown eyes on the waves. Flashes of white suds within the dark blue water tumbled over each other.

"Rain or shine, Nola," Duncan reminded her, pulling her gaze back to his. "I plan to sell everything I made this last month, and you can demonstrate to the customers how well these beauties fly."

She outstretched her arms. "I'll make them fly like—" She smirked. "Hmmm." Her eyes lit up. "I'll make them fly like the dragons I see in my dreams. Like the one Pederick tattooed on my arm," she said, flipping her arm over to reveal the maroon dragon on her forearm. "The dragon I see comes soaring so high above the sky that he looks like a speck of dust." Nola smiled so big, the little dimples on her cheeks widened. "But as small as he looks, his roar is mighty, and his speed is swift. One moment he's there, and then, he disappears behind the clouds."

Her voice quieted to a near whisper, but she simply looked up at her father and smiled faintly.

Duncan rested his arm over her shoulder, giving her a gentle squeeze. "Well, those dreams of yours seem to be more exciting than the fairy tales the villagers tell their children each night." His smile grew wide. "Perhaps it should be you who tells us those stories."

Nola's expression grew somber. "I'm glad they at least get to tell stories, Father. The king—" Her father hushed her, and she stopped at the door before coming inside. She realized her mum could hear her, thus spoke again in a quieter manner. “He can’t continue to get away with what he’s doing. Look at our land, Father. It is nearly dead. Magic—we need it back.”

“Shhh, quiet now. We should not speak of such things. It is what it is!”

Her shoulders slouched. “For now,” she protested.

The Lardbraks’s cottage stood on a small field atop an elevated, flat hill, close to the beautiful cliffs separating the ocean from the dry, brittle land—one hour by horse from the palace walls.

It had been gorgeous once, filled with purple irises and virescent thick trees. At least, that was what Nola’s parents had told her, anyway. She was only a baby at the time when the trees had already begun to die.

The leaves from Zemira’s trees turned to dry crisps, falling from their branches shortly before her father found her floating on a wooden board, and never returned the following year. The grounds shaded to black, and the only life that lit their city was the moonlight reflecting on the water.

Their land was dead, and they had to rely on the king’s monthly food deliveries that would keep them healthy and strong. Half of the produce was overly ripe and molding—taking the lives of about twenty villagers a year. They mostly lived off eggs from their livestock and fish from the ocean, both becoming scarcer by the day.

Decorating the Lardbraks’s cottage was a masterfully carved burgundy front door and grey-colored stones that stretched from the floor to the roof. It was her father’s most admirable masterpiece. The house was small and quaint, but it protected their family from the world around them—until the day came when it could not. The feeling of uncertainty about the future hit Nola when they entered their home and saw her mother sitting patiently, waiting for them to join her for breakfast. A full-plated meal was hard to come by, but that morning they had what they needed to fill their bellies and get through another day.

The pungent smell of her mother's fresh baked bread and omelets permeated the hallway and into the kitchen. The meal was small and somewhat simple—eggs and one potato—but seemed enough for the family of three. Though it was delicious, Val's bread needed to last the entire week, so Nola only ate a small piece.

"Duncan, dear," her mother began, "Nola should not be gallivantin' 'round the forest wit' ye. Look at 'er gettin' scraped up with twigs and dirt and learnin' to use a weapon made for war." Val poured boiling tea into a cup while Nola rolled her eyes, but her mother lifted her chin. "If this is 'bout those dreams ye've been havin'—"

"It's not," Nola said, cutting her off but instantly regretting it. She loved and respected her mother, and she was also aware of the dangers of drawing attention to herself. King Matthias disapproved of the town folk using weapons unless they were part of his guard or part of the wealthy who resided near the palace. That was why her father had to sell his goods at the marketplace. The elite were the only ones who Matthias allowed to purchase that kind of weapon. Yet the feeling of a bow in her hands, despite the king's ridiculous orders, was unlike anything she could have imagined. It was the one thing that truly made her feel alive—the one thing she needed to master to protect herself from her enemy—King Matthias.

"I know you want to protect me, Mother," she said, reaching out and gripping her mother's hand. "But I've had to pretend that I am a nobody my entire life." Nola then closed her eyes tightly. Her parents continued eating in silence, giving her space to think. Slowly, she opened them back up. "I don't want to be nobody. I know there is something better out there for me. And—" She gestured to the kitchen window that faced the path that led to the city. "It's not there."

"Oh, Nola," her father said, drawing her eyes to his. "You have never been a nobody."

Nola shrugged, flashing her parents a fake smile. She wanted to be something other than what she was. She struggled to see that future but needed so desperately to believe it was possible.

Her thoughts had often wandered to the sea; she thought of it as alive, often inviting her to let go of that human part of her and transform into her true self. But she would not. Ever since her parents told her she was a siren and how she came to them, Nola worried she would never be able to change back if she summoned her tail. The curiosity was there, of course, but it did not lessen her fear.

She bathed with rags and soap but never soaked—never sank her legs in water because she feared she would lose them forever.

But that was not the case anymore. Nola wanted to know

where she came from because it was a part of her whether she wanted it to be or not.

The future was uncertain, but she wondered every day what her path looked like. The only thing that made her feel truly happy was training with her father, and though her mother's intentions were not ill, she did not see life without her bow. If only her mother saw her in action with her arrows, she would see she was born for extraordinary things. She was born to fight. And who knew, maybe someday she would use those skills to protect the people from the king who had been destroying their land.

"Maybe, Mother, after today's market, you can see what Father has taught me," Nola said. "Do come. Please."

Her mother crossed her arms and leaned back against her chair, staying silent for a moment before her expression softened. "Of course, I'll be tha'. Though, promise me ye both take up other hobbies. I want ye to be safe from 'arm's way and wantin' this—" She paused and glanced at her husband, who gave a stern look to silence her.

Nola looked up. "Wouldn't learning to fight be the best lesson Father could teach me?" she asked. "The lessons I learned in school growing up are nothing compared to what Father has shown me." She glanced at Duncan and gave him a small smile. "I have the skill to defend myself with my bow, and also by magic."

Her mother blew out a breath. "We still don't know much 'bout that," she said. "And believe us, dear, we want ye to understand everythin' tha' makes ye special." She gripped Nola's hand, giving it a tight squeeze. "Ye did not come to us by chance, dear. Yer father and I know tha' the powers ye were born with are achin' to be released. We see it in yer eyes every time yer lookin' out into the sea. Ye may pretend ye don't want to swim, but yer instincts tell ye otherwise."

Nola lowered her gaze, looking at their hands clasped together, and gave her mother a weak smile.

"It's as though there's a part of me missing by not exploring the siren side of who I am, you know?"

Her mother nodded. "I know ye yearn to explore tha' world. But the king set his mission to destroy yer kind. It's for yer own protection, Nola. Ye shall 'ide yer magic from those who may use it against ye."

"I get it," Nola said, lowering her voice to a quiet whisper. "I understand, but I hate it."

Nola smiled faintly again and gave her mum a nod. She looked to her father, who only winked at her when Val turned to look out to the hills.

"Finish eating, Nola. Your food is getting cold," he said. "We'll discuss this another day, alright?"

Nola flashed a smile to them both and dove into her omelet.

After they had filled up with food, Nola cleared the table and changed into clean clothes. She helped her father load up the stock into the carriage and set course towards the city.

Once they reached the marketplace, Nola spotted three

rows of vendors lining the grey-brick walls outside the palace drawbridge.

The palace was so beautiful, Nola had a hard time averting her eyes. The walls were a clean shade of slate. Every stone, intricately carved, built up the walls gleaming with wealth and exquisite detail. Precious-stone mosaic windows lined the front, accompanying a drawbridge at the center. To the sides, a bridge over a small, rippled river led to the main gates. The marketplace started right at the front of the bridge and ran until it reached the main square.

Nola grabbed a few loose strands of hair coming out of her head wrap and tucked them securely out of view. Her heart was beating frantically, pulsating on her neck. Every time the guards walked past her, she felt nauseous; she worried they could see the fear in her eyes.

Still, she had to remain calm. Nola's father needed her that day because every sale was a plate of food on the table. They could not afford to not sell everything they had. Her father was the best bowyer in all Zemira, so she was confident they would sell out.

The process of carving and constructing a bow was tedious and tiresome, her father would tell her. However, he could sell each one for at least fifty coins, which was enough to buy food for a week.

"There might be quite a rush by high noon, so I'll need you and your mum to be ready to take payment if I'm bagging up the weaponry or instructing them on how to use it," he said. "I made three times as many bows this month, so, I need to push them out."

"Got it," Nola assured. "Do you still need me to demonstrate?"

He smirked. "Only if they're 'bout to walk away from a deal and need a little more persuasion. They'll buy once you show them how fast them arrows fly."

Nola perked up and helped her father set the rest of the bows and arrows along with the wooden table and racks under the tent. She then walked twenty feet from the tent and set up the target board.

"There," she said, "we're ready, Father."

Val, not knowing much about selling weaponry, laid out a table of apple cider brew and muffins she had baked that morning.

"They 'ill need to eat," Val said. "I'm sellin' these, so tha' 'ill be extra money for us. If it gets busy, I'll put this aside and 'elp."

"We've got this, Mother," Nola said, giving her a playful wink."

The morning rush flitted by quickly. It was as busy as her father had assumed it would be. But once it had slowed down to less than one customer every half hour, Nola had become bored.

Being as great of a salesman as he was a bowyer, Duncan had no troubles selling the product he had worked day and night on for the last thirty days. He had not needed her to show the precision of his bows at all. So, she spent most of the time chattering with her mother and helping her pass out muffins and cider.

"Father, may I go for a walk?" she asked him. "I promise I'll be safe. I just want to see the city."

Duncan was counting out the last few coins from the sale before turning to her. "I might need you," he replied.

Nola's shoulders slouched. "I doubt it. I've been sitting here for thirty minutes, and we've seen one customer." She folded her arms and leaned back into her chair. "I've never seen the city other than when I was a little girl, and even then, we were in and out of that chocolate shop before I could count to ten. It's not very often I—"

"Alright. Alright," Duncan said in defeat.

Nola's stomach leapt with joy, but the moment, however, was cut short as she eyed her mother, folding her arms, stomping her foot in protest.

"Duncan!" her mother snapped, shaking her head at him.

Nola glanced at her parents, scrunching up her face in irritation. "I'll be careful," she promised. "I'll use proper judgment on who I speak with. I'll avoid getting too close to the palace gates."

As dangerous as it was for her to venture off and how much she truly understood her mother's protest, Nola'a desire to see more was overwhelming. There was not much to see in her little village; the experiences it had given her for the last twenty years were no longer enough. Her adventurous spirit was aching to be released.

"I'll go wit' you," her mother said. "It does not matter wha' precautions ye take; ye ain't walkin' the city alone."

"Mother, please. I doubt King Matthias will be visiting the marketplace today, anyway. He's probably too busy admiring himself in the mirror." Nola snickered but stopped as her parents' eyes went wide, looking over her shoulder.

A shiver crawled up Nola's spine as she heard a deep voice from behind her.

"What was that you said?"

Her father and mother knelt quickly to the ground. She felt her mother's hand tug at her wrist. She instead yanked her arm away and whipped around to see Prince Elijah staring back at her.

Chapter 5

Prince Elijah's eyes locked in on Nola's, and she gulped. Panic clutched her chest, tugging at every nerve in her spine. He cocked his head while she stood there with an unblinking gaze. The corners of the prince's mouth slowly pulled up into a wicked grin.

She had never met the prince before, but Nola knew it the moment she looked into his eyes; it was him. He was breathtakingly beautiful. His dark black hair and piercing blue eyes highlighted his tall cheekbones. The prince's body was wrapped in a black and silver, well-embellished tunic, and a thin robe draped over his shoulders. He was not burly nor robust like his father, but he had lean muscles perfectly proportioned to his body.

The prince lifted his chin as Nola rushed to bow, but he gripped the cloth near her elbow, suggesting she should stand.

As he touched her sleeve, she remembered her bracelet holding the ruby her birth parents had left her. If she were caught with such a gem, as a commoner, she would be accused of being a thief. Nola discreetly shoved the bracelet further under her sleeve, then closed her eyes for a brief moment to gain her bearings.

"Please, indulge me with your opinion about my father," Prince Elijah said, "your king."

His voice came out smooth and accentuated, but she knew there was malice behind his words. Nola looked back at him, and she swore she saw his eyes shine darker as the prince's smile faded, leaving no trace of the amusement that was there moments before.

She forgot to look down when her nervousness took over, which meant the prince had seen what her eyes did when fear radiated within herself—a small mistake could have given her away. Nola's beating heart pounded wildly against her chest.

"I'm sorry, sir. I did not see you standing there." Nola lowered her head, looking to the ground. "I'm a fool. I don't know why I said that."

A very subtle smirk pulled at the sides of the prince's mouth, but his face remained serene.

Prince Elijah leaned in and whispered, "No, I do believe you meant every word." He inched closer. "Didn't you?"

As panic-filled tears began to reach Nola's eyes, she tried desperately not to show it. She hated crying, especially in the presence of strangers, but right then, she only feared for her life—for her parents' lives—all because she had let her mouth run wild. She had just spoken against the king, which was punishable by death. That was the first lesson her father taught her on their way to the marketplace that day.

Hold your wild tongue, you stupid girl, she shouted in her head.

Nola looked to her mother and father, who both shone dread in their eyes. Duncan shook his head as if pleading for her to be quiet. Nola, however, found her mouth opening, regardless.

"Do you want me to lie or share the truth? Because either would get me punished, would it not, sir?"

She heard a quiet gasp come from her mother's lips.

Prince Elijah placed his index finger on her chin, lifting it to meet his cold-stoned gaze.

"I can keep a secret," he said coolly. "I am more curious about who you are than what you had said about my father. I've not seen you in my city before. You see, I always make a point to know everyone in Zemira."

"We live in Bay—"

"She's my daughter," her father said quickly, interrupting her. "She's nobody, Your Highness."

Nola gave her father a sharp look as he used her own words against her. But regardless of his reasoning, it had hurt. She felt the prince's fingers slip down her jaw, but he did not release it.

"She doesn't look like a nobody," Prince Elijah said, directing Nola's attention back to him. "Will you walk with me?"

She reluctantly held out her hand. "Do I have a choice?"

He took her hand in his and helped Nola to her feet. "No," he said flatly.

Her father quickly stood. "Sir—"

"She'll come with me!" Prince Elijah said sternly.

Nola felt her father leap slightly towards the prince, but she rushed at him, placing her hands against his chest. "Let it go, Father. I never had a choice."

"It's Duncan. Am I right?" the prince asked. "I've heard great things about these bows of yours."

Val and Duncan's attention fixated on the prince, who turned his body to look at the bows dangling from the wooden rack. He traced his finger down the hand-carved limb of one of the longbows, then with a grin, he muttered, "I'll buy one from you—in exchange for twenty minutes with your daughter. I will even pay twice the price."

Nola's eyes went wide, and she rubbed her arms nervously.

"I—" Duncan started but stopped short when Val moved in front of him, shielding her lips from the prince and his guards.

"Shush it, Duncan! Don't provoke the bampot," she said quietly, where only Nola and her father could hear.

Duncan tightened his chiseled jaw before turning back to the prince. "Alright. But take that one." He gestured to the most expensive and detailed bow he had made. "A prince deserves the best and most luxurious of them all. This one took me twenty days to craft."

Nola gave her father a discreet nod. He knew too well how to play the game with the royal family. They needed praise to feel better about themselves. That and he had to make up for Nola's uncontrollable need to say whatever was on her mind. Despite his cleverness, she hated herself for putting them in such a situation.

Prince Elijah tossed a large sack of coins to Duncan,

paying over the asking price as agreed. Then the prince handed the bow to his guard to hold and shook Duncan's hand politely with a firm grip.

"I'll return your daughter in one piece. I am a man of my word," he said.

However, Nola was not sure if it was a promise he intended to keep.

She turned to her parents and kissed them both on each cheek.

"I'll be fine," Nola whispered.

"Shall we?" The prince opened his hand again for Nola to take, and she did it willingly despite hesitating for a split second. She noticed Prince Elijah found amusement in her slight resistance and smirked as he pulled her out from under the tent.

"You know," the prince started as they left the tent and walked down the aisle of vendors. "Most women are usually more thrilled to be in my presence."

Well, she thought, *isn't he just like his father.*

"Prince Elijah, I'm not like most women," she said boldly, referring to the fact he knew she was not human. "But you know that already, don't you?"

"That I do," he said. "Nevertheless, I didn't catch your name."

"Nola," she replied, bowing her head slightly, though her nerves bounced wildly in her stomach. "Pleased to make your acquaintance."

A sudden thought ran through her mind, *Appear friendly, respectful, and the prince shall leave you alone.*

"Quite a unique name, Nola. And, the pleasure is all

mine," he said and stopped abruptly at a jewelry vendor. She watched as he picked up a long, delicate necklace from the front rack. From the fine chain hung a thinly shaped carnelian gemstone at the top. He handed it to her while signaling to his guards to take care of the payment.

"To match those eyes of yours." A smile creased his handsome face as he pulled the necklace around her neck and latched it for her.

Nola's delicate yet strong hands felt shaky, but she hid her discomfort with a smile.

"Thank you, Your Highness," she murmured. Though she felt it polite to keep the peace between the two, dazzling her with jewels would not win her over.

"Elijah," he corrected, "call me Prince Elijah."

She fidgeted nervously with the bottom of her linen shirt until she felt the prince's hand at the bridge of her back. Nola stiffened.

"Are you afraid of me, Nola?" he asked calmly.

She turned to him. "No," she lied. "Well, under these circumstances, a little. I did imply your father was a narcissist."

He chuckled playfully and turned to his guard.

"Leave us," he said in an imperious, authoritative tone, waving his hand in the air.

The guards stood back while the prince continued to escort her down the marketplace corridor.

"You've been forgiven," he continued. "It's not like you're too far from the truth anyway . . ." His voice trailed off, and his attention appeared to have gone to another place.

She let out the breath she had been holding in.

"So," she said, as the prince turned back to her, "I'm not being led to get my head cut off?" Her lips beamed in a self-appreciative way as his eyes searched her face.

"No, I'm not planning to kill you," he said, his lips forming a wicked grin. "Though—I am slightly tempted to steal you away."

He winked at her as if he found humor in his not-so-subtle threat.

"I'm just curious about you, Nola." He paused and leaned in slightly towards her, lowering his voice. "And quite intrigued, I may add," he continued. "A siren—with human parents?"

She shifted uncomfortably. "I'm no threat to your people, Prince Elijah. Being human is all I know."

As he studied her, his unlocked gaze made her want to look away, but she could not. It was as if she was being drawn in by a fishhook, not able to break free from his hold.

"Yet, I can assure you, you will always crave more," he said.

Nola gave him a shy nod. "Oh, yeah, of course. I always wonder what it would be like to be out there, in the sea, but then I'm reminded that Zemira had once been a different place—"

"Before it died?" he asked.

"Yes, Prince Elijah. And I want to be able to fight for it." She pointed towards the seaport. "How can I do that from out there?"

He halted abruptly, standing by another merchant's

booth. The fresh squid lining the table sent an unpleasant odor looming in the air.

"Are you like them?" he said, pointing north. "Are you part of the resistance?"

"No," she answered quickly, "I mean, not like them. But I do believe there should be justice. How can I stand idly by while your father steals more than seventy percent of everyone's profit, while he literally sits on a throne made of gold?"

She wanted to mention how she knew magic was the most beautiful thing Zemira had ever had before the king banished it. But that alone would get a noose around her neck.

"We are suffering enough." She paused, carefully contemplating her next words. "It's inexcusable."

A small chuckle left his lips, and she was not sure if she had taken it too far with her bluntness.

"So, this isn't about the land?" he asked.

"That's not what I said, and quite far from what I meant," Nola appealed.

She looked away from him into the other vendors' tents, trying to think of the right words to help him understand.

Nola turned back to meet the prince's eyes. "Prince Elijah, if your father continues to run this kingdom like we mean nothing to him, then the future generations will be doomed. They will grow into that same destructive nature, ultimately killing every person on this land. We are prisoners to your father's law because it is the only way to survive. He gives us just enough to stay alive—but not enough to live," she explained.

The prince's brooding eyes stared back at hers. Nola was not sure if he understood the seriousness of what King Matthias had done to Zemira.

Even if he understands, does he care? Nola thought. *Or at least care enough to help make changes to how his father runs things?*

Suddenly, a few young women walked by. They were luxuriously dressed. Their tall and svelte bodies were wrapped in exclusive silks, their necks decorated with jewels only a limited number of people in the city could afford. One of the ladies smiled seductively at the prince to catch his attention, leaning forward with her low-cut dress, but his eyes would not leave Nola's.

I am only a commoner, she thought. *Why is he looking at me that way?*

Prince Elijah interrupted her thoughts. "You're different," he said with a disingenuous grin. "I like different." He stared at her with unyielding attentiveness. He courteously waved his hand to the merchants surrounding them. "Perhaps you'd like to join me in the palace sometime—you and I could discuss how we can better serve the people."

Nola felt her cheeks warm. The prince seemed different than what her father said about him, and as much as she wanted to trust him, she did not. The royal family always had a motive for everything they did. Taking an interest in a female siren's opinions—a poor one, for that matter—was so far off. She knew she had to keep her head down from there forward as her father had warned.

Nola bowed her head slightly. "Perhaps," she repeated his words. "Nice to meet you, Prince Elijah."

He delicately took her fingers in his and kissed the top of her hand. It sent a cold shiver up her neck, but she smiled politely and curtsied.

Nola stood still as the prince rounded the corner and walked back through the palace gates, followed by his guards.

She placed a hand on her hip. "Perhaps not," she uttered to herself while rolling her eyes. Nola whipped around to head back to her parents, who she knew were most likely pacing the tent. Right then, she slammed into a tall man's muscular chest, coming to a jarring halt. She looked up. Her heart raced faster than it had with the prince.

"And what does a prince want from a commoner, such as yourself?" the man asked in a slight accent, his deep voice laced with disapproval. The scent of musk coming from the man distracted her for a moment. Nola blinked, realizing the man was gripping tightly to her wrist and pressing his chest up against hers.

She yanked her arm away and said distastefully, "Pirate."

Irritation crossed through her as a smile grew on his face. He had a charming smile, but she still hated it. He was at least a half-foot taller than her, and despite his unkempt facial scruff and his tangled, unruly brown hair, he was rather handsome. As the pirate rested his eyes on hers, Nola's heart hammered. Every fiber of her body was taut with annoyance.

"Placing your hands on a stranger is quite frowned upon where I come from," Nola said.

She stepped to the side, but the pirate moved swiftly, blocking her from passing him. For a short moment, they stared at each other as if they were both hypnotized by a precious jewel. That stare alone caused her stomach to lurch. However, she scrunched up her face and slammed her heel on his toe, which caused him to wince and move out of her way.

"Blimey, woman—"

"Woman?"

"What? Are you not a woman?" he asked, but she only scowled at him.

He bit his bottom lip. "Prince Elijah isn't someone you want to be mingling with, in or outside the palace walls. I'm trying to help you out here by giving you a warning, but clearly, you don't give a bloody hell."

Nola's eyes snuck a glance at the palace walls.

"Oh, I am quite aware of what kind of family they are. It's not as if the prince gave me much of a choice. Nor is it any of your business."

The pirate pinched the bridge of his nose.

"Who are you?" he asked, lowering his voice.

Nola's mouth set in a hard line, not answering the stranger's question.

He gave her a bitter look. "Fine. Get yourself killed. What do I care?" he said, then moved past her, bumping into her shoulder and making her almost tumble to the ground.

"Pillock!" she shouted in his direction, watching him join a group of pirates near a booth selling barrels of rum. "Typical pirates!" she added, straightening her shirt.

Nola tried not to pay much attention to them, as pirates were not known to be the kindest bunch to visit Zemira. They were often spotted at smaller marketplaces near the Lardbraks's village—more than in the city. From what her father had explained, they avoided getting too close to the palace walls.

"Nola!" her parents shouted in unison when she came back to the tent.

"I'm fine, but maybe we should head back," she said calmly, trying not to alarm her parents.

"He knows, don't 'e?" her mother asked frantically.

Nola looked back at the palace gates. "Yes," she said. "But he seemed not to care."

As those words left her lips, she heard a faint cry come from down the line of vendors, closer to where the main entrance to the palace was. The king's guard filed out of the gates, along with two sheeracats.

"Father?" Nola rushed to his side. But as close as they were to the drawbridge, it was most likely that the guards had already seen them.

"Get the 'orses ready," Val said.

"It's too late, Mother." Nola's breath caught in her throat. "They'll see us fleeing and target us."

Nola had always been ready for the sheeracats' visits. It happened twice a year—once after spring and another shortly after the last snow. Sheeracats were much larger than an average house feline. Their limbs were long, their eyes midnight black, their body hairless but rough like tree bark.

It was not their appearance that was frightening; it was

their ability to heighten their sense of smell and sniff out creatures such as Nola—those who held magic.

The Lardbraks had always hidden their daughter well during their visits to Baylin. Their basement was not just an empty cellar. Duncan had created a tunnel that led out of the village and south of the city walls, so if there was ever trouble, trouble involving the king's guard—Nola had a way out.

The wicked creatures would usually sniff around the cottage, looking for something not human. Still, Nola's scent was never strong enough to pique the cats' interest. They would leave and not come back until the next round of visits. However, the market was a new place for Nola—one with no basement or tunnel.

"Secure each exit! No one leaves the marketplace," one of the guards with the most buttons on his jacket yelled from his ebony horse.

The rest of the uniformed men ran down the main vendor hall to prevent anyone from escaping as the sheeracats snuffed out each booth and merchant. The woman who had been crying out was already in their custody. Nola noticed how she kept her hair hidden, pretty much like hers, in a tight wrap around her ears and hair. Her unusually tall body bent forcefully to the ground as one of the guards pulled the scarf off her head. That was when her tiny, pointy ears stood straight up.

The woman was Elven.

They tied her arms behind her back, and she screamed so loudly that a few of the guards had to shield their ears. A little child, no taller than one of Nola's longbows, was dragged away in the opposite direction.

"Monsters," Nola said quietly. "They can't keep doing this, Father. We ought to stop the king."

"Not now, Nola. You're not ready," Duncan scolded.

"Wha' tha' bloody 'ell are ye two jabberin' 'bout?" Val said in a near whisper, but her eyes went wide as the sheeracats snuck up around the corner and entered their tent.

The Lardbraks quickly bowed as they had always been instructed to do when the cats visited. Nola's fingers felt numb as she gripped her hand into a tight fist. She shook and felt her heartbeat in her throat. The cat slowed as it entered her space and sniffed the air.

Go away, you beastly creatures. Leave us, Nola thought in her mind.

She closed her eyes tightly and sucked in a breath, holding it until she felt faint. Her eyes opened, and she looked at the cat. Its dark eyes widened slightly while sniffing the air again, and then it sneezed.

Huh, that's odd, Nola thought.

The sheeracat turned to its mate, and the two stared into each other's eyes for a few seconds as if communicating. The guards nodded and then pulled at the leashes to yank the animals away.

As they walked out of the linen tent, Nola blew out a heavy breath and looked to her parents. "What was that?"

"I don't know," her father replied, aghast. "But we aren't sticking 'round to find out. Once the guards disappear behind the palace walls, we're leaving."

Nola stood and peered down the vendor hall, watching once again the Elven woman screaming for her child being separated and taken into the palace gates. They were both about to be executed for being born different. Nola's nostrils flared as tears of desperation coursed through her.

He must be stopped, she thought, wiping her eyes. She did not care what her father had said about her needing more time.

It was time.

They quickly gathered the remaining bows and pulled down the tent. They were not the only ones rushing to get out of there. The stress created by the vile creatures drove most of the vendors to end their sales for the day. No one ever wanted to be near the palace. Still, the city's marketplace was the only way most villagers could make enough money to meet their tax quota and have spare cash to eat.

Nola looked up at the castle beyond the gate, and, in the distance, she spotted Prince Elijah peering down into the crowd—watching her.

Chapter 6

When Prince Elijah was a small child, his father told him a secret—Queen Serena was not his biological mother. He was too young at the time to understand much of what his father meant. The little boy was not angry or happy to learn such news. Despite his age, he did not dismiss the truth. On the contrary, he was somewhat interested in why his father kept it a secret for so long. The young prince listened intently to the story of how he came to be.

Elijah's birth mother, Gal, was a powerful sorceress. He had always known he had magic in him, yet never understood why he did and his eldest brother, Tristan, did not. It was a gift that his father forced him to keep hidden from the outside world.

"The people of Zemira would hate you," his father had once said.

Matthias told his son how beautiful Gal was. Her hair was the color of night, and eyes the color of deep cerulean blue, hypnotizing any man whenever they locked in on her unrelenting gaze. The king's affair with the gorgeous temptress lasted for months. Matthias was pleased as he was, having his way until Gal wanted more than just a love affair. She wanted him for herself, but Matthias loved his queen.

He tried to make his wrongs right by breaking off the affair with his mistress; however, Gal threatened to reveal their relationship to the queen by sharing she was with child. That child was to be named Elijah, and because she held great power, the sorceress would pass that same power to her son.

The king did all he could to hide Gal and the pregnancy from Queen Serena. He would not risk his reputation among his people. If they found out about it, they would reject that child. He begged Gal to stay away from the palace, and in return, he would shower her with riches if she kept the child a secret.

Nine months later, Elijah was born in the small village of Heyerberg, one hundred miles from the palace. The king looked into his child's eyes and decided he would not be raised in a poor town. After all, a son with magic running through his veins could be an advantage to his reign.

Gal implored Matthias not to take baby Elijah from her. She fought him with every spell she could, but her body was left weak and fragile after childbirth and did not have the strength to destroy him.

"You need to protect his magic," Gal had pleaded, accepting her fate. "Please, Matthias. Use this to protect his magic."

The sorceress handed the king a beautiful emerald crystal and shared with him the power it held. Matthias could hide the child's magic from all who look upon him with a mere touch of the jewel.

"Fascinating," he had said while holding up the gem to the light.

That was when the king remembered that the Newick witches enchanted many crystals in their time, one of those crystals being a key to a weapon. The weapon, a compass, could be used to defeat any kingdom in times of war. And the ruby was the key to unlock its power.

Unfortunately, someone had hidden the compass and the ruby in the sea, where no man could find them.

He looked one last time into Gal's blue eyes. Her weak and defeated body did not bring Matthias to feel loss or sadness at all. Relieved—that he was.

"Thank you, Gal; I will use this emerald to protect our child," the king had said. A lie.

Those were the last words she heard before he smothered her in her bed, taking the baby with him.

Queen Serena forgave the king for his deception and raised Elijah as her own.

All will be well, the king had told himself.

However, King Matthias did not use the emerald to protect his son. Instead, he taught Elijah to hide his magic and only use it when he ordered him to.

As the years went by, Elijah did just that. He suppressed the power that he wanted so desperately to release, and he resented his father because of it.

One evening, Prince Elijah entered his father's chambers, drawn to a safe sitting in the corner of his closet.

"What are you doing in here, son?" he heard his father ask from behind him. The boy startled and stumbled back.

"Father, what is in that safe?" he had asked him.

"Not anything of your concern, child," he replied. "Go back to bed."

"But, Father," he started again, "it's calling to me."

That was when the king understood. The emerald's power was connected to his child, and if that were true, then the power to the hidden ruby would draw him near, too.

The king told Elijah that night about his birth mother, his connection to the gems, and the weapon that would win all wars. No one knew where the ruby and compass were, but if he could use his son to find it someday, then perhaps, he would become almighty.

Years later, that morning in the marketplace, Elijah could have sworn he felt a similar power. However, it did not come from the sea, but a siren girl, right outside his palace walls.

He was drawn by the ruby even though he did not see it with his own eyes. It was hidden somewhere on her, and being a siren, he was not sure what could happen if he tried to snatch it from her in front of the other vendors. The king could not know what she was, or his plan would not play out as he would like.

Elijah entered the palace's gates, dismissed his guards again with a wave of his hand, and headed towards his father's bedchamber. The king stood by his window, looking out like he always did when lost in thought.

"Father," Elijah called.

"You did not slip up this time," his father sneered, turning to him. "That is a first."

Elijah gritted his teeth; his cheeks burned with fury.

His father was never a kind man, but he grew to be someone he despised more than any creature in their world in the last few years. The prince knew his father hated him too, finding him both cowardly and weak. Still, Elijah refused to be manipulated by him any longer.

Elijah sat on the edge of the bed, running his hands over the polished, silk bedding. He would not tell Matthias what he had seen in the marketplace. No. It would be his secret that he knew, without a doubt, the lost ruby was on the siren girl. He knew it the moment he placed his hand on her wrist. It was no secret to the prince what she was because a siren's eyes gave them away when angry or afraid.

He did find it puzzling the sheeracats could not identify the magic in her. It was probably for the best. That could have driven his father to kill the siren girl—and Elijah needed her.

The king turned from the window and approached his son, placing his hand on his shoulder.

"Who was she, boy?" the king asked.

Elijah swallowed. "An Elven woman and her child," he said, hiding the truth from his father.

Matthias's mouth curved into a wicked smile. "Well done. Now tell Mason to cut off their heads."

Elijah quickly stood to his feet. "Why not simply banish them to the Eastland Forest as you've always done?" he said. "Father, that child looked no older than five years old."

King Matthias's warped mind had finally caught up with him. Elijah refused to let his father's deranged ideas of how to rule a kingdom continue further.

"Bah!" The king spat at the floor next to him. Elijah recoiled. "Aren't you as worthless as your mother," the king said.

His father was not referring to the mother who raised him, but he meant his birth mother, Gal.

"Watch what you say next, Father," Elijah warned.

The corners of the king's mouth turned up. "Oh, look at you growing bolder by the day." He straightened his back. "She was a whore who died a slow and painful death. The only kind she deserved."

Elijah bit down hard on his bottom lip before asking, "And what of your wife? The one I called Mother? Did she deserve the kind of death you gave her too?"

"Hold your peace, boy!" The king's jaw tightened, his brows pulling together as if he were disgusted by the memory of what he had done. He paced from his bedside back to the window. "Traitors will eventually meet with death. For some, later than for others, yet they always have the same fate."

"She loved me!" Elijah said, his voice pitched. "She didn't have to love your bastard child, but she did. She should have hated me, but she didn't. Serena loved me when no one else would, even more than you."

The king's face reddened, and he swatted his hand in the air to dismiss him. "You're too naïve and callow to run this kingdom. You continue to prove you are not fit to make hard decisions such as this one! Every time, I am met with disappointment. I'm happy to pass down the throne to someone else."

You don't have a choice but to hand me the throne, Father. You killed your eldest heir, Elijah said to himself, enraged.

He wanted to say those words aloud, but he knew better. Elijah was not a fool, despite what his father thought of him. Then, as sadness clouded his features, he turned his head away from his father to face the door. Matthias snarled and guzzled down his drink and perched on his velvet chair, slamming the mug back down.

"I have given you an order, my son. You want to be king someday; you must let go of that merciful side of yours and start making tough decisions. That Elven woman knew what kind of danger she was putting her child in, and she chose to break the law anyway. Tell Mason to take care of it, or I will make you watch it happen when I do it!"

Elijah bit his tongue, then bowed his head and walked away, exiting the king's chambers. He stormed down the stairs that led to the dungeon where the Elven woman was locked up. The lantern-lit tunnel reeked of elf blood. The prince gagged at the filth.

When he reached the dungeons, he looked to one of the guards leaning against the door leading to the cell.

"Your Highness," the raw-recruit said and stood straight. The young guard, as if caught sleeping, opened his eyes wide. "They're locked in their cells, just as instructed, sir!"

Elijah looked to the guard as Mason walked down the stairs to meet him.

"Mason, my father has instructed that you kill the Elven mother and her child," Elijah said as Mason reached for the lock's keys hung on the wall. Matthias's most trusted guard never enjoyed killing children. Still, it was the Elven child or his head for disobeying an order.

"I'll make it as painless—"

"As you had my brother?" Elijah asked, his voice proper.

Mason cowered to him; his expression dulled as he looked down at his feet. "I promise you; Tristan did not suffer. I made it quick, just like I will with—"

"Right," Elijah said, cutting him off. He swallowed hard, trying not to lash out at his father's right hand. The prince hated his father and what he was doing and after what happened to Tristan, he would not allow the same fate for the Elven family. The blood spilled from a child must end.

Elijah held his hand out, flicking his wrist until black smoke left his fingers. A slow snake of smoke trailed up the young guard's stomach until it reached his throat. It then took the form of long fingers latching around his neck and squeezed so hard the guard's eyes turned beet red. Blood began to spew out of his eyes, ears, and nose. He watched the guard thrash against the door. His chest still rose slowly, but then it stopped, and his lifeless body slumped forward until it hit the ground.

Mason stepped back, preparing to run in the opposite direction. Elijah held his hand out and used that same power to grip Mason's throat.

"Don't worry, Mason, I'm not going to kill you. But it would be wise for you not to cross me. I need you to deliver a message to my father."

Elijah imagined for a moment that it was the king's throat he squeezed. He had fantasized about it every day of his life since his mother died. But he could not kill his father, because if he did, the order of the throne would be taken from him.

According to Zemiran tradition, a king was to pass the throne down to his next kin upon his death, regardless of Matthias wanting to or not. With Tristan being dead, Elijah was going to be king. The only thing that would prevent his right to the throne was if Elijah killed his father with his own hand. The risks were too great.

Elijah released Mason's throat and turned to the guard on the floor.

"You are not to tell him what happened here today! Instead, you'll say the Elven woman and child escaped before you arrived." He heightened his head, and his forehead furrowed. "That is what you will say."

The uniformed man shivered despite years of hardened service in the king's guard.

Elijah continued, "You are safer in my circle than my father's. You will no longer report to him but to me. Am I clear?"

"Prince Elijah—"

"Let me make myself clear, Mason. You do not have a choice," he threatened. "I can use my powers to shatter your spine with one snap of my fingers." Elijah straightened his chest, simmering down the rage he felt course through him.

The prince took a couple of deep breaths, softening the expression on his face. Then he said to the guard, "I am going to need the smartest of my father's servants on my side—and that's you" He stepped closer to Mason and placed his hand on his shoulder. "The king is belligerent.

He only cares about himself. I am trying to help you and our kingdom before he destroys us all."

As loyal as Mason was to the king, Elijah saw how terrified he was of his powers. He would do as the prince requested. Mason would betray his king until the time came when Matthias took his last breath.

Chapter 7

The cellar door outside the Lardbraks's back porch had been locked and latched for nearly a year; the lock's rustic metal bent slightly from the few bad storms after magic vanished. Duncan struggled to pry it open, even after using a few tools he brought from his shed. After he opened the door, they rushed into the basement just below the cottage.

Duncan reached for a bow dangling from a hook on the wall. Then he grabbed a bag with new arrows and placed it on the table next to him.

"Say it isn't so, Duncan!" Val cried. "This entire time, ye weren't trainin' Nola to sell yer bows and arrows, were ye?" Her hands went into fists, watching her husband stay silent as he gathered up more arrows. "Duncan, talk to me, eh!"

"Val—" He rested his hand on the chair next to him and drew a breathless sigh. "I'm sorry, my love."

Nola watched the blood drain from her father's cheeks. She knew he feared her journey more than she did, though their plan had been set in motion for two years. It was not a matter of if, but when she would venture to the sea. That was the day her parents needed to let her go—Val more than Duncan.

Nola turned to her mother. “I’m going to the Eastland Forest to see the Fae queen,” she said.

Val paled, and her mouth snapped shut before she staggered into her husband’s arms. Nola gave her a minute to take it in, then rushed to them both and wrapped her arms around them.

“I cannot allow the king to destroy our land,” she whispered into their ears. Then, as she released the hug, she added, holding out both her hands for her parents to take, “We will all die if the king continues to poison us with his ideology and hatred for anyone who threatens his rule. King Matthias will destroy everything we are.” Nola’s lips drew back in a snarl. “Do you see what is happening out there?”

“Yah,” her mother admitted quickly. “I do, but wh’ must ye be thah one to do it, huh?” she asked, her voice caught in her throat, her accent thicker as tears drew to her eyes. “Ma child, tell me why does it ’ave to be ye?”

Nola felt the heaviness in her chest tighten before she answered, “Because I have a feeling I am somehow special, Mother.” She wiped a tear from her mother’s cheek. “I love you more than my own life. Thank you for saving me. Thank you for becoming my mother—for loving me like no one else has.” Another tiny tear trickled down, that time from her own cheek. Then she continued, “I feel it in my heart, Mum. I believe it is my duty to lead.”

A look of fear passed across Val’s face.

“I am scared but know I will not do it alone. The Elven

warriors live among the Fae, and they are strong and brave. We will fight together," Nola added.

Val tilted her head. "Wha' if 'ey say no?" she asked, "Wha' then, huh?"

Nola shrugged. "I will have to find out when I arrive to see the queen," she said confidently.

Duncan placed his arm around his wife again and gave her a comforting squeeze.

"We ought to trust our daughter; she is stronger than you think," he said.

Val pulled away from Duncan's touch and wrapped her arms around her waist.

"Yer just goin' to get yerself killed! That's wha' yer goin' to do," she said, a hard sob escaping her. "That beast—the king—is goin' to kill ye."

The fear in Val's voice pulled at Nola's heart. She was asking her to trust in the unknown and watch her start a war. Nola needed her mother's strength more than anything. She did not want to leave her like that, but time was running out and if she did not go then, the king's men would stop her before she could leave the shore.

Nola's face lit up as she wiped a tear off her cheek.

"I'd rather fall to protect the people I have been raised to love than turn my back on them and do nothing."

Val drew her lower lip between her teeth and stepped back, placing her hand against the wall as if she were about to collapse to the floor and looked up. A long silence loomed in the cellar, all three of them deep in thought for a good minute.

"Then we—" Val paused, placing her hand on her throat

as if a painful lump was pressed against it. “We need to pack ye some clothes, and—”

“It’s already done,” Duncan said. “I packed her a bag two years ago.”

The Lardbraks stood by the road leading south of their property.

Tears trickled down Val’s cheek as her daughter placed her forehead against hers, lingering for a few seconds. Nola felt her chest tighten in sadness.

Val said softly, “Swim, Nola. Go to the sea, find answers, and become the warrior I ’ave known, yet always feared ye’d become.” She wiped her nose. “It ain’t up to me to decide yer fate.”

Val released her. Then Nola turned and wrapped her arms around Duncan.

“I love you, Father,” she said.

He smiled. “The greatest moment of my life was the day I found you floating in the sea. You were meant to be me daughter, and I am so proud of you.”

Nola’s jaw trembled, but she would not allow herself to cry. She secured the bag's strap around her shoulders, then checked her bracelet, making sure she had the one thing tying her to the sea. A slight moment of doubt crept into her mind—she hesitated.

“Gotta believe, child,” Duncan said as if he had known her thoughts.

Nola smiled; her shoulders slouched. "See you when we win the war and bring back the magic."

Nola had until sundown to reach the docks. Three trading vessels sailed to Queenstown every Monday and Friday. There, she would have to pay the sailors for the remainder of her trip to the Eastland Forest with every coin her father had given her. But she had to move quickly once she reached Queenstown. If she missed the ship, she would have to wait three days in a foreign city.

Brecken's main square was nearly empty; all sailors most likely at the waterfront already, and the shops were starting to close. The lampposts were dimly lit. The lack of breeze promised a relatively quiet evening to Nola's disadvantage. It was a sweltering afternoon.

It took Nola a few hours on foot to get there. She peered behind a weeping willow, keeping to the shadows. Beads of sweat rolled down the nape of her neck. If it were not for the heavy bag around her shoulder, she might not have been so worn.

Nola rested her back against the tree and felt the weight of her body ease and her legs relax. Then she removed the bag and placed it on the ground next to her. She pulled her shoulder blades together and let out a long sigh.

And this is just the beginning, Nola thought as exhaustion settled in her body.

Dried leaves fluttered from the trail, followed by what

appeared to be horse hooves trotting down the dirt-paved road. Nola's eyes turned to the two horses veering the corner, pulling a coach behind, heading in the direction she was going. Brecken was not the safest place for anyone to venture —a city full of crime and violence. Still, it was the only way to a decent ship, and by ship was the only way out of Zemira.

As the horses came closer to her, moving briskly down the road, she leapt forward, standing in their path, holding up her hands. The driver pulled back the reins and halted.

"Move, girl! Get out of my way!" he shouted.

She glanced at the coach. The curtains were drawn, so she was not able to see who was inside.

"Could I get a ride, please?" she asked, nerves twisting in her belly. She had no idea who was in there and feared it was someone from the royal palace, though it did look a bit too worn and tattered to be something the royal family would own.

The driver looked behind him as if he were speaking with someone inside and then back at Nola.

"What's your name?" the hairy man asked, and his eye twitched as he shifted his heavy body in his box.

"Finola," she replied nervously. He probably heard the anxious pitch in her voice, she thought, and that alone could make him suspect she was not trustworthy.

The door to the left of the coach opened slowly, and a woman stepped out. She was tall, with long white hair that reached down to her hips. Her clothes looked like any commoner she had met, and she strolled towards Nola.

"Whereabouts are you traveling to, Finola?" she asked. Her voice was deep but not masculine.

Nola gestured with her head. "Brecken Terrace, the waterfront—just a few miles that way!"

"I know where Brecken Terrace is—that's where we're heading, too. Would you like a ride?"

Nola had not interacted much with people outside her village. She did not trust easily, but the woman did not feel like a threat. However, her father taught her through the years that people could lie and deceive. They pretended to be kind when they were nothing but the sort.

Nola nodded, still doubtful but exhausted. "Thank you. I've been walking all afternoon." Then, she followed the woman onto the carriage and stepped inside. Her shoulders relaxed when she saw a small child sitting on the booth across from her.

"This is my husband, Thomas, and my daughter, Cam," the white-haired woman said, gesturing to her family.

Nola smiled. "It's very nice to meet you," she said, shaking their hands.

The little girl was no older than four, and the woman's husband was a heavy-set man, with a short beard and dark freckles along his nose and under his eyes.

"I'm Sabre," the tall woman said.

"Are you from Brecken?" Nola asked.

Sabre shook her head. "No, but we have business with some friends at the waterfront. You're causing us no trouble at all, I promise. Besides, look at you, you are sweating like you just fell into a lake. You should relax a bit; it's going to be another few miles before we reach the docks."

The horses stepped forward, pulling them along the path towards Brecken's harbor. Nola looked into Sabre's eyes and over to the left of her hair. She spotted her ears slightly pushing out of her long strands.

"You're an elf," she said, immediately regretting it. Elves were spies. Their identity was meant to stay hidden from the enemy. But when those words slipped her mouth, Nola admitted she knew her secret. The woman's shoulders stiffened, and she placed her hand on her sword.

"Please," Nola said, holding up her hand, "I'm not your enemy."

The woman gave her a small smile and released her hand from the sword. "You may have to prove that here in a moment. I hear something," Sabre said, looking out through the curtain. "You might also want to cover that hair of yours too."

Nola felt a nervous twitch in her gut.

My head wrap, she said in her thoughts. She had forgotten it.

"These bastards still won't give up." Sabre pointed out the window. "It's the king's soldiers." The Elven woman glanced to meet Nola's terrified eyes and added, "You don't do anything unless I tell you, understand?"

Nola gave her a nod as she felt the carriage come to a stop. She gripped to the side to keep herself from flying forward towards the others.

"Step out of the carriage. Put your hands above your head so we can see them," they heard a deep voice shout from outside the coach. The muffled sound of the driver answering a few questions alerted the Elven woman. Nola reached forward, gripping hold of the little girl's hands.

"Everything will be alright. I won't let anything happen

to you," Nola assured the little girl. She looked up as Sabre's eyes went wide.

"We should have taken the western route," Sabre said, quickly pulling her hair forward to cover her ears.

"Do you have any weapons?" Nola asked. "Aside from that sword?"

Sabre replied, "Just the one on my hip." She pointed to the weapon in her sheath. "You?"

Nola unzipped her bag, revealing her bow and a tiny clasp-knife.

"Do you know how to use that thing?" Sabre asked dryly.

"Yes." She nodded. "But never on a person."

Awe transformed Sabre's face. Then she peeked out through the curtain again, watching two of the guards approach the coach on their horses.

"Well, you're about to get your opportunity," she said.

Nola's stomach lurched. She had already realized she was about to venture to the Eastland Forest to build an army to go to war. Still, the opportunity to fight an enemy came faster than she anticipated; she was terrified.

The driver opened the side door and whispered, "Sorry, Sabre."

The elf secured her coat over her sword and stepped out after telling her family to stay put.

Nola looked at the man. "Protect your daughter," she said. "I'll help your wife."

"She is not my wife," he muttered quickly. "She's helping us lead the resistance."

Nola learned about the rebels years ago from her

parents. But she had not met a single one—mainly because they were too afraid to reveal themselves. Many had feared retaliation; others had simply left the movement altogether. A small amount of hope reached Nola, knowing there were still others out there willing to risk their lives to save the kingdom.

Nola stepped out of the shabby wagon behind the Elven spy, leaving her bag open and next to the door. They both raised their arms in surrender. Suddenly the guards' shoulders slumped. Their facial expressions changed, as though they believed the women were far from being a threat. Nola dropped her hands and walked back slightly until her right heel hit the wheel of the coach.

One of the men, the skinnier one, rushed forward, pressing his hand aggressively against Nola's chest. He pushed her hard against the side of the carriage, keeping her in place.

"Who are you?" he asked, snapping his fingers at the other guard who climbed off his horse.

"I'm her sister," she lied. Sabre smiled in approval. Nola may not have known much about the resistance, but she was aware they traveled together. Those days, you either traveled with family, or you were up to no good.

A quiet sigh of relief hit her as he eased up on her chest. The man withdrew his hold on her but stayed close so she still could not move past him.

Sabre cleared her throat. "We're just heading to Brecken Terrace's tavern for a drink, sir. Is there a problem?"

The two men exchanged a glance, and the one next to

his horse withdrew his sword and pointed the sharp end at Sabre's cheek.

"Do you have any weapons on you?" he asked, addressing Sabre.

"I have my sword," she affirmed. Not trying to hide it.

"Throw your sword on the ground and show us your ears," he ordered. "Now!"

Nola swallowed hard, remembering the incident at the marketplace. At that moment, it was not her life she feared for the most; it was Thomas's little girl's.

While keeping Nola pinned against the coach, he gripped a silver strand of her hair as she tried to move away. "What's wrong with your hair?" he asked, his breath fanning her skin. His voice alone made her shoulders rigid. The guard's hand moved swiftly to grip her chin; his fingers pressed aggressively into her tender cheeks.

Nola winced, trying to move her face away. She peered over her shoulder, searching for her bag through the crack of the door. The guard was too close for her to position her bow.

She stood still, trying to remain calm. But then Nola saw Sabre standing unmoved, with no plan to reveal her ears—her body drowned in fear.

The man holding her turned to talk to the other one. Nola saw her chance. She slowly reached into her bag and gripped her knife, closing her fingers around the handle. Nola was lucky he did not feel her moving. Then, she carefully pulled the weapon out without making any sudden movement and kept the knife close to her thigh as the guard held his eyes on Sabre. The instant the guard turned back to Nola, she brought the metal tip up straight and plunged it up into his throat. His eyes shot open as blood spurted out his throat and onto her face. She yanked the knife out and used her foot to kick him away, then tossed the bloodied knife on the ground.

Nola hastily drew in a deep, audible breath. Her wobbly legs buckled, causing her to stumble back a step. Leaning against one of the horses, she felt bile rise to her throat before puking over its side. She spat the sour taste from her mouth and looked up; her hands shook uncontrollably.

Nola's head fogged over, and all she heard was Sabre urging her to run. Simultaneously, the Elven woman came to a warrior stance gripping her sword as the other soldier tried to flee in the other direction.

Flashes of confusion came next. All Nola saw was a crimson blood pond expanding from the guard's corpse. She then heard the echo of a low cry and then silence.

Nola glanced down at her trembling hands and saw her blood-stained fingers. They did not look like her hands. She still was not sure what had happened.

She licked her lips unknowingly, tasting the blood that was not hers. Nola recoiled, staggering over to a fallen tree and leaning into the trunk, inhaling the herbaceous scent of wet bark. Any scent to mask the smell of death.

She had never killed a man, yet she was about to convince an entire land of elves and fairies to start a war with her. Her own doubts crept within her mind.

I don't think I can do this, Nola thought, then sat on the branch stagnant until she heard Sabre's voice calling her name.

"Look at me, Finola."

She looked up at Sabre's eyes. "I—I'm sorry," Nola stammered, feeling her heart pounding beneath her ribs. "I didn't know what else to do."

Sabre shook her head, placing her hands on each side of Nola's face. "I know you're scared—"

"Scared?" Nola repeated. "No." She shook her head. "I'm not scared, Sabre. I'm terrified."

The Elven woman released her, stood straight, and glanced over her shoulder at the coach. "You did what I would have done. That is what any warrior would have done. You protected that family over there. Remember that."

Did she say, remember that? Of course, she thought, knowing she would never get the image of stabbing a man through the throat out of her mind. Ever.

Sabre walked to the carriage, putting her sword away, and said something to the man. Then she kissed little Cam on the forehead and closed the cabby's door. From her cloak, she pulled out a small leather bag and gave it to the driver. It was heavy, Nola could tell. The fat man made a weird salute to her and tugged at the horses' reins. A few seconds later, the carriage was out of their sight.

Nola looked around the dark trail. "What—what do we do now?" She did not recognize her own voice.

"Now," Sabre started. "We walk the rest of the way. Wherever you are heading, you better get there fast because they'll come looking for those soldiers, and then they'll come looking for us." She extended her hand. "Come on, get up."

Nola gripped her hand so the elf could help her to her feet. She felt numb all over her body, but if she did not pull herself out of the fear and shock, she would not be able to find her feet to flee.

Sabre handed Nola her bag. Her hands shivered so badly she had trouble wrapping the strap around her shoulder.

Nola pressed her palm against her chest, taking a few heavy breaths until she felt the trembling subside. She had to keep moving.

The Elven spy was right—they were going to come looking for whoever killed those men.

After parting from the spy, she sped through the forest, not stopping until she reached the docks at Brecken Terrace.

By the time Nola entered the port, all she wanted to do was sit and not move. She immediately inhaled the pungent odor of garbage from the alleyways. The smell of rotten fish and old beer was overwhelming to her siren senses. It also did not help that it was a humid and miserably hot day. Whores loitered the streets. Drunken pirates and tired patrons flooded the taverns. Nola could not help but stare at the scene. She had not seen a place like that before. Baylin, unlike Brecken Terrace's pier, was quiet, peaceful, and pleasant.

Sweat beat down her forehead, making her hair a tangled mess. She spotted a nearby bench, and despite the grime and filth that coated the wood, she sat on it, leaning back to catch her breath.

Nola pulled off her cloak and used the sleeves to wipe

off any trace of blood from the guard she still had on her. Once she finished, despite the metallic smell of blood on the fabric, she put her cloak back on, covering her hair with the hood. She looked down at the ground, trying to hide her face, as a homely old man walked past her.

The stranger tipped his unkempt hat. "Eh, lassie. You got some money for me? Or, how about you and I—"

"Get lost!" she snapped, feeling as though drops of boiling water trickled down her spine as she fumed with rage. Sudden anger trembled throughout her body as she met the man's gaze. He blanched, watching her eyes change. Nola kept a stern expression on her face until he took off running in the opposite direction. All the emotions were so new for her. She rubbed the back of her neck, feeling her fidgety hands going wild, so she placed them between her thighs for a still moment. Nola licked her lips as she felt thirsty and could still taste the coppery, bitter taste of blood on her tongue. She needed water to wash it away.

Standing up and dusting her cloak, Nola walked down the street and found a few barrels with fresh water. As she washed up and drank, loud, boisterous laughter rang from a grotty old tavern across the road. Her entire body still felt as if it had fallen into icy waters—her blood ran cold from worry.

Nola blinked, catching her breath one more time, before heading towards the tavern.

Chapter 8

"How about that be your last drink, mate? Eh?" Lincoln said to Hill evenly. He took the skinny buccaneer's empty mug from his hand and placed it on the bar.

The Sybil Curse's crew was used to the days and nights of getting sloshed until they passed out. However, given they needed to leave Brecken Port that evening and journey to the Eastland Forest, Lincoln had to get Hill sober, even just for a few hours while they left Zemiran waters.

Hill braced himself on the corner of his chair, nearly tipping it over as he maneuvered his way back to the bar.

"Fill 'er to the brim, wench," he said sluggishly to the barmaid, ignoring his captain's request.

The skinny pirate flinched, bracing himself for the slap that did not come.

"Aye," Lincoln muttered quietly to himself, "this isn't going to end well."

The barmaid yanked the empty mug from the counter and gritted her teeth. "Who ye callin' wench, ye bilge rat?"

Hill flashed his yellow teeth and looked down, staring at her full and voluminous bosom. "Are ye flirtin' wit' me, darlin'?" he asked, speaking to her chest.

Her shoulders stiffened—her nostrils flared. "Get out of me tavern!"

A slow smirk reached Hill's lips right as her brother, Edgard, walked in from the back, folding his arms over his puffed-out chest. Lincoln had met the lad a time or two during their visits. He owned the bar with his sister, Sarah, and they had not encountered any issues for the most part. Until then.

A stern glare rose on Edgard's face. He growled at Hill, his lip curling up to show his teeth.

Hill's smirk faded quickly to a flat line, not stepping back. He stood stiff, swaggering back and forth on his heels.

"Edgard, he ain't worth it, Brotha. We're just dealin' with another drunken princock." Sarah leaned forward, so close that Hill was forced to look into her eyes. "I said, get out of me tavern, worthless spine." She smirked at her own remark while he continued to stare at her heart-shaped lips.

Hill 'Tipsy' Penny was not a fighting man, nor sharp-witted. And, despite the woman's brother glaring him down and being three times Hill's size, he leaned forward, placing his elbows against the bar. She, too, moved closer, meeting him halfway.

"What's the matter, pirate," she said, as the smile on her lips grew wider, "had yer tongue pruned?"

No, Hill was not a fighting man, but he sure knew how to start one.

Lincoln watched his mate close the gap between them and plant a kiss upon her lips. Then he decided to push his luck, wrapped his fingers around her shirt's collar, and pulled her closer, deepening the kiss.

Edgard immediately rushed to land a blow on Hill's gut as he pulled him from his sister.

Then, the fight broke out.

Kitten and Mazie watched the encounter from a distance, staring at Edgard, who lunged at Hill. Boots pulled his peg leg off and brought it savagely at the back of his head like he was swinging a bat.

As with any other harbor tavern, at the fall of one man, the ones around engaged in the brawl.

"Fight! Fight! Fight!" the crowd chanted.

Beer soared through the air. Empty rum bottles crashed on the floor, and one or two teeth flew by as the punches arrived.

Mazie shone Kitten a look, her teeth flashing a half-smile before her fist came out and crashed into the nose of a male patron at the table next to them. The man had only been minding his business.

When he sprang forward to defend himself, she raised her knee, connecting with his nose. Lincoln watched as the lad tried to flee the assault, wailing and throwing his hand up while red spewed from his bloodied face. Mazie gripped the clothes at his shoulders and hurtled him across the table with one heave.

"Bloody hell, Mazie!" Lincoln shouted.

Ardley slapped his knee and tossed back the last of his

drink as Edgard struggled to hold Hill and defend himself from Boots.

"Bloody hell to the lot of them," Lincoln shouted to Ardley as they watched Hill, who wobbled around every time Edgard swung his fist at Boots.

"We should really break this up and finish here. We ought to get our supplies," Ardley reminded him, still gripping his mug tightly in his fist, shouting over the banter. "We only have three hours before we head out to sea. As fun as this is, Captain, we don't want to draw any more attention to us."

Lincoln nodded, pulled his boucan knife from the sheath, and hurled it across the room until it hit the bar, the blade sticking into the wooden surface. Boots and Edgard broke their fight, both staring at the weapon that stood upright between them.

Sarah pulled Hill from her brother's grip and slapped the lanky pirate hard against the cheek. "Scallywag!"

He placed his hand against his cheek and smiled as if he had been under a love spell.

A loud moan came from the back of the bar. They all turned to see the lad still in Mazie's grasp. Boots lifted his peg leg again to strike Edgard while he was distracted, but Lincoln held up his hand.

"Enough, Boots! Let the poor man be."

While trying to balance on one leg, Boots reconnected his peg leg and gripped Hill's arm to pull him away from the bully. The rest of the crew scurried to their tables to finish their drinks while Edgard tried to get his bearings to stand straight.

"Perhaps next time," Kitten said, laughing under her breath, "ye, grog blossom, give us a li'l warnin' before ye assault a town local."

"And miss out on all the fun, lassie? Don't pretend ye didn't take a likin' to that brawl," Hill said, watching her wink at him to let him know she was only teasing.

The buccaneers had their share of fights since they formed their crew, but it had been a while. Lincoln hoped that brawl was enough to last them for the entire trip until they hit dock again.

The front door swung wide open, drawing the crew's attention to look up.

Lincoln watched a woman walk in, her eyes growing wide as she looked around at the tavern full of bloodied patrons, half on the floor, many with a busted lip or eye.

Ardley handed Hill a glass of water and forcefully sat him down on a chair. The barmaid resumed her post while her brother patched up the wound on his forehead. Their casual response showed it was not the first time a random altercation broke out in their tavern.

Lincoln glanced straight at the woman; she had her head down, but he could tell her eyes searched swiftly for the bar. He noticed she appeared troubled as she marched with extreme trepidation. It was almost as if she did not want to be there. Or she did not have a choice.

Lincoln's stare would not leave her as he watched the woman pad across the tavern to the bar. He noticed her clothes were worn, ragged. Suddenly her eyes flashed to his table as Hill laughed; Lincoln recognized her as the one from the marketplace with whom he had made himself a complete buffoon.

The beautiful woman had captivated him that day. He was somehow glad to see her again. But one thing was clear —she did not belong in that tavern.

Perhaps she is from the north side of the city, he supposed. He then saw the long bag she wore over her shoulder, so he thought maybe she was just traveling through.

Lincoln's eyes narrowed to the red-stained spots on the front of her shirt, and then over to the tiny drops on her cloak's sleeve.

He watched her intently as she pulled her hood off her head. Her gaze met his for a few seconds before turning away.

What is she doing here? Lincoln thought. He would never forget that face, nor those fierce eyes.

Lincoln's attitude had been slightly out of place that morning. He remembered being coarse, but he could not help himself. He felt drawn to protect whoever the girl was from the royal family. They were beyond evil, and she was anything but.

Ardley stomped his foot, pulling Lincoln away from whatever spell she had on him.

"What happened to you, matey?" Ardley asked, clearing his throat and arching a brow.

Lincoln ignored him as the woman waited for the barman to notice her.

"Captain, we need to leave," Kitten suggested. "The Eastland Forest is a seven-day journey, and there's talk of a storm rollin' in."

Lincoln held up a hand to silence Kitten to eavesdrop on the conversation at the bar.

"What do ye want?" Edgard scowled at the woman, wiping the blood that was dripping from his nose onto his sleeve.

"Water, please," her voice pitched.

Sarah moved past her brother and looked at the woman for a long moment before throwing her hands up. "Well, ye got money for us?" she asked.

The beautiful woman drew in a deep, audible breath. "For . . . for water?" Her voice shook when she spoke.

"Nothin' is free, darlin'. Now pay me a pretty penny or get out of me tavern!"

Lincoln rushed to the bar. "Sarah, love, I will pay for the girl's drink. It's the least I can do," he said, placing three coins on the counter. "Is that enough?"

Sarah nodded and took the coins, placing the money in her register.

The woman looked up at Lincoln again, who was nearly a foot from her, and smiled. "Thank you—" Then her face grew grim. "It's you."

"Aye, it is me," he said, gesturing a dramatic bow and moving his open palm forward.

She rolled her eyes, picking up the drink. "Thank you for the water, pirate," she said, seemingly annoyed with him, and did not look up again.

The woman fumbled with the mug before bringing it to her lips—gulping it down until she finished, then placed it back on the counter.

Lincoln sized her up. She was drenched in sweat, but he

only smelt her herbaceous fragrance. It was almost like the warm scent of spring.

He folded his arms and shifted on his heel. “You don’t look like you belong in these parts of town,” he said. “What is a girl like you doing in a dingy tavern in Brecken Terrace?”

Lincoln was simply trying to unwind each secret she held firmly. He flashed her a playful smile that reached his jade-green eyes.

“Just out for a jog,” she said dryly, “and I ran out of water.” She lifted her mug and smiled back.

His gaze went back to the blood on her clothes, and as she turned, he noticed a smudge on her chin. Lincoln reached out, causing her to flinch as he ran his thumb across her skin. He pulled back and rubbed the tips of his fingers together.

“Is this your blood?” he asked, his smile slipped. “Are you hurt?”

Her shoulders went rigid, and her jaw clenched as she drew a deep breath. “No, it’s not my blood,” she answered, bringing her voice to a quiet, almost inaudible whisper.

Something flickered in her eyes; she had secrets—that was certain. Lincoln wiped his fingers over his shirt but kept his eyes glued to hers.

“Pardon me.” She placed her mug on the bar and tried to move past him, but he did what he had done at the marketplace and blocked her path.

Lincoln looked down as she wrapped her arms around her waist—clearly showing her frustration.

He cleared his throat, speaking with confidence and

vigor, "I realize now I wasn't my charming self this morning when we first met—"

"My father taught me to avoid the likes of pirates," she said, cutting him off. "What he told me didn't paint a man like you to buy a girl a drink."

Lincoln smirked again, shrugging a shoulder. "Did your father piss on the wrong pirate?"

Wrinkling her nose and a glint of irritation crossing over her features, she replied, "Well, that is a bit crude."

"I'm only trying to be honest," he added. "And if that means I'm crude, well, then, aye, I do believe I am." He leaned to the side, resting his elbow on a stool next to him, keeping a warm grin on his lips. "No offense to your father, but it appears that he may have deluded your mind. We aren't all violence and bloodshed."

The moment the words left his lips, he chuckled to himself, watching the patrons in the tavern avert their eyes from his crew after what had just occurred before she walked in the door.

She raised a brow, looking at him questionably.

He flattened his smile. "In all seriousness, I—" Lincoln glanced over to his crew, "—*we* would never hurt a lady," he said, trying to sound as genuine as he felt.

She smiled for the first time. "Those, about random bar fights, aren't the stories my father told me," she corrected, pausing for a beat. "And I need to leave." The woman secured her bag over her shoulder, keeping it from sliding down her arm. "Thank you for the water, truly," she said, and started to walk towards the door.

He shook his head. "Nay, wait. I have offended your

father. Please allow me to apologize," he said. Lincoln rushed after her. He could not allow her to go.

She narrowed her eyes as he caught up with her at the door and pressed his hand against it but pulled back quickly when she looked daggers at him.

"What stories did your father tell you?" he asked, genuinely curious, but also, he did not want her to leave.

A glimmer of agitation flickered in her eyes. "Pirate, if you don't move out of my way—"

He loomed closer to her—the heat of her quickened breath warmed his cheeks. She did not move a single inch. Lincoln's stomach twitched at the excitement. For a moment, he lost his voice. Instead of saying anything else, he shifted on his heel, backing up a step to give her space.

Lincoln cocked his head, fire burning in his lust-filled eyes. She looked down as a mischievous grin reached his lips.

The silence looming between them was driving him mad. All he wanted was to reach out, but the woman was clearly angered.

She cleared her throat before saying, "I must leave. Now, I—"

"Name," he said, a smirk reaching his lips. "Just tell me your name."

She smiled meekly, adjusting the hood over her hair a little further down her forehead. "Goodbye, pirate."

"I'm Lincoln," he said, but she would not look up. "Captain Lincoln."

She pressed her foot against the door and her hand on the knob and let out a weak breath. "I'm Nola." She quickly placed her hand over her mouth as if she had said something wrong.

"It's a beautiful name," he said, watching her hand fall to her side. A peachy hue rose to her cheeks. "Why are you so afraid to tell me your name?"

She nibbled on her bottom lip, turning the knob to open the door. Lincoln's smile broadened as he took another step back, giving her space to move past him.

"You did not see me here today." That was the last thing she said before stepping through the door into the shadows.

Lincoln immediately regretted letting her go, but it was evident she was running from someone—the blood on her clothes.

Nola, he repeated the name in his mind.

"Hm. You are quite a captivating woman," he whispered to the warm evening wind.

Lincoln let the door close, sauntered back to the bar, and winked at the barmaid. "We'll be off ourselves. Don't tell anyone we were here. Eh?" he said, placing a stack of coins on the counter. "Sorry for all the fighting."

"Another day, 'nother brawl." The barmaid smirked back. "Ye weren't here. Now bugger off before ye draw guards into me business."

Lincoln turned to his crew and rested his hand on his pistol, but only felt the empty holster at his hip.

"Oh, bloody hell," he fumed.

"What is it, Captain?" Mazie asked, resting her arm over his shoulder.

"That girl."

"Did she reject you or something?" A shrill of laughter left her lips, but when he did not respond, her grin turned into a concerned frown. "She drove you mad, then?" She removed her arm and leaned against the barstool next to him, waiting for his reply.

"I thought it was the latter until I discovered she stole my pistol from right under my nose."

Chapter 9

"Is this the last of it, Captain?" Kitten asked as she heaved a crate of fresh produce onto the ship. Finding healthy food to eat in Zemira was nearly impossible those days. The pirates had to pay a few extra coins for the merchants to sell them that much.

Lincoln nodded. "We're still waiting for Ardley; he's picking up medical supplies from Doctor Bailey." He turned to Hill. "You fill the water barrels?"

The still drunk pirate stood quickly, staggering a bit. "Aye! Six of 'em, Captain," Hill replied sluggishly.

Boots reached out his hand for Mazie, helping her up from the Jacob's ladder. Once on deck, she pointed towards the east.

"Captain, are you seeing this?" she asked.

Lincoln glanced at the horizon and saw the dark, threatening clouds rolling in. Glowing white lightning hit the water, brightening up the sky around it. The waves picked up, rocking against the ship, and Lincoln knew if they did not leave within that next hour, they would be stuck on the shore, riding out the storm.

The sound of the rain hitting the deck was pleasant, but storms often deceived the sailors. When rippling waves started rolling over the calming sea, any experienced sailor knew what the near future held—it was a matter of being prepared. Most ocean storms were worse closer to the shore. However, there were others that if the ship was too far from dry land, a crew had to hold on tight to the mast. As a ship captain, the main worry was for a wave to crash against the broadside, for it would sink even the most stable of ships.

"Time to turn in early and sleep below deck," Boots suggested. "If there's a storm comin', we should probably go lookin' for Ardley."

A glint of irritation shone in Lincoln's eyes. Ardley's lack of punctuality was wearing on him. His mate never hesitated to engage in small talk with anyone for longer than necessary.

"Nay. We'll give him another hour, and then I'll be the one looking for him." Lincoln turned to the crew, barking orders. "All hands hoay!" he shouted.

Mazie turned to the crew. "You heard the captain! All hands on deck!"

The buccaneers quickly began to ready the ship seconds before Lincoln felt a raindrop hit the tip of his nose. The storm was coming sooner than he predicted.

"Batten down the hatches!" he shouted. "Everyone below deck!"

The storm was about to hit, and it was going to hit hard.

The crew turned in for the night—all but Lincoln. He stared out into the city and placed his hands on the polished cedar rail, not caring about raindrops coming down and soaking his night clothes.

Aside from a few flickering lights across the pier, he could not see much beyond the dock. Lincoln turned on his heel, walked to the mainmast, reached into Ardley's coat, and pulled out a pipe and a box of dry matches. Then he peacefully walked to the back of the ship and sought shelter under the stern deck's canopy as he lit the pipe and inhaled. His elbows rested against the railing as he filled his lungs and then blew it out slowly, releasing a thick cloud of smoke.

Lincoln did not smoke, not since he was a young lad, but that night he would. The scent of the tobacco wafted in the air, mingling with the filth of the city streets.

He would not miss Brecken Terrace, but his thoughts went back to the woman he had met that afternoon—Nola. His pulse jarred in his throat when the image of her face flashed in his mind. She was someone he was leaving behind. Brecken was not the place for a girl like that.

And she has my pistol. Lincoln bared his teeth at that thought.

The king's plan to rid Zemira of magic and everything else that made it beautiful was finally coming to an end. The once gorgeous land was more dead than it was alive. Lincoln saw it when they walked the streets that day, and that girl—the blood on her shirt was not hers, but she looked far from someone who would do anyone harm. But then again, she had stolen from him.

Those pretty eyes had fooled him. She was only a thief —a bloody good one at that. Lincoln would let it slip if he did not love that pistol as much as he did. He had never had someone rob him from right under his nose.

His eyes hardened, finding it hard to believe he was fretting over a woman he did not know.

One thing was sure, whoever Nola was, Lincoln ached to unravel every dark secret she held hidden. Every mystery encompassing her devoured his thoughts. The moment he had seen her in the marketplace, the desire to have her was irreversible.

"Captain?" he heard Mazie say, sneaking up under the canopy from behind him, her clothes not soaked like his.

Lincoln looked over his shoulder. "You should get back below deck, sailor," he joked.

Mazie huffed. "Always looking out for others, but not yourself." The side of her lip twisted up. "You're still thinking about that girl, aren't you?" she asked in a smooth voice.

A frown tightened his face. "Nay!" he said, his words brusque. "*She* is the last person I want to think about."

Mazie glared at him skeptically. "Sure! Whatever you say, Captain."

His eyes looked to her briefly, then back to the sea. "Doesn't matter. All she saw was a blathering fool, giving her the perfect target to steal from. I'll know better next time I see a pretty face like that."

Talking to Mazie about the girl at the tavern and how his lungs warmed as he thought of her was the last thing he wanted to do. The corner of his mouth lifted, and he ran his hands gingerly through his wavy hair while the ship rocked back and forth.

"Hope Sybil holds up this round. This foul weather has done quite the number on her, hasn't it?" Lincoln said, turning back to Mazie. He drummed his fingers over the edge.

"She's been doing alright," she replied with a soft smile. "More than what you expected when you stole her, at least." She looked out into the ocean. "I think back then, we didn't know what to expect, even when I joined you. It terrified me —stepping on a ship that creaked every time you sneezed." She flashed a smile before that smile faded to a frown. "Bah! The waters have been dreadful, that's for certain. But you could not have asked for a better crew of buccaneers who have kept her for the most part unscathed."

"Aye," he said. "It is the unshakable loyalty from our crew that has held this ship together."

Lincoln gave her a meek smile as he thought back to the day a crew of pirates welcomed him on their ship. The moments that followed were when he realized that being a pirate was his destiny.

"When I joined Wentworth's crew all those years ago," he continued, "My only thought was to be this seafaring man with no ties to dry land. There was no place to be other than out here, searching for my own crew to sail the wide-open ocean—with complete and utter freedom."

His smile grew a little wider as nostalgia set in.

"They cannot touch us anymore, Mazie. Not out here. And if they do, I'll die, even sink down with my ship, protecting my mates. That, I promise you."

Mazie gave a lopsided grin as she reached for the pipe. She held it up to her nose for a beat before lazily resting it to her bottom lip, sucking in a puff of smoke.

"I'd say you picked a damn good bunch of buckos, Captain," she said in a hoarse tone, clearing the smoke from her lungs. "Besides, it's absurd to believe we wouldn't go down with you. We took an oath, remember?" Mazie turned back to the purplish horizon and rubbed her arms as prickles of goosebumps rose on her skin. "Blimey. I don't recall Zemira ever feeling this cold at night, eh?" she said. "It was bloody hot this morning."

Lincoln nodded, though he was indifferent to the chilly breeze blowing through the ship. "Aye, things have changed. 'Tis not the same place it was ten years ago."

Mazie held the pipe to her lips again, holding it for a bit longer. She coughed that time as if she had taken a little more into her lungs than she had planned.

"This shit is terrible," she said, handing it back to Lincoln while watching a barely noticeable smile edge his lips through the cloud of smoke.

"Yeah, but it's helping me, so I don't jump overboard and go looking for her," he confessed. He placed the pipe on the damp balustrade, his throat already feeling parched from the number of grog shots he had earlier that day. "A pirate doesn't stand by and allow anyone to steal from them, Mazie."

Her brow rose. "And what would you do if you found her?" she asked.

Lincoln stared at Mazie long enough for her to turn away. "Alright, I'll leave you alone to wallow in self-pity.

We start our long voyage at dawn, Captain. We all need rest."

Nola hurried towards the oceanfront, holding the pistol in her palm with hands trembling so forcefully, she felt she would drop it.

What was I thinking, stealing from a pirate? Nola thought as she hid in the shadows of a fetid alley.

She snuck between two storage chests used to stock supplies for the trade vessels and leaned against the wall, placing the bag between her legs.

Nola stared at the docks, shivering from the coldness of the night wind. Once she felt calmer, she focused on her surroundings—the laughter in the city streets, the waves crashing against the rocks.

She looked around for the trading vessel her father had mentioned, but it was not there. The only ship docked was a pirate ship. She could tell by their flag. Then, as her eyes narrowed in on the ship, she noticed a name written on the side—Sybil Curse.

"Fuck."

She looked ahead at the coastline; the rocky cliffs towered high above the sea. If she traveled back north, keeping flush to the rocks, she could stay hidden, she thought. Nola could probably reach another port, a few miles northward, but it was much closer to the palace walls than Brecken. That alone would be more reckless than hopping aboard a pirate ship.

Lightning crashed down on the ocean as the raindrops thickened. Nola needed to hide before the eye of the storm came in, and there was only one place now that would take her to where she needed to be. She had overheard one of the female buccaneers mention the Eastland Forest at the tavern; they were traveling there. No stops in Queenstown. It was a free ticket to the Fae kingdom, where she needed to go.

A rush of fear stormed through her body. "Well," she said out loud, her beating heart not agreeing with the words that came next. "I never thought I would be saying this, but it looks like I'm going to be a stowaway on a pirate ship."

Chapter 10

Lincoln held Ardley's pipe out for him to take as he met the crew below deck.

"Nice of you to finally join us," he said, watching Ardley place his pipe in his coat pocket and lean back against one of the barrels.

"Sorry, Captain," Ardley said, then turned to pull out his psaltery from behind him and strummed a string.

Lincoln watched Boots outstretch his hand towards Kitten, gingerly grazing her chin with his fingertips. She turned away as her face blushed from his touch. Then he invited her to dance. Boots was a decent dancer despite his missing limb.

Kitten landed a gentle kiss on his cheek as she nestled into his arms.

Lincoln smiled as he leaned back against a barrel, with his elbows bent and hands behind his head, watching them flit across the wooden floor in a graceful waltz. Sadness stabbed at him like a dagger to his chest. He had a love like that once nearly six years before, but she destroyed every part of him when she vanished without a trace. After resting his eyes, his thoughts went to the day they met, but he only felt an emptiness in the pit of his stomach.

No, he thought, *I cannot go back there.*

Lincoln had to think about something else—anything else. So, he thought about the story Boots had told him on more than one occasion about how he and Kitten met. It was the kind of love story he wanted but would never have.

Kitten's father was a ship captain who sailed for nearly forty years with Boots's father—his first mate.

The two lovers dancing before their captain were raised as best friends until Kitten's father went down with his ship. Boots returned to the sea, never to see Kitten again—that was, until Lincoln invited them both to join his crew and sail the open waters.

The rest was history.

As Ardley played a smooth song, Boots ran his hands down Kitten's bare arm. Then he laced his fingers around her voluptuous curves and pulled her closer to his chest. She twirled in a circle before Boots swaddled her in her caramel-colored dress. He then bent her backward; she arched as her head fell under his hold.

A smile reached her lips while he wrapped his arms around her waist, squeezing her rear with the other hand. Kitten raised an eyebrow and gave him a provoking wink.

That familiar look of desire flashed in Boots's eyes before he pulled her towards his face. His lips touched hers in a tender kiss.

There was an indescribable connection as their bodies

continued to sway to the soothing sound of the psaltery. The rest of the crew watched them in silence as Ardley hummed to the melody. Their dance stopped abruptly when a tall wave crashed against the boat. The ship rocked harder as the storm picked up. Boots and Kitten held to a barrel while the others gripped their mugs tightly. It was a priority to keep their sanity—their booze—from toppling over.

The storm was fierce; the howling wind roared under each crash of the thundering booms across the sky.

Mazie trudged towards Lincoln, plopping down next to him, and slung her arm over his shoulder.

"Something bothering you, Captain?" she said sluggishly, her voice pulling him from his thoughts.

"Nay," he lied, holding out his hand. Lincoln faked a smile and spoke more eloquently than usual. He asked, "How about a dance, Mazie?"

"Naaaah," she said back, forcing a playful scowl. "You aren't my type."

The captain dropped his hand.

"No need to look so dour; I'm not asking to take you to bed, matey. C'mon, only a dance."

"How 'bout a drink instead?" she asked, resting her head on his shoulder and lifting her mug.

He snorted. "Cheers, then."

They clinked their mugs together and guzzled down what was left. Lincoln's eyes wavered from Mazie and signaled Hill to mosey over with the rest of the bottle to top them off.

That night, the crew could relax, dance, and drink while the storm passed. The next day, however, the slate clouds would clear. The sun would guide their journey to the Fae, where the breath of life and magic would give them the anticipated peace they had been craving for months.

Nola hurried to the ship once she heard thunder blast through the sky. She hoped the storm would drown out any noise she would make breaking into the pirate ship.

She noticed the gangplank was not set out, so she needed another way inside. Then she saw the vessel's Jacob's ladder, but to reach it, she had to jump. Backing up slowly on the dock, she sucked in a heavy breath, knowing that if she did not catch the edge exactly right, she would fall into the water.

Nola took off running as fast as she could, and once her toes felt the edge of the dock, she leapt. Raising her hands high in the air, her fingers caught the last of the rope. She let out a sigh. But as she beamed, her right hand lost its grip. Her bag started slipping from her shoulder.

"Shit!"

The tip of her middle finger caught it, but barely. Nola's left hand clenched tightly to the rope, and she climbed to the top. She swung her body and flung the heavy bag over the railing but nearly lost her grip again, feeling beads of sweat running down her forehead.

Once both her hands held steady, she took three calming breaths before pulling herself up. She leaned back against the wooden balustrade, waiting for her nerves to settle before finding a place to hide.

Nola tiptoed on the deck towards the back of the ship, found a small latch, and pulled it up. She slunk into the hallway, closing the door behind her, latching it, and then looked around in the silence. The old cedar floor squeaked as the waves wobbled the ship—saltwater leaked from the ceiling onto the already damp walls.

Nola had never been in a pirate's ship before. It was mesmerizing, but she had no time to look around as much as she wanted to. Before Nola opened the first door, she stopped to listen to the music but was not sure where it was coming from; it came from somewhere below the main deck. After closing what looked like the captain's quarters, she carefully opened every other door as she worked her way down the small and cramped hallway. Finally, she found a dry place to hide—a supply closet.

Nola hurried into the closet, eyeing a mop, a few metal shelves, a bucket, sponges, and old dirty rags.

The pungent stench of mold and decay stung her senses. She had worked on her town's farmland when she was much younger, so Nola had had her share of nauseating smells, but what she smelt in that closet was different.

Nola grabbed some of the rags and stuffed them into the bucket, closing the lid over it, and perched herself in the corner, pulling her knees up against her chest. She felt the sea rock the ship from under her and closed her eyes. It was going to be the longest night of her life.

Bringing back magic comes with a price, she thought.

As that thought resonated with her, she leaned against the wall, settling in for the night, her ears focusing on the clattering sounds in the room. With her head pounding, exhaustion took over. But her eyes shot open as she recognized the unmistakable sound of guards nearing the pier. Horses trotted closer and closer. Chiming bells warned those in Brecken Terrace—they were coming for her.

Chapter 11

"How much did you take, Ardley?" Mazie asked, eyeing a large crate filled with medicine and bandages near the corner where he sat.

Ardley shrugged. "I hate stealing, but we needed medical supplies," he explained. "Remember that poor bloke we tried to save last year on the northern shore? We didn't have enough antibiotics to save him and—"

Lincoln held up a hand, not satisfied with his rambling explanation.

"You thought stealing from the king was the way to do it?" he asked, his blood running cold. "Ardley, we may be pirates, but we live by a code! Never, ever steal from the king."

Ardley huffed. "In my defense, Captain, it was not the king I stole from; it was his doctor, who refused to sell me what we needed." He spoke slowly as if it was the only way Lincoln could understand his reasoning. But Lincoln was not a fool. Ardley's actions were reckless.

"Bloody hell!" Lincoln cursed. "We leave now. That bell that sounded off was the sign of a traitor or thief. They'll be coming for our ship first. Storm or not, let us prepare the Sybil Curse and get the hell out of here." He turned to the crew and began barking orders. "Kitten, you pull us out. Hill, put down the damn drink and help me raise the sails!"

"Aye . . . aye, Captain," he said, saluting with his index finger.

Lincoln watched as his crew hustled to their duties, preparing the ship for their seven-day voyage. He prayed to the Almighty Gods that his ship would withstand the storm.

"Ow!" Nola groaned.

She hurriedly grabbed a dirty rag from the bucket to place against her head as soon as she felt the blood ooze from the wound. She pressed it firmly against her skin, hoping to stop the bleeding. The last thundering crash had pulled a strong force against the ship, rocking it so hard her body slammed against the shelf next to her, the steel bars scratching into her forehead. She was not sure how deep it was, but the bleeding would not stop.

"You'll be okay, Nola," she said aloud, talking to herself.

She looked around frantically in the small storage space. In the far-right corner was a tackle box. She rushed towards it and thought, perhaps there was something inside she could use to help stop the bleeding.

Nola pulled open the lid and spotted a few musty-smelling sponges. That was all she could find, so it would have to do.

She grabbed the cleanest one, pulled a small piece from

it, and placed it on her wound, hoping to fill out the tiny cut made by the shard of metal. It felt like an inch long, but thankfully, it did not feel too deep as she cleaned around it.

Then, she cut along the bottom of her shirt with her pocket knife and wrapped her head to keep the sponge in place. She tied it off at the back, then crawled to her post and buried her head in her hands, carefully avoiding the wound.

Nola did not know what time it was, as it was so dark down there already, but the sounds and cries above deck began to taper off after a moment. Perhaps they were sleeping, or maybe the storm was so fierce that the ship had lost its crew.

As her head throbbed, her body went rigid when footsteps descended the stairs below the main deck—she was not alone.

"If Hill would only put down 'is damn bottle once in a while, perhaps 'is scrawny li'l body would be able to withstand the boats rockin' durin' a storm," a woman's voice said.

"Bless the man's 'art—he's not been able to handle his drinkin' since he joined the crew. We need to put some meat on him so he can keep up with us. He drinks like a little girl," a man's voice replied.

"And wha' the bloody 'ell does tha' mean?" Her voice climbed an octave higher. A flirtatious giggle followed before she said, "Oh, Boots, we don't 'ave time for tha'."

"Just tryin' to cheer you up, my love."

Oh no, Nola thought. *Oh no. No. No. No.*

Nola heard a thump against the door and saw the

shadows of feet near the opening below it. Still, her thoughts about what was about to happen against that door was the only thing she could focus on. That was until Nola felt a furry creature run over her fingers. Her hand flew over her mouth, muffling the scream, but the yelp was louder than she expected. The two behind the door stopped their movements, followed by complete silence.

Nola was not ready to blow her hiding spot. She knew she would eventually get caught, but it was sooner than she anticipated; she ran cold to the core.

"Boots, wha' was tha'?" the woman asked.

Nola felt her palms go clammy.

"Ah, Kitten, it was only the sound of me lips smackin' against your beautiful neck," the man she called Boots hummed.

"It came from the closet," Kitten said.

"Aye, it was probably a rat."

"Ain't no bloody rat, Boots. It sounded like a scream."

"Blimey," he huffed, "we can continue this later. They'll be expectin' us on deck, anyhow."

The door swung open, and the two pirates looked down at Nola, with confused expressions crossing their faces. With her hand still covering her mouth, she slowly ran her palm down her face, looking up at them, whose eyes would not leave hers.

Nola looked at Kitten, scanning her long brown hair that reached her hips, broad shoulders, and perfectly sculpted legs. She wore a black tricorne hat tilted to the right and a black bandana around her neck. Her skin was light tan, like she had spent days basking in the sun. Nola narrowed in on her eyes; the left one, sapphire color, and the other, bright ochre—it almost looked like liquid gold.

The other buccaneer, Boots, was at least a foot taller than Kitten. His clothes were baggy, overly accessorized with ropes, scarves, and leather. His goatee, which reached right below his chin, was dark brown, his skin light but not pale, and his eyes chestnut brown. On each ear dangled a golden-plated earring hoop, and he wore a hat to match Kitten's, but the color was a bright maroon like most of what he was wearing. As Nola sized him up, she noticed he only had one leg—the other made from wood. For a short moment, she wondered how he had lost it.

Do something, she thought. *Say something.*

The pirates' eyes swept her up and down. "Nope, not a rat," the golden-eyed pirate said.

Nola blinked.

Kitten turned to Boots. "Well, say somethin'."

Boots's eyes narrowed, and his rust-colored mustache arched at the ends. "Arrrrgh!!"

Kitten slapped him in the arm. "Don't be a damned fool," she said, then looked back at Nola.

Boots scrunched up his nose at Kitten and said, "Well, look at what we have here; a stowaway."

When Nola did not move, he gripped the hilt of his sword, but thankfully, he did not unsheathe it.

Nola had not realized how fast her breathing was until Kitten stepped forward, placing her hand on Boots's knuckles, which rested on the hilt of his cutlass. "Easy, Boots. Look at 'er. She's scared witless." The female pirate looked down at Nola and smiled kindly. "I recognize ye, darlin'. Yer the girl who 'ad me captain smitten back at the tavern last night."

Nola lowered her brows. "I think you're mistaken," her voice shuddered.

Kitten flashed a smile again and stood up, folding her arms while cocking her head to the right. "I'll be honest wit' ye, girl, 'e is a bit upset 'bout his pistol."

Nola was not sure why the pirate giggled when she said that, but it did help her feel the sense of security she would need to calm her nerves.

"Can you help me? I need help, but I have little money," Nola said.

Boots's lips spread into a wide grin. "Did you hear that, Kitten? She wants us to help her for free."

"Not free," Nola refuted while clambering to her feet. She gripped the rack next to her to keep from falling.

Boots outstretched his arm. "Need a hand there, darlin'?"

"No, thank you, I've got it," Nola said. She still smelt the revolting scent crawling out of the closet. "Mind if I step out of this closet, though? It smells like piss."

Kitten chuckled. "Oh, the captain isn't goin' to like this, but I'll try to talk 'em down, eh?"

Nola thought about Captain Lincoln. He was cruel at the marketplace, but she saw something other than a ruthless pirate at the tavern.

She looked down at her wrist and began to untie the leather rope wrapped around the ruby. Her father had given her only but a few coins. The ruby would have to do; it was the only valuable thing she had to offer. Nola gripped her fist around it and let out a painful sigh.

She hesitated. The ruby was the one thing she never wanted to part with—it was what connected her to her birth family. It was everything she had left from them. But it was giving up the jewel or walking the plank.

The two pirates exchanged a glance as Nola held out the gem from her bracelet and the coins. "Here," she said, "Your captain can have these."

Boots reached out, taking the ruby in one hand, and pocketing the coins. His eyes grew wide as he held the red, sparkling jewel between two fingers.

"Well, shiver me timbers," he said. His eyes gleamed at the ruby.

Kitten leaned forward to get a closer look, her mouth agape. "Blimey. Did ye steal this?" She turned to Boots then back to Nola. "Who the bloody 'ell are ye?"

She used her father's words. "I'm nobody."

Kitten's brows knitted together, taking the ruby from Boots's fingers into her own hand. "Well, *nobody*, where did ye get such an expensive lookin' jewel? I know real ones when I see 'em!" Kitten questioned. "This 'ere's a ruby—and not any ruby!" She rolled the gem around in her palm.

"It doesn't matter where I got it. Take it. It's yours if you don't kill me."

The lady pirate gave Nola an inquisitive look and turned to Boots again. "Wha' shall we do, love?"

He shrugged. "Bring her to the captain, I guess?"

"And what if 'e decides to kill 'er?" Kitten asked.

Nola stiffened.

Boots looked over Kitten's shoulder and creased his brow. "She's too pretty to kill. He might . . . you know."

Is he serious? Nola thought.

Kitten slapped him hard against his shoulder with the back of her hand.

"—the 'ell, Boots! Don't be a pig," she said, turning to Nola. "I give ye me promise, the captain won't lay a finger on ye, got it?"

Nola nodded. The woman was a pirate, and her father taught her better than to trust their kind. Yet, Kitten's eyes were gentle, and she had a subtle feeling she could trust her.

The wooden floor creaked from behind them as another female pirate hurried below deck. The two pirates both turned to look over their shoulders at her.

"What's taking you two so long? I cannot stand the smell of puke all over the deck! I just cleaned it this morning," the woman said.

Boots and Kitten moved aside as the female pirate's dazzling eyes went round. Then, she stepped closer to the closet, giving Nola a better look at her.

Her raven-black hair, which fell to the middle of her back, adorned her slim face and gorgeous cheekbones. Her skin was the color of a moonless night with eyes so dark they almost looked black. The pirate's attire was not as loose and frumpy as the others. She wore different shades of black, and every piece was snug against her skin, showing off her slender curves.

"Well, what do we have here?" the black-eyed pirate asked, a smile pulled at the side of her lips.

"Stowaway," Kitten said, "But look at this, Mazie!" she continued, handing her mate the jewel.

The one she called Mazie held the precious gem between her fingers and looked back to meet Nola's eyes. "Grab her," she instructed. "The captain needs to see this. And her."

Boots reached out, taking her arm lightly. Nola stepped forward.

"You don't need to hold on to me," Nola said. "Where would I go?"

Boots shrugged. "Go on, then," he said, pointing to the stairs that led to the deck. "The captain is this way."

Not one of them said a word as Nola followed the lady pirates down the hallway and up the stairs leading to the deck. Boots staggered behind her as if to make sure she did not run. Once on deck, Nola eyed a tall, skinny pirate whose body slumped over the ship's rail. When he lifted his head, his clothes were soiled from collar to knee.

Kitten tossed a mop in his direction. "Clean up yer mess, mate. We 'ave more important matters to address with the captain," she said, now looking around the ship. "Where is 'e, anyhow?"

"What the fuck is this?" Nola heard a deep voice hiss from behind her. Boots turned her around to confront the familiar face.

Since she had last seen him, Captain Lincoln had trimmed his beard, revealing what she had not noticed before because of all the scruff—a thin, one-inch-long scar just inches to the right of his lips.

Nola had to crane her neck to look into his eyes. She had

not noticed how towering he was before—as tall as her father, maybe more. He had a strong jawline and perfectly sculpted facial features as if whoever created their kind had taken time on such a beautiful masterpiece. He had changed into a black blouse, with the top buttons undone, showing off his chest. Her eyes could not help but stare at his strong muscles under his shirt. Despite the scowl he wore over his seductive pink lips, his eyes looked gentle as he glared at her. Lincoln was not wearing a hat like the other pirates on the ship. A lock of wavy brown hair fell slightly over his eyes. She wanted to reach out and brush it away.

Nola stepped back instinctively, but Boots gripped her arm in a tight hold, making her wince.

"Boots, let go of her," Lincoln ordered. "It's not like she can escape from the ship if she were to run." The corners of his eyes crinkled.

An unsettling feeling hit Nola straight in the gut. The man was right. There was no escape, even if she wanted to. Though she was a siren, she had not used her tail since she was a few months old. She could not risk sinking to the depths of the sea.

As Boots released his grip on her, Mazie tossed him the jewel.

"What is this?" Lincoln asked.

"We found the girl in the supply closet downstairs. She offered us that," Boots answered for her, gesturing to the jewel and not bothering to mention the coins Nola saw him pocket for himself.

Lincoln stared keenly at the ruby and blew out a

whistle. Nola swallowed and focused on the hard lump pressing against her throat. There was a small moment at the tavern where she thought she had seen only a man—one who called her name beautiful. However, the man before her was a pirate who had her life in his hands, and he could do whatever he wanted, and no one could save her.

"Well, isn't this the finest piece of pirate booty I've ever laid my sight on?" he said. His eyes glinted on hers and not the ruby. Her stomach jumped as he drew his lower lip between his teeth.

Lincoln closed his fist, gripping the jewel firmly. Unlike the other pirates on the ship, there was no hint of a smile or kindness on his face. He glared at her with malice. Nola took another step back as his eyes darkened.

A slight unreadable grin pulled at the side of his lips before he said, "Pull out the plank."

All the color drained from Nola's cheeks while a cold tremor ran through her body.

"You—you are to kill me?" her voice stammered.

Nola planted her feet as Boots's fingers wrapped around her arm in a firm grip. She quickly looked up, fixing the captain with an incredulous, unblinking stare. "I paid you, you bastard," Nola added boldly, but only a wry smile tugged at his mouth as he waved a hand in the air.

Boots glowered at him. "Captain?" he said, releasing some of the pressure he had on Nola's arm.

Mazie stepped in front of Lincoln and tried to place her hand on his shoulder, but he slapped it away.

"Captain Lincoln. What are you doing?" she asked. Her voice was authoritative to match his own.

Lincoln scolded her. "Step away, mate. She doesn't belong on this ship!" he said through gritted teeth.

Mazie looked at Nola with apologetic eyes and shrugged. She then nodded at Boots, who pulled her away from the crew and towards the ship's broadside.

Nola squirmed her body, trying to wrest herself free from the pirate's grip. "Please," she pleaded, "don't do this!"

Once they reached the starboard side, a burly, redheaded pirate and the lanky-looking one grabbed the wooden plank, stretched it outward towards the sea, and secured it to the deck.

"Get on," Boots said; his voice cracked.

"Tell me what I must do to change his mind," she pleaded, her skin shivering with fear. "I'll do anything!"

Nola's eyes swam with tears. Despite her encounter with the guards and the night at the tavern, it was the first time Nola had cried since she left her home. In fact, she had not shed real tears in years. She fled because she wanted to save Zemira, but all that planning, training, and running would be for nothing. Nola could not fail her people, especially at the hands of a pirate.

Boots resumed a fierce scowl across his lips while tightening the grip around her arm. "You'll do as—"

"Captain!" Kitten shouted. "She paid us. Let us just take 'er where she needs to go. Look 'ow terrified she is."

Kitten placed her hands on the captain's chest, but he shifted to the right, causing her to drop her arms to her side. Boots rushed Nola to the slim board and pushed her out.

She stood there, looking at the horizon, trying not to lose balance.

Suddenly, a loud shot rang over the deck. Nola, unable to turn and see what was happening, clasped her hands over her ears to muffle the sound. Lincoln stomped lively towards her and onto the plank until he stood mere inches from her trembling body. He turned her around. Her knees shook, barely able to keep herself from balancing on the board. She blanched as he lifted a pistol, pointing at her forehead. He threatened to end her life right there.

At least a bullet would be quicker—and less painful, she thought, *than the heavy waves slamming my body against the ship.*

Nola's muscles quivered when she looked into his eyes. Lincoln's beauty had blinded her. The captain was a monster and nothing like the man she thought she met at the tavern.

"Please don't do this!" she begged, squeezing her eyes shut. Tears ran down her pallid cheeks before she continued, "I need your help, Lincoln." Nola watched his eyes evade hers when she had said his name.

Lincoln did not move; his nostrils flared with each breath he took. After a few silent seconds, she looked past him, eyeing the faintest hint of the sun rising from the east. It was the only haven she had at that moment. If she dropped into the sea, her legs would change—but what if they did not? The water would consume her, and she would sink to the bottom of the sea. With twenty years of steering clear of the water, she did not know how to swim.

Nola closed her eyes, knowing every breath she took

could be her last. After a moment, she opened her eyes again, looking back at Lincoln.

"I have nowhere to go," she said, her voice soft, defeated. "Please, Lincoln. I—I need your help," Nola stammered, embarrassed at how her voice sounded. She could feel all eyes on the deck fixated on her.

The captain pulled his brows together. His head tilted to the side, still pointing the pistol at her.

"Help?" His cold voice caused her heart to thud beneath her chest. "In what world would a pirate help the very person who stole from them?" He gestured with his head towards the west. "Were those bells for you earlier? Did you steal that jewel from the king? Because if you had, you are walking off that plank because I want no part in King Matthias's feuds. We don't need the royal guard on board my ship. And you," he said, inching the pistol closer where the barrel brushed against her skin, "are going to get us killed."

"The Eastland Forest," she said quickly, her voice cracking. "I just need safe passage to the Eastland Forest."

Lincoln's lips drew back in a snarl, not speaking for a long, torturous moment as if he were contemplating if he believed her.

"Humans aren't allowed in the Eastland Forest. You've wasted our time." He sized her up, then lowered the pistol down to her chest and cocked his head. "What do you want with the Fae people, anyway?"

Nola was sure he would continue to press for answers. She owed him the truth. That was not her ship, after all. She was on their territory and was most certainly putting their lives in danger by being there—at least once the king or his son realized she had fled on their ship.

"Zemira isn't the same place it used to be," she answered.

"No shit." A small chuckle left his lips. "What does that have to do with visiting the Fae? They won't welcome a human. You are aware of that?"

"I don't care," she said confidently. "I have no other choice. I'm going to the Eastland Forest, and you are going to take me there."

She looked over as a snort came from Mazie, who looked up and met Nola's eyes. Her eyes told a different story—that of a captain who would never hurt a lady.

Nola somehow managed to suppress her fear from coming to her eyes. She tried standing tall, not to show Lincoln how truly terrified she was of him. She worked so desperately to appear brave.

"I'm just a poor village girl who is tired of the king destroying everything we love," she said, "and I need the Fae's help to stop him."

Amusement flashed in Lincoln's eyes. He cocked his head, withdrawing his pistol, and slowly lowered his hand to his side. Her rapid heartbeat slowed a bit. Nola dropped her shoulders, finally able to relax the tension that was building up in her neck.

Lincoln reached out his hand for her to take. She hesitated, unsure if what she said was enough, but she grabbed his hand anyway and followed him off the plank.

The captain pressed his lips together as if he were considering her words.

"I'll tell you what—" He lowered Nola back down to the deck, "—I'll take you to the Fae, but while you're on my ship, you are to be my prisoner. You will do everything I tell you to do, or you'll become shark bait!" He bit his lip.

As ruthless as his threat was, a thrill bounced in the pit of her stomach.

Lincoln stepped closer to her. "There must be retribution for your crime," he added.

Nola's excitement dissipated.

"My crime?" she said, giving him a slight scowl. "What crime have I committed?"

Lincoln chuckled, throwing his head back, and flashed her his perfectly straight teeth. A dimple creased on his right cheek, hiding the tiny scar.

"You stole my pistol," he fumed. His tone matched the grimace on his pretty face. "I've had it since I was twelve years old." His smile faded as he fidgeted with the one in his hand. "This one doesn't have much sentimental value."

Lincoln was so close to her now she felt his warm breath caress her cheeks.

"I want it back," he ordered.

Nola let her gaze wander leisurely down his face, searching for the man she met at the tavern. As she looked into his eyes—he was not there.

Nola's expression closed up as she clutched her bag. The pistol was in there. Even though she did not know much about firing a gun, it was the only protection she had since leaving the tavern. Sure, she had a small bow, a few arrows, and a knife, but a pistol gave her more protection, especially after what she had done.

Lincoln stepped in her direction when she did not move. "I've never had a man steal from me and walk away!"

A brave smile pulled her mouth to one side.

"That's because I am no man. I'm a woman, remember?" she said, recounting what he had called her the first time they had met at the marketplace.

A sexy yet intimidating grin widened across his features.

"You can have your damn pistol back," she said, reaching into her bag with trembling fingers.

Lincoln's eyes held a flash of amusement as he looked down into her bag. "You can hand over the rest of those stolen weapons while you're at it," he ordered, taking the pistol from her hand, but she shook her head.

The captain signaled with his finger to Boots, who grabbed the entire bag from her.

She scowled. "That bag and those weapons belong to *me*. Please—"

"Everything you have is mine until I release you," Lincoln said. "This is my ship. You own nothing."

She flinched as he reached out suddenly. His fingers traveled across the piece of cloth tied around her forehead. Nola felt her heart thump in her throat as he touched her. That same feeling ran down her body to her toes.

"What happened there?" he asked. The touch of his skin warmed Nola's cheeks.

She placed her hand over the wound but winced a little as her fingers pressed into the sponge she had used to stop the bleeding. The darkness was no longer in Lincoln's eyes

—his demeanor shifted to something soft and almost kind as if there was a glint of compassion in him.

Nola swallowed. “The ship rocked during the storm, toppling me over in the storage room. I cut it against a metal rack.”

He signaled with his hand to the redheaded buccaneer standing near the ship’s mainmast, who came running over. “This is Ardley, our . . .” He brought his hand to his mouth and tapped his chin. After a second, he continued, “Doctor, I guess.”

“I’ll patch that right up, madam,” Ardley said. “Come with me.” Lincoln gave him a stern look, and the redheaded man straightened his back. “Uh . . . you’ll come with me!”

There was a clearly fake glower over his face. Nola could see that his crew did not approve of the captain’s ways, and she had wondered if she could use that to her advantage.

Ardley took Nola’s hand gently and pulled her with him, and she felt everyone’s eyes on her back as they stepped down to the crew’s quarters.

Chapter 12

The buccaneers looked daggers at Lincoln, but they knew better than to let their tongues run wild to protest what he had just done to the girl.

In the years the crew had been on the Sybil Curse together, he had only taken the lives of men who deserved it, the ones who attacked or stole from them with malice—never being granted immunity or mercy.

Lincoln made the death of his enemies a quick one, though. He was not a man who believed in torture, even if a pirate deserved it.

But with Nola, Lincoln watched the crew look at him as if he had lost his mind. Lost his mind over a crime as inconsequential as stealing a pistol. It was clear she had only stolen it to protect herself.

Boots paced the deck—tapping his peg leg against the wooden boards rapidly.

"Hill?" Lincoln called.

"Yes, Cap—Captain," he said, his voice sluggish as he blinked rapidly, widening his eyes the closer he approached.

Lincoln looked down at him with an unreadable expression across his face.

"Please, clean up your own mess, would you?" He kept his voice calm and steady. Stress on deck was not what they needed right then. The storm had passed, but the danger Lincoln knew that woman was about to bring upon them far exceeded what himself and the crew had ever encountered at sea.

Lincoln sauntered towards Nola with his eyes set down to the wooden floor, which creaked with every step. The stowaway girl sat on a little wooden chair where Ardley had tended to her wound.

He replayed in his mind what he had done earlier to her. Though he was not too keen on helping a fugitive and was mildly agitated she had stolen from him, all that changed when he saw her on his ship. She was there. The girl from the tavern he thought he was never going to see again was there.

Lincoln hated himself for pointing his pistol at her. However, if he had not shown her that side of him, she would have never confessed why she had boarded his ship in the first place.

Nola looked up as Lincoln stepped closer to her.

He gave her an expression that was quite indecipherable, hoping she could not read him.

"You're not very good at the ruthless pirate act, are you?" she said.

Amusement crossed his features and he narrowed his eyes at her. He had no doubt she was somewhat afraid, but he, deep inside, hoped she would warm up to him.

Nola shifted uncomfortably, but her gaze would not leave his dim eyes.

"Hm, you think you can read me?" he asked, lowering his mouth to hers but stopped mere inches from her lips. "What secrets do I have, Nola?"

The pirate's eyes raked hers, and she gulped. "I may not know your secrets, Captain Lincoln," she admitted, "but I know true malevolence when I see it."

He turned away and eyed Ardley, who mumbled a melody to himself, seemingly trying to pretend he was not listening to their conversation.

"Your eyes give you away." The smile on Nola's lips was meek. "I see you," she muttered proudly.

Lincoln matched her smile, placing both hands on each side of her hips to trap her where she sat. "Aye. And I see you, too, Nola."

She swallowed but kept her body poised.

The silence between the two was both awkward and intriguing, but they rarely diverted their eyes from each other. Ardley shifted uncomfortably, distracting himself with the medical equipment next to him.

Lincoln stepped back, taking a seat at the table where Ardley sat.

The girl who had been pressed on his mind since he met her lowered her head. Guilt tore at him again for how he had treated her; he should not have behaved that way despite his reasoning.

"Did the wound need sutures?" Lincoln asked Ardley, taking his eyes from her for only a short moment before looking back into hers again.

Ardley straightened up, shaking his head.

"Nay. It wasn't deep enough. I treated it with frankincense and bandaged it properly. It is her headache I'm worried about. She said she hit her head rather hard."

As Nola continued to stare into Lincoln's unrelenting gaze, his jaw relaxed as a sudden warmth rose inside his chest.

Lincoln stood, sauntering back to where she sat. Once he was in front of her, he reached out for her hair, running his fingers through the silver strands. When Nola flinched, he lifted his fingers and stepped back just as he had at the tavern when she blenched from his touch.

Nola trembled under his fingertips as if he had frightened her then. He wanted to tell her not to be afraid of him because he would never hurt her. Never.

"Why does your hair grow in three different colors?" he asked, but when her lips pressed together, he snickered. "Guess it doesn't matter."

Be kind. Nola needs to trust you, Lincoln reminded himself.

"Is this where you take me down into the darkest room of the ship and chain me up like a prisoner?" Nola's voice came out with distaste and resentment.

He raised an eyebrow and rested his hands on an old coffer next to him.

"No, not a dungeon, but don't expect any special treatment on my ship if you're to stay above deck. Your jewel will only cover us to take you to safe passage. But I still need to feed you, so you will work on the deck and help my crew whenever they need." Lincoln slowly smirked and winked at her. "And do whatever I need help with." He could not help himself, but when the words left his lips, he immediately regretted it.

It was a bad habit, saying dull-witted things to get a reaction. That was the one lesson Wentworth taught him and the one trait he hated the most about himself.

Lincoln's not-so-subtle insinuation hit a nerve, he was sure. Nola's nostrils flared, and she looked down as her fingernails dug into the wooden chair she sat on.

"You'll sleep in my quarters while you're here," Lincoln added, drumming his fingers onto the coffer.

"I'd rather be shackled in a dingy dungeon or that revolting supply closet again," she said, her voice barely audible.

An amused expression crossed his features as he glared down into her eyes. Ardley excused himself, not making eye contact with either of them.

Nola swallowed. "I am not a whore, nor will I ever be," she seethed. "Even if my life depended on it."

A playful smile reached his lips. The girl's answer satisfied him enough. "Good," he said. He stood and leaned against a column, folding his arms. "I have a cot I keep tucked under my bed. You'll sleep there."

Nola seemed to be studying his words before she nodded, followed by a faint blush creeping up her face, giving her away. Lincoln let out a small chuckle at her response and stood straight again.

"I am dead sure the blood on your clothes is not yours, though. I will not ask whose blood it is—or used to be—but please get yourself cleaned up. After you clear this mess, there's a bathtub in my room."

She nodded before she said, "Aye, aye, Captain."

Lincoln walked away with a smile adorning his face.

Nola, as instructed, went down into the captain's quarters to clean herself, but as she had done her entire life, she would not submerge in the water. She used a rag to wipe herself clean and rinsed her hair with seawater left inside a bucket. Then, she stopped and allowed herself to feel the water trickle down her spine. For a few minutes, Nola forgot she was washing away the reminder she had taken a life. The stench of the alleys in Brecken Terrace and the cleaning closet's fetid smell flowed down the drain blended with the guard's blood. However, Nola was beyond thankful for being able to bathe. After a couple more minutes of relaxation, she took a deep breath and reached for a towel Lincoln had left for her. She patted it gently to dry off her skin and then cleaned up the floor.

Nola pulled her hair up high atop her head, creating somewhat of a bun to keep the long strands out of her face. She thought of putting on a robe she saw hanging by an old dresser as she looked at the stains on her shirt. Nola did not want to overstep, so she dressed again in her dirty clothes and turned on the bed lamp in the corner of the room.

Her head still pounded mercilessly from her wound.

What she needed was to eat and rest her body. Lincoln had told her Mazie would come to retrieve her after she cleaned up, so she sat at the edge of the bed and looked out through the small window in the corner of the room. As the silence loomed over her, she thought of her parents and if they were safe.

Would the prince report to his father that I, a siren, had been living among them? Nola wondered. *And then come after my family to find me?*

She then thought of the captain, remembering how she felt around him at the tavern. Even with the pistol pointed at her forehead, she saw through the pirate's eyes and into a man who was fighting something he hated about himself. She knew deceit. Not because she had met a man like that, but because she had lied to everyone around her. Her parents forced her to lie to hide her identity.

However, she remembered her father's words that pirates only cared for two things. They desired the wide-open sea and endless amounts of treasure. There would be no remorse from their violent battles, their endless thievery, and no enemy deserved mercy.

According to her father's stories, they would kill sirens because they felt threatened by them. The king often hired corrupt pirates of the Portland Sea to slaughter the undersea creatures.

At that moment, while staring out the window, Nola realized something that had slipped her mind earlier.

Lincoln can see magic, she told herself, *but can he see me?*

"You can hang that towel back in the bathroom," Mazie said from behind as she walked in, carrying a bundle of clothes. Her footsteps clumped against the wooden planks. "You'll need to dress differently if you want to blend in. Your clothes are terrible, and they don't look like what a pirate would wear." Mazie threw the bundle on the bed. "Put that on."

Nola held up a pair of black, tight leather pants and an all-black shirt, and lying flat on the bed was a black scrap of fabric.

"You want me to wear this?" she asked. "What's wrong with what I'm wearing?" Nola looked down at her clothes, which were not terrible, she thought. She was wearing brown pants and a long burgundy, sleeveless shirt that exposed her shoulders and back. The collar of her shirt came high on her neckline, just as her mother had sewed it. Her mother made all her clothes. But there was nothing special about her attire. It was plain, dull, and as simple as her simple life.

"Yes, I want you to wear *this*. You are out in the Portland Sea, milady. We need you to not look like a girl from a small, poor village. If you do not look like a pirate, then anyone who approaches our ship will ask questions we aren't going to answer. Then there'll be fighting and bloodshed, and, as much as I crave every part of that scenario, we don't have time for that. We're on a schedule right now, and you can't become more of an inconvenience."

Nola felt very small at that moment. She barely made it off land and had entered someone else's home—if that was what they called their ship. She expected the pirates to help her when they were not even sure what they were helping her accomplish.

Nola nodded. "I understand," she hushed, looking down at the dark red spots on her top.

Mazie smirked as she walked past her and stopped at the door.

"You meant to say, 'Aye, matey,' eh?"

Nola reciprocated with a humorous smile. "Aye, matey."

Mazie turned on her heel, heading back to the stairs as if she were already annoyed by Nola's presence. Once she reached the steps, she turned to look at her. "Bear in mind, girl, if you cross my captain again, he may not be so lenient on your punishment next time."

Nola nodded, unsure if she believed her. The female pirate was hard to read, that was certain, but one thing Nola knew was to stay out of that one's way.

"I'll remember that next time," Nola said.

Mazie flashed her an obviously fake smirk, flaring her nostrils as she walked out of the captain's quarters.

Nola put on the pants, securing a rope to keep them from slipping off. She fanned out her hands, running her fingers down the slick material of the pants. She and Mazie were close to the same size, but Nola's waist was slightly thinner. The pants also felt a bit itchy, but nothing in her bag was anything that the crew would approve of. Everything looked like what she was wearing when they caught her, which apparently, was not pirate enough.

After pulling Mazie's shirt over her head, she heard footsteps descending the stairs again.

Lincoln stopped on the last step abruptly, and his eyes met hers. He sized her up, giving her a look of approval, his teeth gleaming with a broad smile.

"That outfit suits you," he said.

She was aware that the outfit revealed a lot more than she was used to near her breasts. And, she had nothing to cover herself with. Lincoln only stood there, with his elbow pressed against the stair's railing. Nola liked how he looked at her, even though it was only with lust-filled eyes.

She held the bandana out. "How exactly do I wear this?"

Lincoln continued into the room and once he stood in front of her, he reached up, removing the thread she had used to tie her hair, and allowed it to fall against her back. As his fingers lightly touched her skin, she sucked in a breath. His eyes stayed on hers as he smoothed out the front of her hair and proceeded to wrap the piece of fabric around her head, tying it off at the back. He reached around the front and lightly touched a wavy strand that had escaped the bandana and tucked it back in.

Nola lightly fluttered her eyes when his fingers grazed her neck as he trailed his hands back down. She turned slowly to stare into his eyes, his lips creating a perfectly flat line. Lincoln let his hand fall to his side, but not before a chill ran up her back. Nola was not sure why he had dropped his hand so abruptly.

She opened her mouth to speak to break the silence, but he said, "I was telling you the truth at the tavern when I called you beautiful, Nola." He paused, a small smile reaching his lips.

Nola's cheeks turned pink as she remembered how she felt at the tavern when he spoke to her. Her body reacted to that one word. Beautiful. Her stomach muscles fluttered.

"Actually, you didn't," she said, watching his brows knit together. "You said my *name* was beautiful."

It did not matter to her; the words still made her feel something she had never felt in her life. Desire.

"Did I? Hm, well, I guess I didn't say out loud everything that came to my mind that day." His dimples creased as he smiled at her.

"Thank you," she said, watching the sincere look in his eyes.

It was as if everything he had done to her earlier had not happened. She would not forget it. But the way he treated her then, like a friend and not his enemy, gave her hope. Maybe her time on the ship would not be as scary and life-threatening as she believed it was moments before he came into that room.

Nola also was becoming aware of the changes in her body when he was that close to her. He smelled so good she almost had to hold her breath. Maybe it was cedar, like his ship, but there was something else.

Musk? Something citrus? Nola thought, trying to figure out why she liked it so much.

Though difficult, she willed her eyes to look away as an uncomfortable feeling took over her.

Don't, Nola, she thought. *Focus on why you are here.*

"Very well, um—" Lincoln said, looking flustered like he was not sure what to say next. "We should give you a pirate name."

She giggled softly. "As much as I appreciate the gesture to include me among your crew," she said politely, "I do like my given name. And besides, I don't believe I truly need a pirate name. I'm only on the ship for seven days."

He flashed her a playful smile. "It's not as if my mates use the pirate names we picked for each other, anyway." Lincoln let out a small chuckle. "It is more of an obligatory act when you join a pirate crew. At least it was for us." He winked. "I'll think of something that fits you beautifully."

She mulled over the idea. "Very well," she said softly, "Captain."

"Lincoln," he corrected. "Please, address me as Lincoln." Nola nodded as he stepped back, sizing her up one more time and smirked. "You look like a pirate now."

"Not ruthless enough," she said.

He dropped his smile, his expression taking on a more serious tone. "May I ask you a question?" Lincoln said.

"Sure."

He walked to the back wall, folded his arms, and leaned backward, pressing his shoulders against the wooden paneling.

"What did you mean by stories back at the tavern? Say, the stories your father told you?"

She shifted. "What made you think about that?"

Lincoln shrugged. "I know I haven't treated you kindly since you broke onto my ship." He raised a brow. Nola pressed her lips together, feeling guilt tug at her again for coming aboard uninvited.

"They were just stories, Lincoln."

She wanted to say, but could not, was that her father told her to be wary of pirates. He painted them as bloodthirsty thieves. However, that was not what worried her the most; sirens feared the pirates sailing above them, and the pirates dreaded them equally. She was more an enemy than a mere stowaway girl.

"Very well. Perhaps you can share with me those pirates' tales on another night."

She gave him one mute nod, trying to quiet her thoughts, but as the captain turned to head back up on the deck, she called out, "Lincoln?"

"Yes, Nola."

"I'm immensely grateful you are helping me. Truly, I am. I can't repay you, other than the ruby—"

"I'm not taking your ruby, Nola," he said hastily.

She lowered her brow with a sudden relief hitting her body. "Thank you," she said. "Thank you, Lincoln; I cannot tell you how much I appreciate that gesture."

He pointed his finger past her at her bag against the wall.

"I placed it back in your bag. I put it inside a tote with a strap to keep it more secure. If a pirate out here were to see something like that dangling from your wrist, they'd cut your hand off to get it."

Nola's stomach jumped.

"Mazie and Kitten are on deck waiting for you. They will give you your assignment for today. The crew can be a bit unruly from time to time, but we do our share to keep this ship tidy," he explained. "Everyone works, but don't worry, there's plenty of time to enjoy these waters. Just not today."

The sudden shift in his mood and demeanor towards her was unexpected but comforting.

"The ship took quite a beating during the storm," he continued, "and we need to get her back to her ol' self."

Nola nodded eagerly.

Despite loving her chores and to-dos at her father's workshop, she had never felt useful.

"Aye, Captain," she said, saluting him. Her gesture only caused a slight, barely noticeable smirk on Lincoln's lips.

When Nola stepped up to the main deck, she looked out to the water, staring at the waves. She inhaled the scent of wet cedar and rum. Then, as a reminder of being safe, Nola allowed herself to close her eyes and let the salty air fill her lungs. There was something she had not felt since the storm hit the night she broke onto the ship. Peace. No danger lurked in the waters—it was tranquil, serene, almost perfect.

Boisterous laughter drew her attention to the ship's stern while Kitten and Mazie had to shout over the loud clamor for Nola to hear them from the other end. Both pirates stood by the broadside holding a fishing net and throwing their morning catch into empty barrels lined by a prep table.

"They all seem so lively this morning," Nola said as she stood by Kitten.

The female pirates exchanged glances. "It's the first time in weeks we've 'ad an afternoon where we weren't tossin' 'bout the deck from the ill weather plowin' through the sea," Kitten explained. "If I believed in the gods, I'd think they be tryin' to murder every one of us." She snickered to herself. "But we're still standin', aren't we now?"

"Still standing?" Mazie pointed her finger at different parts of the ship, babbling stuff Nola did not quite understand.

She followed Mazie's finger, trying to catch what she meant. The deck was covered in ocean filth, along with several new cracks in the old wood. Half of their black flag had been ripped—pieces of it spread out along the deck.

"Is that what you call this?" Mazie said, her face taking on a bitter scowl. "Look at this mess."

Nola somewhat agreed; everything was in bad shape. She did not get a look at the Sybil Curse before the storm. Still, it must have seen better days. Nola had spent most of her time hidden below deck during the storm. That morning, after being caught, she had not looked around to see the wreckage. All she could look at was the plank under her feet and then Lincoln's deep green eyes.

"Don't ye worry, we will get 'er up to 'erself in no time," Kitten assured. "Mazie, toss me that orange one, will ye?" She held up her hands. "Make sure they be dead before ye toss them over, eh. They are squirmy li'l things."

Mazie tossed her a bright orange fish, the size of a large boot, then pulled another net out from the water, all by herself. At least twenty fish fell from the frayed net and hit the deck.

"Ever kill a fish before, Nola?" Kitten asked, placing the fish in a large sack.

She shook her head. "My father was a fisherman," she

explained. "But he never showed me how to catch and prepare. I just ate it."

Nola smiled at the memories of her father bringing home bunches of fish to provide for his family. A tear crept at the corner of her eye at how he would wait until she and her mother finished dishing their own meals before grabbing one for himself. Often, he would go without his supper so his family could have a bigger meal. Nostalgia hit her. Nola missed them so much already.

Mazie rolled her eyes and pulled a knife from the sheath at her hip. She bent down and stabbed the fish clean through its bottom. Nola's stomach cringed a bit; the slight rocking of the ship did not help either. Kitten leaned forward, grabbed a knife herself, and started showing Nola how to do it.

Kitten placed the gutted fish inside a sack as Nola held it open. Mazie continued descaling her own and tossing them into another bag without uttering a word.

Once the bag looked plenty full, Kitten signaled Nola to follow her below deck. As they entered the kitchen, Nola scanned the room, peering over at the stove, which was already boiling water. The scent of lemon and what she thought was maybe cinnamon filled the air. The space was mostly empty, but it was tidy. A long wooden table with eight chairs sat in the middle of the room. Several barrels stood in each corner, along with at least ten crates loaded with bottles of rum.

It is, she thought, *a ridiculous amount of rum.*

Aside from the piles of fish, the table was laden with seasonings and fresh vegetables.

Nola heard her stomach rumble. She had not eaten since she fled her home and looking at all the fresh food had reminded her belly she needed to eat.

Kitten rolled up her sleeves and hummed a song to herself as she finished piling the fish on a wooden board next to her. Then she pulled out a large cutting knife.

"We are on cookin' duty today," Kitten said. "Not my cup of tea, but frankly, this is much better than wha' the men are doin' 'bove deck—cleanin' the 'ead." She pulled a cleaver from a drawer and dropped the heavy blade on the dead fish, separating the neck from the rest of the body. "It all can become a bit tedious at times—the days blendin' together. But ye should not worry 'bout tha', ye 'ere for no more than seven days."

Kitten spoke fast and her accent was as thick as her mother's.

Nola arched a brow. *Did she say 'head?'*

"Kitten, what did you mean by the head?" she asked innocently.

The pirate snickered, trying to stifle a laugh. "The 'oles in the deck under the bowsprit, lady. The shitters!"

"Oh." Nola was quiet for a moment.

The captain had a closed-off lavatory in his room. It was not fancy, but it at least had a curtain to give her privacy.

Nola had no time to see where the others went to the bathroom. She did not want to know much after that.

"Um, will we have to clean—"

"Nay," Kitten said, swishing her hand at Nola. "Not you, anyway. Mazie and I may be ladies, but the captain treats us like every other buccaneer on this ship," she explained.

Nola stared at the fish and the kitchen supplies surrounding her.

Kitten snickered. "Judging by tha' look on ye face, I'm to guess tha' ye 'ave not done 'ard labor."

"On the contrary, Kitten, I grew up helping my father on our farm, but cleaning up . . . a bathroom." She pointed up towards the deck with a smile on her face and said, "No, neither of my parents ever asked me to do that."

Kitten chuckled under her breath. "Ye ready to stop chattin' 'bout piss and shit and cook some fish?" she asked hastily, pulling out the rest of the panfish and slamming them on the kitchen table.

Nola chuckled and nodded her head.

"Bloody hell!" Their eyes looked up as Mazie stormed into the kitchen. "He had one job! One bloody job!"

Kitten wrinkled her nose. "Hill, again? Wha' did 'e do now?" her voice pitched.

Mazie folded her arms. "Bless the man's 'art. I love him dearly, but the captain needs to stop giving Hill duties when he knows too well he is going to screw up." She ran a hand down her face. "I'm surprised that a captain who's meticulous about every detail on the ship, who is picky about his crew and how we run things, trusts someone who can barely stand on two feet."

Nola bit the inside of her cheek and stepped back to give Mazie some space. But by then, the pirate was already pacing at the far end of the kitchen, stopping abruptly at a chair, then slumped down, her mouth agape.

"We won't survive five days." Mazie snarled.

Kitten's eyes widened as the realization hit her. "He didn't get the water while we were in Zemira, did 'e?"

Mazie looked up, shaking her head slowly. "Aye. We are down to one barrel of freshwater. The idiot filled the other ones with rum."

"Blimey!" Kitten cried, placing her knife down on the counter.

"Mazie," Nola called before the pirate opened her mouth. "How long will the water last?"

She shrugged her shoulders, giving Nola a bitter grin. "Now that you're here—half a day, maybe less."

Nola frowned, leaning back against the counter, resting her palms against the cool metal. Mazie pressed her lips together, taking a slow breath.

"Sorry," Nola said, her voice softening, her gaze falling over Mazie's. Then she fell silent, her stomach tightening so hard she felt like puking.

"I'm not trying to be rude, Nola," Mazie said, "but in normal circumstances, we'd turn around and head back to Zemira to fill those barrels. But no, now we can't go back because we are harboring a fugitive."

Nola stepped in Mazie's direction slowly, stopping by her side. "I understand your doubt in me being here. But, if we don't see the Fae queen—if we don't stop King Matthias, there won't be a Zemira for you ever to go back to. Not for water, food, medical supplies—because it will no longer exist."

Mazie's face hardened. "Well, you'll find really quick it's not only Zemira that's dying." She looked through a round window and into the deep, blue sea. Nola could see the sorrow in her eyes. "Ten years ago, we could look out, watch hundreds, maybe even thousands of mermaids swimming the ocean. Dragons soared above us." She became silent, biting her lower lip. "Matthias, he—"

"You see?" Nola said. "Is this the life you dreamed of?" She realized the moment Mazie furrowed her brows and flared her nostrils that she had overstepped.

Mazie stood to her feet, getting so close to Nola she felt the heat of her breath on her forehead. "You don't know a damn thing about my dreams," she said curtly, before turning to move past Nola.

Once she reached the doorway, she stopped, turning back around.

"It doesn't matter that you're here. The water we have still wouldn't be enough for us," Mazie explained, her voice modulated. "The sea isn't clean, Nola; we can't drink from it. Sure, we bathe in it. We can clean with it. But we can't drink or cook with it." She threw her hands up. "We need to stop in Westin to get water."

Kitten blinked, her arms folding around her curvy waist. "Ye sure 'bout that?"

Mazie's face scrunched up. "Nay, Kitten, it is the last place near these bloody waters I want to be." She closed her eyes, looking perturbed. "But we don't have a choice. I'll warn the captain."

Nola swallowed the nervous dryness aching in her throat. She had endangered the crew just by being there. Sure, it was not her fault Hill had not filled those barrels, but her presence only complicated things. Without clean water, she was not sure she would even make it to save the kingdom. If she were to die out in the sea with Lincoln's crew, her parents would never know.

Mazie turned on her heel and headed up the stairs. Nola paced back to where Kitten stood, still working on the fish.

She let the silence dwindle in the air before she asked Kitten, "What is in Westin?"

A small smile formed on Kitten's lips as she looked up to meet Nola's gaze.

"The nomadic families of the ten kingdoms, Nola. Tha' is, if they are still there."

Chapter 13

The crew's voyage to Westin took them nearly a day and a half. Lincoln knelt where the shore met a grassy field and let out a long sigh. Then, gripping firmly to the lush greenery between his fingers, he pressed his forehead against the ground.

Nola was transfixed by the scene before her. The ramble and chanteys of the crew as they descended the canoe muffled as she watched Lincoln focus on the peacefulness of the wavy grass. Then, when he came back to his knees, she noticed the solace in his eyes as if he had longed to see something real—something beautiful. Nola knelt with him, placing her hand over his in a bold gesture. She relaxed her shoulders, allowing herself to sink in the warmth of their touch.

Nola's feelings were awfully confusing to her. She had only known Lincoln for such a short time, but what she felt, especially at that moment, made her heart flutter. Just watching his eyes change to pure joy at the near sight of a plant was like looking at a small child staring into his mother's eyes.

"What does this feel like to you?" Nola finally brought herself to ask.

At first, Lincoln did not answer, just gazed at the green grass, running his hands gently over the prickly texture.

"A dream," he answered after a long pause. His tone was soft and serene, almost like the quiet whistle of the wind before the storm. "It feels like hope, Nola."

Hope. The one thing she tried so desperately to cling to because it was all she had left. The hope to make it to the Fae and save her people. The hope that someday, the life Lincoln held between his fingers would flourish again on her own land and save her people.

The meadow stretched along the shore, thousands of feet in each direction; it almost looked endless. A wall rose several feet tall along the shoreline until it reached an entrance. The towering bronze gates were covered in long, radiant green vines climbing to the top arch, with budding rosewood-colored flowers lining the edges.

Nola felt the urge to cry as she admired the captivating sight. She had seen colorful vegetation in paintings—never so close or with her own eyes. Nothing compared to seeing it for the first time before her, to touch and smell.

As Nola spun around, she eyed Mazie approaching the gate and link her fingers around the latch, but it was locked. A large crow, which sat atop the gate, looked down at her—glaring even. Mazie then moved over as Lincoln walked past her, fiddling with the lock himself.

"It won't open, Captain," Mazie explained. "It's not as if I have the key."

Lincoln leaned forward, his forehead pressing between the bars of the gate.

"Harry!" he shouted.

Right then, Nola noticed a chubby man leaning up against a tree a hundred yards away, sitting on his rear. He looked as if he was lost in a sleepless slumber.

"Harry! Get your ass over here and open the damn gate." His voice was a little louder that time.

Nola watched the burly man with a full beard stifle a yawn with his fist, then narrow in on Lincoln; his eyes grew.

"Over here," Lincoln said, waving his hand through the gate. The man jumped to his feet and scurried over to the gate, tripping on a few rocks along the way.

"Lincoln!" he called cheerfully. "What are you doing here? This is a nice surprise!" He looked over Lincoln's shoulder. "You and your crew haven't been eaten by sirens yet?"

A jolly smile pulled at Lincoln's lips. Nola, on the other side, when she heard the man say siren out loud, felt her shoulders perk and her body stiffen. Because the captain had stayed focused on the bearded man, the change in Nola's demeanor went unnoticed.

Lincoln said playfully, "We aren't taken down that easily, Harry." He gestured to his crew. "I've acquired quite the valiant and brave crew of hearties these last ten years."

The man huffed. "Well, look at that. Has it really been that long?" He scratched his head. "It feels as if it was only yesterday you snatched up Mazie and took off to the sea." The odd man smiled widely. "Well, time sure has passed by us all, hasn't it?"

Lincoln nodded as if to dismiss the man's comment, then shifted his body, opening a path for the crew. The man looked at Mazie—she swallowed, her head hanging low.

"I can't believe it, Mazie. Look at you, all grown up." He held out his hands as if wanting to draw her in for a hug.

She finally met his eyes. "Am I welcomed here, Harry?" she asked shyly.

The man dropped his hands and gave her a quizzical look, his bushy eyebrows pulling together, creating a large wrinkle between his eyes.

"What in the—" Harry threw his hands up. "You honestly believe your mother won't be thrilled to see you after all this time?"

Nola's lips parted, the realization hitting her that Westin was Mazie's home—at least, it used to be.

"Come, dear, she'll be hard to find today with it being the Westin Harvest Festival. We have had ships coming and going all morning. The best festival we've ever put on."

Nola stepped closer to the man. "What happens during the Westin Harvest?"

He squinted at her as if everyone should know about the festival and said, "Well, aren't you a pretty lady. Come here." And he opened his arms wide, gesturing his fingers his way.

Nola kept her feet pinned to the ground. The man was a hugger, and she most certainly was not.

"Ah," he huffed, waving his hand in the air to assuage her. "I might be fat and ugly, but I won't bite."

Nola finally smiled, her cheeks turning pink. She may not want to hug him, but she thought him to be a silly, funny man.

"Sorry, sir," she said. His eyes were friendly, but she was guarded—always had been.

Lincoln moved past Nola, patting the man on the back. "Do you have a carriage for us while we're here?" he asked. Nola smiled as she realized he was trying to distract Harry enough to lose interest in her.

The man nodded again. "I've got horses. But it's going to cost you about—"

"Oh, bloody hell, Harry, give us the damn horses," Mazie barked.

He raised his hands. "Fine. Fine. Fine." He gestured to the rest of the crew, who stood quietly behind her. "I've got only four. You will have to double up on the white one and brown one—they are my strongest—oh, and Jet! Lincoln, you can ride Jet with Miss Beautiful; he is strong but needs a firm hand."

Nola felt uncomfortable immediately as she realized Harry was referring to her.

"Aye, we'll take what you have. Thank you, mate," the captain said, signaling the crew to gather up their bags and swords, which were scattered over the grass.

They followed closely behind Harry to the horses—one white with cute freckles all over, two black, and one light chestnut brown with a large black ring around one of her eyes. Nola and Lincoln paired together, while Mazie shared one with Hill. He was going to need someone to steer the horse. The lanky pirate was still smashed from all the drinking an hour before.

Boots made himself comfortable on the white horse, then reached out to grab Kitten's hand to pull her up, sitting her between his legs. She leaned into his chest and looked back, sneaking a kiss against his dry, salty lips.

Despite being on the heavier side, Ardley climbed quickly to the horse, took hold of the reins, and looked to the captain, waiting for him to lead the way into the city.

Harry adjusted his vest and looked over to the crew, gesturing to the trail. "The festivities are over by the new fountain." He shook his head. "Not that old, rusted witch; she didn't quite make it through the last storm. Beshy built a lovely clay creature that resembles more of a dragon than a bird." He sauntered to Mazie, who looked down at the man. "You'll see all the new tents we've put up. Your mother is at the far end, yellow tent, with a grey cloth over her table. She's been doing quite well today."

"What is she selling this time?" Mazie asked. "Crystals, gems . . . dirt?" Her words were laced with sarcasm, and she averted her eyes from Harry.

The man laughed, handing Mazie the reins to her horse. "She doesn't do readings anymore. Not since after you left."

Mazie swallowed; her face hardened as if she was not a bit pleased with the reminder that she had left her family to venture into the sea. "Fine, whatever," she said dryly, pulling the reins down until the horse galloped forward, Lincoln and Nola already heading down the path.

The ride to the town was quiet, other than the rustling within the trees surrounding them. Nola looked over her shoulder, and Lincoln gave her a comforting smile. He wrapped his arms around her waist, pulling her closer back between his thighs. The captain leaned forward, and she felt his breath against her neck. "You look like you could use some entertainment," he said. "This is the one land you will enjoy."

"Is this Mazie's home?" she asked quietly.

"I can hear you, lassie," Mazie mumbled.

Nola bit her bottom lip. "So, this is where you grew up—you miss it here?"

"Nay," she snapped back quickly. "And nay again."

Lincoln chuckled. "Mazie's family are travelers. They never stay in one place for more than a few years," he explained. "I'm genuinely surprised they are still here." He looked over his shoulder. "Mazie, it's been at least ten years since I met you here, hasn't it?"

Mazie nodded but did not comment further.

Nola looked around. "I haven't been anywhere other than Zemira my entire life," she said. "I'm excited to explore, either way."

Lincoln gave her another tight squeeze around the waist. She was not sure what all that meant; the way he touched her, the way his hands glided across her stomach when he gripped tight to the reins. Either way, she enjoyed his touch.

After a few minutes where everyone rode silently except for Hill's drunken chants, Lincoln spoke up.

"We're here," he said.

Nola looked around, admiring the busy multitude around them.

The horses trotted slowly along the barely paved road. Nola was enthralled by the commotion. Boots and Kitten giggled as she pointed to the food stands. Ardley encouraged Hill to sober up as Mazie tried to keep him on the horse.

Nola had tears in her eyes as she watched the people laugh, eat, and celebrate life. They all turned to look at the travelers, musicians, and dancers performing on a stage to their right. Lincoln pulled back to halt their horse as a willowy man riding a unicycle zoomed by. The sun had set, yet the city was bright, illuminated with the glow of lights lining the streets and wrapped around each of the blooming trees.

"This is beautiful," Nola said, her stomach fluttering with elation. "I've never seen anything like this in my entire life."

Lincoln leaned over her shoulder. "I was here for over a week when I visited ten years ago. It happened to be the time of the harvest festival. The nomads use nature's herbs and crystals and harness the elemental magic for each kingdom they visit. It is—"

"Quite beautiful?" she added with a slight smile over her features.

"Aye, it was quite memorable, to say the least," he said.

Nola kept her neck turned, looking into his jade eyes and the handsome smile imprinted on his lips. She nibbled on her lip nervously as his gaze fixed to hers, then turned back to the lights.

The glow lit up hundreds of colorful tents, colors Nola had never seen before—colors she did not know even existed. Despite it being dusk, the lights lit up the sky with fireworks booming into the night, lighting up the gorgeous, unique scenery surrounding them. There was a long stage to the left, decked with thousands of flowers and garlands. A couple dancers and what appeared to be goblins moved about the tents surrounding the square. Nola had read about the traveling nomads of the ten kingdoms, but the way they looked was not what she had pictured in her mind. The books had it all wrong.

Their outfits were eccentric—almost glowing—several with makeup painted thick on their face.

They look different, just like me, Nola thought; the instant comfort connected her to those the world looked at as strange and weird. If not in Westin, at least, they would have been in Zemira.

"What happens during the festival, Lincoln?" Nola asked innocently, not turning that time. She could not will herself to look away from the spectacle.

"Ah, well, I guess you wouldn't know such celebrations since small villages like yours haven't had fresh produce in nearly two decades," Lincoln explained. "But in every town they visit, they reap the harvest from the fields. Then they sell the product here to give thanks to their gods for the good season." He pointed around at the tents surrounding the city streets. "Anything you see here is free," he reiterated, bringing their horse to a stop.

Nola smiled. "This is beautiful, Mazie," she said as Lincoln swept her up and off the horse. "Why did you leave?" she asked, oblivious to the fact that she was stepping again on the ground.

Mazie's dark brows raveled into a glower as she sucked in a breath. "It wasn't like I wanted to leave—I was dead to my mother, and if it wasn't for the captain here, who knows where I would've ended up."

"Oh," Nola said. "I'm so sorry, I didn't—"

Mazie raised her hand. "Just because Harry greeted me with open arms—doesn't mean . . ." She paused, looking irritated. "Gah! You're so stupidly naïve—"

"Raven, that's enough!" Lincoln scowled.

Mazie's body visibly tensed. Nola had not heard Lincoln use her pirate name since she met the crew.

It was clear to Nola that Mazie despised her, and she was not even trying to hide it. She also wondered how much more she would hate her when they figured out that she was a siren and had lied to all of them.

After Mazie rolled her eyes and looked back at the city, Nola noticed a somber look in her eyes. Kitten rushed to her side and held her hand as if to comfort her friend.

When they all had their bags on their shoulders, Lincoln led them to a yellow canvas tent at the far end of the main road and there stood a woman holding a curtain open. Her long black hair, dreaded in thick locks, fell to her hips, and a dark tattoo wrapped from her shoulders to her nails. She wore a colorful red lace dress draped over the front of her chest, with beaded lining over the collar.

Once inside, tall canvas walls surrounded them, lit by incandescent lamps on every corner of the room. The tent was embellished with garden leaves climbing up the walls, dried-out flowers scattered about, and jewels and stones placed on each table, creating a brightly lit sanctuary. An earthy aroma drifted in the air. It was pleasantly inviting.

"You're back?" the woman said as Mazie moved past Lincoln to stand in front of her.

"Mother, you haven't aged a day," Mazie said wryly.

Her mother laughed. "My magic has done well for me over the years," she said. "And what say you, daughter? Have you learned to fly yet?"

Mazie's jaw tightened. She quickly turned away as if consciously fighting to contain her untamed tongue from saying something she would regret.

It was clear to Nola that Mazie's mother's remark—whatever it meant—was intended to hurt her. And judging by her scowl across her face, she had let it sting.

Mazie looked at her mother sharply; a begrudging expression shone on her face. "I daresay, Mother, you are still a raging bitch," she sneered.

Her mother threw her head back and cackled, and of course, that only caused Mazie to hiss through her teeth.

Nola found it interesting how tough Mazie behaved towards her and the rest of the crew since she met her. However, she appeared a lot more vulnerable, as if her mother knew exactly what to say to get under her skin.

"Kala," Lincoln called heedfully, stepping between the two women.

Mazie turned from her mother and folded her arms defiantly, then began to mumble obscenities under her breath.

"We have quite the voyage ahead of us, but my crew and I are lacking the amount of water to get us to where we need to go," Lincoln said, looking at his crew. "In fact, we are all feeling a bit parched. So, any food and water you can offer would be deeply appreciated. Also, I would be much obliged if we could fill our barrels. We only need enough to get us to where we are sailing to. If you may," he asked, gesturing out his hand and giving her a slight gentlemanly bow. "Do you have room here for at least a night? We won't stay long—"

Kala nodded to Lincoln. "Of course, handsome," she replied. "I'll always have room for you, and please, our well has been plentiful these past few years. You'll find enough water for your needs."

The pirates' faces lit up when the woman said they could stock up on the water.

Nola let out a breath of relief.

"This way," the woman said. Kala walked out of the tent, and the crew followed, looking on to the festivities. "You can use our carriages to transport the barrels." She looked over her shoulder at Lincoln. "However, we are using them for the time being." She smiled, but it faded quickly as she eyed Harry running their way. "Harry, get back to your post."

The fat little man stopped next to Lincoln, smiling with eagerness. "And miss out on the party? Get out of here!"

Kala laughed. "Fine," she said. "At least go bring our guests some water. Make yourself useful."

"And grab us some food too, ye fool!" Hill shouted as Harry dashed towards the stage.

Kitten quickly swatted at his head. He staggered back in surprise.

Kala caressed her dreadlocks. "So many new faces this time visiting us, Lincoln." Her eyes scanned Nola's. "Are you going to introduce me to everyone?"

Lincoln gestured to Boots. "Sorry. Right. These two here are Boots and Kitten—" he pointed to his right.

Kitten grabbed at her dress and bowed, while Boots gave the woman a curt nod.

"—and over there is Ardley," he finished.

Ardley hunched forward, placing his hat to his chest and gesturing a bow. "Ma'am." He tipped his hat, then put it back on his head.

"And that there, near your tent, touching your skulls lanterns, is Hill."

Kitten raised her hand to her face as she watched her drunken comrade. The lanky pirate looked like they had just scooped him up from a random dock.

Lincoln smirked. "And this here is Nola. She's new to our ship." As he said her name, a smile lit up his face, and he ran a hand through his chestnut-colored hair.

Nola felt a blush rise on her cheeks. She found it interesting how flustered he looked, especially after treating her like an enemy a few days ago.

"Well, hello, dear," Kala's voice drew Nola's eyes back to her. "You are . . ." The woman reached out and took her right hand.

Oh, no! Nola froze.

The woman's touch shot a bizarre energy through her skin, and she knew, in that moment of fear, her eyes had changed for Kala.

". . . quite different looking," the woman finished.

Nola's shoulders relaxed, and she flashed a tiny smile. "I will take that as a compliment. I know my hair is a bit strange, but—"

"Yes," Kala hummed, "it must be the hair."

The comment held a hidden meaning. The nomad woman was not talking about her hair—she was referring to her eyes. Kala knew she was a siren.

Nola cleared her throat, bowing her head slightly. "It's very nice meeting you." She looked around. "This place is breathtaking."

Kala smirked. "And you are welcomed here, any time," she said.

Quietly and slowly, Nola let out the breath she held in, then shimmied her hand from hers. She did not want Kala to know her secret, but it was too late. However, given how the woman kept her lips sealed, Nola allowed herself to relax.

"Come now, join the festivities. Mazie, everyone will be thrilled to see you," Kala said.

"Yeah, I'm sure," Mazie said bitterly, turning away from her mother again.

"Don't be melodramatic. You know the triplets are a little lost without their best friend." She sneered at her daughter. "You owe them an apology, you know? You took off without so much as a goodbye!"

Mazie's hands went into fists. "I don't owe them shit!"

Lincoln chuckled. "I'd love to meet your friends and family, Mazie," Lincoln said, placing a hand on her shoulder. "We were so busy the last time we were here fixing up the ship that I didn't get a chance to meet everyone."

"You aren't missing much," Mazie belittled. But she drew

in a deep breath before saying, "Gah, where are those ridiculous creatures?"

As the crew stepped out onto a field, they could see that multiple tents, vendor stands, and tables full of food encircled a large stage at the center. Everything covered with white and red lights made it look more like a carnival than a peaceful town.

Maybe this is what life is like when people are happy, Nola thought as a few dancers moved past them to the beat of the tambourines.

The crew walked to a couple tables next to a tent that looked like a bar and joined Harry, who delicately arranged a feast for the visitors. Ardley, Boots, and Kitten sat together on one side and grabbed a plate. Hill managed to balance himself as he joined them to eat. With only a couple of seats left, Lincoln pulled one out and nodded at Nola to sit on it as he followed Mazie to the bar. Kala sat next to her—somewhat fascinated by her.

"Ever been to a harvest festival?" Kala asked Nola. "We do them in almost every city we visit."

She shook her head. "I never have. Zemira doesn't celebrate like this."

"You're from Zemira?" Kala asked, seemingly surprised.

"Yes, in a small village south of the palace walls. I have lived there my entire life," she explained. "My mother grew up in a city several hours north of Baylin. After meeting my father, he built her a cottage with his bare hands. We lived in that home ever since."

Kala smirked. "Well, that is quite interesting."

Nola watched Lincoln, who sat at the bar, glance over

their way and give her an odd look. Kala stood and came up behind three women. The ladies immediately turned around to see where she was heading. They were tall, slender, and incredibly beautiful.

The one on the left had short blonde hair with hints of rose-toned strands; her dress had cleavage falling all the way down to her belly button, and she had a gorgeous yet intimidating gaze. The one standing in the middle wore her long brown hair straight down to her hips, where it met the beads on her colorful skirt. The mascara on her long eyelashes made her turquoise eyes look ravishing. They giggled as the third girl with tight curls that reached the middle of her back, wearing a long dress and with bare feet, said something in a low voice.

"Mazie! It can't be!" the curly brown-haired girl shouted.

"Veronika," she said flatly as the girl leapt into her arms, giving her a tight squeeze.

Veronika turned to Lincoln and licked her lips flirtatiously, with her arm still dangling over Mazie's shoulder.

Mazie rolled her eyes. "Oh, bloody hell," she cried, brushing Veronika's arm off her shoulder, then gestured to the other girls, saying, "This is Samantha, Nichole, and—"

"Veronika," the woman finished for Mazie, her eyes still transfixed on Lincoln. "Care to dance, pirate?" She held out her hand. "This is a night of celebration, and you all look bored out of your wits," she babbled on. "No one sits around and mopes during a harvest festival!"

Samantha stepped forward. "I've been fermenting our

own brew if you'd like to try some," she said, swaying where she stood. "It's delightful."

Nola, noticing the trio's encroachment on Lincoln, sauntered towards the bar, a little jealousy shining in her color-changing eyes.

"Homemade brew, you say," Nola said. "Sounds intriguing."

Samantha snickered, turning to Nichole. "Go grab a mug for the pretty girl."

Nola smiled. "Thank you, I'd love to try some."

Lincoln grinned at Nola and gestured to the dance floor. As she stepped forward to go with him, Veronika stepped between them, taking Lincoln's wrist, and in a split second, she yanked him towards the center of the field. A small smile reached her lips. The look on his face as the music played, and while he moved to the beat, had made her happy.

He caught her eye and shrugged, but all she did was wave her hand in the air, showing Lincoln she did not mind. Kitten pulled at Boots's shirt to drag him after them, and Hill and Ardley followed behind to the dance floor.

Nichole giggled to herself. "Oh, tonight is going to be fun!" she said with enthusiasm in her voice. She curtsied to Nola and swung around, chasing after them. Right then, Nola noticed, dangling from behind the beautiful girl was a long, thick, black tail.

Chapter 14

"What is she?" Nola asked Mazie once they were left alone at the table. She waited for Mazie to brush her off and not answer her nosey question. However, when she smirked for the first time since they arrived at Westin, Nola's shoulders relaxed.

"They are called maukibas," Mazie explained.

Nola raised a brow.

"Before my father died, when I was five, he found a beautiful egg on one of our trips to the Southlands. He thought it was only a stone at first, but when it hatched, three little hatchlings came out." She pointed to the three girls dancing on the field with Lincoln. "They are more human-like now." Mazie shifted uncomfortably; her smile dulled. "Veronika and I—"

Nola smiled at the realization. "Then go dance with her, Mazie," she said. "It's quite obvious she's only dancing with Lincoln to make you jealous."

Mazie looked up. "Nay. That was a long time ago," she explained. "We didn't end things in a friendly manner."

Nola opened her mouth to speak but held back. That

was the first time Mazie had been cordial with her. She was afraid the pirate would close up to her again, so she shifted her attention back to the crowd.

"Go ahead," Mazie said without looking at her. "Ask me what is pressed on your mind."

Nola smiled. "Very well," she started reluctantly, clearing her throat. "Why do you hate me so much?" she asked. "It can't just be because I broke into your ship."

Mazie turned and looked at Nola, but her eyes were soft.

"Don't be ridiculous. I don't know you enough to hate you," she said.

Nola scrunched up her face and pressed her lips together.

Mazie shrugged. "You remind me of someone who broke my captain's heart, and I'm worried it will happen again, and I will have to mend those broken pieces . . . again."

Nola nodded. "I see." She let out a breath. "Who was she?"

Mazie stood straight. "Her name was Sybil."

Nola's stomach tightened. "Like the ship?"

She nodded. "Lincoln named the ship after the woman he almost married, yes. But the bitch left him the day they were to take their vows. A woman who, until very recently, still had his heart."

Mazie paused and stood up to step closer to Nola until they were within arm's reach.

"As much as it pleases me to finally see him happy again, I know where this will end." Mazie bit her lip. "Nola,

Lincoln was bewitched the moment he saw you at the marketplace. He acted like a buffoon because he already cared about a girl he did not know. It has been less than two days and I see the way he looks at you. And in five days from now, all that goes away."

Mazie looked back at the stage as Nola's subtle grin faded. The pirate shot her a look as if she pitied her, then slammed her mug on the table.

"Okay, I'm done talking," Mazie said, marching past her, brushing against her shoulder.

Nola sat silent, sucking in a breath. *Great.*

Her eyes turned back to Lincoln on the field. Nola could not deny the attraction she had for him; that was clear. But Mazie's words were a reminder that the two could never be.

She was a siren, and he was a pirate.

Nola's mission was never to board a ship and fall in love with the captain. She was a monster in a pirate's eyes. And Lincoln was falling for someone he did not know.

As they danced, Lincoln coiled his hands over Veronika's shoulders and moved with the music. He looked hesitant to place his hand on her hip, but she gripped his wrist, directing his hand to where she wanted it to go. He looked up as a dancer jumped off the stage and moved towards Lincoln, joining the two.

The dancer paraded herself in front of Lincoln. Still, his eyes stayed on Nola's. Startlingly, she felt a rush of jealousy climb up to her throat. But recalling her conversation with Mazie, she smiled back, waving her hand at him to continue dancing. Nola knew she had no right to feel that way.

He is the captain of a ship, and he is only taking me where I need to go, she reminded herself.

Nola sought to convince herself that her feelings resulted from the new and exciting experience, and none of them meant a thing.

While the people danced, she sat alone at the table—a spectator who did not belong.

"You and I need to speak," Kala spoke from behind her. Nola turned around, wrapping her arms around her waist as a slight cool breeze swept between them. The woman may have looked kind, but the energy Nola felt whenever she was close to her was anything but. She could not tell what it was; it just felt off, like a magical force was circling her—warning her.

"You want to speak with me?" Nola asked, surprised, but then it dawned on her.

Of course she would want to speak with a siren posing as a human who had just entered their city, Nola told herself.

"Sure," she agreed, turning back to her.

Kala inched forward. "Do they know?" she asked. "About what you are?"

Nola looked down, shaking her head. "No," she replied. "I don't believe so anyway."

"Good. Mazie has her own demons to deal with. It is better that way."

Nola looked up. "Why do you care what they think of me?"

"What I care about is my daughter," Kala confessed.

"I would never hurt her."

"Oh, I believe that. A true siren would have slaughtered

that entire crew by now." Kala's eyes searched hers. "You are a delicate one."

Delicate one? What the hell does she mean by that? Nola cursed in her head.

She was no delicate flower, but Kala was right; she would not—purposefully—hurt anyone. At least not a crew who was trying to help her get to where she needed to go.

"They are helping me, Kala. I'm on a journey to save my family. To save Zemira," Nola said as she stood from her chair, trying to avoid the conversation.

Kala got up and walked by her, looking skeptically.

"You want something else, don't you?" Kala asked.

Nola's mind drifted as she thought about her question. She shrugged. "I want to know who I really am—I want to swim."

Kala interrupted, ". . . How about finding out who your parents are?"

She nodded in silence.

"I guarantee, whoever they are, they've not forgotten about you. If your parents are still alive, that is. A mother never forgets or stops loving their child," Kala said.

Nola frowned. "It seems, though, Mazie thinks you hate her," she said. "Unless this is how you have always treated each other."

Kala let out a small laugh. "Mazie was young when she left. Her hatred towards me runs deep." Her smile slipped. "Especially after what happened the week she left."

Nola's forehead creased.

"You want to know what happened, don't you?"

Nola nodded eagerly. "Yes. I do want to know."

Kala walked towards a path and Nola followed closely behind until they reached a bridge. “Mazie and her sister believed they could fly.”

Nola’s lips parted. “Like a fairy?”

“Like a bird,” she corrected. “A raven, to be exact.”

They stopped at the center of the bridge and Kala leaned against the rail, falling silent.

Nola perched her hands on the rail as she saw Kala’s shoulders slouch. The woman let a long sigh escape her withered lips.

“I don’t understand,” Nola said.

Kala turned to overlook the river they stood over. It was another beautiful sight. The clapboard-sided bridge covered in blueish-green moss created a perfect arch leading across the water. At the other end was a forested glen, where weeping willows and shrubs formed a stunning path.

The water looked crystalline, even in the darkness of the night. Straight ahead, Nola saw a full moon shining bright and looking as if she could reach out and touch it.

“Mazie’s sister,” Kala started, drawing Nola’s attention from the view she did not want to avert her eyes from, “—her twin, actually.” She swallowed, her eyes glistening with tears. “Her name was Bay. She and Mazie were always getting into trouble. Then one day, her sister stood on this bridge, standing right over the railing, and jumped.”

Nola’s mouth gaped open. “She—”

“No, she never wanted to hurt herself,” she corrected before Nola could finish her question. “She thought she could fly. See, I had told my children that they could be anything they wanted to be. Bay wanted to be a raven, of all creatures." Kala wiped her cheek as a few tears trickled down. "She thought them to be the most beautiful creature in the world." She ran her hands gingerly over the bridge railing. "Once I told Mazie I was wrong to tell them that, something snapped in her and she lost her mind."

That explains why Mazie is the way she is, Nola thought before Kala continued.

"Mazie struggled to accept what had happened that day. She also believed *she* could fly—like her sister—and that something had gone wrong. Then, a few days later, she said that she saw Bay soaring through the clouds . . ." Kala's voice trailed off.

"I'm sorry," Nola said remorsefully. "I'm so sorry. I should not have asked you."

Kala shook her head, closing her eyes. "Needless to say, after I convinced her Bay was dead, I stopped being my daughter's favorite person, of course. Mazie became aggressive, hostile—especially towards me. One day, out of nowhere, she began to destroy everything in her path. Tore down a few tents, knocked everything off the shelves from a couple of businesses. She became so uncontrollable that we had to tie her down."

She removed her hands from the railing and turned to Nola. There was complete silence between them as a small tear reached one of Kala's eyes.

"That day, she became an outcast. That was, until Lincoln showed up here, looking for food and supplies to repair the damage on his ship. And he was looking for a crew at the time. So I was happy to send her away. But after she left, that burning, aching feeling in my chest felt like I was dying. I lost a child to the river and the other one to the sea."

Nola leaned back and looked up. "Why did you tell me this?" she asked. "You could have told me no. I am but a stranger to you."

Kala smiled lightly. "Because you are a lot like Mazie."

Nola chuckled. "I doubt that. She's brave, and I'm—"

"Bravery isn't what makes you strong, Nola. Bravery is to keep going despite one's fears. You are wrong to believe Mazie does not fear. She fears greatly."

Those words resonated with Nola. Her father taught her bravery was the one trait needed to help her save her kingdom. She always thought if she was afraid, she was not brave.

Kala lifted her hand and stroked Nola's cheek.

She froze.

"You are a siren," she said, "but you're something else, and you know it, just like my daughter did." She dropped her hand. "She may not have wings to fly, but she was born for more than traveling from one place to another, using magic she never understood or wanted. And I had not realized that until she was gone. Seeing her today, though her face reveals a lie of bitterness and resentment—true happiness hides behind her eyes."

Kala played with her long dreadlocks as she looked out at the moon's reflection over the river.

"Find that magic inside *you*, Nola," she said. "I am a strong, nomadic woman, with the power to harness the elements of this world, my dear. We see things others cannot." She stood straight, reaching out for Nola's hand, touching her again. That same eerie feeling reached inside her, and she tensed.

"Two nights ago, I had a vision of Mazie on Lincoln's ship," Kala said, a strange expression crossing her features. "In that vision, I saw her fly."

Nola felt in danger. The numbness at her fingertips made her pull back from Kala's touch.

"A vision or a dream?" she asked Kala.

She smiled. "They are the same to us, little siren."

Nola thought for a quick second about what Kala had said. She was unsure how all of it worked: traveling witches, visions, humans flying without wings. But she would allow the world of magic taken from Zemira to become a reality in her life.

Perhaps letting it all sink in would help her better understand who she was. And the powers she held. Nola was unsure what meeting Kala meant, but she could be the key to learning how to use her own magic at will.

Loud laughter echoed from the festival, drawing both the ladies' eyes towards the field.

"Come, Nola. Relax for a night. Then, you and the crew should leave in the morning."

Nola agreed with Kala, bowing her head as she watched her saunter back to the field. They docked in Westin looking for water, but things were getting strange; it was time to leave. Her eyes darted towards the east, where they had anchored the Sybil Curse. She longed for the boat she had boarded only a few days ago.

Nola's thoughts spoke to her, *There is something odd about this city, and I cannot place my finger on it.*

Her gut told her something was not right while her heart hammered inside her chest every time she breathed.

"We need to get out of here," Nola whispered, so low, it might have been a mere thought.

When she returned to her senses, Kala had disappeared into the darkness. She peered around, looking for Mazie's mother, but the sound of a breaking branch cracked through the trees. Nola quickly looked over her shoulder; her face blanched as a disembodied being stared at her from in between the leaves. A heavy shiver coursed the entire length of her spine; her skin prickled painfully, and her breath caught in her throat.

Nola turned to run, but as she blinked, the image before her disappeared.

Chapter 15

"Nola!" Lincoln called out, rushing through the hills by the river towards her. "Are you alright?"

His eyes shone with worry as he looked at her horror-struck expression. Lincoln reached for her silky hair, removing a few of the silver strands from her eyes.

"I've been looking everywhere for you," he confessed.

His mere touch provoked a rush of excitement through Nola's body.

She opened her mouth to tell him about the conversation between Kala and her and the unsettling feeling she had about that place but hesitated.

Perhaps it is all in my head, she thought. *Why should I worry him with my own paranoia?*

"I didn't want to dance," she said, "so I went for a walk."

Of course, it was a lie. Nola wanted to be the woman in Lincoln's arms as he curled his fingers around her waist while they moved to the beat of the music. She looked at him pointedly, trying to erase the ominous dark eyes from her mind that watched her moments before through the trees.

"I'm a bit tired," Nola continued. "I think I'll turn in for the night."

He laid his hand to the side of her neck, and his thumb landed close to her lips. He retracted quickly when her shoulders heaved.

"Sorry. I—" Lincoln said.

"Don't be," she said, biting her lip, feeling utterly embarrassed by her reaction.

Nola had not meant to pull back, but his touch had taken her by surprise. His fingers against her bare neck were provoking. She could still feel the ghost of his fingers against her skin.

Lincoln stepped forward boldly, raising his hand again, slowly reaching for her cheek.

Nola wondered if his heart was racing as fast as hers. His fingers ran down her delicate jawline until he seized her chin and gripped it gently. Then, he tilted her head up to look deeper into her eyes. They both got lost in each other's gaze for a few moments. Unmoved. Serene. Slowly, Lincoln slid his hand up her jaw and to the back of her neck, lacing his fingers through her hair—a warm, welcoming shiver tickled her spine.

Lincoln's intense stare made her feel wanted. With a reassuring smile on her face, she sucked in a soft breath and took an unconscious step closer to him.

He did not pull back.

After a minute of silence, Lincoln's lips trembled as he spoke, "I've not treated you kindly since you boarded my ship. I should have never pulled out my pistol on you. I shouldn't have—"

"You don't have to apologize, Lincoln. I'm not upset." She felt her hand shudder as she rested her palm over his muscular chest, leaning into his touch. Nola bit the inside of her cheek. "I mean, I was at the time, but looking back, I know that wasn't—"

Lincoln's lips collided with hers—eager and wild. His hand gripped the back of her neck. She moaned. However, with her hand still planted on his chest, Nola pushed away, breaking their kiss.

Parting her lips, she drew in a breath and said, "This is mad, Lincoln. We've only known each other for a couple of days."

He pressed his forehead to hers, bringing her closer to him, slowly gliding his fingers down her arm.

"Time seems to stop when you are at sea—it feels much longer." Lincoln leaned forward, whispering into her ear, "Doesn't it?"

Being wrapped in his arms clouded her mind, distracting her from the world around them.

Nola closed her eyes as a cool breeze prickled the back of her arms; her hair danced in the wind.

A sudden sorrow crashed at her heart as he pushed back, creating a gap between them, just as she did.

"I'll ask Kala where she wants us to sleep," Lincoln said, holding out his hand for her to take. "I'll get you settled, and then I will gather my crew." He squeezed her hand as a whimsical smile played on his lips. "But I'll lay with you tonight."

Her heartbeat quickened with anticipation to be so close to him for an entire night.

"This is a strange place. I don't want to leave you alone." Lincoln reached out and framed her face with his rough hands. Then, he leaned forward until she felt his breath on her ear, "I don't ever want to leave you alone."

Neither do I, Nola thought as he escorted her to the camp.

As Nola crawled into bed, she looked up to see Lincoln leaving the tent.

"Goodnight, Lincoln," she called.

He stopped at the entrance, gave her a charming wink, then disappeared as the canvas entrance closed behind him.

Her heart longed for the pirate when he left her alone in the tent. Well, she was not entirely alone; Hill laid curled up in a corner, already passed out. The drunken buccaneer snored so loudly she wondered if she was going to be able to fall asleep.

Nola leaned back, staring at the netted skyline above her. The night was black with only the dim light from the moon coming through the trees, and not even the sound of the music could be heard any longer.

She closed her eyes.

That kiss.

Mazie sat alone at the edge of the stage, staring at the grass below, wiggling her toes.

"They cleared out already?" Lincoln asked her, joining her at the stage.

"Aye," she said. "It's like nothing has changed, Captain."

He gave her an inquisitive look. "How do you mean?" he asked.

"This place—my mother! Everything seems untouched by time, you know?" She stopped suddenly as a clutch of panic twisted in the pit of her stomach. "They should have been venturing off to another kingdom by now. Instead, they are—"

"Stuck?" he said.

"No one has aged a day." Mazie looked over Lincoln's shoulder. "Even the children, Captain. In the ten years since I've been gone, they look the same." She scrunched up her face. "Fucking magic."

He chuckled at her comment and held out a beckoning hand. "Enough. Let's go. You and I made each other a promise; you are over what happened. I can't imagine what it'd be for us not to—"

"Age?" she said.

He dropped his hand, giving her a frustrated look.

"Isn't that what you were about to say?" She pointed towards her mother's home. "They used magic to keep themselves young. After they forbade me from trying to use magic to bring my sister back!" A tear of frustration fled her obsidian-colored eyes. "I tried, Captain. I tried to bring her back before you found me, and I was shunned by every person who ever loved me."

"You're drunk, Mazie; let's get you to bed." He reached out again, but she slapped his hand away.

"Fuck you, too!" A look of disdain flared in her eyes. Yet sudden guilt hit her like a heavy brick crushing at her chest.

The moment those words left her lips, she wished she could take them back, but pride consumed her.

Mazie slid off the stage and staggered across the grass, catching herself on a table. "Sorry, Captain, it's just—"

"It's okay."

She planted her feet to keep herself from falling over. "No, I have to say it," she breathed. "The part that hurts the most is that even after ten years, my mother hasn't even apologized for blaming me for Bay's death." She looked up, wiping a tear falling down her nearly perfect cheekbone. She wiped her face with the back of her hand as she said, "I know my mother wishes it was me who tried to fly that day."

Lincoln placed his hands on each side of Mazie's cheeks and looked her deep into her eyes.

"So, what if she does?"

Mazie gave him an odd expression.

"Listen to me. When have you ever cared what someone thought of you? Even your own mother?" He dropped his hands and crossed them over his chest. "You left this place because you didn't give a shit about this life. The way they treated you after Bay died—you're better than anyone here—especially your mother."

Mazie gave him a subtle nod, but as she turned to walk on her own, she heard a feminine voice in the distance.

"I'll take her to bed, Lincoln."

They both looked up as Veronika padded across the lawn, picking up a glass of water from a table next to her.

"Here." Veronika handed Mazie the mug, but she gagged it out immediately after she drank.

"The bloody—" She spat on the ground. "Tastes like dirt." She looked around. "I'll take some whiskey if you have some."

Lincoln smiled. "Thanks, Veronika," he said, nodding for Mazie, who still had a scowl pointed at the nasty water.

Veronika held up her hand. "Care to dance with me?" she asked her, not acknowledging Lincoln's presence any longer.

Mazie's vision blurred, spinning around like the sky was closing in on her. "There's no more music."

"We'd make our own songs, remember?" she replied, pouting her lips.

Veronika gripped Mazie's hips and pulled her close to her, wrapping one hand around her waist, giving her a tight squeeze. "We used to dance to no music—once upon a time."

Mazie laughed sluggishly. "Oh yes, those were the days, weren't they?"

Lincoln bowed at them both and excused himself.

Mazie stepped closer to the girl she once loved, who also inched forward and landed a kiss upon her lips. But when she felt Veronika's tongue run across her teeth, she stepped back.

"What are you doing?" Mazie asked.

"I've missed you," Veronika said softly, pouting her lips again. "Everything is different now. Stay."

Mazie's gaze blurred again. "I—"

Veronika moved towards her, but that time swiftly, gripping the back of Mazie's head and pulling her in for another kiss. The girl's tongue claimed hers, swirling around seductively while dancing to the music of their own. Mazie's eyes shot open and pushed her back, creating distance between them.

Kissing Veronika was not new. But that intimate moment was not what Mazie remembered. It felt different. Wrong. She *tasted* wrong.

"I can't," Mazie breathed. "I can't do this with you—not anymore."

Veronika frowned. "You seem a bit moodier than you used to be," she accused. "You sure have changed!"

Her complaint sounded venomous.

Mazie pinned her with a cutting glare. "Aye, I have," she said. "I refuse to accept you and everyone else we have grown up with to turn me into something I am not. I should have never come back." She staggered back, holding her hands up as if pushing towards a barrier.

"I can help you back to the tent—"

Mazie flipped up her middle finger. "Fuck off," she cursed, feeling herself spin again, holding back the vomit she knew was coming. She tromped towards the tent, running her tongue over the bitter taste she still had in her mouth.

Placing her hand on the zipper of the tent, she quietly pulled it up. She peered inside before she walked in, eying Nola curled up into the captain's arms. Mazie sneered in their direction. She was pissed. But, luckily, she spotted Hill in time, lying on the far end with all four limbs sprawled out. She placed both hands on her head, feeling vertigo hitting at her brain, then stumbled forward a few feet, face planting into her pillow.

Fuck, I am wasted! She gathered her thoughts.

Then she pushed herself up to the sudden guttural cries that rang in the distance. They sounded like small children wailing out in pain. Her breath quickened before the wails died out, blending into the sounds of nature around them.

"What the hell was that?" Mazie whispered to herself, waiting to see if any of her mates woke from the sound.

Morning came quickly as if Nola had simply blinked.

She looked over at Lincoln, who was still sound asleep, her body molding comfortably into his arms. Nola pressed her nose against his shirt, inhaling his scent, and felt him shift, moaning into her hair, but his eyes remained closed. The feeling of belonging consumed her. His touch, smell—everything.

She wondered if he felt the same way. Of course, it was too soon, but she could not shake that kiss the night before from her mind.

Nola looked up through the canvas screen lining the tent's ceiling, with her arm still wrapped over Lincoln's chest. The sun had barely risen—the moon was no longer above them.

A low rumble gurgled from her stomach—she needed to eat.

She scurried out of bed, pulling a dress over her head, and exited the tent. A few of the town folk were already bustling about and opening their shops. Others seemed to be decorating the stage and setting the tables. Everything looked oddly similar to the night before.

Hmm, they cleaned up last night's mess quite quickly, she thought.

Nola took that as an opportunity to explore the small town before the crew awoke.

As she stepped onto the grass, her ears opened to loud screams echoing in the distance. She panted, feeling anxiety slap at her chest.

Nola tried looking past the eerie haze creeping through the trees, but it was nearly impossible to peer through the main road.

The lush green meadow tickled between her toes, but when she looked down, the grass shriveled into decay, the dry twigs slicing into her skin. Nola stepped back, aghast. Her brows pulled together. She ran her hand through her hair nervously and looked up as she heard a rustling noise coming from behind a tree in the distance.

"Hello," Nola heard from behind her, drawing her attention away from the haunting surroundings.

She pressed her hand to her chest, feeling her nerves jump from the sound of her voice.

"Didn't mean to startle you," a small woman said. "We've not met before. I'm Sugar." She held out her hand. "I hear you are part of the pirate's crew. I've never met a real pirate before."

"Oh, no," Nola corrected, "I'm not a pirate. I'm just traveling with them."

The woman looked to be the height of a small child, but she was very much a woman. Her breasts were large, her hips wide, her hair a peachy hue, like a brightly lit sunset. Her skin was pale, with black freckles below her eyes, and right above her top lip was the faint scruff of a mustache.

"I've heard my people talking about you," she said, holding out her hand for Nola to take.

"Oh?" she said in reply, but she felt reluctant to give the woman the greeting she wanted. Instead, Nola stepped back.

The small lady gave Nola an unusual expression but seemed to brush it off as she perked up. "Yes, we are all so delighted to have you here with us." She tilted her head. "It's been nearly a decade since we've had visitors who stayed more than an afternoon."

"That's quite a long time," Nola responded flatly.

"Too long, really. I do remember the boats that pulled up to the shore . . ." Her voice trailed off. "Are you staying for the festival tonight?"

Nola blinked as a strange chill washed over her, but then her body went taut with raw fear as a loud explosion rang in her ears, causing her to jerk back. She stumbled over her feet. Her bare heels hit the stone-covered road, feeling the rocks pierce her skin. When Nola looked over her shoulder, the woman took off sprinting, disappearing into the fog creeping over the street like a flowing, translucent river.

The wind blew a chilly breeze against her cheeks. The moisture from the fog rolling over her skin felt slimy. She tried, unsuccessfully, to wipe it away with her sleeve.

"Right," Nola said aloud, "because that was not weird."

As the fog cleared out, she began to see more tents with a few signs connected to them. She had reached the part of town where all the vendors had their small businesses. One of the tents, a red one with colorful rags and beaded strands hanging from the top, caught her eye. The sign was freshly painted, so she assumed someone was inside.

"Hello?" she called as she walked through the beaded curtain door.

The dusty wooden racks were bare. Nola creased a brow.

"Anybody here?" she called again.

Nothing.

Nola left the red tent and walked to the next one. She continued down the road, looking inside each of the town's businesses. Suddenly, a couple of children ran past her, giggling while they chased after a ball. She hurried behind them, but as she turned to the back of the canvas tent, they were gone.

As she continued her search, she found no one inside any of the canopies.

Nola ran her hand through her hair nervously. *What is this place?*

"Have any of the food tents opened yet?" she heard Kitten ask from behind her. She yawned as Nola turned to face her.

"I don't know," Nola replied. "I came here trying to find a place to eat, but everything seems to be abandoned. I heard a strange explosion in the distance and came to see where it came from but—" she waved her hand to the sign above her, "—I mean, the open signs are out, but no one is here. That sign over there even has fresh paint on it."

"Explosion? I 'eard no explosion. Hope everyone is

alright! Anyhow, wha' I really need is a coffee," Kitten rambled on, rubbing her eyes to wake.

"Am I crazy?" Nola asked, running her hand through the front part of her hair. "You didn't hear it? It was deafening."

Kitten shook her head, her brows knitting together.

Nola looked back to the road to try to spot the little woman she had seen. "It was so hard to see with all the fog. I was afraid to venture too far from you guys, and then this woman—"

"What?" Kitten continued to gaze at her with wonder plastered on her face. "Wha' are ye babblin' 'bout?" she asked, scratching her head. "I 'eard no explosion and—" She pointed to the sign. "The signs are fallin' apart."

Nola quickly looked back up, and Kitten was right; all the signs were worn and damaged. "I swear! They were . . . moments ago—" She turned to Kitten. "I know what I saw."

I am not crazy! Nola said to her thoughts.

"Hm, I believe ye! I thought it was just me, but this place seems off, doesn't it?" Kitten asked. "I barely slept last night, and this shiver creeps up me back every time I look at someone in the eye." She leaned on a heel, pulling her coat tighter around her body. "My eyes were closed last night, but—"

"You felt like you never went to sleep. Didn't dream?" Nola completed Kitten's sentence.

Kitten's mouth fell open.

Last night's sleep felt strange. Nola's mind had drifted into darkness and her body appeared to have floated above the sheets. The numbing feeling of being watched crept through the tent and her dreams were filled with memories from her past. Nola had not dreamed of anything other than a bright red dragon soaring above her for at least a year.

Kitten nodded.

"We must wake the crew," Nola said. "We need to leave."

Kitten followed her closely until they reached the tent. Everyone still slept. The two ladies began tapping their shoulders until they all opened their eyes.

"Lincoln," Nola whispered. "Lincoln, wake up."

His eyes darted at hers, letting out a soft groan, and sat upright. "What is it, love?"

"We—we need to go," she said, her voice stammering, "Now."

The captain's eyes held a puzzled look.

"Is it morning?" Mazie asked, rubbing her eyes, then gripped her head. "I'm going to need another drink to kill the pounding in my temples."

Nola's lips formed a flat line. "It's just at sunrise."

"What has you so spooked?" Mazie asked, sitting up and reaching for her shirt.

Nola looked away. "This place," she said. "Everything about this place."

"Welcome to Westin," Mazie said, slipping both her feet in her pants and pulling them up slowly. "I'll go find my mother. I'm famished."

As Mazie left the tent, Nola turned Lincoln's face to meet his eyes. "Lincoln—"

"I know. I felt it last night, too," he affirmed.

She nodded. "I'll gather my things, but . . . what about the water?"

He shook his head. "We'll think of something else," he

said quietly as if someone was listening behind the tent. "Let's go."

As the captain and Nola rushed to the long road leading to the shore, they looked to where Mazie stood. She was frozen still, looking into the street. The entire town of folk stood stiff, staring back at her.

The rest of the crew staggered out from their tent, looking lost in thought as if unsure of what was happening.

All the color ebbed from Nola's cheeks while her stomach lurched. "Lincoln?"

To the crowd's right stood the triplets, with Kala standing next to them. An unsettling grin lined their lips. Kala's eyes looked more somber than the disgruntled expression crossing over the others' faces.

"Leaving so soon?" Veronika asked Mazie.

"We've missed you," the triplets said in unison, their voices morphing into one. But they did not sound like themselves; they sounded different to Mazie.

Veronika linked pinkies with Samantha, and Samantha with Nichole. The three stood so close they were touching shoulders. Then their tails rose high, wrapping around each other until the three women's bodies morphed into one, resembling someone with a completely different face.

"We have so much to catch up on," the transfigured woman said. "Won't you join us?" There was an echo in her voice, as if the three girls were still there, sharing one mind and body.

"Is that normal?" Nola asked Lincoln quietly.

He nodded but stepped back, reaching his hand out across Nola's chest to push her back with him.

"Mazie, back up," Lincoln warned. But she did not move at first; she stood there—stunned silent.

Then, Lincoln called her name a second time. Mazie slowly and cautiously stepped back until she was standing between Kitten and Boots.

Ardley's eyes widened. "Normal to morph into one woman, aye, but they're . . . they're—"

"Dead," Mazie breathed, the ominous silence looming in the air. "They're all dead."

Chapter 16

"I think we best be goin', mates," Boots said carefully, his voice a quiet purr. He reached out, gripping Kitten's arm, and pulled her close to him. "Not doin' ghosts today."

Kitten's face turned ashen as if frozen with fear. "Captain?" she called out, wrapping her arms around her love and squeezing him tightly. "We can't exactly fight somethin' that's already dead."

Not everyone had seized up their swords when they left their tents. They were largely unprotected and defenseless. Not that a sword or pistol would do so much as fly through the dead entities, who no longer looked human. They looked more like monsters, hungry to devour whatever stood in front of them.

Lincoln rested his hand near his sword at his hip. Nola felt relief that he had not left it in the tent. Her blood ran thick in her veins as they watched the creatures before them take a step forward.

Seeing a spirit for the first time felt as if someone was pouring icy water down her spine. The lump in Nola's throat refused to slide down to give her a chance to breathe.

The ghostly figures crept closer to the crew.

"Please, don't do this," Mazie begged at the triplets, but it sounded like her voice died in her throat.

The morphed creature tilted its head and glared at the crew. Their eyes were vacant, almost hollow.

Mazie's hands shook as she rubbed the back of her elbows. Her entire body shuddered with each step the creature took closer to her.

"What happened to you?" she asked the unliving beings. Her voice cracked. "Tell me, what has happened to you that has taken your life? Why are you here? Why—" she rambled on.

"The King of Zemira and his men slaughtered us one by one," they echoed. "The magic we bound to this land has kept us here, in this state, repeating the same horrific day over and over again, trapping us, unable to escape." The creature shrilled so loudly, the crew had to clasp their palms over their ears. "But we feel so alive at the same time. It is beautiful on the other side. You'll see."

Mazie dropped her hands, gripping to the pistol she never left behind. Tears pooled into her eyes as she pointed the barrel at the mob. For a moment, her eyes caught a glimpse of her mother moving through the crowd.

"Mother?" she called. "I'm so sorry." She wiped a tear falling down her face with the sleeve of her coat. Her voice quivered, "I'm so sorry this is happening." Sadness clouded her beautiful features.

"Don't be, dear. I'm not sorry. Look at us. If you die here, on our land, you're reborn." Kala's expression grew weary. "Though I did tell you to leave. You should have been on your ship by now." Her mother held out her hand. "Might as well join us. I will help you reach the other side."

Her mother stepped forward, then halted. She appeared frozen where she stood, like a predator, waiting for the right moment to strike.

Lincoln closed his hand around Nola's wrist, pulling her closer to him, then wrapped his other hand around her waist, rubbing the chill that reached under her shirt. She exhaled, watching the vapor of her breath dance in the wind. The air itself was not crisp, but the entities had somehow turned the atmosphere around the crew to an icy fog. There was a small moment of silence before Kala stepped forward again and hissed—the entire town charged right at them.

"Run!" Mazie shouted rapidly, not bothering to look back as she turned on her heel, waving her hands at her comrades. "Everyone, run!"

Lincoln gripped firmly to Nola's shirt, tugging at her. The crew sprinted towards the gates, leaving their belongings behind.

"Run faster," Ardley shouted, turning his neck to give a hasty glance behind them.

Nola heard a yelp to her right. As she turned, she saw that Hill had hurdled over a fallen tree. He tripped, his head colliding with the thick roots spread across the trail.

"I'm okay, I'm okay!" Hill shouted, jumping back to his feet, pressing his hand over a bloodied gash on one of his temples.

The buccaneers stormed through the forest, with Mazie

leading the way. Nola avoided looking back as she hurried next to Lincoln, but they were close.

The Sybil Curse's crew stopped abruptly at a tall, stony barrier—higher than the walls at Westin's gates. Nola glanced quickly to see how close the mob was. But the ghosts were gone. She sucked in a breath, looking back to the fence. "What is this?"

Mazie slid her hand down her face. "I—I don't know. This wasn't here when I left ten years ago. We took the wrong path," she explained with panic in her tone. "Shit! Shit!"

The pirates turned quickly as they heard a heavy gasp come from Mazie's lips. A cold chill ran between them, causing the hairs on the back of Nola's neck to stand straight.

"Mazie," a soft voice whispered. Mazie's eyes widened as she saw who stood behind her.

She immediately covered her mouth with both her hands.

"Bay? Bay, is that really you?" Mazie gave her a shaky smile.

Lincoln stepped forward. "Mazie, that isn't your sister anymore. That's not her."

The town of ghosts had stopped following them—surprisingly—but Bay was there.

Mazie reached out to her twin sister, trying to brush her fingers against the spirit's cheek.

A split second before Mazie could graze Bay's skin, her hand sank through the spirit's body, turning into a bright beam of light instead.

"We can't touch. Not yet," Bay explained. "The bridge is over there, Mazie, remember?" She pointed towards the old bridge. "All you have to do is jump, and we can be together again," she said. "Fly, Mazie. Fly like a raven."

"Mazie, look at me," Lincoln interrupted the ghost. "Mazie!"

His first mate snapped from the trance her sister had over her and fixed her eyes on her captain.

"That's not Bay," Lincoln said again. "That—thing is not your sister!"

When Mazie looked back to Bay, her face was almost unrecognizable. Tousled. Decrepit. Then, the spirit arched its neck beyond how any living creature ever could. Nola and Kitten averted their eyes in disgust. Following a gurgling sound, hundreds of white maggots began crawling out of her mouth.

Mazie's jaw clenched before letting out an ear-splitting scream, toppling over her feet until she fell hard on her back. Bay's spirit looked up as Lincoln wielded his sword over his head.

"Sorry, Mazie," Lincoln said as the sword sank, slicing through the creature. The apparition crumbled before their eyes into dust.

Mazie wiped her tears as she watched the wind pick up the ashes and carry them far away. She, trying to catch her breath through the thickness of the air, mumbled, "I don't know what the bloody hell that was, but I'm not staying around to find out."

The wall was still behind them. The only way back to

the shore was through the city, where more of those creatures would be waiting for them.

"There!" Nola shouted, pointing to a tree. "We can climb to the top branches. It is tall enough. Maybe we can jump to the other side."

Lincoln beckoned the crew. Time was ticking and their lives depended on that tree. It was their only way to escape.

The crew ran to the old tree. First, Lincoln laced his fingers and shot Nola a look for her to go first. Then Ardley and Boots helped Kitten up.

"Come on, my love. Latch onto the edge of the wall. I've got you," Boots began, grabbing hold of her waist to hoist her over.

Mazie, agile as she could be, helped herself and Hill onto the trunk and up a few branches. Once all the ladies were safe, the four men climbed, boosting their legs onto the next branch. Lincoln reached the top, securing his hands on the stone wall and looked over. The ship was about a mile down to the left of the wall.

"It's quite the drop, but we can do it," Lincoln assured Nola. "I've got you." He girded his arm around her chest, cradling her in a possessive hold. "We'll jump together."

She nodded, wrapping her arms around him tightly before Lincoln let go of the wall. Nola let out a whimper as she felt a sting at her ankle when they plunged to the sand.

Lincoln looked down at her. "Are you okay?"

She nodded. "I think so."

The sound of the waves crashing against the seashore gave Nola a sudden relief.

"We're alive! We're alive!" Hill chanted.

The captain clutched Nola's arm and picked her up from the sandy shore. He then ran his hand over her hair, tucking a few strands behind her ear.

"Almost home," he whispered.

A faint smile reached her lips as she looked over at the rest of the pirates jumping back to their feet.

"Everyone okay?" Lincoln asked.

"Aye, Captain," Hill said.

They picked up their pace on the beach until they reached the rowboat, climbing aboard and rowing to their beloved Sybil Curse.

Mazie plopped on the deck, pulling her legs up against her chest. She did not speak; she just sat there.

The rest settled on the ship, scattered and exhausted. Nola looked up to Lincoln as he uncorked a bottle of rum with his teeth.

"It was all a lie," Nola finally said. "Not just the people but the land, the party, the colors—it was all an illusion."

"Aye," Lincoln affirmed. "For all we know, they died years ago."

Nola ran her hands restlessly down and up her arms. The goosebumps refused to leave her skin.

"Will that happen to us when we die? Being trapped like that?" Nola asked. "Repeating the same day over and over again, as if nothing has changed?"

"Nay," he replied. "They're witches of nature, love. Even Mazie gave up that kind of power when she became a pirate. I believe when we die, we become fish food." He smiled, despite their grave situation. "And I'm okay with that."

Nola watched Kitten pad across the deck, kneeling next to her friend. The life within Mazie's eyes looked bleak. Empty. It was as if her own soul had been ripped from her body.

"Not everyone ye love is dead, Mazie; we be here wit' ye," she told her. "I'm so sorry 'bout what 'appened to yer mother. I'm so sorry."

Mazie wiped her eyes. "Don't bother, Kitten." She swallowed a gulp of bitter saliva. "We need to continue our journey. We need to get to the Eastland Forest and Nola to the Fae queen."

Her firm tone drew the eyes of every buccaneer to stare at her intently. She stood up and began to pace around the mast.

"But our journey will not stop there," she continued. Her expression was fierce, determined. "I say we join Nola on taking down the king." She looked up to meet Nola's eyes. "The war started with Matthias, but it ends with us."

Lincoln nodded and glanced at his mates.

"Aye," they all agreed in unison. It was no longer Nola's fight alone—it was all theirs.

Chapter 17

Mazie lifted the lid to the barrel and stared blankly at the last of what was left—enough water for one mug each.

"Bloody hell," she mumbled.

Anxiety stirred in her stomach as she gazed silently at the empty mug, tears glistening in her eyes. Mazie hated crying more than she hated anything else, but she could not hold the tears back at the thought of dying of thirst. She did not want to die—not so quickly, anyway—not until she avenged her family's death.

Reaching inside the barrel, she ladled up some water for herself, then placed the lid back. She strode across the deck, slumping down at the back corner, and leaned against the railing next to the stairs. Mazie wiped the tears from her eyes and looked out to where the white clouds met the surface of the water. The sun had not set, not entirely. It hovered over the horizon, brightening up the thin line drawn by the ocean.

When she first stepped onto the Sybil Curse, Mazie swore to always protect the crew and the ship. And that was precisely what she planned to do. As she sat there by the steps that led up to the quarterdeck, she wondered if Zemira would ever be at peace.

Were those creatures in Westin just a manifestation of my family, she wondered in silence, *or were their spirits trapped in some eternal purgatory?*

One thing was sure, King Matthias had to die. He slaughtered them all—he slaughtered innocent children.

The pirate would mourn their deaths, regretting not having a chance to say goodbye. But she would move on quickly and not look back. What happened to those she loved made her feel rage and hatred. She was not going to let it slip.

Nola dressed in a nightgown, pulled one of Kitten's sweaters over her head, and walked up the stairs to the top of the deck. She had not seen Lincoln yet after she had gone downstairs to bathe. Feeling well-rested and tidy, she wandered to the front of the ship. Then, pulled herself up to sit on the railing, holding on to the shrouds, and stared at the waves lightly crashing against the side.

"Tell me, Nola," Lincoln said, distracting her from the foamy crests. "What exactly were you doing at the marketplace when we had first met?"

Memories of how angry he had made her that day flashed over her mind. But he was no longer the brusque man she had encountered at the market. She felt as if she had finally seen him for who he truly was.

"How do you mean?" She arched her thin brow, then gave him a cunning wink.

Lincoln nibbled on his bottom lip, then stepped closer, resting his hands on the edge, looking out to the sea with her.

"You didn't look like you belonged in the city," he explained, turning his head to her, "and the only people allowed to attend are either vendors or the city folk."

"Oh." The nerves fluttering in her stomach disappeared. She still had her secret. "I was there with my parents," she answered. "My father, he's a bowyer. He's the best there is in our town—the entire kingdom, really."

A jaunty smile crossed his face, and he ran his hand through his tousled hair. "That is quite an art," he acknowledged. "And you were there to sell the product?"

She nodded. "Demonstrate, actually," she said. "We have to sell everything my father makes—or we don't eat."

Nola watched the smile on his face fade away. She was not sure if it was pity that moved swiftly across his face or guilt because her family was poor. Maybe it had bothered him that she was not someone more . . . special—someone who deserved to be near the palace walls.

"Baylin," she continued, "the village where I'm from, has been the only home I've ever known." She leaned forward and fiddled with her fingers but when she felt Lincoln's hands rest on hers, she stopped and looked up.

"Don't feel ashamed. Many of us have fled home, running from something. We all have our problems, but you and I know it is mostly because of what the king of Zemira has done."

She watched Lincoln shift on his heel. It was clear he hated the king as much as she did.

So, he fled from somewhere too, Nola thought before he continued.

"How bad has it gotten?" he asked. "For the village folk?"

She straightened up her back as she sucked in a heavy breath. Then she let it out, exhausted by simply thinking about it.

"The king collects more than half of my father's income. He's taken most of our cattle, and—" She paused, being cautious with her words. "But that was a few years ago," she noted. "King Matthias ignores the fact that our crops are dying, and if no one does anything soon, my people are going to starve to death."

He stepped closer to her unexpectedly and placed his hand against her cheek tenderly, and though it looked like he wanted to say something, he did not. Instead, he only peered deep into her warm-honey eyes.

Nola's siren eyes fought not to turn white as desire devoured at her heart.

Please don't change, Nola begged her eyes.

Oftentimes, she felt her iris change when she was scared or angry, and apparently, that situation was no different. She could not control when they turned, but she fought it.

She narrowed in on his mouth, which alone caused an intriguing quiver on her pink lips. The feeling of his touch against her cheek sent a warm feeling down her chest.

Nola could not afford to dwell upon her feelings for Lincoln. She had found herself distracted again from her mission.

She concentrated on memories of her parents, her people, and the very purpose for coming onto that ship. However, her mind and heart leapt at the sight of Lincoln standing before her.

Nola broke the silence between them as he continued to stare at her, waiting.

"And what about you, Lincoln?" Nola cleared her throat. "Where are you from?"

"Someplace I vowed to never return," he said, turning from her. His face hardened. "A place where I could never hope to be free, where its king destroyed everything *I* loved."

Is he from Zemira? Nola wondered. *There are nine other kingdoms in their world.*

He turned back to meet her eyes. "Now, my place is here on this ship, and I am going to help *you*, love, to fight for that freedom I never had."

She hopped down from the railing and narrowed the space between them. Lincoln immediately placed his strong hand upon her cheek as she said, "My father has trained me my entire life for this."

Nola dropped her head to the side, resting her cheek on his hand, taking in the warmth of his touch.

Closing her eyes, she continued, "You can leave me with the Fae people, Lincoln. This isn't your fight." His eyes shifted from hers for only a moment as if her words tugged at his heart.

Lincoln dropped his hand to his side. "I disagree," he said. Nola felt a sense of relief hitting her at her core. To tell the truth, she was terrified. Though she did not want the crew to be in harm's way, the idea of them fighting along with her gave her hope. Nola was devastated when she first left her home. She thought she would not have enough strength to do it, but with the captain and his crew in her corner, maybe they could defeat the king.

"My father taught me three things about life," she started, thinking back on her childhood, "and I'll never forget them."

"And what are those three things?" Lincoln asked.

She smirked at his hasty inquiry. "Never leave food on your plate." Her smile grew wide. "Never trust a pirate—"

He chuckled, giving her a cocky wink. "Oh, is that right?"

There was a slight twist at her lips before saying, "Well, he's had his share of run-ins with those who weren't like yourself," she explained. "He spent a lot of time out to sea, and some pirates—"

"You don't have to explain. I understand." Lincoln crossed his arms around his chest. "What's the third thing?"

Her expression changed; a more serious one took over her features. "Fight like a warrior and be merciful only when you are given mercy."

Lincoln turned out to the seas and began humming. Then he rested his hands back on the railing and drummed his fingers against the wood to a beat.

"He sounds like a wise man," he said after a while.

"He is. I—" Nola rubbed her eyes, holding back the tears, allowing her sight to get lost in the fading pink painted on the horizon, the blue darkness of night quickly approaching.

When she looked back up, Lincoln's hand was outstretched.

"Dance with me, Nola?" he asked, his tone gentle.

She shook her head and rolled her eyes with a grin. "There's no music," she said.

Lincoln stepped closer to her. He gently brought his hand to her hair and twirled the front locks with his finger. She giggled when a shiver skittered down her neck as he tucked those silver and maroon strands behind her ear.

A smile across his face made his dimples crease.

"Listen carefully."

Nola quieted her breathing and focused. There was music—a song—but it was only someone's voice.

Kitten, Nola thought.

The golden-eyed pirate stood at the other end of the ship with the rest of the crew surrounding her.

Nola's eyelashes fluttered faintly. "She sings beautifully."

"Aye, shall we join them?" he asked.

She nodded. Lincoln placed his hand on her lower back and escorted Nola across the deck.

Hill leaned against the mizzenmast, with his legs crossed at the ankles, nibbling on a biscuit and an overly ripe apple. Ardley sat on a short stool—his pipe hung immobile from his mouth. The white smoke slid from his nostrils, clouding around his pointed nose. Mazie sat straight up against the helm and combed her long, jet-black hair with her fingers, seemingly lost in thought.

Lincoln piled a few sacks and laid a quilt for him and Nola to sit together on the cedar floor. Boots moved over to give them some room and wiggled his messy brows at the captain.

Boots laughed and leaned his back against the side of the ship. His eyes locked on Kitten's, and she sang to him.

"I think we all look back with glee.
T' th' ships we sent t' th' bottom of th' sea.
Th'ir crews all drowned 'cause th'y couldn't breathe.
Sent beneath th' waves like . . . scum!"

She bowed then took off dancing. A side smirk crossed her face as she wobbled on her heel.

"Now th' sun's so hot, time's almost up.
No water t' e'en wet th' bottoms of our cups.
We may have just run out o' luck.
Fish food we'll be when 'tis sun comes up."

Everyone sprang laughing, raising their glasses high and shouting, "Drink!" It was rum in their mugs, of course—because rum they had plenty.

"But let's think back t' th' song o' th' wires.
Th' flash of a blade when th' cannon fires.
Th' billow o' t' sheets and t' creak o' th' masts.
We chose this life, and we know it can't last.

We've paid the price. We'll stay afloat.
There ain't not leaks on this fine boat.
We'll find a spring and drink our fill.

Then off t' find, our next fine kill!"

She belched, placing her closed knuckle over her mouth.

"It may look bleak but show some spine.
Afore I put ye t' th' cats 'o nine.
Lubbers 'ave their yards, but I 'ave mine,
An' they anchor th' reefs in th' gale.

But we'll find land, just follow me!
We'll take our rats, an' set 'em free.
On a sandy isle with trees o' green
With water as clear as ale!"

Kitten looked around with a sluggish grin fleeting across her lips. "Sing wit' me, ye bastards!"

The crew raised their glasses high, then sang with her the final verse.

"Steady now, 'cause we can't slip.
But mark me words, we'll end this trip.
It's up t' us t' outlast this ship.
'ave courage, face yer fears!

Now rum we 'ave, but it's all f' naught.
It can't be drunk 'cause it's all we've got.
If we do, then we'll meet our ends like sots.
Let's die like buccaneers!"

Boots scratched his hairy belly, then shouted Kitten's name from across the deck.

"Why don't you chasse your voluptuous little tooshie my way, love?"

She flashed a sluggish smirk and tumbled forward, falling into his arms. A passionate kiss landed upon her lips, and his hand wrapped around her neck to pull her even closer. Then, he slowly traced his other finger down to her décolletage.

"Aren't I one lucky bastard," he hummed before leaning down and pecking small kisses between her breasts.

Mazie averted her eyes from the lovebirds, then stood and stumbled forward, sitting next to Lincoln and Nola.

"Here, drink up, you two!" she shouted while holding two mugs to their faces. "You both look miserable. It's depressing!"

Nola took the cup and stuck her nose in the drink, inhaling the sharp scent. It smelt like freshly poured glue.

"Thank you, mate." Nola cheered.

Mazie smirked. "I'm your mate now?" She caressed the edge of her hat, shooting Nola a cunning look, then said, "If you can drink like a pirate, then you may call me whatever the hell you want."

"Oh, that may be a challenge, Nola," Lincoln teased. "No one can outdrink Mazie."

"Aye, we've got 'bout seven bloody barrels of it now," Boots said, wiping red lipstick from his chin. "We can just drink until we die, really." He chuckled to himself.

Suddenly, everyone fell silent.

The reminder that they were out of water hit all seven of them.

"I'm in for the challenge then," Nola said, trying to divert their attention, and placed the mug to her lips. She took one sip, trying not to heave at the bold flavor that bathed her tongue.

It was not as if she had not had booze before, but strong liquor was a luxury in Zemira, and only the elite who resided could afford it. A time or two, she and a few village girls snuck out of their houses, fled to the nearby city, and drank the leftover booze thrown out behind each tavern. It was always the old kind that no longer tasted good, so the bar could not sell it.

It tasted horrible, but it did the trick—if they drank enough of it, anyway.

Nola chugged her first drink since then. The Sybil Curse's crew looked perplexed yet fascinated by their new addition. They all began to laugh as the bottom of her mug hit the floor.

"It's on!" Nola shouted.

"It's on, matey!" Mazie said as she raised her drink and said, "To our journey!"

The pirates brought their mugs together and toasted to the days ahead.

After several rounds of cheap rum, they all rested. Mazie relaxed her head on Hill's shoulder. Ardley still puffed his pipe, slowly blowing out a cloud of smoke, sending the pungent aroma of tobacco wafting in the air.

Kitten sat comfortably between Boots's legs; his arms

wrapped around her waist. She leaned back to rest her head against his muscular, hairy chest.

Lincoln turned to Nola, who was still by his side. "Hey, beautiful."

A faint flush tinged her cheeks. "Yes?"

He swallowed. "Tell me one thing about you?"

The realization they had not talked much about each other rose in her mind. She liked that Lincoln was interested in her, except, of course, she could not reveal the fact she was born with a siren tail.

"I—"

Lincoln reached out, and she stopped her sentence short, then lost track of time looking into his beautiful eyes. He brushed his thumb over her lips and played with a few strands of hair hanging over her shoulder—a familiar gesture she loved.

Lincoln lowered his hand down from her shoulder, and nerves twisted in her stomach. Nola wanted to talk to him; she had to. But then that moment was over.

"Nola," Mazie called.

Nola did not want to look away; that was certain. She could stare into his eyes forever.

Mazie clambered to her feet. "You said your father was a bowyer, eh?"

Nola nodded.

Mazie gave her a side smirk. "Can you shoot an arrow and not miss?"

After nodding again, she said with pride, "I've never missed. But I've never practiced on moving targets."

Kitten raised her head. "I've got an idea. If we miraculously survive these next four days," she said, "we can 'ave Hill run around the deck, and then ye can practice!"

Hill broke out in a hard laugh at the joke directed at himself. Mazie looked down at him. Her expression hardened as she walked to the broadside and faced up to the full moon. The conversations around the crew muffled before Nola pulled Mazie from her deep thought.

"Now that we're—you know—mates," Nola stated, "I'd love to hear the story behind your pirate names."

Boots let out a laugh, sticking his fine leather cavalier boot in the air. "My father gave me the name Boots, but once I lost me leg, the crew thought No Leg was fittin'. But I prefer the name my father gave me. Now that I can only wear one of these, I guess I could be called Boot."

Kitten and Hill snickered at his joke.

A small smile shone on Nola's lips before she said, "May I ask?" She gestured to his peg leg.

"I wish I had a better story for you, like a crocodile ripped it off," he explained. "Nay, I got bit by a snake, and the doctor had to cut it off before the venom reached me heart."

Nola gasped. "Oh, Gods. I'm so sorry," she said.

Boots burst into laughter; that time, the entire crew joined in. A teasing quirk pulled at the corner of his mouth. "Just yankin' your chain," he said.

Nola smiled. "A crocodile bit it off, didn't it?"

He nodded. "Aye, the damn bastard ripped it clean off."

Kitten pointed to her eye. "And I was born with this eye, so Golden-Eye seemed fittin'."

"Oh, I thought Kitten was your pirate name," Nola admitted, confused.

"No, dear, Kitten is my very given name! Love every letter on it!" she said. "It's funny. We all gave each other names we rarely use."

Hill smirked and lifted his mug, joining in. "Mine is a bit fittin', too," he said. "Tipsy."

And so, on went the crew saying the whys and wherefores of their pirate names: some interesting, some not-too-much. She learned that it was Ardley who had stitched Boots's leg up after the crocodile attack and joined the crew shortly after.

Nola felt among friends—real friends—for the first time in her life. She even felt safe, understood, and a weird sense of belonging.

After Ardley sat his pipe down and pointed to his hair and big round belly to explain the reasoning for the name Big Red, Nola turned to Mazie, and waited.

"You want to ask me, don't you?" Mazie said, her lips curling up and her fingers drumming against the deck.

"Would you tell me if I do?" Nola asked.

She snickered. "No bloody chance." Mazie banged her mug down and took out her boucan from its sheath, slamming it into the deck.

Nola shifted, looking down at the knife.

"Bloody hell, Mazie," Boots said, "You don't need to kill everyone's buzz every time you hear somethin' you don't like." He scrunched up his nose. "Even behind that droll deviltry, we see you for who you are. So relax, mate, or sleep it off."

Everyone fell silent, watching a sneer cross over Mazie's lips. Then she threw her head back and laughed, releasing the tension she had created.

Nola suddenly felt a bit suffocated, even in the open air. She searched her mind for any other topic to shift the conversation.

"This rum—" She cleared her throat, breaking the silence. Nola already felt the liquor hitting her senses. ". . . is delightful. I've never tasted anything like it." She acquired the taste, but it still burned.

Lincoln folded his arms over his chest and gave her a subtle wink. As he opened his mouth to speak, Kitten chuckled, leaning up from Boots, who had nestled his lips into her hair.

"First off," Kitten said, "ye need to eliminate the word 'delightful,' like right now, from yer vocabulary." She held up two fingers. "Secondly, 'ave ye 'onestly not 'ad rum before?"

Boots wrapped his arms around her waist and pulled her back against his chest. She snickered, wiggling back between his legs.

Nola smiled for only a moment before her smile turned into a small frown. "I haven't, actually. We were always too poor for a drink like this."

The crew blasted into laughter, so hard they held their stomachs.

"Oh, my love," Lincoln started, his laughter tapering out. "I don't recall the last time we ever paid for the rum."

Nola smiled. "You stole it?"

He tipped his head. “I’m a pirate, milady. That is what we do.”

Boots wiggled his shoulders, swinging his arm over Kitten’s head, grasping her waist again. “In our defense, we’ve never stolen from someone who didn’t deserve it.”

“I see,” Nola said.

She was not judging them either way. They survived that long by doing what they did best, and she respected them for it. After years of having everything taken from them, if her parents’ lives were not at stake, she would have done the same to the king.

There was another moment of silence. No one made a sound other than the waves gently crashing against the side of the ship.

Hill pulled out what looked like a banjo and began to play, as Nola felt fingers lace between hers.

“How about that dance?” Lincoln stood to his feet, keeping her fingers locked around his.

She nodded, and Lincoln escorted her to the center of the deck, wrapping his strong hand around her hips.

He caressed her hair gingerly as he ran his hand down her body, his fingers stopping at the bridge of her back.

“Your presence on my ship has troubled my mind, Nola. You have been making it impossible for me to focus on leading the crew,” he said playfully, edging closer until his chest touched hers. “Your beauty is pleasantly distracting, to be honest.”

A small frown raced over her thin brows.

Pleasantly distracting? Nola thought. *What does he mean by that?*

However, the moment was perfect. Lincoln's words made Nola feel intrigued, wanted. Her body—her mind—responded in a way she had not expected. It was a strange feeling, a tingling sensation almost, under her navel.

It was then when he looked at her with lust. There was *desire* in his eyes.

You do not know the real me, Nola thought as his piercing eyes continued to leer at her.

The truth was, if he did, Lincoln would probably let her go, she thought.

Nola had deceived him. Her body wanted him, but she, deep down, knew he would never forgive her. She had deceived all of them.

Hill strummed his banjo. He played a soft melody, and Lincoln twirled her to the beat, leaning her back before bringing her up to his chest.

"Lincoln?" she whispered.

His hand quickly rose, cupping her chin.

"Nola?" he sighed, looking down at her, his eyes penetrating hers. At the same time, he curled an arm around her waist and tugged her even closer to him.

Goosebumps from his sensual touch crawled up her spine. She had not realized her brows had knitted into a frown until he slid his thumb over her forehead. That alone relaxed every part of her face, forcing her to let out a calming breath.

"What is it?" he asked soberly, his eyes holding her captive.

Nola gave her bottom lip a slight nibble, trying desperately to find the words to speak.

"Do you believe it possible for a person to change?"

Nola paused briefly, waiting for his answer. Her father had told her haunting stories of pirates and their war with sirens. Her kind was painted as monstrous creatures, and pirates were simply defending their ships.

"Why do you ask that?" Lincoln inquired. But he got no reaction from her. He then turned his gaze to the stars.

The pirates from Nola's father's stories were nothing like the man she danced with. They were nothing like his crew. Kind. Loving.

Lincoln stared back at her. "No," he answered. "I don't believe people can change. We just are who we are. Anything other than that, it's putting on a facade to fit in and make people comfortable."

"That's like saying we cannot grow or become better people," she replied, "Isn't it?"

Lincoln's face remained serene yet unreadable. Nola was getting used to that look ever since she came onto their ship. She honestly had no idea what was going through his head, and it drove her mad.

"I was not born a pirate, Nola. I became one because my heart desired the sea, and nothing else," he explained. "No one could take that from me, even if they tried, and I wouldn't sacrifice who and what I am for anyone."

"I would never want you to," she explained, realizing the way her words could have been misinterpreted. She was speaking about herself—not him.

"What's wrong?" Lincoln asked, his forehead puckered.

She inhaled a sharp breath, her thoughts muddled as

she fought to get the words out. "Lincoln, I need to tell you something—"

"Captain!" Mazie shouted across the deck, gesturing to Ardley. They turned to where he sat, his body slumping against the mast. "Ardley doesn't look so great," she said. "We really should be searching for land. We need drinking water."

"We could always drink each other's piss!" Boots shouted.

Kitten rammed her elbow into his rib. "Why ye always so crude?"

He wheezed. "The bloody hell, woman! I'm serious, love." Boots pressed his hand against his ribcage. "My throat is already parched by drinkin' all night."

Ardley cleared his throat, sitting up a bit. "We should get to it," he said weakly, "We need a plan. Whatever we have left will only last us a day."

"Then perhaps we all best stop drinkin', instead," Kitten said. "It's makin' our thirst worse."

Mazie stood abruptly, grabbing Lincoln's mug that sat abandoned next to the helm.

"I'd rather drink Hill's piss than stop drinking," she said, knocking back what was left. She used her tongue to lick the rim after she saw it was empty. "Fuck! Where's the barrel?"

Hill grabbed his crotch. "Too far of a walk, lassie. Bring that mug over here, Mazie; I've got a ragin' fire hose ready for ye."

"Nay," Lincoln said, waving his hand at Hill to sit back

down. "No one is drinking nobody's piss." He released his hold on Nola. "How much is left?" he asked Mazie.

Her shoulder lifted in a shrug. "Nothing, Captain. There's nothing left." Mazie glanced at Ardley again. "The Eastland Forest is still four days away. We won't survive without water."

"Aye," Lincoln said.

Nola lowered her brow and brought her arms around her waist. Lincoln looked defeated, and that alone caused her stomach to twist in knots.

Lincoln on the deck, planting his elbows on his knees, and massaged his temples. A tinge of apprehension shone in his eyes.

"There's one other city before we reach the Fae, but they are known to kill pirates. They *will* attack for blood."

"Bloody 'ell, Captain," Kitten spat, "What kind of a place is this?"

Mazie placed a hand on his shoulder. "Captain, forgive me, but I've sailed with you for almost ten years now," she said, "and there's nothing between here and the Eastland Forest."

Lincoln looked dubious about his own plan. But Nola knew that whatever it was, they had no other choice.

"Nothing you can *see*, Mazie," he said.

Lincoln's first mate dropped her hand as he stepped back. He searched a pocket in the inside of his vest, taking out an old, rusty compass. The artifact pointed east.

". . . But this ship is about to go through one hell-of-a-journey to get to it."

Chapter 18

The crew sailed north for what felt like hours before the sea began to change.

"What the hell is happening, Captain?" Ardley shouted, panic reflecting in his voice.

Nola and the rest of the crew looked ahead, watching as dark grey clouds hovered low over the sea. Suddenly, a waterspout began to form, swirling around, threatening the Sybil Curse. The ocean then pulled down, and amid the thunder and rain, a massive whirlpool appeared.

"Batten down the hatches, hearties! 'Cause this will be quite a ride!" Hill yelled from the crow's nest.

The pirates held onto the railing as the ship rocked back and forth, resisting the current.

"We're goin' to die!" Kitten cried as she gripped at the taffrail. "Wha' do we do, Captain? Wha' do we do?"

Boots turned to Lincoln as his eyes stared at the storm. "Is that a bloody maelstrom?"

A slow smirk reached Lincoln's lips as his crew clung firmly to whatever they could hold on to.

"Not quite, matey. 'Tis a door into another world," he replied.

Nola shook her head in disbelief while a chill crawled up her spine. ". . . A world? Inside the sea?" she asked, aghast.

"Aye," Lincoln answered. "And we better hold on tight because we're about to sail into it."

The current was stronger with every second; the waves crashed forcefully, landing on the old wooden deck, sweeping loose barrels and everything else on their path.

Kitten squealed as Boots's hand slipped from the railing and he was nearly washed away by a wave. Luckily, he caught himself on time, gripping a pole as tightly as he could. Nola appeared just as frightened as Kitten. She dug her face into Lincoln's neck, clinging firmly to his unbuttoned shirt.

Suddenly, Ardley shouted at Mazie, "Here!" as he tossed the end of a rope to her, and with all the strength he had left, he pulled her to him.

Lincoln remained calm but held Nola firmly against his chest.

"Don't be afraid!" he whispered to her ear, wrapping his arm around her waist.

It was not the first time Lincoln crossed that portal. In fact, Wentworth, his previous captain, and his crew, had visited Dratose several times during Lincoln's early days as a pirate. It was never a pleasant visit, but Wentworth always took a gamble to get what he wanted from the people who lived there.

"Are you fucking mad, Captain?" Mazie shouted at him,

the rope slipping from her fingers as she swung to smack him. Ardley quickly reached out and yanked her elbow to pull her back.

The Sybil Curse fell into the whirlpool, and it spiraled them down as they sank deeper into the hole. Nola looked up, watching the sky above vanish before her eyes. All she saw was water swirling around them.

"Kitten!" Boots shouted, stumbling forward, failing to hook his hand over hers. She reached out to grab him as he fell when his wooden leg shattered in half.

"Gotcha!" she said, pulling him next to her.

A nervous feeling hit Nola as she watched the crew struggle.

Lincoln looked over her shoulder. "You okay, mate?" he shouted. Boots gave the captain a nod and waved his broken peg in the air as Kitten held him up.

"This bloody piece of junk!" Boots laughed, tossing the broken peg leg onto the deck.

Lincoln shook his head. "Hearties, hold on tight now!"

The deep, blue ocean swallowed the ship. Everything turned black. There was no water, no air, no light. It was a complete void. For a few seconds, they ceased to exist, only to suddenly re-emerge into another world—a cold, frozen world.

The water settled on the ship. The sails hung low, heavy from the icy water. They all opened their eyes and took a minute or two to adjust to the bright turquoise sky around them. Shocked, the pirates stared at a tall glacier wall in front of the ship. It had a cave-looking shaft as an entrance.

"Blimey! It's quite chilly, ain't it?" Kitten said, squeezing the freezing water from her dress.

Lincoln pulled a few blankets from an old chest and handed them to his mates. When he got to Nola, he took the liberty of wrapping the blanket around her himself.

Her eyes gleamed at the blue glow coming from the water surrounding them. The sight was precious to behold.

"Wow," Nola said, watching the heat of her breath dance before her.

The color of the sky changed to a light shade of pink where it met the glacier. There were no clouds and an immense amber moon shone above them.

"Is there a place to dock?" Boots asked, pointing to the cave. "Or are we headin' inside there?"

"If we want clean water," Lincoln said, "That's where we will find it. All the water is pure, but it is too frozen out here to even get it inside the barrels. It will be easier inside where the climate is slightly warmer."

"I'll grab us some dry clothes," Mazie said. "We'll die if I don't." She rushed below deck as Lincoln stood at the helm, steering the ship towards the cave.

The sound of the ship cracking through the ice silenced the pirates. All but Ardley, who slumped against the mast in his weakened state, looked at their surroundings. It was truly majestic, and the crew took in the world around them: the colors, the massive walls of blue ice, and the crystal-clear water below.

Hill focused on his breath breaking through the chilly air, creating a fine mist in front of his chapped lips.

The ice cap slowed the ship as they entered the cave,

making way amidst massive, towering glaciers on either side.

Once inside the cave, the pinkish hue dimmed but was overtaken by aqua-blue rays shimmering over the ice around them.

This is incredible, Nola thought.

"Kitten, drop the anchor once we reach that turn," Lincoln ordered, pointing at a fork in the cave.

"Where do those paths lead?" Nola asked.

"One leads to the city, the other back to the sea," he explained. "It's easier to sail ahead than try to turn the ship around."

Nola helped Kitten turn the windlass and drop the heavy anchor.

"Let's get them barrels and I'll be needin' my cane as well until I fix up me leg," Boots said, heading below deck, Kitten and Hill following closely behind.

As the crew went about their duties to prepare the ship to retrieve the water, Nola listened to Lincoln's story about their last encounter in that place. Her chest gave a nervous twist hearing about the bizarre creatures that lived on that land, and the unnerving feeling Lincoln had that somehow, they were not yet aware of their presence, as the last time they were not so lucky.

"My old captain, Wentworth, was a damn fool," he said. "He had not cared about the danger lurking in this cave. Despite the risk, he still did all he could to steal from the people, so we were met with cannons and ferocious creatures that wanted nothing but blood. And we got it.

Wentworth lost several men that day and I swore I would never return."

Nola placed her hand on his shoulder for comfort right as Mazie returned to the deck.

"Captain, how in all these years have you not told us about this place?" she asked, tossing a handful of garments on the deck.

A small frown edged his lips. "Oh, my dear Mazie, this place may look beautiful, but 'tis what nightmares are made up from. I never wanted to return here so I kept this awful wonder to myself. The creatures that live here will, without a doubt, kill us if we are caught. So, we must be ready to strike back if they pose a threat."

Boots, Kitten, and Hill reappeared, each dragging a barrel across the deck. Mazie then passed out the waterproof coats, boots, old gauntlets, and hats. Nola zipped one of the jackets tightly around her body and grabbed a pair of gloves from the stack of clothes.

"How do you get the water into the barrels?" Nola asked.

"We'll have to use the pulleys and rig the rope until it reaches the sea. It's strong enough, but it's going to take us a while," Lincoln replied.

Boots prepared the pulley and began coiling and securing the rope around the first barrel.

"Ardley," Lincoln called to his mate, "I need you to stay below deck. You are in no shape for this weather." He watched Ardley's already pale cheeks slowly turn blue.

"Come on, mate," Hill said, "I'll help ye down the stairs."

Hill wrapped his arm under Ardley's armpit, grabbing

his hand with his other and carefully, yet stumbly, helped him to the captain's quarters.

"It's bloody freezin'," Boots said once the barrel was tied off.

Even with layers of warm clothes, their limbs had already begun to stiffen. Their bodies were nowhere used to that temperature.

Mazie exhaled heavily, watching her breath fog before her eyes. "It's been a while since we've been in this kind of weather, Captain," she said.

Nola peered ahead as a soft echo sounded through the cave. She was not quite sure what she was looking for, but she still had a baleful feeling. It appeared to her as if someone or something had been watching them.

Nola gave Lincoln an anxious look. "What do we have to fear here, Lincoln?" she asked.

He frowned before he hesitantly answered, "Gnomes."

A polar breeze caused Nola to shiver, or maybe it was fear. "As in, tiny creatures with red pointy hats?" she asked. He inched closer and wrapped his gloves over her already frozen fingers.

"Fairy tales, Nola. Those are just the fairy tales King Matthias made for the children to believe their parents. These gnomes are small, yes, but they look a bit different than you've probably been told they look like." He turned to his crew. "They don't speak our tongue and they don't welcome visitors, especially those who plan to steal from them."

"Bah!" Mazie huffed. "This is hardly stealing."

He shook his head. "They won't see it that way."

"Then perhaps we get those cannons ready and our weapons, just in case," Nola interrupted.

Lincoln nodded. "Aye, that's a good idea. We barely made it out of here alive the last time we did this."

For the first time since Nola fled Zemira, she felt a sense of courage. She ran to Lincoln's quarters to grab her bow. Having it close gave her that power and bravery she needed. It made her strong.

Mazie took a deep breath and drew in the crisp air before turning to Boots. "Let's get that water, shall we?"

Boots heaved at the pulley, lowering the barrel down to the water. Once the water rose to the barrel's brim, he and Lincoln grabbed the rope together and rigged it up.

"Nola, grab the other end," Lincoln ordered.

She rushed to the side, and she and Kitten helped pull the end up over the railing to keep it from tilting over. They secured the lid and shimmed it to the side, leaning the barrel up against the mast.

"The next one," Lincoln said.

They secured the rope and lowered the barrels down, one by one, until all four were filled.

Nola watched as a heavy sigh of relief left Lincoln's shivering lips. They had their water; they were exhausted, but not out of harm's way. Not yet.

Nola filled a few empty mugs and passed them around. They had to quench their thirst before heading back. Mazie took two and raced below deck to give one to Ardley.

After Mazie returned, she helped secure the last barrel's lid while Lincoln hurried to the helm.

"Are my lips blue yet?" Hill asked, joining the crew on a bench. He rubbed his hands to keep them warm.

Mazie held out a beckoning hand to help him sit by her. "Like a blueberry," she teased.

Hill settled his rear at the end of the bench, cupped his hand over his lips, and blew out the heat.

"Sorry, lads! This is all my fault." He looked up. "I'm never drinkin' again."

Kitten snickered. "Well, we all know that's a bloody lie, but we still love ye."

Hill gave her a weak smile. "I can't feel below my waist," he said. "That's a bad thing, ain't it?"

Kitten nodded as Boots wrapped his arms around her waist to keep her warm. He shot her a strange look.

"Anyone else feelin' like we're being watched?" Boots asked.

Kitten nodded. "Aye."

Mazie leaned her head on Hill's shoulder and held out her hands. "My fingers feel like heavy bricks," she said, trying to pull her Monmouth cap over her ears, but she struggled to grip it.

"Frostbite already, darlin'?" Hill asked, laying his long fingers gingerly over hers.

"Thanks, mate," she said, taking his hands to keep hers warm.

Suddenly, as the ship moved slowly onward, movement caught Nola's eye.

"Lincoln?" Nola shouted back. "Look." She pointed ahead. "What is that?"

Lincoln's eyes narrowed at the fork, watching a little raft

move through the water, with two tiny gnomes sitting on top.

"Fuck!" he cursed under his breath. "Let me do the talking."

The crew peered over the edge as the barge pulled up to the side of the Sybil Curse.

Mazie jumped to her feet.

"Best you keep your tiny little asses on that raft, will you?" she said boldly, ignoring Lincoln's order. "We're just heading out. No harm done."

Lincoln tightened his jaw.

The two gnomes were no bigger than the size of Lincoln's forearm. Their eyes were bright red and warts covered their scaly skin from their bald heads to their toes.

Nola swallowed down her nerves. The creatures looked nothing like what her father described when she was a little girl.

Mazie stepped back as the two tiny beasts boarded their ship. She quickly placed her hand on the cold metal of her pistol as if ready to draw her weapon and shoot.

A grim little gnome stepped forward; his rheumy eyes twitched as he spoke.

Mazie's brows furrowed. "Sorry, I don't speak ugly little vermin," she berated. Her shoulders visibly stiffened as the little being crinkled its pointy nose.

What is she doing? Nola thought. *Has the dehydration caused Mazie to lose her mind?*

"Mazie!" Nola whispered from behind her, but the pirate only waved her hand in the air to brush her off. Then the other gnome spoke, but that time he shouted, pounding its fist in the air.

"I said, I have no idea what you're jabbering about, but it sounds to me like a threat!" Mazie fumed, turning to Lincoln. "Captain, we can't risk an attack," she called. "May I?"

"Aye," Lincoln said, running a hand through his hair, "blow the man down."

"No!" Nola shouted again, but her warning was too late. Mazie closed her finger over the trigger, her eyes glowing with excitement as she extended out her hand. She fired off two shots at the gnomes and watched their tiny bodies fall backward into the water. The sound of gunfire echoed loudly through the cave.

Lincoln watched as Nola covered her mouth, preventing a wail. She backed up, then looked out and around the cave as if she were looking for someone.

Boots peered further over the edge. "Well, it's a good thing we got our water already. The sea is turnin' red now."

The buccaneers looked up and scrunched up their faces at him, but then their attention drew to Nola, who cried out.

"What have you done, Mazie? Why didn't you listen? Why did you shoot them?"

Mazie rolled her eyes, placing her pistol in the holster at her hip. "When you are a pirate, Nola, you shoot your enemies first before you ask questions," she explained distastefully. "If not, we'd all be feeding the fish tonight."

"But," she started again, her voice trembling, "They were letting us go."

Mazie huffed. "So, you speak gnome all of a sudden?"

Nola looked at Lincoln, whose eyes darkened, his brows knitting together.

"Wha—you didn't understand them?"

How could they not? Nola thought. She had heard everything they said as clear as her own thoughts.

"They told us we could leave and that they'd forgive us for taking their water if we just left without sailing through their city." She ran her hand through her hair. "They were not threatening an attack. They were letting us go." A feeling of terror rolled within her stomach.

Lincoln's face paled. "Bloody hell! Listen."

A loud bell rang from a distance, echoing through the cave.

"Great, now we've started a war." Lincoln turned to Kitten and Boots. "Weigh the anchor!"

The crew fanned out across the deck, preparing to leave but not before gathering up the weapons needed for combat. As Lincoln steered the ship to the right to exit the glacier, he pitched a fearful glance over at Mazie. Their faces blanched watching another ship enter the cave. It was a smaller vessel but stocked with cannons and tiny gnomes. Their artillery was pointing right at the Sybil Curse.

"Well," Mazie said. "Looks like we're going to have our war sooner than expected." She winked at Nola.

Nola glanced up, averting her eyes from the ship nearing theirs. "If that cannon goes off in this cave, we'll all die."

Lincoln gripped the helm and pulled right, veering towards the sea. Shortly after turning the ship, a blast from a cannon came their way.

He skillfully steered the ship to a sharp left, the cannonball hitting the side of the ice, instantly cracking the glacier up the wall. Tiny shards of ice fell on the ship.

"Bloody fuck!" Kitten shouted. "We don't 'ave a choice, Captain!"

"Aye, Kitten. Go!" Lincoln shouted.

Kitten ran to the Sybil Curse's chase cannon and turned it towards their enemy's ship, which was only a hundred yards away.

Nola pulled her bow off her shoulder while Boots unsheathed his sword and held it in front of him.

Hill only sat in the corner, curled in a ball, with a bottle of rum.

"Fire in the 'ole!" Kitten shouted, their ship's cannon firing off towards the gnomes.

The cannonball hit the side of the small ship near the bow. The wood burst in all directions while several gnomes flew off the ship and scattered along the water. The creatures left standing on board screeched and wailed.

"Fire!" Boots shouted that time as the craft sailed closer. Kitten did not miss. The thirty-two-pound cannonball hit lower, causing the ship to split, and half the crew, maybe twenty or thirty of the little creatures, fell under their deck as the ship collapsed at the center.

Lincoln looked up as the rest of the tiny gnomes leapt high in the air and landed on the Sybil Curse once they were closer.

Ardley came up from below deck, his sword already swinging and ready to defend the ship. He came down with one swift blow but missed as a gnome locked onto his leg, digging its serrated teeth into his ankle. Ardley tried to shake him off, but the gnome held tight, digging deeper into his flesh.

Nola rushed to him, pulling her bow back and releasing an arrow towards the gnome attacking his ankle. Crimson blood sprayed over the deck as the sharp tip cut through the back of its neck. She ran to Ardley, who held his hand to the wound as blood oozed from his ankle.

Mazie shot a couple rounds of her polished revolver. The gnomes dashed about the deck like little crickets. But it was not enough; there were too many.

Lincoln left the helm and pulled out his sword, swinging at the devilish monsters.

"Boots!" Kitten shouted, leaving the cannon and dashing to him as he laid his back on the deck. He had four gnomes on top of him, biting down into his flesh.

"Oh no!" she shouted. But before she reached Boots, four arrows flew by her, piercing into the hearts of each attacking gnome. Kitten turned around to see Nola behind them.

"Thanks, lassie!" she said, practically sobbing with relief.

Nola smiled, despite her heart beating hard against her chest—a mix of satisfaction and horror. She rushed to the dead gnomes and pulled her arrows out, placing them back in the quiver. But as she turned, Lincoln had several gnomes latched onto his back and neck. He had his sword, but he appeared to be struggling to defend himself with it.

A lump of rage grew in Nola's throat.

She turned, her eyes scanning the scene, watching her

friends being attacked. Nola had felt helpless before, but that was different. She cared about them. They were her allies. Her friends.

Nola felt her instincts speak to her; it was not new, but she embraced them that time. She backed up slowly, standing tall at the stern of the ship, and sang quietly to a near whisper. She tried to push away the doubt in her heart.

She sang a melodic song, drawing in her powers. Nola did everything to focus on her siren call while the harrowing images played out in front of her.

One by one, the tiny gnomes dropped to the deck into a sleepless slumber.

A few yards ahead stood the last gnome to fall; she looked straight at it. A sardonic grin pulled at its lips before he charged towards her across the deck. She lifted her elbows and hesitated for only a second before the arrow sprang from the bow. The gnome launched into the air, avoiding the arrow, and slammed its vile, bald head against her chest. She flung back against the rail, then they toppled over and into the frigid water.

Her fingers dug into the gnome's shoulders, taking it down with her as they both sank. She released the gnome as he opened his mouth, flashing his jagged, sharp teeth. What came next was a savage screech. Bubbles clouded the space between them. She gripped the arrow she still held tightly in her palm before stabbing into its chest. The gnome let out a bubble-filled cry before its corpse sank into the water. Nola felt herself begin to panic and tried to swim to the surface. She had to get out of the sea before it was too late.

Nola sank deeper. She flailed her hands up to reach above the surface, but she was already too far down. She felt a strong pull between her thighs.

No, she thought. Not now. That was the first time she had felt her tail begin to transition.

But before they fully connected, a pair of strong hands gripped her shoulder and pulled her up.

Once on the surface, Lincoln gripped the ladder and the crew helped pull her up the rest of the way. They laid Nola down, still not fully conscious.

Hill ran over to cover her with a dry blanket. She looked down; her human legs were intact. However, the inside of her pants had ripped when her legs tried to come together.

She felt the draining weakness through her body and all she wanted to do was lay her head down on Lincoln's chest.

"My bow!" she cried out.

"Leave it, Nola. It's already sinking to the bottom."

It was all she had left of her father.

The captain's jade-green eyes settled on hers.

"Are you okay?" Lincoln asked.

Nola clutched at his arm; she did not care if he saw what happened in the sea.

"A gnome knocked me off the ship," she started, "after I missed." She bit down hard on her bottom lip. "I missed, Lincoln."

He chuckled.

"I thought you never missed," he pointed out teasingly.

She smiled weakly. "Well, the bloody thing moved."

Lincoln caressed her pale-blue lips with his thumb. She

shivered, taking in a heavy, exasperated breath. "But you . . . you saved me," her voice stammered.

Lincoln wrapped his arms around her, trying to keep her warm. Nola's eyes wavered from his and she buried her face into his shoulder, her teeth chattering.

"Let's get these little shits off our ship," Mazie said, looking around. "By the way! What happened?"

The gnomes remained scattered all over the deck.

"I don't know," Lincoln said. "I haven't a bloody clue." He gripped her again, tightening the blanket more securely around her as her body went stiff.

Boots staggered to one of the gnomes and poked it in the stomach with his wooden cane. They heard a loud snore from the little thing.

"It's sleepin'," Boots said.

A knot twisted in Nola's stomach.

Kitten bent down and lifted it up in the air, turning the ugly thing to face her. "Maybe that's their thing," she observed. "When they get too excited, they sleep?" She turned to look down at Lincoln.

A brow rose high above Lincoln's right eye. "All at once?"

Mazie nodded, but they all quickly glanced up. The ice above them cracked loudly and large pieces of ice fell all around the ship.

"No time to figure it out," Lincoln said. "Let's get out of here."

"I'm okay," Nola said to him, sitting up as his arm slackened around her waist.

Lincoln buried his face in her hair and gave her a gentle kiss on the top of her head. He sprang to his feet, rushing to the helm, while the rest of the crew tossed the sleeping gnomes into the icy waters.

Nola laid in the captain's cabin, wrapped in a blanket. She towel-dried her hair, dabbing the tiny drops of water dripping down her neck. She looked up, placing the damp rag next to her, and glanced in the mirror on the wall. Color had returned to her cheeks.

Nola heard the sound of Lincoln's boots clomping down the steps that led to the room.

"Here," he said, handing her one of Kitten's dresses once inside the cabin.

She held it loosely in her hands. "A dress?" Nola said, lowering a brow.

He shrugged. "You somehow ripped the last clean pair of pants Mazie had. This will have to do until we wash our clothes."

Nola narrowed her eyes above his right shoulder. She had not noticed before the scratch marks over the curve of his neck.

"Are you okay?" She reached out. Her delicate fingers ran down his neck but avoided the marks.

He smiled widely. "Aye. Those little bastards were quite savage. But I'll survive."

Lincoln's playful smile grew somber as he looked down at her, scanning her for injuries.

"My cheeks' pallor found its color again," she said. "I'm alright. Really."

He then ran his hand down her messy, damp hair but stayed silent. Lincoln's tousled hair spilled over his right eye. She wanted to reach up to move it away and look into his emerald eyes, but she did not. He was acting strange, distant, and she was not sure why.

Nola tilted her head and studied the expression on his face instead. "Is everything okay?" she asked. "What is it?"

His gaze ran down her face. "When you fell into the water, I thought I was going to lose you," he said.

She frowned. "Do you have me?"

He did not respond as if an internal conflict ate at him.

Lincoln withdrew his hand from hers and looked at her intently with his brooding eyes. "I, um—"

Nola then heard Boots's voice bellowing, "Heave," above deck.

"Stay down here until your body feels a bit better; I have something to tend to."

Nola nodded. "Sure," she whispered as he rushed out of the room.

A shiver of emotion ran through her body. Something had happened between her falling into the water and after they re-emerged into the Portland Sea.

Is he afraid of something? Nola wondered. *Afraid of me?*

She sank into the mattress.

He knows because he saw, she thought to herself. *He saw my tail.*

Once Lincoln ascended to the top deck, she dressed quickly, wrapped the blanket back over her body, and followed him.

Nola rounded the corner but stayed close to the door,

watching from a distance. Lincoln reached out his hand below him, his back to hers, and helped lift a woman to her feet—a siren.

Nola had never seen a siren up close, but even then, she still could not see her entirely from where she stood. Mazie held out a white robe as if they had been expecting her. The woman used it to wrap around her body.

Then Lincoln's hands reached her shoulders and he escorted her down the front entrance to the deck.

Nola's heart hammered hard against her chest. He knew that woman, and they were not enemies.

Suddenly, Mazie turned to face Nola.

Only a small pout reached Mazie's lips before they disappeared below deck.

Chapter 19

Nola massaged her knees as she stared down to where her skin had begun to join between her legs. She closed her eyes, and the uncomfortable memory flashed before her—it burned, even though she was submerged in frigid water.

It was an odd feeling, the tug from her tail, willing her legs to blend into one.

Strange, yet invigorating, she thought. It was as if her mind and body had both revitalized. A new life that should have always been a part of her.

Nola had not expected Lincoln to risk his life for her, but he had. She could only think about his strong hands yanking at her shirt, pulling her out of the sea that was meant to swallow her.

Nola leaned back against a small barrel at the ship's stern and folded her arms across her chest. She kept her eyes glued to the captain's cabin door, where he and the mysterious siren were having an in-depth conversation.

The crew and Lincoln were alive and away from that dreadful place, but the woman's presence meant they were not out of danger. Only eight hours earlier, Lincoln had peered into Nola's eyes and promised her she was safe with him.

Perhaps I misread those feelings, she thought.

It did, however, answer two questions that had been occupying her mind.

The first: the woman in there with Lincoln proved he did not fear a siren. It made Nola wonder how wrong her father's stories were—that pirates and sirens were sworn enemies.

Secondly—Nola shook the thought from her mind. She suspected he knew about her tail.

Boisterous laughter came from below deck across the ship. Nola strolled down the main corridor towards the stairs to the kitchen and inhaled the scent of fish and fresh herbs. She would be more useful helping Kitten cook supper than moping on the damp wooden deck. She needed to stop obsessing over the siren woman holding Lincoln's attention for nearly a day.

Nola took one step before she heard Mazie call her name from across the deck. She looked over at the pirate, who threw a sword at her feet while holding another.

Nola glanced down at the blade and slowly raised a brow.

"You look as if you need a distraction," Mazie said.

Nola shrugged. "I guess I need something to do."

Mazie smirked. "Something other than thinking about the captain, I presume?" she asked.

Nola laughed lazily. "You presume wrong. I barely know him, so what do I care?"

Of course, the lie did not come off naturally. Nola sounded more defensive and annoyed than truthful, and she was quite aware that the eyes that looked back at her were not fooled.

Nola cared greatly for Lincoln, more than she was willing to admit. But she felt guilty for wanting a man who did not want her back. One moment, he would lightly touch her lips with the tips of his fingers, getting lost in her eyes, and the next, he evaded her.

Mazie took a step closer until their noses almost touched. "You can dress, walk, and talk like a pirate, but you will fool no one if you can't fight like one." A smile curved at the edge of her lips. "Let us practice what skills you have when you must battle with your hands," she said.

Mazie dropped her sword and brought her fists up near her face.

Nola huffed. "You want to fight me?"

Mazie shrugged her shoulders. "I saw you take out a handful of those little gnomes like you were born to fight, but you lack confidence in your skill, so you'll need to practice." She cracked her knuckles like she was ready to strike at Nola right then and there. "You almost got yourself and our captain killed when you allowed something the size of a rat to knock you off the ship," she fumed, then stepped back, her closed fists out front.

"How about we try the swords first? I might need a tad warming up," Nola asked.

Her father taught her how to use weapons, but not how to fistfight. From time to time, he did bring her with him to see illegal combats outside their village. He had once been a skilled fighter until her mother asked him to give it up and start a life with her.

Nola reached down and picked up the sword at her feet. She felt the weight in her palm and instantly swung it towards Mazie, who dodged it and leapt for her own sword, gripping the hilt and pointing it up to her throat.

Nola froze.

Mazie cocked her head and grinned. "Impressive," she said. "But you hesitated."

Nola smirked. Having any kind of weapon in her hand gave her a sense of security. However, a bow and arrow would have been a much better fit.

"Let's fight, then," Mazie said, her smile growing wider. She raised her sword up and swung towards Nola, but she turned, meeting the pirate's weapon.

Adrenaline coursed through Nola's veins before she swung the sword forward with accuracy and precision, almost stabbing Mazie through the chest. Still, the female buccaneer quickly blocked the hit, matching her skill—her lips pulling into a scowl.

They danced around and exhausted each other. Mazie jumped forward, kicking her leg out, landing her heel into the back of Nola's knees. She flung forward and smacked her face against the deck.

"Ow," Nola cried, holding her right hand to her forehead to check for a wound.

Mazie rolled her eyes. "You might swing that sword like a warrior, but you fight like a child." She reached her hand out to help Nola to her feet, then tossed her sword on the ground. "Have you warmed up yet?"

Nola frowned before shifting her shoulder back with her arm bent at the elbow, then swung up, smacking Mazie hard on the nose. She cupped her hands over her nostrils.

Nola backed up her left foot, her vision speeding up to see her next move. As Mazie came forward, Nola's hand came up and gripped her fist, blocking the hit. She felt her muscles clench as Mazie resisted her hold.

They dropped their hands, taking a step back from each other.

"Nice block," Mazie said, "but still only an amateur."

Nola scowled at her remark. "How's your nose?" she mocked back.

Mazie's lip curled at her remark. She pulled her fist back, bent her knee, then slammed her fist hard against Nola's gut.

She coughed, not believing Mazie had walloped her so hard. Nola let out a groan, wincing at the fierce blow to her stomach.

"Seriously, Mazie?"

"You are as good as dead if you continue to fight this way, Nola," she said. "You want to lead an army to war with the king?"

Nola flinched, watching Mazie slide her sword her way with her foot.

"You'll have to kill someone at some point. You'll have to fight for your damn life!"

Nola looked up, straightened her back, and pulled her shirt up to check on her belly.

"You didn't have to punch me that hard to make your

point," Nola hissed, looking down at the bright red mark right above her birthmark.

She heard a faint gasp come from Mazie's lips. When Nola looked up, she was eyeing her birthmark. It looked like a shark eye shell.

It took Nola a moment to realize what was happening. Her parents had said that birthmark was the marking of a siren, and Mazie was staring right at it, dumbfounded.

"Please—" Nola started, panic dancing around in her stomach.

Mazie threw her hands up. "Stop," she said, cutting her off. "Is that your little secret?" She stepped back. "Oh, you lying bitch!"

Nola stepped forward. "Please, I'm not going to hurt any of you."

Mazie breathed out a quiet chuckle. "You think we're afraid of you, little siren?"

Nola shrugged and shook her head. "No, actually. I don't," she said. "But I lied to you. I lied because I'm scared."

Mazie pulled her eyebrows together and looked towards Lincoln's quarters, letting out a sigh. "We all have secrets, Nola, but the captain is falling for you. So, you better tell him what you are, or I will."

Mazie then leaned down to pick up her sword and swiped it up, placing it into her scabbard.

"We're done here."

Chapter 20

Once the sun began to set, Nola headed into the kitchen to help with dinner. There was a bit of chaos as she looked around. Kitten rushed from each side of the kitchen, pans and silverware scattered over the counter, food laid out and not quite prepared. Hill and Ardley sat in the corner of the kitchen, tossing back their mugs. But Nola's eyes focused on Mazie slumping forward and staring down at the empty plate.

"Need help in there, my love?" Boots asked while descending the stairs, securing the buttons on his breeches after returning from the loo.

Kitten placed two cooked sea turtles on the counter, steam rising from the meat. "Not unless ye wash those filthy 'ands of yers," she said, looking up with a smile.

"Is the captain joining us?" Nola asked, turning to Mazie, who looked up, expressionless. "Does he not dine with the crew anymore?"

Mazie pulled her cup to her lips and smirked at her. "Oh, he's been entertaining our siren guest," she said. "I'm actually quite surprised you haven't asked about her yet."

Nola glared at her.

A sardonic smile flickered on Mazie's lips as she slammed her mug on the table. "My guess is that you haven't told the captain that you're a fish?" Mazie accused, not even trying to hide the volume of her voice.

Nola squinted her eyes. "One cannot speak with another who does not want to be spoken to."

The floor creaked next to them as Kitten walked up to the table. "What are ye two jabberin' 'bout?" she asked, placing their food in front of them.

Right then, the door swung open and Lincoln entered, visibly drunk, and staggered to the table. He gripped to the edge and stopped, his eyes glossed over Nola's, and for a moment, despite his drunken state, she saw that same man who cared about her. She saw kindness but also sadness. Something was wrong.

Lincoln gave her a cocky smile and plopped on the chair across from her. He reeked of booze and cigars. His masculine jaw was marked by a light scruff, and his hair was untamed and slightly greasy.

"Hey!" he said as he looked up towards Kitten, who was still preparing their supper. "Dinner not done yet?"

Pompous bastard, Nola thought.

She had not noticed him behaving so rudely towards any of his crew members since she had stowed away on his ship.

Lincoln snapped his fingers at Kitten, who rushed over a plate of food. But, instead of placing it in front of him, she held it there and looked at him with a stern, accusatory glare.

"Someone 'as 'ad a bit too much rum. Eh, Captain?" she said. "How 'bout ye take yer own damn plate."

Nola thought it was a bold move to speak to the captain that way, but it seemed as if Kitten had not cared at that moment.

After a moment of awkward silence, he slapped his knee, throwing his head back and letting out a hearty laugh. "Aye," he said, then took the plate from her and placed it in front of him.

Lincoln stared at his meal. "Again?" he said.

Fish and white rice had become the main dish on the ship since they had one more mouth to feed.

Nola watched, perplexed, as he devoured his food without a fork, using only his fingers. It was a bit distasteful and strange to see such a good-looking man eat like he was a wild beast.

"Pardon me," Nola said, moving her seat back and standing, staring down at him. "I need some fresh air."

Nola rushed out of the dining room and climbed the stairs to the main deck. She took in the cool evening breeze, but as she went to close her eyes, a white robe blowing in the wind caught her attention. Nola's eyes spotted the woman she had seen earlier. She was leaning up against the balustrade, looking out into the water.

"Hello," Nola shouted. The woman turned and looked back at her while Nola took a few more steps towards her—cautiously, of course. She did not recognize the woman, but the closer she got, an odd feeling grew in her chest. It was like they were connected in some way.

The siren's hair was a bright, coppery red. It fell

gorgeously down to her hips. Her eyes were a glistering white, almost as if they were translucent, like tiny little opals sparkling around her pupils. Nola was intrigued by the woman and her beauty.

The white-eyed siren turned away to look out at the full moon; it had created a beautiful glow above the surface of the water.

Once Nola stood by her, she turned to meet her eyes.

"I'm Pearl," the woman said.

"Nola," she replied.

The redheaded siren greeted, "Yes, I know who you are." She stopped and crinkled her nose. "And you want to ask me something, don't you?"

Nola nodded. "It's not a question, per se," she uttered. "Only that I know what you are, and—" She stopped, pressing her lips together before asking, "You are here, on a *pirate* ship."

The woman's smile grew. "You're right. That isn't a question. Unless you are wondering why it is that I'm not trying to kill them?" Pearl asked, gazing towards where the crew was dining.

". . . But the stories I've heard—"

"You've heard but not actually experienced?" Pearl's grin faded.

"I wasn't raised in the sea."

"Interesting," the siren woman said. "Then, it's quite unfortunate you were raised to hide and fear the very thing you are."

Nola lowered her head in shame. "I don't want to feel this way."

The woman reached out and brushed Nola's fingers. Nola looked up as Pearl said, "We are not all like them." She released her hand and gestured to the sea.

Nola looked over and stared out into the water. "But sirens do kill men. Do they not?"

As they stood silent, the woman turned to Nola and stepped closer to her until they were almost touching.

"Don't fear or hate what you are, Nola. Embrace the darkness, just as you embrace the light."

Nola thought about those words. Yes, she felt like a decent person her entire life, despite her anatomy, but nature had a way of taking its course. So, she would have to accept it, or she would lose herself.

"Lincoln has avoided me since you came upon the ship," Nola said. "He knows what I am, doesn't he?"

The woman nodded. "He knows."

Nola's stomach twisted into a sickening knot.

"But he's got more pressing matters he's dealing with at the moment. Which is why I had come to the ship in the first place—to deliver a message," Pearl explained.

Nola's eyes shone in confusion; the white-eyed siren stepped closer to her and placed a gentle hand on her shoulder.

"I did what I could to assuage the situation, Nola. Lincoln expected me to be gone by now, but I couldn't leave until you and I spoke," she said. "Lincoln doesn't hate sirens, he never has, but he's not happy you lied about it. However, you did what you had to do to survive. I get that, but he is—" She stopped, sucking in an exhausted breath. ". . . Let's just say, he has been hurt before, and you remind him of that loss and pain he once had."

Nola squeezed her eyes shut for a quick moment.

"We have an enemy in common. The war between pirates and sirens is irrelevant when that enemy threatens to destroy our kind—one siren at a time—one pirate at a time."

Nola thought about the king and everything he had done to destroy not only their kingdom, but all creatures who held magic.

"You're safer on this ship than you are out there," Pearl continued, gesturing to the sea with her head. The woman then pushed away, placing her hands again on the rail. A grim expression on her face made Nola feel uneasy.

Something is wrong, Nola thought.

"What is it?" she asked.

Pearl looked up. "A few days ago, the night you fled, Prince Elijah put out an order to hunt you down."

Nola's eyes shot wide. Her suspicions were true. The bells were for her.

"Believe me, Nola, the prince is more terrifying and dangerous to our kind than Matthias is and will ever be."

"Why wouldn't Lincoln tell me this himself?" Nola asked.

"Because his own guilt is clouding his judgment," Pearl explained.

However, Nola still was not sure what that meant.

"Prince Elijah wants you for something. I promise, we sirens will search for that answer because we look after our own!" she said, then looked at the waves rolling over each other. "You must be completely honest with the crew, though. You ought to ensure their trust, or they will not follow you into battle—and you also need to be honest with yourself."

Since Nola was a child, she craved answers to who she really was, but at the same time, those answers were her greatest fear.

"How do you know all this?" Nola asked.

A faint smile grew on the siren's face. "It's not just the Fae sending spies," she replied, then turned abruptly to discover Lincoln had been watching them, who knows for how long.

His arms were folded across his chest.

"Take care of yourself, Nola." Pearl stepped back, giving Nola an apologetic stare.

Then, the copper-haired siren pulled the robe off her shoulders and dove over the ledge, her tail forming before her hands hit the water.

Lincoln drifted over to Nola. She turned on her heel to face him. The look in his eyes gave a sudden shift in the atmosphere around them.

"What did she say to you?" His voice was ice cold.

Lincoln smelt of rum and cinnamon, and his near presence, despite his intense stare, made her want to melt into his arms.

She did not respond.

After a long moment of silence, he stepped forward again, placing both hands on each side of her. Nola gasped at how close he was to her.

"What did she tell you, Nola?"

Though Lincoln's voice was softer than before, almost to a whisper, it was pitched with irritation.

Nola tilted her head up. "Only what I already suspected —the prince is after me, but no one knows why," Nola said. Her stomach twisted but was somewhat relieved. She then noticed a flicker of concern in his eyes, but it was quickly replaced by distaste—her deception then unfolding.

"Sounds like you've kept a pretty big secret since you came upon my ship," Lincoln scolded.

She gritted her teeth. "Do you not have secrets, Lincoln?"

One of his eyes twitched.

"Because everyone hides their true self. Even you!" Nola frowned.

The captain shook his head slowly.

"You're right," he said, "I have lied to you. But you are on *my* ship, so I don't owe you anything."

A flush crept up her face.

"How long have you known I'm a siren?" She instinctively pushed back, but all she felt was the damp rail pressing into her back. "It's when I fell in the water, isn't it? You saw my tail?"

Nola was afraid of him at that moment, yes, but the truth was out.

He shook his head. "I saw you sing," he said. "It didn't matter how quiet you sang; my eyes never left yours, even while I was being attacked by a herd of gnomes—I saw you sing. And knew then what you were doing because I had seen it before."

Nola gnashed her teeth, confused.

"Sybil," Lincoln answered the question she asked with her eyes.

"Sybil?" Nola remembered what Mazie had told her in Westin. Her mouth fell open before asking, "Sybil was a siren?"

He nodded, pointing at her chest, landing his finger between her breasts. "Just like you."

The ship suddenly felt like it was rocking. That or Lincoln's touch made her head spin. She looked up with slight surprise in her eyes.

"You loved a siren, and yet you push me away and look at me right now as if I'm a monster!"

He shook his head. "I'm not pushing you away, Nola! I'm trying to save you, and being on this ship—" Lincoln stopped, running his hand through his hair as his eyes turned weary. "We should have never agreed to help you!" he said.

Unexpectedly, Nola let out a sob, feeling like her chest was being crushed by a heavy blow.

"I'm not her, Lincoln!" she spat out. "I would never hurt you."

He slammed his palms against the wet wood, causing her to jump. "You already have!" His tone changed. It cut like ice. She cowered to his voice, lowering her head to the ground. "Just show me already. Show me that side of you." He gripped his hair and shouted, "Stop hiding from me!"

Seeing the rage in his eyes, Nola's fear disappeared and was replaced with her own anger. She turned to see the crew standing behind him, drawn to the sound of his shouting. Her eyes blazed with a fury she did not want to feel.

Nola punched her fist against her own chest. “I can’t, Lincoln!”

He moved closer towards her, regardless of what she was. “Show me, for bloody sake!” he shouted.

“Stop!” She held up her hand. The heat burned at her chest; her skin tightened with each breath.

Nola was scared.

She looked down at her hands, the color changing to a slight maroon.

“Step back.” Her eyes implored him to listen. “Lincoln, you need to step back.”

His expression hardened, not listening to her plea, and he stepped closer to her in one sudden movement. He reached out and tightened his grip around her chin. Lincoln shifted her jaw so she would be forced to look him in the eyes.

“Do you have any idea how much you mean to me?” Lincoln asked.

The tension in Nola’s skin eased. Her heart fluttered wildly the more he encroached in her space. Lincoln squeezed her chin a little bit harder.

“Why did you have to lie to me?” he asked with desperation in his voice. “Why are you hiding your true self from me?”

“Because I thought I was a monster in your eyes.” She tried to look away, but he held her chin still.

As Nola felt the pressure on her face, she remembered the

guard in Brecken, who trapped her between his arms. She blinked slowly, and when her eyes opened again, they felt like fire, as if hot flames were pressed against the back of her eyes.

"Maybe I will take back what I said about you being safe," she continued. "You want to see what happens when you corner a siren?"

Her stomach did a flip as his thumb rubbed gently against the skin of her jaw as if she had not threatened him.

Nola's body burned as he inched towards her—her breasts pressing up against his.

"You need to let go of me," she begged, trying to hide her growing wrath as he continued to stare into her eyes. Nola looked down at her fingers again. They looked different, coarser, almost scale-like.

"Lincoln, please stop!" Kitten shouted from the other side of the ship.

Nola's temples pounded heavily with each beat of her heart, and it got worse the more he hovered over her. It all seemed as if Lincoln were pushing her, testing how far she would change.

She wondered if he wanted to see her that way.

The man she cared for so dearly was not afraid of what she could do to him.

Finally, Lincoln released her and took one step back.

Nola placed both hands against his chest, pushing him even further away. The whites of her eyes turned grey, moving in circles as the anger fueled her. For a moment, Lincoln appeared afraid.

Good, she thought. *Be afraid.*

They both breathed heavily as the silence continued to loom between them.

"You're drunk," she scoffed, "sleep it off." She wiped a tear falling down her face as Lincoln staggered back, his mouth agape.

The Sybil Curse's crew looked at Nola, appearing more leerier of the siren than their captain had been. She knew her eyes beamed fire, her skin felt rough and coarse, but she relaxed with each step Lincoln took back.

"Captain, I think you need to listen to her," Mazie said calmly from behind.

Seconds before, Nola wanted to attack him, kill him and the crew. But Kitten and Mazie standing up for her made her realize they cared about her too. Nola locked eyes with Lincoln and saw genuine fear and remorse. She finally realized what was happening.

His shoulders sagged. "Nola, I—"

She held up both her hands. "Don't, Lincoln. Just leave me alone."

He had pushed her too far, bringing out that side of her she did not want to show.

"Lincoln, what the 'ell were ye doin' to 'er?" Kitten said as she approached behind Mazie. She turned to Nola. "Easy. Take a deep breath, will ye?"

Nola glanced at Kitten, and then back to Lincoln, feeling her anger finally subside.

She quickly became aware of her equally irrational reaction. Lincoln was drunk and upset, and she had let him get inside her head. She was not afraid of him; she was angry. Her blood pulsed, but she had to focus on becoming calm.

Ardley, Boots, and Hill had their hands hovering over their weapons. Nola could see the fear in their eyes. However, Mazie had a slight smile pulling at her lips, and amusement glinted in her midnight-black eyes.

"I'm fine, Kitten," Nola assured. "I just need your captain to back away for a minute."

Boots stepped forward. "Captain, you best sleep off whatever is goin' through your head, mate," Boots said, "what were you thinkin'?"

Lincoln's face flamed with remorse. "Nola, I didn't—" he said, breathing heavily through his nose, keeping his eyes locked in on hers.

"I've never meant to hurt you, Lincoln, but if you ever come at me like that again, I can promise you, I will defend myself." She looked away. "I was raised by humans, but since I left Baylin, I don't even recognize myself. I don't know how to control it."

Nola stepped closer to the captain, but Hill moved between them, pointing his pistol at her head as a warning. She stopped and stepped back.

"That blood you saw in the tavern," Nola continued, "do you want to know who it belonged to? I took a knife and plunged it into a guard's throat because he cornered me like that. So, do not test my limits and threaten me."

Lincoln's face twisted as he nodded. "I know. I don't know what came over me."

"Boots, it's okay," Nola said as Boots tried to grip

Lincoln's arm to pull him away. "It's me I'm more concerned about. I'll see myself below deck."

Hill lowered the pistol as Nola walked between him and Ardley.

Before she descended the steps, she watched Lincoln run his hand through his hair restlessly. His eyes displayed a sort of grief and deep guilt before she turned on her heel and headed below deck.

Chapter 21

"Captain, may I come in?" Mazie's voice called from outside the captain's quarters, placing her ear against the door to listen in for any noise. She knew he was awake as the bed lamp shone brightly from beneath the crack.

Mazie waited in silence.

She thumped lightly against the wall, hoping he would grow tired of the annoying noise and let her in.

"Go away," he finally said dryly. His tired voice was muffled through the door.

Mazie had witnessed, on more than one occasion, the captain losing his temper. But never had she seen him feel such remorse for him to hide in a room, wanting to be alone.

The Lincoln she knew would drown his sorrows in a bottle of rum while going about his duties as their captain. Because that was something he was good at—letting it go.

She suddenly heard movement from inside the door, then Lincoln pulled it open and stepped back, allowing her to enter.

"You aren't going to leave me be, are you?" he asked, stepping to the side as she walked by him.

"You would not have picked me as your first mate if I didn't make you natter out those feelings of yours, would you?" She tossed a hand up. "Bah! You need me to ask you what is wrong because everyone else up there is mad at you right now. You provoked a fucking siren, Captain!"

Lincoln's lip twitched, but aside from the involuntary reaction, he did not respond. He only leaned back against the wall with his arms folded across his chest. His eyes were flushed, his cheeks a peachy hue under his scruff to match the change on his face.

Mazie was always cautious around her captain when he felt troubled. She knew he would not dare lay a finger on her. However, his behavior from earlier was indeed scary and very unusual. She figured he would have sobered up enough to talk rationally.

"I only came here to check if you wanted to talk about it, but clearly, you are not ready to—"

"Is Nola okay?" Lincoln asked, sounding almost like he was out of breath.

Mazie placed her hand on her hip. "I cannot speak for the siren," she started. "But my guess is she is not. Her face is still buried in my pillow. Nola can stay in my room for as long as she wants. Hell, I know she doesn't want to be near you!"

Lincoln ran his strong hand through his hair. "Fuck!" he shouted, stepping towards the door.

Mazie rushed to block him from leaving his room. "Easy, Captain. You're a man and have no clue how a woman works, but I'll say this once. Give her the damn space she needs. She will come to you when she is ready."

His breath was heavy. "Raven," he started, using her pirate name. "I'm not going to hurt her." His voice was soft but troubled. "I don't know what happened back there. She—"

Lincoln pressed his lips together, his nostrils flaring.

"Shit. I need to tell you something."

Mazie relaxed her shoulders and stepped back. "Have at it, Captain," she said.

Lincoln had always been forthright with his crew, but she knew everyone held secrets and they had a right to them.

"That other siren who came upon our ship, Pearl," he started, reluctance in his tone. "She, uh, told me some unsettling news. I took my shock and horror to her words and unleashed those feelings upon Nola. I was drunk and reckless, and for that, I'll never forgive myself!"

"You're not going to start weeping, are you?"

He shot her a cold sneer. "This is serious, Mazie."

"Blimey! Quit beating around the damn bush and tell me then." Her expression hardened. "Is it because she's a siren?"

Lincoln swallowed, shaking his head. "No. None of that matters, Mazie. I do not care that she is not human. Shit. I don't even care that she lied about it."

"Because you care for her?" she asked.

He nodded. "Deeply," he confessed. "But that isn't the point."

Lincoln ran his fingers nervously through his hair, his

mouth forming a straight line. "Prince Elijah has set to capture Nola. He's on one of the king's ships, heading our way, and he will not stop until he has her. For what reasons, I do not know. He would not go out of his way for only a thief. That's for certain."

A side smirk reached Mazie's perfect mouth. "Let the pansy come. We will fight the bastard."

Lincoln looked heavenward. "It's not that simple. We could only wish—"

"Sure, it is," she said sternly. "It's always that simple."

He shook his head.

"I never left my home by my own choice, Mazie," he said, watching her forehead crease. "Zemira was my home," he confessed, watching her dark eyes widen. "Elijah is my brother. And King Matthias is my father."

Her eyes grew even wider.

Oh shit! Mazie thought as her jaw went slack before she could utter her next words. "No. Bloody. Way."

Chapter 22

Lincoln buried his face in his hands as embarrassment flooded his veins.

Nola was still asleep, so she would not yet learn it was his own brother who was after her. Sharing his true identity with her would be entirely different than it was with his hearties.

Mazie had called the crew to gather, and they all stood in Lincoln's room, waiting for him to explain himself. Beads of sweat trickled down his neck as a nervous twitch tugged at his chest.

Lincoln looked up slowly.

"Will you stop looking at me like that," he said to his mates, who stared at him with an unblinking gaze.

Mazie ran her hand over her face. "So," she started, "let us get this sorted. You're Prince Tristan?"

"No!" he shot back. "I mean, yes! I was. My father tried to have his men kill me and throw my body into the ocean. I miraculously survived and washed up on the Eastland Forest's shore."

Lincoln saw Kitten's lips part in shock. The first time the

crew docked on that land, he acted as if the Fae kingdom was as foreign to him as it was to them. It was a secret he swore to keep until he gave his last breath.

"The Fae people healed me with their water," Lincoln continued, "but after a few months, I had to leave. They could not care for a human—a young lad for that matter—nor did they want to. I boarded one of their ships and sailed with them until they found a pirate ship—Wentworth's—and bargained with them. They promised to share some of their magical water with the crew if they took me in. Wentworth always had desired what belonged to the Fae, so he gladly accepted."

Mazie and Kitten exchanged a look while he told his story.

Lincoln smiled. "That, and he needed an extra hand on deck. I became a pirate that very day."

His eyes drifted from the crew as if lost in thought.

"Anything at the time was better than being my father's son."

Lincoln omitted the notion that he always thought it was the merfolk who saved him. Or perhaps it was just a miracle he did not drown that night. Wentworth was a cruel captain, but he gave young Lincoln a second chance at life without being forced to return to his father. Wentworth was an ally to the king. However, he never exposed Lincoln's identity and for that, he was grateful.

Boots stepped forward, his head slightly tilted low.

"Should we start callin' you—?" he started.

"Don't you dare call me Prince," Lincoln said.

"You're not!" Mazie said. She flared her nostrils as if the

title Prince sent an unwelcomed, bitter taste to her mouth. "Like you said, that isn't you anymore. You're a fucking pirate, and though you've lied to us, you son of a bitch, you're still my captain."

The door creaked behind them.

"Lincoln?"

The crew turned to Nola standing in the doorway.

Lincoln's stomach lurched, but he quickly rose to his feet. Nola's hands trembled; her eyes were swollen as if she had been crying all night. However, she stood straight and managed to give them all a small smile.

"Let's go, hearties," Mazie said, signaling for the crew to head back above deck.

Lincoln swallowed the nervous dryness in his throat before moving from the bed and sauntering towards her. There was a gleam in her eyes that settled on his, causing his stomach to flutter wildly.

"I know that wasn't you back there," she started, her smile fading. "I'm sorry for what I did as well," she continued. "It felt like I had no control. As if my will power to shut it off was—" She rubbed her arms nervously. "I should have never—"

"Nola," he sighed, watching her shoulders sag; shame flushed his own cheeks. "Don't apologize for something you had no control over." His eyes narrowed as he searched her face. "It is I who should be apologizing."

Lincoln reached his hand up, placing his palm softly against the curve of her neck. Nola nibbled at her bottom lip, trying to look away, but he lightly gripped her jaw and stepped closer. "You did what was natural for you." The corners of his mouth turned up as he whispered the words, "Oh, beautiful siren." His voice came out like a purr as he caressed her neck.

The burning shame of guilt sent a blush flowing down his face.

"I—" Lincoln closed his eyes slowly because looking at Nola's eyes stopped the words from coming out of his mouth. "I have something I must now confess."

For that following hour, Lincoln told Nola his story.

He was born in a palace as Prince Tristan of Zemira. His mother, Queen Serena, brave and valiant, sought to save their kingdom by working with the Fae. The day he turned eight, his mother shared her plan with him. She wanted to rescue her children from the king and set sail to the Eastland Forest to live among the Fae. But to gain their trust, she wrote a letter, warning them that the king was coming for them. And the young boy was to deliver it to a vessel sailing East. The plan failed and his mother was taken away. She regretted it until the moment she died to Whale's Tongue, that she had involved her own child—dooming his future.

"Your mom was a brave woman, Lincoln!" Nola said. He placed his hand on hers as faint tears formed at the corner of his eyes.

"The darkest hours came next!" he continued, "I looked into the guard's eyes with pleading desperation. I was terrified! No child should walk the plank! I just stared at the darkness of the Portland Sea. Only a spark of regret flashed over Mason's eyes as he plunged his sword into my stomach and slammed his heel against my knees to push me off and into the waters." Lincoln's face blanched at the memory.

He remembered vividly the pain growing in his gut as the crimson-stained waters carried his little body away. The young prince blacked out as the frigid water enveloped his body. Hours later, his eyes opened to bright, sunset-colored leaves falling gently to the ground. A fairy held his shoulders down against a soft linen sheet. Another Fae girl laced her fingers over the wound, while a third Fae poured a warm crystalline liquid across his bleeding cut. It then began to heal before his eyes.

"There. That is my story; magic healed a dying prince, and a pirate was born."

Nola felt better that night after Lincoln shared his own secret. She grinned as she watched his bare chest rise and fall from her cot.

Pirate or prince, Lincoln or Tristan, you are the same to me, she said in her thoughts.

The story of how Prince Tristan died was somewhat different throughout the kingdom. Some rumors claimed he had fled to the sea and was killed by a vicious storm that had hit that night. But that was all it was; the kingdom held a funeral, and the Zemirans lost a prince.

The unsettling news about it all was that Prince Elijah was coming for her. Nola assumed those bells were for her back at Brecken Port, but she did find it strangely odd and ridiculous he would go through all that trouble over merely a sea creature. But then again, she had killed one of the royal guards.

But traveling for seven days over a guard? Nola questioned.

One thing was sure: nothing had changed about her mission. She would sail to the Eastland Forest and demand war against the king who had destroyed her land. Whether that king was the father of the man she was falling in love with or not.

Nola climbed out of bed and wandered over to the bookcase across the room, scanning over the books lining the shelves.

"Could this be . . . a map?" she whispered to herself, eyeing a bronze-colored paper stuffed in the corner.

Nola gripped the tattered map and unfolded it slowly and carefully, trying not to rip the sheet.

But before she laid it flat, she heard Lincoln wake and say from his bed, "Careful, that's one of my most prized possessions." He smirked as he walked to her. "Well, aside from that pistol you stole from me."

Nola's cheeks flushed with embarrassment. After their long conversation earlier that night, the mere sight of him caused a timid feeling in the pit of her stomach. She fiddled with the bottom of her shirt and stepped back. Their talk, though slightly awkward, had given Nola a fresh start. The honesty—the closeness—and realization that the two had pretended to be something they were not. Despite it all, neither of them cared about what that truth was. They no longer had to hide from each other.

Lincoln took the map gingerly between his fingers and moved towards his bed, lying flat on his back.

"Buried treasure?" Nola asked. "Such a pirate thing to have in your possession." She smiled sweetly.

He chuckled and looked up. "Something like that."

Nola hesitated before approaching him. Once they locked eyes, he held out his hand. "Join me, please."

"Wait, Lincoln, I need to say something first."

While still standing next to his bed, she sucked in a breath.

Nola continued, "I need you to understand why I must go to war with your father." She nervously licked her lips and lulled her voice into a gentle whisper. "He is destroying everything that made Zemira beautiful before I was born. He is killing innocent people—children. I must stop him. I know he's your father, but—"

"Nola, it's okay! No explanation needed; I get it," Lincoln said. "He is as dead to me as I am to him." He paused a beat and then placed his hand on her fingers lightly, rubbing the top of her hand. "Nothing has changed. We will still fight with you."

Nola did not expect that kind of reaction, but she was grateful he recognized the king for what he was—a monster.

Lincoln gripped tighter at her hand and pulled her onto the bed.

Then he placed his hand to the side of her head and caressed a long purple strand that fell right above her breasts.

"Still," he said, "we first have to convince the Fae queen that war is the only way to defeat him."

Nola nodded.

It was true the Fae queen had been sending her spies—but it had been for their own protection. She had never attacked a single human in the two decades since the conflict with Matthias began. Starting a war meant losing some of her people, and Nola was not sure she would be willing to do that. Despite the spy slaughter, the Fae finally lived peacefully in the Eastland Forest, and the Zemirans had given no reason for them to help.

Nola thought hard about putting the Fae at risk, but what other choice did she have? There was no one else. And they had every reason to despise the King of Zemira, as much as she did. Matthias had banished them and killed the Fae king. There was no retaliation or retribution for what the king did. The Fae had surrendered.

Nola watched Lincoln clutch the map between his fingers.

"And what about that?" she asked, signaling to the map. "Did you ever find your hidden treasure?"

Lincoln shook his head.

"Nay," he replied. "But it was all I could think about a few years back." A smile adorned his charming face. "Monsters live on that island. We barely made it out alive that time."

She smirked, despite his mention of monsters. "You stole the map from Wentworth with no intention of ever going back?"

"Aye. I did not want the idiot to have it. Wentworth was too stubborn of a man to let it go. He would risk the life of anyone on his ship, over and over until he got whatever treasure it hides."

"How did you take the map from him?" Nola asked.

His brows bounced up. "It's a long story, but the Fae queen wanted the treasure this map led to but wasn't willing to risk her own people to get it. So, she sent pirates to do her bidding. The cave, where the treasure is supposed to be hidden, is filled with wealth beyond what any pirate could imagine. If we retrieved her treasure—" he pointed to a bright red X near a cave, "—then we could have anything else we eyed inside what she called everlasting fortunes."

Nola could only imagine the adventures a pirate encountered. The stories of stony-hearted freebooters exploring islands for treasure were told quite often in her land. It all seemed so exciting to her.

A treasure, she said in her mind.

That is all she would need to help her mother and father to never go hungry again.

"I am not a prince anymore, Nola. I went from a scared little boy who hated his father to a pirate whose life belonged to the sea. The idea of a hidden treasure and the freedom I've had out here are things I would've never experienced behind palace walls." He laid his hand on her cheek. "Every plan I have had since I took this map never came to fruition. However, I now have a glimmer of hope."

She smiled. "Except soon, I'm leading us into a war."

"As should you, Nola."

She shrugged. "Maybe," she said, then bit her lip. "Can I ask you one more thing?"

"You can ask me anything, my love," he said, running his finger along the lines of her palm.

My love, she said the words in her mind. *If only he knew how that makes me feel.*

"Sybil," she started, "will you tell me about her?"

Nola instantly regretted the question. She had asked Lincoln to share a vulnerable part of his life, to talk about someone who destroyed his heart, but when a small smile pulled at the corner of his lips, her shoulders relaxed.

"When I left Wentworth's crew, I went seeking for a ship of my own," he started. "The Sybil Curse was a trading vessel at the time, and in bad shape too, but I wanted her all the same. She was called The Cauvery at first and I kept that name after I stole her. Mazie helped me fix her up and set sail. Four years later, I met Sybil."

"A siren," Nola stated.

He smiled and nodded.

"Sybil was the first siren I ever encountered. I was barely in my twenties. At the time, it was only Mazie, Kitten, and Boots on the ship. I heard a female voice out into the sea, and it was the most beautiful song I had ever heard. It echoed in the distant waters. My tired eyes gave in to her temptation, and I veered my ship towards the sound.

"She came up to the edge of the ship, and as I got close, she pulled me into the ocean with her. I don't even want to know what she was going to do to me, but before I lost consciousness, she pulled me back up to the surface and returned me to my ship."

Nola cocked her head. "She returned you?"

"Aye," Lincoln said with a smile, describing the memory. "The crew was passed out from her siren song while Sybil frantically blew air into my lungs while still contemplating on whether she should be helping me at all."

Lincoln paused for a second or two as he caressed Nola's fingers. Then he continued.

"I looked back to the stunningly beautiful, blue-eyed temptress who rested her gaze on me." His smile faded. "We had stared at each other for what felt like hours. At that moment, I thought it was love at first sight. Looking back now, I wonder if it was. After one year together, she vanished. I fell into deep despair. It felt like a curse—desperately struggling to pull myself up."

"The Sybil Curse," Nola said flatly. "What a fitting name."

He smirked. "Quite fitting."

Lincoln's eyes looked downcast. Nola wondered what he was thinking at that moment but stayed silent, allowing him to get lost in the memory.

Nola rested her fingers over his hand but did not squeeze. "I'm sorry about Sybil," she said, "and I'm sorry you never found that treasure."

He chuckled. "Oh, the stories of that island would give you nightmares, my love."

A look of curiosity crossed over her face. "Oh, do tell."

"There are deadly creatures who reside there," he started, watching her lips part. "And Wentworth knew it before we arrived. His idea of being a pirate was bent on war and unprovoked violence. Wealth was all he cared about. Not me, nor the crew." He turned until he faced her. "My former captain was the kind of pirate who sullied the reputation pirates once had. He was a traitor, even to his own kind. I hoped to never become that, but I have become somehow lost." He inched closer, placing his hand over her cheek. "However, that hope came back when I found you."

Oh, that touch again, she hummed in her mind.

"I feel the same way," she said. "When Matthias started killing spies, my adoptive father found me floating in the sea and took me to Baylin. I was raised by incredible parents but at the same time, I had to hide the fact that I was not human. As much as I understood and feared that life, you cannot help but embrace it when you feel the magic inside you. I craved it."

"Nola," he hummed, "you do not have to hide. Not anymore." Emerald flecks shone in the depths of his eyes.

"Lincoln." Her soft murmur was drowned by the sound of loud bellows above deck.

Slowly, the crew's shouts and laughter died away. Silence fell, broken only by the creak of the ship and the lapping of the water. Lincoln's breath rasped in his chest. Nola fought the urge to lean into him, to feel the length of his body against hers.

Nola wanted to say more; she wanted to tell him the truth. She was falling in love with him and she would love him even in his darkest hours. But that intense need to confess that love to the man before her was quickly smothered by the weight of self-doubt, and she did not know how to rid herself of it. So, she said nothing.

Nola peeped at the porthole, breaking the locked gaze they had on each other. Pink wisps were breaking through the midnight blue of the skyline.

"It is nearly daybreak." She sighed, pulling up a small smile to mask the little quivers in her voice.

Nola straightened up onto her feet, sensing a shake in her knees, one that had become all too familiar around him lately.

"Should we join the crew for breakfast?" she asked, about to spin away, when five taut fingers wrapped around her wrist.

"Nay," he said. His husky voice was low and urgent.

She glanced down at his hand. It had a sense of possessiveness around it. Expectedly, the rippling in her belly fluttered higher. "Lincoln, I—"

"Stay here, with me." It was not a request. He brushed his rough fingertips over her wrist. Slowly, the distance between them narrowed as he reeled her towards him, eyeing her as if she were the most beautiful creature he had ever seen. And she let him, without struggle, until he had her imprisoned in his hold.

Nola's breath hitched.

I don't think we'll be joining the crew this morning.

Chapter 23

Lincoln's strong arms wrapped around her waist, pulling her hard against his body. Nola watched the fire in his eyes and a pleasant warmth went soaring through her chest. His gaze hovered over her lips.

A moment passed, where nothing but the sounds of their not-so-steady breaths collided.

Cupping her cheek, Lincoln lowered his mouth to hers. The kiss was untamed but not fierce; the urgency burned inside her chest.

"Lincoln," she hummed as his hands dipped to her waist, his weight pinning her back to the wall in a gratifying trap, sending surges of warmth down her spine.

Using his tongue, he coaxed Nola's lips to open for him. She submitted without hesitation. His hands roamed up from her waist, tracing the curves of her hips. She could feel his arousal as he kept her pinned against the wall. Swept by a whirl of conflicting sensations, especially those of a siren where everything was heightened, she sucked in an exasperated breath to calm her body.

"Lincoln, I—" Nola lost her words again as he tightened

his hold around her. A quiet groan left his throat as he opened the space between them.

Lincoln's hand returned to her cheek. "My darling, you have taught me how to love someone more than myself," he said as the edge of his thumb brushed along her chin. "Something greater than the sea."

Nola's heart pounded so hard, she had to clutch her chest to get her bearings. His eyes settled on her while she tried to string her thoughts into words. Then, Nola reached up, taking his rough face between her hands, running her fingers along his tiny scar. At her gentle touch, he leaned in again; that time, he did not linger on her lips.

Lincoln's mouth dipped, making its way to the arches of her neckline. Every inch of her neck he kissed passionately, awakening a fresh sensation in her. Nola shuddered with each soft kiss against her skin; she had barely come to grips with his touch when his palm reached up to stroke her breasts.

"Please . . . don't stop," Nola breathed into Lincoln's ear, but her moans and words were incoherent. Her body was being thrown into a storm of pleasure. Her hands eagerly reached under his shirt, craving the smooth touch of his body. Lincoln reared back an inch, untied the knots of his shirt, and pulled it over his head, tossing it to the side. Nola gaped at the rigid muscles running up his body. Shyly, she brushed the dip of his chest with the tip of her trembling fingers.

Nola could not help but stare before she tucked into him, seeking his warm touch. Lincoln held her gently as her lips caressed his chest. She froze when he began to undo her bodice. Lincoln pulled back.

"What is it, my love?" he asked in a gentle whisper. He tucked a silver lock of hair behind her ears. "I won't do anything you don't want me to."

Nola took a deep breath before nodding into the crook of his neck.

"I want you, Lincoln. I want all of you."

Lincoln swiftly unlaced her bodice and cast it aside. He stepped back and let out a slow exhale, staring at her figure.

Then, he reached out, threading his hand into her hair, tugging back her head gently to kiss her collarbone. His mouth trailed down to her chest, unleashing on her tender breasts. Nola shivered, intertwining her fingers into his unruly hair, pressing herself against him.

Just as a quivering wave took her to the peak, Lincoln lowered himself on his knees, his eyes leveling with her navel. A flash of awareness yanked Nola back into her body.

"Wait," she said as her hands darted to cover her birthmark.

A smile skewed his lips, and he pulled her hand away tenderly from the mark. "It's okay, Nola. I want to see it."

She lowered her hands reluctantly, allowing him to see her birthmark—the small shark eye symbol over her slender stomach.

With the most delicate movement, he leaned in and brushed his lips slowly across the mark, kissing it gingerly.

Nola felt her knees give way under a new tide of emotions. Lincoln hastily straightened, catching her hips to steady her. They stood there for a moment—a moment that seemed to stretch for hours. Then, their quickening breaths and their heated bodies asked for more than a simple touch.

Lincoln whispered by her ear. "You took hold of my heart the moment you entered that tavern and stole my pistol."

She bit her lip.

"Maybe I was not the only one who took something that day," she said.

His mouth crashed against hers, his large hand encircling her nape in a firm, taut grip. The sheer pleasure from his powerful, possessive grip ignited the heat inside her.

Their unbridled bodies would not let go as Lincoln lifted Nola up and held her into the wall once more. That time, her breasts rubbed against his bare chest and her legs linked around his waist. It was the most explosive sensation Nola had ever experienced.

Her mind shouted at her with every spark of pleasure.

When Lincoln took a firmer grip and swung her away, she let out a squeal. He hoisted her up into his arms and proceeded across his quarters, kicking things out of his path until they reached the bed. Lincoln laid her down smoothly and immediately began tugging impatiently at the rest of her clothes' ties, hurling them across the room.

He sucked in a breath, his eyes glinting with want as he devoured her naked form. A pink blush raised to her cheeks. Nola was tempted to draw the silk sheet over her body, but she swaddled herself with his torso instead. She molded into him, rejoicing in the closeness of his touch. He untangled himself from her for a moment and pinned her hands above her.

"Finally." He toyed with her, blowing away a few strands of her hair that were floating over her lips.

"What?" she asked.

"This is how I imagined you ever since we met." His tone dropped. "On my bed, in my quarters, breathless." He drew in, lips teasing hers with tiny kisses under her earlobes. "Naked." His brow rose. "And completely at my mercy."

A low giggle left Nola's lips but stopped short as mischief gleamed in his eyes. He quickly began unbuckling his belt.

Air hitched in her throat as he kicked free of his trousers and moved over her, his broad frame sweeping over hers. Lincoln's torrid breaths brushed her skin as he drew in closer, his erection pressing onto her thigh.

When Lincoln's hands started to move, though, stroking upwards along the inside of her legs, she stilled.

"Oh," she gasped. "Um—"

His movement paused. "Do you want me to stop?"

Nola's eyes twinkled. "No, just go slowly."

Lincoln gave her a cheeky smile as he continued running his fingers up her legs. She arched as his fingers trailed between her thighs.

"Oh my—!"

Her fingernails reached out and gripped hold of his hair, giving it a tight, aggressive squeeze. The feeling was quite exhilarating; she wanted it more than she had ever wanted anything in her entire life.

Lincoln's touch made Nola's head spin—unlike anything

she had ever felt. She moaned as she arched her back upward into a beautiful abyss of ecstasy.

Nola laid gasping, pleasure still wrapping around her like the gentle foam from a receding tide.

"Lincoln?" She watched him position himself over her, his arousal parting her thighs.

"Nola, I need you. Now."

She writhed beneath him in complete and utter surrender, then wrapped her legs around his waist, and their bodies became one. Nola winced, her hands coiling around him in a lustful grip.

Bathed in sweat, the world around them seemed to pause—there was nothing but pleasure and passion.

Lincoln deepened himself into her while she let out a quiet moan. Nola opened her eyes to see him over her, loving her like the sea desperately needing the moon.

Their bodies moved to the beat of a wave. Lincoln bent to hug her tight, placing his hand at the bottom of her spine. She wrapped her arms around his shoulders, allowing him to lift her slightly from the damp sheets, bringing her mouth closer to his ear.

Lincoln smirked as she let out a quiet moan again.

Lust and passion encircled her senses, making it hard for her to even think.

Please, don't ever let me go, Nola thought as he gripped the back of her knee to pull her in closer.

Then suddenly, the last of their barriers burst, and they scaled the peak of pleasures together. Nola cried out his name, her fingernails raking down his shoulder, leaving light marks against his skin.

Blissfully exhausted, they collapsed beside each other, catching up on their breaths. Nola laid against him; their legs entwined. Physically, she had never felt more nervous, more vulnerable. But in her heart, Nola had never felt safer or happier than she was at that moment.

She noticed a fresh scratch on Lincoln's shoulder, one she had left in the heat of the moment.

"I cut you," Nola whispered. "I'm so sorry."

He laughed, the vibration humming through her. "Fear not, beautiful siren. I have had worse."

"From enemies?"

"Aye."

She paused. "And from past lovers, too?"

He responded with nothing beyond a faint smile.

A bitterness coiled in her belly. "Oh."

"Is my beautiful siren jealous?" Lincoln drew himself up, resting his elbow against the mattress. His smile widened into a grin as he propped her slender body onto him. "None of those mattered to me. You do." His voice took on a serious tint, one it so seldom did. "Not until you, Nola. I have never felt for anyone what I feel for you."

In a beat, Nola's insides softened. She leaned in and kissed him.

"And I have never felt for anyone what I feel for you, Lincoln," she whispered as their lips parted.

The two lovers continued to exchange a few kisses as they rested on one pillow, their bodies molding into one. Around them, the ship rocked and creaked, but none of those noises muffled their heavy breaths. An old, dusty lantern swung on its hook, casting rolls of shadows and light across the captain's cabin. Overhead, they heard the clomping of a few boots and the distant sound of laughter.

"Do you think they heard us?" Nola asked, a grin pulling at her mouth.

"Of course they did." He ruffled her hair. ". . . With you crying my name out louder than a wildcat."

Nola scrunched up her nose teasingly.

Lincoln rested his head beside Nola's, his breath fanning her cheek. "You are everything to me."

Nola sighed. "And you to me."

His eyes closed. "I am but a ruthless pirate, Nola," he reminded her.

She interlaced her fingers within his until they were a tight knot. "But you are *my* ruthless pirate."

"And you are my siren."

She giggled. "What a pair we make."

Eventually, silence blanketed the cabin when they grew too tired.

The couple fell asleep in one another's arms, while outside, the sea lapped against the ship and the sun continued to shine.

Chapter 24

A faint moan left Nola's lips in her sleep. The heat of her breath tickled over Lincoln's muscular, bare chest. As he leaned in to draw in her scent, his ears honed in on the explosive sound of pattered footsteps scurrying across the deck.

Lincoln sat bolt upright, instinctively gripping Nola's arm to wake her.

"Don't move," he barked in a subtle yet firm tone as her eyes sprang open. His mouth formed a hard line as he listened again intently. "No matter what you hear, do not leave this room."

Nola sat on the edge of the bed, still waking from her slumber. Lincoln's eyes stayed fixed on the door as if someone would come storming into the room at any given moment. He felt panic begin to rise, the aching stab of his fast-beating heart caught painfully in his throat.

He crawled out of the covers and rummaged through their clothes, which were scattered across the floor. Lincoln found his trousers and quickly put them on. Then, he peeked through the porthole.

"Blimey!" he whispered quietly to himself, then turned to Nola. "Pirates!"

"The not-so-friendly kind?" Her voice quivered when she spoke.

Lincoln nodded slowly, not wanting to terrify her. Still, she needed to know the grave danger unexpected visitors posed when sailing the seas.

"Most likely," he said, watching her stand up straight, pulling the sheet to her chest. "Please, Nola," he begged, "get under the bed and do not come out unless you hear my voice."

Nola squinted, looking towards the door.

"Nola!" his voice hardened that time, causing her to look up.

She put on the dress Kitten had given her and looked back over to him. "Is it someone you know?" she asked.

"I have to go see." Lincoln moved swiftly in her direction and grabbed her arm but loosened his grip. "But get under the bed, my love," he implored. "Please."

Nola glanced up to meet his eyes; she nodded, then turned swiftly to crawl under the bed.

Lincoln rubbed the back of his neck vigorously before he removed his coat from the hook and hurried upstairs. The approaching pirate ship crashed against the side of the Sybil Curse, causing the crew to grip the ledge to keep from falling overboard.

"Sorry, Captain," Boots said, "We were shittin' around in the cannon room. We didn't see them comin'."

"Hoist the black flag, Boots," Lincoln instructed. He

turned to the crew standing behind him. "Do not attack unless it is clear to be an ambush."

The Sybil Curse's crew stayed poised.

Ardley gave Lincoln a curt nod while his hand rested on the hilt. "We've got this, Captain."

A deafening sound of gunfire shot across the ship. Mazie muffled her ears as they all squatted down. Lincoln winced as he heard the agitating voice of his old captain calling out his name.

Fuck! Fuck! Fuck! It can't be him, he cursed in his mind as one of Wentworth's men tossed their grappling hook over to the Sybil Curse.

Lincoln looked over the railing towards the opposing ship's deck. He spotted the captain and shot the old bastard a scathing look.

"Damn you, Wentworth. What are you doing?!" Lincoln shouted, signaling for his crew to raise their weapons.

Wisps of smoke hovered near his old foe's lips as he tossed his pipe onto his deck. Wentworth always had appeared cordial at first. However, Lincoln knew the malice behind those eyes. The trust between the two buccaneers shattered the day they parted over ten years ago.

Lincoln glanced at his crew, watching Hill stagger on his feet with his hand over his right cheek. A bullet had grazed his skin, and though it did not imbed itself, it had fueled the captain with rage.

Wentworth was an evil son of a bitch, but he had never tried to kill them. Resources were too valuable to any pirate who sailed the Portland Sea. Most—if not all—crews knew of the Sybil Curse and the consequences for those who dared cross them.

"Sorry, mate, this lad 'ere is new to our ship. He can't even 'andle 'is own pistol," Wentworth said, turning to a young boy, shaking in his boots. A taller lad tossed a pistol over to Wentworth, who caught it mid-air. The clearly terrified boy stepped back as the old captain tipped his hat, then shot at the boy, grazing his cheek to match Hill's.

Lincoln exhaled, pressing his lips together to hold his tongue. It was none of his business how Wentworth punished his crew.

The boy squealed, backed up another foot, and tripped over his own feet. He was shaking and shielded his bleeding, boyish face as Wentworth slowly approached him, crouching down to meet his terror-stricken eyes. He took the pistol and pointed it at the boy's chin, using it to lift his face.

"Ye fuck up like tha' again, and next time I'll aim between yer eyes," Wentworth muttered. His broad nostrils flared.

Lincoln had no clue what Wentworth's intentions were, but with Nola hidden below deck, he did not want them there. His plan was to get the other crew inebriated enough to lose interest and leave.

"Can we get you and your crew a bit of rum?" Lincoln asked casually with a fake smile across his lips. "We've got plenty of it."

An uneasy feeling hit Lincoln in the pit of his stomach —their presence made him feel on edge. Wentworth was a haughty lecher. He would not hesitate to take a woman as beautiful as Nola for his own enjoyment.

"Nay," Wentworth said, "we were just visitin' Zemira and took plenty for our voyage. We were there shortly after ye left, Lincoln. We missed each other." A slow grin formed on Wentworth's lips, making the wrinkles under his eyes more pronounced, showing off his age, and he had aged quite a lot the last decade. "You was busy while ye were there, weren't ye?" he asked in quite an aggressive manner.

Lincoln faltered as he observed the way Wentworth moved from his own ship to Lincoln's. It was not hostile, but he knew the man could not be trusted. It had been years since the two sailed the seas together, and one thing was certain: the old man standing before him held no loyalty towards him anymore.

"We heard a bit of commotion while we were there," Lincoln replied, "however, we fled as soon as we heard the bell chime."

Wentworth chuckled to himself and looked over Lincoln's shoulder. Lincoln had not realized he was gripping his fist so tightly he was drawing his own blood in his palms.

"Did ye now? That's interestin'." Wentworth cleared his throat. "Ye have always been a curious man, Lincoln. Ever since ye were a li'l lad and I took ye in. Ambitious. Determined. Ye proved to me ye could be a captain of yer own ship someday. Now, look at ye," he mocked, then cocked his head. "Wit' the bells chimin', ye didn't have the slightest curiosity as to what all tha' ruckus was 'bout, eh?"

"None of my business," Lincoln said too quickly, then

turned to Boots, who went for his sword but only hovered his hand on the hilt.

Hill, no longer able to stand on his two feet, tottered back, slammed his shoulders against the mast, and sank to the damp floor. He wiped some of the blood oozing from his wound.

Wentworth's lips curved into a crooked smile—a grin Lincoln was familiar with, which told him they were ready for an attack.

"How do you want to do this, Wentworth?" Lincoln glanced at the young boy, still shaking, covering his cheek. "Perhaps your men would be more suitable to sailing with us than being afraid of their own captain. Lead—not dictate, right? Isn't that what you taught me?"

Wentworth clicked his tongue between his slightly crusty lips.

"I ain't forcin' them to be on me ship." His disapproving glare turned into an amused smirk. "They're welcome to leave the crew at any time, but we aren't departin' until I 'ave the siren. I've been offered quite a bounty for 'er." The grin on his lips reached his eyes as he looked at the others standing behind Lincoln. "Do they know yer secret?" he rattled on. "That yer not a *real* pirate."

Mazie sprinted forward with her pistol gripped tightly in her hand. Lincoln turned swiftly, stepping in front of her, and wrapped his arms around her shoulders in a tight hug.

"Don't, Mazie. He's trying to provoke us to start a fight. He is not worth it."

Wentworth was clear as to why he was there—they would have to fight to save Nola's life or die trying.

Lincoln quickly drew his sword, and without a second thought, he swung it at Wentworth, who shifted his shoulder to the right. The tip of Lincoln's blade reached the top of his shoulder, grazing his coat enough to slice through it, but unfortunately not his skin.

Wentworth drew his own sword, the blade nicking Lincoln's thigh. His left hand flew to his new wound, and despite the pain, he continued swinging his weapon.

As Lincoln wielded the sword above his head, Ardley kicked Wentworth forcefully against his backside, sending Wentworth hurling forward. Once he was flat on his back, the rest of Wentworth's crew jumped aboard the Sybil Curse.

The racket above echoed through the walls. But Nola's ears narrowed in only on the footsteps stomping quickly down into the captain's quarters. Stopping at the entryway.

Nola felt a lump in her throat as she swallowed quietly as beads of sweat dribbled down her forehead.

As much as her heightened senses could help at that moment, she was too afraid to focus. Her ears stopped with the silence. Until a creak of the wooden floor was right next to her.

The hairs at the nape of her neck prickled.

"Come out, li'l siren," the intruder's eerie voice called out. "Can't keep me captain waitin'."

Nola muffled a high-pitched gasp with her hand—tears rolled down her cheeks and dripped to the floor. Her eyes changed suddenly as the room got a lot darker. She squinted, trying to make sense of the space around her and where the intruder was.

She sucked her lips inside her mouth and held her breath as a pair of large boots cast a shadow by the bedside. Whoever the pirate was, he annoyingly whistled to his own tune.

"Boo!" the man barked, lowering his head under the mattress, extending his dirty fingers out to Nola and seizing her arm.

She wiggled back, her feet pressing against the wall. He tugged and pulled her wrists, yanking her from under the bed with his grimy, elongated fingers, and wrapped his bony arms around her waist. The tall pirate whirled her around, flashing a self-satisfied expression across his face. She recoiled, and the pungent smell from his clothes drifted under her nostrils.

He smiled, and she immediately eyed his crooked grin revealing more missing teeth than Nola could count. A patch covered his left eye, and a thick pink scar stretched over his right eyebrow, causing the side of his face to droop. As he let out a laugh, his breath made her gag. Nola tried to turn away, but he gripped her jaw, pulling her gaze back to him.

"Well, aren't ye pretty!" The pirate lowered his gaze down her body. "Me captain is goin' to have fun wit' ye," he said, running his tongue along what was left of his yellow-tinted teeth.

"Oh, you reek of trash!" she ranted. Insulting the man was a bit mindless. Saying nothing was better. However,

Nola thought if she was going to die, she might as well give it everything she got.

The pirate chuckled and gripped her jaw harder, and she watched his veins bulge from his neck.

"Ye know? I reckon I've changed me mind. Looks like ye 'n I will be havin' a party afore I hand ye o'er."

The man's hand flew to the front of her neck while he wiggled his fingers around his crotch.

Nola scrunched up her nose before she spat in his face.

Right after he placed his hand against his nose to wipe it off, his eyes bulged, and blood spewed from his mouth. Nola quickly backed up as his grip released. She looked down. Her then-white eyes went wide. A knife stuck out from his back—blood began coloring his dirty shirt.

Nola quickly pulled her hands back to her mouth to stifle a scream. The pirate fell to his knees, drowning in his own blood. Mazie stood behind him, bloodied knife in one hand, and lifted a finger to her lips.

"Shh," she said quietly, pointing to the stairs, and signed with her head to follow.

Mazie grabbed Nola's hand, and they ran up to the deck, creeping around the corner to the back.

"We'll take the rower boat, but we need to—"

Heavy footsteps stomped towards the women. Mazie turned and held out her knife.

"Grab the sword in my sheath," she said quickly. "Do it. Do it. Do it!"

Before Nola could grip the hilt, a pair of strong arms wrapped around her waist and hoisted her in the air, pulling her away while Mazie was fending off her attacker.

Nola felt the sharp, cool metal of a cutlass against her throat as they reached the center of the deck.

The moments that followed seem to slow as the muscular freebooter dragged her closer to where the intruders stood.

Nola was entirely benumbed to everything happening around her; she was beyond terrified. Not because a pirate had her life in his hands, but because she realized what a damn fool she was.

This is over before it even started, Nola thought. *How could I ever convince the Fae queen to fight with us to protect Zemira, and the magical creatures in their world, when I cannot even defend myself?*

Nola felt anything but gallant or courageous. She felt weak, defenseless, and even embarrassed.

The pirate holding her whistled. Lincoln came to a screeching halt the moment he saw Nola trapped within the pirate's arms. The other buccaneers pulled their weapons high to each of Lincoln's crew.

Nola opened her mouth to call for Lincoln but was met with a piece of rolled-up dirty cloth being stuffed inside her mouth. The man's fingers felt greasy against her cheeks as he tied a thick rope around her head and over her mouth to keep the cloth inside. Her scream was muffled—she could not sing to summon her powers.

Nola heard another pirate rush up the steps behind them, but she did not see his face.

"'Tis not down there, Captain. I ransacked each room."

Nola narrowed her eyes on their big-bellied captain, wondering what they were looking for.

"Aye." Their captain stroked his long beard. "We shall leave without it."

Nola lowered her brow; an unsettling feeling hit her while observing his intimidating appearance. The man looked to be in his late forties but was somewhat handsome for his age, aside from a few wrinkles under his eyes, a bright chestnut brown. His hair was as black as coal, wavy, and reached to the middle of his back. A bandana wrapped around the top of his head and tied off on the side, with a thin gold chain hanging to the end. His shirt was tucked tight into his trousers under a black vest.

The man locked eyes with Nola and flashed her a lopsided grin.

"Lincoln, perhaps we can duel another time, mate. She comes with us. Either that or I can slaughter yer entire crew," he said.

Lincoln glanced briefly at Nola, right as the old man held up his sword, inching closer to his throat.

"Get out of me way, lad, or I'll give the order for Russell to cut 'er clean through the chest."

Nola refused to blink as she eyed Lincoln. The handsome captain she cared for so dearly could not move. At that point, Lincoln's crew had surrendered their weapons to the floor. No one could do anything to save her.

Still holding his sword, Lincoln leapt at the other ship's captain but was met with a sword through the stomach.

A muffled scream left Nola's lips as a cold rage welled deep within her.

The enemies' captain snapped his fingers, signaling for the pirate to hold her in place. Her eyes grew wide as he placed his hand on her cheek—a miffed glare in his eyes. His hands felt like rough leather as he moved his grip down and held firmly to her wrist, yanking her body forward until she landed against his solid, broad chest.

"Hello, me li'l dove." His lips flattened to a grim line. "I'm Wentworth, by the way. Prince Elijah is expectin' you."

Chapter 25

The haunting image of Lincoln lying flat on his back with his hands covering the bloodied wound burned Nola's mind. Ardley was last seen tearing a piece of cloth from his shirt to stop the bleeding.

Please don't come for me, Lincoln. I'm not worth your life, she pleaded in her mind. *Stay on course to the Eastland Forest and survive.*

Nola flinched as Wentworth reached behind her head to remove the gag.

Once the pirate captain freed the knot and tossed the cloth and rope to the floor, a scowl grew on his sun-wrinkled face.

"I must warn ye," Wentworth said, "Yer siren call only works on weak-willed men." He smirked. "And that—I am not."

Nola placed a hand on her right cheek, rubbing where the rope had burned her skin. "I—"

The pirate held up a hand. "And I 'old no affection towards anyone, not even me crew. Slaughter 'em all, for all I care."

Dread crept up to the pit of Nola's stomach. She turned away from him, not wanting to look into his cruel eyes any longer. Instead, she scanned the deck and saw the rowdy crew of buccaneers scattered about the ship.

The vessel was quite different than the Sybil Curse—clean and lavish. An extra mast stood mid-ship; their flags were not frayed and tattered like Lincoln's. His crewmembers were all men—large and burly, not much unlike Wentworth himself. The one called Russell, who had held his cutlass to her throat, stood near the front of the ship with a bronze tobacco pipe between his lips—black smoke drifted around his head. A menacing expression flitted across his lips as he sneered at Nola. A pulse jarred in her throat.

One pirate she had not seen until then stood at the mast, lowering one of the finely made pieces of cloth to the ground, while another turned the helm to a hard left, shifting the ship west.

Wentworth huffed when Nola stood idle, her eyes still fixed on her surroundings—memorizing every part of the ship until it imprinted a permanent image in her mind.

"Hustle those damn legs of yers, siren." Wentworth yanked her by the elbow, but she put up a struggle, dragging her feet lazily against the deck. "I'll haul ye over me shoulder if I 'ave to," he warned. His voice took on a savage edge to it. "Move tha' pretty li'l ass of yers!"

Be the worst prisoner he has ever had, she told herself.

Nola tried to tug her arm away from his hold. "I will walk at my own pace, you filthy pirate!"

A quick flash of fury gleamed in her eyes, the iris

changing color in a deadly warning. She hoped he had seen it.

"So—" Nola's voice cracked before swallowing, "—you can take those disgusting hands off me." She attempted to pull away from his hold, but his grip tightened around her arm. Nola felt a tear slip from her eye, but she was too furious to wipe it away.

Wentworth threw his head back and chuckled before whipping her around to face the sea. He pushed his broad chest against her back, and his fingers dug painfully into her shoulders. Her heart thumped harder against her chest, nearly taking her breath away.

Nola glanced at the horizon. *I cannot go back to Zemira,* she said in her mind, nerves rippling low in her stomach.

The Sybil Curse was falling far behind them. Her breath quickened. It was the same feeling she had when she left her home.

When Nola glanced over her shoulder, Wentworth's eyebrows pulled into a sardonic glare, right before he slammed his forehead against hers. She felt a rush of blood tinge against her skin. Her hand flew to her forehead.

What the hell was that? Nola thought, rocking her head back and forth in utter disbelief. *Oh, you bastard. You are going to pay for that one.*

"Let tha' be a warnin'," he breathed into her neck. "I don't like feisty, li'l dove. What I desire is respect and absolute obedience. If I don't ge' it, I am not opposed to harmin' a lady."

Nola froze, contemplating how far he would go to hurt her.

Wentworth turned her fully to face him, flashing a jaunty smile.

She continued to rub her head while examining his every move. He appeared on edge as if she alone made him nervous.

Excellent.

Nola dropped her hand to her side. "What does Elijah want from me?" she asked.

He shrugged. "Not a bloody clue. Nor do I care."

When she gave him a scowl, Wentworth gripped her jaw and lifted her face up to meet his. Once their gazes locked, he loosened his grip on her chin but did not release her.

"Ye seem to be an invaluable piece of some grand scheme of 'is. That I know," he answered. "He 'as already set sail to meet us halfway in the middle of the sea. He 'as no plans to 'and ye over to the king."

Nola narrowed her eyes. *No, this is not about me being a siren or about killing that guard—it can't be.*

"Not that I care what lies in your near future," Nola said, "But the royal family holds no loyalty to anyone. The prince will kill you once you hand me over." She bit the inside of her cheek, trying so desperately not to cry. "And Lincoln—he'll come for me."

"Oh, I'm hopin' for that," he said arrogantly, "because we get paid a vast amount of gold to deliver Lincoln and his crew, on top of what 'e 'as promised me for ye." He chuckled to himself; a cynical smile played on his lips. "Let's think of ye as bait, shall we?"

Nola grappled again within his hold, but he gripped harder around her elbow.

"You have known Lincoln since he was a child," she spat. "How could you do this?"

She felt blood rush through her veins as he tossed her to the pirate who had held the sword to her throat. He reeked of smoke and a scent that reminded her of the dirty dumpster in Brecken Terrace she had passed in an alleyway.

Nola looked up into Wentworth's wicked eyes again.

The pirate tilted his head to the side, and a glint of sobriety flashed in his eyes. "Lincoln stopped being me comrade when he abandoned me ship. I gave that fool everythin' and—"

"So, this is about revenge?" Nola scolded. "That's pathetic!"

Wentworth snarled, commanding another pirate with a snap of his fingers. The entire crew went silent as the man pulled at her arm to follow.

"Put 'er in me quarters," Wentworth said. "I'm done with 'er blabberin' tongue."

His fingers gripped hers as she tried to wrench free.

I'm getting out of this, Nola told herself, *even if it means killing his entire crew with my bare hands.*

"Kitten, grab his legs," Mazie cried. "Help me!"

Lincoln's eyelids were heavy as he felt himself go in and out of consciousness. His feeble attempt to move was met with sharp stabs against his cold and clammy body.

Scads of fingers ran over his wound, and stabbing pain pulled at his stomach. He could not keep himself conscious enough to see how bad it was. Lincoln's heartbeat started slowing down, and as he opened his mouth to speak, a sensation of cool liquid ran down the side of his navel. He stopped.

Is that water? Lincoln thought. *Blood?*

It stung for a short moment before his eyes rolled back. Then blackness.

"Captain?" Kitten called. "Keep yer eyes open, will ye?"

Lincoln opened one eye slowly, then the other. His vision blurred, trying to make sense of the space surrounding him. His hand instinctively landed where it hurt the worst. It felt cool and sticky.

"Keep your hands off it, Captain. We had a bit left of honey from the market. Let it do the job," Ardley said, prying Lincoln's fingers from the wound.

He moaned as he felt another sharp stab.

"How bad is it?" Lincoln asked. He rubbed his eyes with the one clean hand and blinked again.

Ardley blew out a puff of air. "Do you want me to lie to you?"

"Great," Lincoln said breathlessly.

"You're alive, for now. You son of a bitch!" Mazie cried. "But I'll kill you for scaring me like that."

"Good to see you too, Mazie." He cleared his throat. "Sorry to disappoint, but I'm not going anywhere yet."

Ardley straightened his back as Lincoln spotted Hill passed out in the corner of the room.

"Ten sutures. Give it, uh . . . two weeks, maybe?" He redressed the wound with a clean piece of gauze and tape and stepped back slightly. "You're damn lucky."

Lincoln scanned the room. Assuming Boots was steering the ship, a sudden panic hit Lincoln in the chest.

"Nola!" He tried leaping off the table, but Boots and Kitten pressed their hands against his chest, pushing him back down. "Where is Nola!?"

Kitten took a hasty glance at Mazie, then locked eyes with Lincoln. "I'm sorry, Captain," she said, resting her hand on his shoulder. "Wentworth 'as taken 'er."

"No!" he bellowed, but a sharp, stabbing pain shot into his gut. "Fuck!"

"Stop moving, you fool," Mazie cried. "You're not healed yet, and if you keep moving, your stitches will rip straight off."

Lincoln's lips curled into a scowl before he saw Ardley move forward again.

"Mazie's right. You will have to lay down for the remaining days to the Eastland Forest; let us handle the ship. She is second in command, so she will lead us to where we need to go."

He turned back to his first mate. "Turn the ship around, Mazie," he ordered. "This bloody minute!"

She shook her head, avoiding his eyes. "Nay, Captain. We aren't going back there. Not without an army," Mazie explained, looking down at him. "It's too dangerous, and you know it. Maybe we were fools thinking we could lead this fight with her. We are going to get ourselves killed. All slaughtered by your father—"

Lincoln's expression hardened.

"The king and his evil spawn," she corrected. "This isn't our war to fight! Aye, I thought it was, but all it really is, is vengeance. I don't think she—sorry, we—are enough. We were wrong and should have minded our own business like we always do."

There was no longer a vestige of reasoning in Lincoln's eyes.

"No, Mazie," Lincoln said, "that is where you're mistaken. It is my brother who wants her. My father most likely sent him to do his bidding. For whatever reason, she is of value to them, and I need to find out why. I need to save her."

Lincoln closed his eyes tightly, and for the first time in a while, he felt a tug of emotions hit him at his core. He had not felt that kind of pain since he had lost Sybil. The only woman he had ever loved.

Sybil, he said her name in his mind.

The one woman who kept him looking out at sea all those years, hoping one day he would find her.

And when he had finally moved on, allowing his heart to heal, the sea had new plans for him. Rum, countless women, and booty—a life any pirate would dream of, but he never wanted for himself.

Until he found her. Nola.

That beautiful, kind siren had shown him there was hope after all. She made him *feel* again.

"We have to go after her. I will not lose her, too, Mazie," Lincoln said. The next words burned in his heart and would stay there forever. "Because I love her."

Chapter 26

Fear and confusion crippled Nola as she stood at the center of the captain's quarters.

Wentworth's hand searched for the bed lamp in the darkened room. When the space around her lightened up, she searched every wall for another exit, but there was none.

Nola peered into the eyes of her captor, who stood under the door frame with his arms crossed leisurely over his broad chest, blocking her only escape.

Leather-bound books lined the walls. One row of books was held up by a decorative atlas of the ten kingdoms of the world. Shades of bronze and silver decorated the shelves; coins, gold, gems, and ancient-looking compasses.

Nola was fascinated to see such valuable artifacts up close. She wanted to touch the smooth surfaces of such priceless possessions. Clearly, they had stolen everything in that room.

A small bed stood in the corner, with two large red pillows and silky black sheets. A beige blanket draped at the end of the bed, loosely covering a long bronze chain that dangled to the floor.

The sight of a chain and cuff made her stomach lurch.

Nola glanced up, right as Wentworth cocked his head to the side. A disconcerted sneer grew on his lips, sending a shiver down her spine.

"Now what?" she asked nervously. "Chain me to your bed with those shackles?"

Amusement glinted in his eyes. "I can't 'ave ye divin' into the sea, now, can I?"

Wentworth padded across the room and stopped in front of her.

She refused to step back. "I don't know how to swim, you buffoon, if that's what you are afraid of."

An unreadable expression flitted across his face. "I'm not afraid of anythin'." His voice was low and menacing.

"No, you are, aren't you?" she tested. "If you don't deliver me to the prince, you're afraid he will kill you."

A slight flare of his nostrils gave him away.

Nola frowned. "You don't have to do this, you know?" she said with pleading desperation. "Please, Wentworth. You can return me to the Sybil Curse, and you can sail far from this place." She bit the bottom of her lip. "Or you can help me fight against the king."

He raised a brow and let out a snort. "Fight against the king? Ye are madder than I expected."

Wentworth glared at Nola for a long moment before reaching out. She flinched as he traced her neckline with the tip of his wrinkly fingers. Then he pulled up her sleeves and ran his touch along her wrists.

"What are you doing?" she asked. "Why are you touching me?"

"Where is it, Nola?" he asked calmly.

She quirked an eyebrow at him. "What are you looking for?"

"Don't play coy, li'l siren," he said, stepping forward. "The ruby. Where is it?"

My ruby? Nola thought. *How does he know about my ruby?*

She shook her head. "I don't know of any ruby," she lied. "And if I had, why would I hand over such a precious gem?"

Memories of her time with Prince Elijah at the marketplace crossed her mind. The bracelet was under her sleeve—he could not have possibly seen it, and if he had, the prince was showered in wealth. Why would the prince care about a ruby the size of a fingernail?

"All hands on deck!" They heard a distant bellow from the crew above.

Nola looked up. "What's happening?" she asked as the ship rocked more than usual.

Wentworth smirked. "Welcome to the Portland Sea, siren; another storm is comin'." He pointed to the bed. "I want ye there," he ordered.

Nola did not move, so Wentworth took hold of the back of her neck, shoving her forward. She turned quickly, clawing at his face, but he slammed his fist against her jaw. Blood dripped slowly from her lips as every nerve in her body cried out in sheer pain.

You will pay for that one too, you bloody bastard!

The shock of the blow stunned her. Nola placed her

hand against her burning skin and cowered to him. She licked her lips, tasting the copper on her tongue.

"I'm going to kill you," she said under her breath.

Nola assumed he had not heard. That or he ignored her threat—a stupid threat at that. Provoking a merciless pirate alone made her a damn fool.

"Ye can fight all ye want," he continued, "but yer puttin' on that cuff."

She eyed the chain connected to the frame.

Nola scowled. "You are honestly going to chain me up like an animal as I sit on this hard floor?" she asked, aghast. "I cannot swim, and I have no weapons to defend myself."

The unnerving feeling hit her again. She had no protection. They could do whatever they wanted, and if her siren call would not work on Wentworth, her only hope to survive was nonexistent.

He huffed. "Prince Elijah mentioned ye were raised by humans, but that does not mean yer instincts won't take over the moment ye 'it that water. Have ye ever seen yer tail? Ye surely look nothin' like the sirens I 'ave seen in me days as a pirate."

It was true; she looked human. Her parents suspected it was because she had been out of the water since her father found her. She had perhaps evolved into a new form of a siren. However, they had another theory. Maybe she was not fully siren. Perhaps human, or something else.

Wentworth placed both hands on the mattress and leaned forward. "Put it on," he said.

Resisting the captain was useless, and Nola knew it. Putting the cuff on felt as if she was giving up, though she knew she was not. She vowed to herself to fight when the opportunity arose.

Nola clamped the cuff and dropped it, listening to the clanking sound of the chain hitting the floor.

Letting out an exhausted breath, she asked, "Do you have any water for me?" She settled herself as comfortably as she could on the floor while a stream of emotions took over her body. They were not the typical response when she was afraid. Something was wrong.

He nodded. "I'll get ye water once yer secured." Wentworth reached out and placed a hand on her cheek. "Ye do look quite pale," he observed. "Are ye ill?"

She closed her eyes for a moment, feeling the room spin.

"I—" Nola glanced at the cuff. A strange sensation came over her body as if she were wrapped in a blanket of scorching heat. "No, I—" She held a hand to her forehead, feeling as if her body was floating above the clouds. "Something is wrong, Wentworth." She glanced up; her eyes felt hazy. "Uncuff me."

Nola's siren senses dwindled into nothing while hearing the distant echo of the pirates on deck. Her eyes rolled back and she entered a blackened murk in desolate darkness.

Prince Elijah held firmly to the Voleric pendant, keeping it secure in a tight-fisted grip as he clenched it to his chest.

He felt the siren's presence at that moment. He sensed the power of Nola's fear as it enveloped his mind. Elijah also connected with her unfaltering courage, despite the danger she had put herself in.

He shut his eyes.

"Focus!" he whispered.

Suddenly, a light shined brightly through the window like an intense beam of energy cracking through the glass. The sun warmed against his eyelids before opening to Nola being chained to the end of a bed.

Ah, there you are, he thought.

Elijah watched as Wentworth placed a damp rag to her forehead, but it would not do her any good, not until he woke Nola from the spell.

Elijah's mind transported him to another place where Nola stood alone, looking bewildered. She turned on her heel to look into his blue eyes. A mossy tree stood, with burgundy leaves falling slowly to the ground, surrounding the two in a colorful field of beauty beyond what either of them had ever seen. It was magical.

"Nola," he said softly.

Her eyes widened as she took a step back. "Where am I?" she asked. "How am I here?"

Elijah straightened his back before sauntering across the blossomed ground as if gliding on a sheet of glass.

Nola was trapped in a space he created inside her mind.

"You're on a pirate ship, but your mind is somewhere else until I release you."

He watched her trail her fingers over her arms nervously. "Is this a dream?"

Elijah nodded slowly. "My magic created this space, but the subject is not of my creation."

"You're—you're in *my* dream?" she asked.

He nodded again, right as a dragon flew above them, soaring through several white parting clouds.

Elijah smirked. "That is what you dream about? Dragons?"

Nola's eyes burned with anger—it amused him.

"Very well," he said, watching the dragon disappear back into the sky as if she had willed the image away.

She closed her eyes as if trying to harness her own magic, but she had no power there. As her eyes shot open again, Elijah flashed her a small smile. Even if she wanted to wake, she could not. Nola hesitantly reached out, and as she stroked his cheek, his eyes widened at her touch. He could not only see her but smell and feel. The magic of the Voleric was truly magnificent. After she withdrew her hand from his skin, she stepped back.

"Are you going to tell me why you've sent pirates to capture me?" she asked.

He lifted an eyebrow in amusement as he locked eyes with her. "You have no idea, do you?" he said.

Elijah inched towards her and reached out, placing his hand on her colorful hair. She did not flinch or move from his touch but watched as he ran his fingers through her locks. He cocked his head, more curious about her appearance than the reason he had brought her there.

"I'm fascinated by how human you look," he said. "A siren, yes, but you are no monster, Nola. Instead, you dedicate your life to saving the people of Zemira, more so than your own kind."

Her features flinched.

"I seek to fight for all the races, Prince Elijah." She stepped back. "But what do you fight for?"

He gave her an icy glare, not expecting such a direct response.

"I fight for myself," he replied through gritted teeth.

She gave him a mocking grin. "Not surprised," she said. "So why do you need me?"

Elijah ran his hand through his hair and took one step back, giving her space. A slow grin pulled at his lips. "Because I want to kill my father," he said.

Nola's lips parted. "You—"

"He murdered my brother and my mother." He pressed his lips together. "Well, he killed both my mothers."

Elijah watched her shift uncomfortably.

"I'm sorry about your mothers, Prince Elijah; I truly am. But you need to listen to me," she began. "Your brother—"

"Do you feel that?" he asked, closing his eyes. "Something is happening outside this realm," he said. "Out there." He pointed up.

She turned, both watching herself now at the center of Wentworth's quarters.

"On the ship?" She turned back to look at the prince, who was mere inches from her face.

He nodded. "You're not safe, Nola," he warned. His warm breath brushed against her temple. "You need to swim, now. Get off that ship and swim to me."

Nola shook her head. "What? Why—why do you need me?" she asked again.

"I need your power," he explained. "And I need the key."

"A key? What key?"

"Your ruby, Nola. It's the key to the Kroneon."

Her eyes narrowed. "My ruby?" she asked. "My ruby is a key?"

Elijah's jaw tightened when her expression changed. A sudden uncomfortable feeling caught in his throat and she fanned out her hands and placed them over her chest.

"What's happening to me?" Nola asked.

His face grew into a scowl. "Get off that ship and swim, dammit! Swim, Nola."

With his last words, she opened her eyes.

Nola watched Wentworth hover over her, pushing down on her chest as if he were trying to revive her heart.

She sat bolt upright and turned to him, breathing heavily as she was ripped free from her dream-prison.

"Wha' the bloody hell was that?" he asked.

Nola shook her head, knowing she could not tell the man what she had seen.

"I have no idea," she replied.

Nola thought about the prince's warning. Examining the pirate before her, she realized she was uncertain who her real enemies were. Prince Elijah had sent that crew to bring her to him, yet his plea was to flee that same ship and go to him.

"Ye scared me witless," Wentworth said. "Ye can't die on me now."

Nola closed her eyes tight with irritation. "Listen to me,

Wentworth. You cannot take me to the prince. Do you understand?"

Regardless of what Prince Elijah said, she did not trust him more than she trusted the pirates who took her.

Neither staying with Wentworth and his crew nor swimming to the prince seemed like a good option. Both could or would get her killed. With both, she would have no freedom.

Wentworth grabbed her arm and helped her to her feet. He had removed the cuff when Nola had passed out.

"Yer a stupid girl," Wentworth said. "Ye talk nonsense. The prince has offered me quite the treasure if I bring ye to 'im, whole," he explained. "The amount of the bounty 'e offered will 'elp buy me another one of these ships." He released her arm and picked up the chain from the bedpost.

"Be quiet and I'll get ye some food," he said.

Nola's heartbeat sped up at the idea of being chained up again. She stared at the cuff and back to meet Wentworth's eyes. "No."

Wentworth turned to her slowly. "No?" he repeated, but when his eyes widened, she felt a slight sense of power, as if she may have been finally getting through to him.

But he was not looking at her. He looked past her through the porthole.

Nola furrowed her brow and turned around to look with him. Through the porthole and under the water, she spotted a thick tentacle moving past the glass. Terror overtook her face when it went out of sight, and a large eye moved within view, looking into the room and right at her.

"Aye," Wentworth said through a shaky breath. "'Tis a

bloody Kraken." He caught her wrist. Fear flashed in his eyes before he said, "Guess none of us 'ill be makin' it back to the prince alive after all."

"Wentworth?" Her voice cracked, backing from the window and into his chest.

"We're no safer above deck than we are trapped down 'ere," he said.

"I'm not dying today, pirate!"

She wondered what was going through his head as he went silent.

"Well, there's always tha' one thing ye do," he finally responded.

She turned to him and shot him a quizzical look. "The thing I do?"

"Sing, Nola," he replied, placing his fingers against her lips. "Use tha' li'l siren call of yers. Sing the monster away from our ship."

She shot him a scowl. "You can't be serious."

True, she had done it before on tiny, nine-inch-tall gnomes. But what he was asking from her was to repel a Kraken.

When they turned back to the window, the monster was gone.

"Well, I think we 'ave a problem," Wentworth said, followed by blood-curdling screams above deck.

Nola looked up, hearing the buccaneers' guttural cries and the pounding of feet on the main deck. She ran up the stairs and looked around. The Kraken's tentacles had wrapped around the ship's front half, tilting it on its side. She felt a jolt, and part of the boat split through the center, and another one of its tentacles broke through and grabbed the young boy who had shot Hill. It took hold of his waist and yanked him off the ship and into the sea.

Nola sprinted to the mast and climbed up as fast as she could. She held to the flag and swung on a rope dangling next to her. Clenching tightly, she pulled herself up until she settled inside the crow's nest and looked down.

One by one, the creature yanked each pirate from the deck. The pirate called Russell tried to cut away the tentacle gripping his leg, but it was too strong, and it flung the man into the dark, churning waters. Wentworth only watched the destruction of his ship and crew.

Nola closed her eyes, sucked in a breath, and began to sing. It was not music, but it was a calling, a melodic sound that vibrated inside her chest. She felt her body tingle as she harmonically echoed the cry over the sound of the violent waves.

After a few seconds, she was controlling the beast's movements.

Nola felt her eyes glow; warmth radiated from under her eyelids. When she opened her eyes, the creature had tossed the last standing buccaneer and waited close to the ship. Wentworth was face down on his stomach, pistol in his hand and blood spewing from his side. Nola looked down at the old pirate who hurt the man she loved. Rage filled her heart, and she felt no mercy when she gave the Kraken the final command.

Kill him, she ordered.

The creature wrapped its tentacles around the

remaining floating pieces of the ship, crushing Wentworth with one blow.

As the Kraken pulled the captain's lifeless body into the sea, the mast tilted forward until she released her grip and fell into the sea with it.

As Nola hit the cold water, she sucked in a breath before her head sank under the sea. Suddenly, her eyes felt like someone had forced them open. A light that was not there brightened the sea, giving her a clear vision of her surroundings. She watched as the Kraken swam away from the ship, dragging Wentworth's corpse with it.

Nola stared in awe at the gorgeous reefs surrounding her and the schools of fish circling her body.

As she expected, her legs began to pull together at the thighs, tugging again like they had before. Her limbs felt free, her skin rough as the hairs on her arms stood straight.

The dress she wore remained intact, but she felt the wet fabric loosen where her tail had formed. Nola gathered the courage to suck in a breath at the sight of a maroon fin moving under the dress. As water entered her mouth, it filled her lungs and the pressure shifted to her chest. She breathed out, water bubbling in front of her, and her breathing settled. It felt as if she had sucked in air from above the surface.

It was a strange feeling, but she continued to inhale and exhale until she no longer noticed the difference.

Nola paused and looked around, the ocean looking as clear as the world above. She saw every detail, from the small forage fish to the algae a few hundred feet below her.

Not knowing if the Kraken would return or how much

longer it would be under her spell, she swam off quickly to find safe land. There was such an exhilarating feeling in her tail as she moved through the water. It was an odd yet familiar feeling as if it were embedded in her genetic memory.

At least a day had gone by when she noticed a slight change in depth, possibly leading to a sandy shore. She swam to the surface and saw what appeared to be hundreds of charcoal-colored bark trees drooping over each other.

Her father had once told stories of such a place; a dark, swamp-looking land where King Matthias would banish traitors to live out the rest of their lives: the Marsh Wetlands. If the Kraken could not kill her, that place surely would. However, swimming for almost a day had exhausted her. She had to rest.

Nola hurried to the shore using the energy she had left. She then buried her hands in the grainy sand, resting her face on them, and closed her eyes to sleep.

Chapter 27

The Marsh Wetlands

Nola's eyes opened as the sun rose on the eastern horizon. The sweltering heat of the swampland was quickly draining whatever strength she had left.

She assumed she had slept on the shore for nearly a day. Her hair was sticky, damp, and covered in green algae. A look around was enough to notice her tail had transitioned back.

Her head pounded with every cluck of the insects within the marsh. Turning, she dipped her toes in the warm water and felt the small waves crash over her ankles—the water soaked her skin, quenching her thirst.

Would this be a part of me now? Nola thought. *My body becoming one with the sea while adapting to the siren change?*

Her body felt a bit dry as if the air around her was no longer natural to her. Either that or the sun had burned her skin, leaving an itchy sensation.

Nola's eyes shimmered with tears. She felt grateful to be

alive but mortified for what she had done with the Kraken and that dreadful crew.

Sweeping the front of her hair from her eyes, Nola glanced at the barren, desolate land. A circle of trees rose above a cloudy haze, lining the dark sand and growing into the murky water.

Faint whispers tickled her ears, echoing an eerie sense of life within the swamp lurking amidst the trees.

Nola's legs felt fatigued as she rose to her feet to stand straight. Her muscles ached where her legs had changed. As she tried to step forward, intense pain pulsated between her thighs.

She only took one step before her toes sank deep into what felt like thickened quicksand. With every movement she made, her legs dug deeper in the mud. A hard surface leveled between her toes. At least it would not swallow her entirely—it was not as deep as she feared. Nola wiggled her toes to free herself from the trap, but the mud became dense, not allowing her to move much further.

Great! Nola thought.

The air felt thick, making it harder for her to breathe since the moment she awoke. Fog crept through the trees, and the moisture in the air pulled beads of sweat over her brow.

The Marsh Wetlands was the most frightening of all the lands Nola had read about in books. It was where the king sent people to die a horrible death. Nola thought it was not far off from what she had imagined Zemira would turn into someday. Misery. Loneliness—until everyone withered away into nothing.

The leafless branches hung over the ground as if the trees themselves were crying. Even the sky above looked different, like the world's beauty could not touch such a place.

After several uncomfortable minutes, Nola's shoulders slouched. She let out a long sigh and pressed her fingers into the mud. As she tried to pry the dirt away from her skin, a dark shadow appeared just a few feet from her. A boy, much younger than her, knelt on the ground with his hand outstretched.

"Need some help, miss?" he asked in a joyous tone. "Looks like you've gotten yourself into a mess." A radiant smile shone on his face as he continued to hold out his hand for her to take.

The peculiar boy had a thin, sallow face. Loose strands of his shaggy wheat-colored hair fell over his eyes. Several scars covered his face as if an animal had savagely clawed at his skin.

Though apprehensive about the stranger, Nola accepted his outstretched arm, gripping her fingers around his feeble little wrists. He pulled back, helping her lift her feet from her trap.

Nola felt relief as she slithered out of the muddy hole and plopped down on a large rock.

"Thank you," she said, turning to the boy who seemed amiable and full of life as if a place like that had no effect on his mental wellbeing.

Nola immediately wondered how he ended up in the Marsh Wetlands. He was too young to be punished for a crime by the king. He was no older than the age of twelve.

"Is there anything edible around here, do you know?" she asked, realizing at that moment how famished she was.

"Yes. Yes, of course," the boy said, pointing to the forest, "This way."

She clambered to her feet and maneuvered cautiously between the trees. Her brows pulled together as she mulled over the place surrounding her. Nola's tired legs managed to keep up with the mysterious stranger, moving deeper into the swampland.

She trailed closely behind the boy through the muddy water, feeling the wet twigs scrape against her shins. Each step felt more nerve-wracking than the one before.

"Over here," he said, pointing to a tall, thick tree with a manmade ladder leading to the top. "After you, madam."

"Nola," she said, stepping onto the first wooden rung leading to the treehouse. "Please call me Nola."

"My name is Jastris. It is pleasantly nice to meet you, Nola."

The young lad appeared somehow elated, despite being in a place designed for death and despair.

Nola was relieved that even in a place as terrifying as the swamp, she felt safe with him. However, she would not let her guard down. She had learned throughout her life that looks were deceiving to one's sinister ways.

She inspected the ladder leading to a treehouse about thirty feet high.

They entered the tiny home, which she was quite impressed by. The house was built with bamboo and string, roped around the edges to keep it secure. A little table made from wood stood in the corner, with a small bowl crafted from a coconut. It was hard to imagine anything growing in a place like that. But it was a relief to Nola, knowing there was something to sustain those sent there.

"How long have you been here?" Nola asked, genuinely concerned for the young boy.

He shrugged. "All my life," he answered in a melancholy tone.

"All your life?" she asked, aghast. "You . . . you were born here?"

He gave her a curt nod.

"Where are your parents, Jastris?" she asked.

An easy, languid smile crossed his features.

Shrugging, he replied, "Dead, I presume. Everyone dies, don't they?"

Her forehead wrinkled as she watched the sullen expression on his face shift. It was as if her question alone had disrupted their cordial connection. She wiggled uncomfortably, leaning back against the wall of the treehouse.

After wrapping her arms around her knees, she said, "We all need someone, Jastris." She hesitated, but only a moment. "If you would like, I can send a ship to come for you once I get to safe passage. You are but a child."

"Nah," he growled, "I like it here. I—" He stopped.

Nola cocked her head. "You what?"

The boy smiled and looked out the window, extending his frail arms upward in a weird manner. However, he stayed silent.

Then he dropped his hands to his side and peered

through the hole where the ladder was, then leaned towards it and jumped.

Instinctively Nola reached to catch him, but he was already gone.

"Jastris!" she shouted, moving over to where he had disappeared. He could not have made a jump like that—he had not used the ladder.

"Hello!?" she shouted, panic rising in her chest.

Did he honestly jump to his death? Nola asked herself, running a hand through her messy hair.

She scooted to the window and looked down, then over to the door which led to the ladder again.

Panicked, Nola moved to where she had climbed up. Then, she placed her feet on the ladder and headed back down. Once she reached the ground, she looked around. The boy was nowhere to be found. If he died after such a drop, his body would have been at the bottom, but it was not.

Are my eyes and ears playing tricks on me? Nola asked herself. *Did I imagine that boy?*

The latter was a possibility. It was the first time Nola had breathed underwater, and she had been traveling for nearly a day. Perhaps the lack of oxygen was causing hallucinations.

Utterly alone amid the marsh, Nola glanced around, feeling an unnerving fear run up her spine. The only certainty she had was that she was somewhere between the portal into the land of the gnomes and the Eastland Forest. Only a day's swim in the sea before she would be safe.

The swamp's mud appeared relatively compact, and the

air thinned as she approached a large clearing. For the first time, she was able to see through the trees and into the early dusk.

Find food, then shelter, she thought, for the dangers of the Marsh Wetlands lurked around her, watching her every move closely.

Nola's body still felt fatigued, so she let her body sag against a tree and quickly fell asleep.

The calming silence lasted for a few long hours before the wind roared, disrupting Nola's sleep. Her eyes shot open, not realizing how long she had slept, but she assumed most of the night, as the sun had already begun to rise.

How in the—? She rubbed her head. *If Lincoln continued course, they would be arriving at the Eastland Forest by sunrise.*

Time moved quickly in that strange place.

Nola rubbed her eyes, the perception of the world coming back to her.

Not a dream.

The field was bleak, and a sense of being watched again crawled up her skin. Though she was hungry, she did not feel the need to find water. Her body felt refreshed as if the seawater had absorbed into her skin, giving her the needed replenishment.

Cattails brushed against her ankles—tickling her skin as she moved through the marsh. She straightened her back as she spotted movement ahead.

Nola waited a moment in silence before calling out.

"Jastris?" She ran her hands down her arms nervously. "Jastris, is that you?"

A couple shadows through the trees made her step back.

The entity whipped by erratically like some wild creature was bustling through the openings of the forest.

Then, it stopped.

A lump caught in her throat.

"Jastris?"

That time she whispered so softly; she barely heard her own voice. As Nola paid closer attention to the tree line, a chilling sensation trickled down her neck. It felt like a feather had brushed up against her skin. She squinted her eyes, trying to draw a sense of the image before her within the darkness. Still, it was not bright enough to see her surroundings, only the moonlight shining down on a small hill at the center of the clearing.

A beam flashed towards the middle of the hill. Nola's mouth gaped open. It was not a hill; it was piles and piles of . . . bones.

The ghastly place reeked of death and decay.

I will not suffer the fate of dying in this place, she vowed.

Nola stepped back again, her hand covering her mouth. The sulfurous scent of the marsh was replaced by the rancid smell of decomposing bodies. She had to choke back the bile rising in her throat.

The same sensation tickled her skin again; that time, she quickly reached back and grabbed hold of the entity which taunted her. However, her fingers slipped as it sped towards the trees.

She was not alone.

Suddenly, Nola saw a tiny, blue, translucent light zip past her out of the corner of her eye. A long animal-like tail stuck out from the light.

She sucked in a breath. *What in the—*

A shrill sound swayed by her. She swiftly reached up, muffling the noise as it pierced in her ears. The blue light moved briskly around the trees and over to the mass of corpses. It circled the pile until it stopped, staying hidden behind the bones.

"Hello?" Nola stammered, still smelling the acrid scent before her. "What are you? Come out!"

She heard the shuffling of feet before Jastris rounded the heap of bodies until he stood next to them. Nausea rose to her throat.

"Did you prefer me in the form of a boy?" he asked. "Or—"

She gasped. "Wha . . . what are you?"

The boy gave her a sharp look. "Hm. Well, I've had a few names throughout the years. But I prefer a will-o'-the wisp."

Despite being a magical creature herself, Nola had not seen such a mystical being, nor heard of one.

"Did you do this?" Her voice trembled as she spoke, gesturing to the massacre before her.

"Oh, this?" His eyebrows shot up as a cynical smile twisted his lips. "No, milady. He did, though. The one who lurks in the forest." His head cocked. "Wendigos must eat."

She felt her heartbeat pounding in her throat. "A wha—?"

Unexpectedly, a grumble echoed behind Jastris. The boy moved to the side as a skeletal figure slowly crawled around him, extending its long limbs with each step, never taking his eyes off Nola.

Its grimy paws pressed into the mud, making a pattering, squishing sound.

The creature's bleached bones stuck out through its crusty fur. Its head was the color of burned wood with midnight-black eyes and lips covered in dried blood. The eyes sank deep into its skull, creating a ghastly appearance.

Nola refused to blink as a subtle, deflated expression flashed briefly over the creature's features before its lip curled.

Jastris's eyes burned into hers, leaving no trace of kindness in them.

"Fear him, siren," he said in a strange, soothing tone. "He does love the taste of fear." The boy stepped forward, standing next to the creature. "It is okay to be afraid."

Nola shook her head but felt frozen. Her mind said to step back, but her legs would not move.

The wendigo's lips curled further, snarling at her; her limbs turned to ice—she was utterly horrified.

Nola swallowed down the lump in her throat to be able to speak. "Jastris," she choked out as the color drained from her face.

"It was genuinely nice to meet you, Nola." The boy stepped back. "But Prygus has to eat now," he said, his threat calm and eerie. "He likes it when they run." He gestured to the forest. "He'll give you a head start."

Another thick snarl escaped the wendigo's bloodied lips. It bared its pointed teeth as its mouth quirked upward, twisting its warped face. As the creature crouched low, the bones on its elongated spine protruded even more from its back.

The wendigo's features darkened; it let out an ear-piercing screech which sent Nola's legs sprinting away on their own.

Nola quickened her pace, only to hear the sound of footsteps rushing through the forest behind her. The crackling of leaves was close; panic surged through her veins.

I am going to die.

As the thought left her, she tripped over her dress and stumbled to the ground.

Nola watched the creature leap high through the air. She lifted her hands as it came crashing on her, immediately sinking its teeth into her shoulder.

She screeched at the stabbing pain but willed herself to fight, kicking her legs up to give space between her and the wendigo as it tried to nip at her flesh.

An eerie sound rang out of the creature's mouth as it grated its teeth. Nola shifted to the right, feeling dizzy from the pain, but kept moving as she felt another bite, that time on her leg.

Her mouth let out a strange noise before her siren call boomed through the swamp. The trees toppled down, and mud shot out around them.

She screamed again, letting off a loud, vibrating blast throughout the forest.

But the noise that came from Nola was not what she had expected; it was foreign—a siren's sonic scream.

The creature swiftly covered its ears as if the sound of her voice shattered its eardrums.

Nola quickly jumped to her feet and rushed to a thin

branch lying on the ground. Anything she could use as a weapon. The creature was still on its knees, its head bent back as it watched her. The ache in her shoulder from when it bit her was nothing compared to the panic rising in her chest. The wendigo watched her intently with its black eyes as she lifted her arm, the stick's sharp end pointing its way, but she stopped moving towards it when she noticed something strange. It cowered before her.

Is this creature submitting to me? Nola asked herself, letting out a nervous breath.

Prygus dug its claws into the mud, its head lying low. The dingy-colored fur on its back stood straight, as if afraid of her.

It did not matter what control she had over that thing; the smell of rotten flesh was still vivid in her memory. She had to get off that cursed land.

Nola looked around the forest one more time before tossing the stick on the ground and dashing in the opposite direction towards the sea.

Chapter 28

The Eastland Forest

The Sybil Curse had been docked on the Fae's land for only an hour before they were caught. Lincoln had not expected to steal their magical water without a snag along the way. However, he had hoped he could heal himself before the queen's protectors arrested them.

Nola is still out there, he said to himself, *and we do not have time for the theatrics from the Fae people.*

Lincoln and Mazie stood before Queen Cassia, who drummed her fingers on her throne's armrest, appearing bored. Her long white hair fell over her shoulders, framing her beautiful, fair features.

The Fae did not need opulent quarters to display their wealth. When they were banished from Zemira, they left with only what they could carry on their backs. However, the world they had created in the Eastland Forest was beyond glorious. Floral vines lined the walls to the skyline, and the intricately sculpted wood fixtures were carved by their most skilled workers. The handmade grand hall was made with elements of nature and magic.

The queen fluffed out her claret-colored dress, running her fingers through her long blonde locks before clearing her throat after a long, agonizing silence.

She signaled to one of her protectors to bring Lincoln forth.

"A pretty face with flattering words," she noted, her tone brusque. "You and I both know the wings of a fairy may be tender, but our punishments are surely not."

The queen's threat caused Mazie's eye to twitch.

Lincoln knew well enough that even the most civilized conversation with the queen would not change how the Fae felt about pirates.

The Fae culture was quite unconventional. They held no loyalty towards anyone but themselves. At least, it had been like that since they were banished. Lincoln did not blame them, but it still aggravated him how crass the queen was towards them.

Lincoln turned to Mazie, knowing how much her pride itched at her. He watched his mate flex her fingers once or twice before shifting her weight on her heel to lean towards him.

"Are we honestly asking for permission?" she whispered into his ear, wrinkling her nose in distaste.

It is that, or she sets her dragons on us again like she did five years ago, Lincoln thought without answering her.

"For once, Mazie, I need you to keep your brutally candid tongue zipped!" he whispered back.

Lincoln looked up as Queen Cassia's azure–silvery eyes sparkled.

"Make your presence here worth my time, pirate," the queen said, her lips quirked in amusement as she tapped her heel on the tessellated tile.

Lincoln straightened his back and gently bowed his head, placing his right hand on his chest.

"Years ago, we betrayed you, Your Majesty," he said. "I had come for selfish needs as I went looking for my fiancé, Sybil." He cleared his throat. "And in return, my first mate —" Mazie snickered under her breath as if recounting the memory, "—she, um, had a heart for once and attempted to steal your pixie."

Mazie's fists tightened, baring her teeth. "—Who you have imprisoned like an animal." Her cold eyes stared intently at the queen. They waited for a curt remark, but it did not come.

"Pretentious bitch," Mazie cursed silently.

Lincoln stared daggers at Mazie. But she pressed her lips together in a defiant sneer.

"Ah, yes," the queen added. "I remember that day well. Your skill as a thief is quite impeccable. If it were not for the fact that our trees had eyes, you'd probably have gotten away with it."

Mazie shrugged her shoulders.

"But your pretty face paid the price for your crime, didn't it, Lincoln?" Queen Cassia continued; a hint of mockery edged her lips.

Lincoln's fingers instinctively reached up to his face,

running gingerly over his scar. "Aye, Your Majesty," he said, choking down his own pride.

"So why have you come back?" she asked flatly. "Clearly, you have not learned your lesson."

At that moment, Lincoln was glad he told his crew to stay behind on the ship. He did not trust the Fae people, that was certain.

"Well, originally, we set out to steal your pixie again," he confessed daringly, not caring about the repercussions. "But everything changed when a siren came upon our ship over seven days ago. We were only trying to take a little bit of water because I've been injured, and I'm losing strength by the minute."

The room was silent for a short moment. Suddenly, an Elven protector approached the queen slowly and whispered something in her ear.

The elves were a stunning race. The protector's white hair was the length of his neatly embroidered robe, which flowed with each movement he made.

The queen raised a brow and dismissed the Elven man.

"Oh, Lincoln, I do not care if you drink our water. What I do find interesting, though, is this siren you speak of? She boarded your ship?" She leaned back against her throne and smiled. "This story has become a lot more interesting. Go on."

Lincoln cleared his throat. "She was taken by Wentworth. By now, they most likely have reached Zemira, and—"

Queen Cassia's exaggerated laughter reverberated through the grand hall. "Oh, stop," she said, standing to her feet. "Your siren is alive, pirate. My dragons found her five miles off the coast. She escaped Wentworth on her own." A smile reached her lips. "She even took on a Kraken."

Lincoln's eyes widened. "She . . . she's alive?" He ran his hand over his face. "How—"

"Lincoln," Nola's voice came from behind him. He turned quickly to see Nola standing between two of the queen's protectors, wearing a long scarlet dress and sparkling tiara upon her head.

He rushed to her, sweeping her up in his arms. "Nola! You're here," Lincoln said, dropping his hands to her waist. His gaze wandered slowly down her body. "Why are you dressed like a princess?"

Her honey-colored eyes twinkled, but she pressed her lips together.

"Because she is a princess," the queen quickly answered for her, stepping down from her throne. "Our efforts to find the lost princess after King Matthias's army attacked our land were to no avail. We believed she died along with her mother, Maydean."

"The siren queen?" Lincoln asked, turning back to Nola.

Nola placed her hand on his cheek, caressing her thumb gingerly over his skin before she dropped her arm to her side. "Lincoln, my father was King Argon of the Fae."

Nola watched him as his eyes widened before glancing over Lincoln's shoulder at the queen.

"Cassia is my family," Nola said. "Recognition swept over me the moment my toes touched the soil. The land, the dragons, the elves—the memory from my infancy is still engraved in my mind."

A princess, he thought—*a Fae princess.*

Muddled thoughts warped his mind, causing confusion. He was happy she was alive and there in his arms. But he also saw clearly how unworthy he was of her.

It was not just because she was a Fae princess, but because his father had murdered both her birth parents. He was asking for her to love him, regardless of the family he was born from.

Lincoln stepped forward, closing the gap between them, burying his face into her hair. If whatever he had with her was to end, he would make that moment last for as long as he could.

He slowly leaned in—his long fingers intertwining between the strands of her hair. His mouth claimed her lips, relishing in the savoring taste of her tongue. The need to never let go, if only to breathe, wrapped deeply in Lincoln's mind and body. As their lips parted, he kept a possessive hold on her—his mouth swelled from their touch. He ran his hands down her cheek, wiping away a fallen tear.

"Lincoln, I—" A smile flitted across her mouth. "I love you."

Lincoln relished in her words. Being away from each other those last two days had burned in his heart. He could finally touch her again. Feel her warm fingers on his skin, not wanting to let go. Not then. Not ever.

Lincoln placed his hand over hers and muttered softly in her ear, "And I love you. Nola. I love you with all my heart."

Nola clung to his strong shoulders as he peered down at her with adoration in his eyes. Seven days; it had only been seven days, and yet his heart throbbed for a girl who told a different story than his. Her story was of a warrior who left her land to fight for an entire nation—a girl who wanted to be ordinary but was not.

Nola's eyes peered down at her dress. She looked up to Lincoln's torso. "You are bleeding, my love," she said.

He nodded. "I need the Fae's water."

Nola quickly looked up to address the queen. "Please heal him from his wound, Your Majesty," she begged. "And then I shall share with you the true reason I ventured here."

The memories of her days at sea were fixed pleasantly on her mind, reminding Nola she would never go back to her human life. At least, not to how it was before. The teak-brown forest's woodsy scent and the bristles of straggly moss covering the trees brought her the peace of a magic land. A place that long ago would have been a part of her—part of her Fae life. A life that was taken from her.

Nola placed her hand on the grass and closed her eyes. It was real. Not an illusion like it had been in Westin. Life there grew and thrived. And it was magic which bound her powers to it.

She looked up, watching the crew from a distance as they walked about the ship still docked fifty feet from their coast. It was better that way, at least until they had ensured the Fae's trust.

Lincoln's head was cradled in her lap as one of the fairies lifted a goblet and let the tepid water run down his wound. Nola stroked his hairline as his skin healed before her eyes. The tiny fairy left them alone in the field as they waited for the queen to meet them there.

Nola began telling Lincoln about the Kraken attack on Wentworth's ship. She told him about the exhilarating feeling of using her tail for the first time, the dream where Elijah appeared, and the nightmare in the Marsh Wetlands.

Lincoln reached into his back pocket and pulled out the sack with her ruby inside. She extended her fingers as he placed it in her palm. Nola reached inside the little bag and ran her thumb over the jewel's smooth surface to affirm it was there, safe. Then she pulled her hand back and tied off the rope.

"Lincoln, your brother is after this." She held up the sack. "We need to find a place to keep it safe."

His eyes narrowed. "What would he want with the ruby?"

Nola shrugged. "Elijah says it's a key." She placed the sack in her pocket. "A key to something called the Kroneon. I have so many questions after the last few days."

She tried to recall more of the conversation she had with the prince, but the memory had become lost in her mind.

Lincoln's eyes looked dull. "Like why a wendigo would submit to a siren?" he asked.

Nola recounted the time she spent in the Marsh Wetlands—barely making it off that dreaded land alive.

"Yes," she said, "that too."

Suddenly, the ground shook beneath their feet, the trees rattling around them. Lincoln and Nola turned their heads right as the queen climbed off her dragon.

"Nola's mother was among the Shelei species of sirens. Maydean passed that power down to Nola." Cassia held out her pale hand to help Nola back on her feet. Then, the Fae queen stretched out her hand and brushed her fingers along the silver part of Nola's hair. "You have dominion over all species. You can control them with your mind, and they are obliged to submit."

Nola's mouth fell open.

"Well," Queen Cassia continued. "All aside from your own species, of course. You cannot control Fae or the sea folk."

Nola swallowed; it all made sense, given the recent events.

"But even with those powers, Nola, you still have much to learn about who you are."

Nola turned to the queen. "I know who I am, Your Majesty. I may not know everything, but I do know my purpose. And I refuse to leave this land without your help."

The queen waved a hand in her face and turned on her heel, walking away. "The humans have destroyed all that I love," she said, and the look of scorn and bitter resentment flashed across her face. "Why should we risk our lives for your cause?"

Nola knew it would not be as easy to convince the queen as she had hoped it would be. "Because magic is the only thing that can save us. You may not feel for them as I do, but my family is all I have."

"Your family, and your rightful place, is here, Nola," Cassia said. "Nowhere else, but here."

Nola shook her head. "With all due respect, Your

Majesty, but this—" she removed the tiara from her head, "—is nowhere near to where I want to be. I am not a princess. I am a poor village girl. The only future for me is fighting for my people. But for that, I need your Elven warriors."

They were interrupted by Mazie walking up the shore.

"Queen Cassia, what has happened to your land?" she asked, looking around. The colors still shone bright, the vegetation fruitful, and the water was so clear they could see every detail of the shells buried within the sand. However, the trees were split, and there was nature's waste scattered along the sandy beach.

The queen's bright eyes shone with annoyance. "You mean all this?" she said, gesturing around them.

Mazie nodded. "Aye."

Queen Cassia's shoulders slouched. "We have a giant problem." She gestured with her hand at one of the most ancient trees on their land—one that stood taller than the others.

"The creature has eaten our crops, destroyed our homes, and not even my warriors can tame the beast."

Her tone sounded exhausted as if they had been battling that giant for years and had simply given up.

Mazie snickered. "You have thousands of warriors on your land, and you can't kill a mere giant?" she mocked, folding her arms across her chest.

Nola was used to Mazie's arrogant tongue since she had met her, but a sudden nervousness hit her to see her speak so candidly to the queen.

"You believe you are skilled enough to kill a giant?" the

queen asked Mazie, knitting her brows together as if to study her face for any sign of doubt.

Mazie puffed out her chest. "With a few flicks of my sword, I can have it dead by sunrise."

Queen Cassia plastered a smile on her face. "I see." She fell silent for a couple seconds. "I'll make you a deal. You kill my giant, Mazie, and you can have that little pixie of mine."

Mazie's eyes widened. "Are you serious?" she asked, surprised.

Clearly enthralled by the queen's proposal, she held out her hand. "You have yourself a deal, Your Majesty," Mazie said, bouncing on her toes in anticipation. "I will kill your giant, and then I will leave with your pixie."

The queen did not shake her hand.

"Done! But not today, pirate, for we have more pressing matters at hand," the queen said as she turned to her niece. "Nola, you are asking my people to risk their lives for humans. It goes against everything we stand for. And you, being part Fae—it should concern you, too."

Nola folded her arms stubbornly. "What is the purpose of having Elven warriors if you're not willing to use them? The Fae have magic, and what about the other creatures on this land?" She looked up, watching the two dragons circling the coastline in the distance. "If we all fight together as one, using magic to destroy him, we will win. My queen, King Matthias killed your brother. That alone should be enough for you to fight!"

The queen flinched. "I cannot make that decision today. It is not about me, Nola. It is about what my warriors are willing to do for a race that has banished us for two decades—humans are nothing to us. Not anymore."

Nola nodded. "I understand."

"I don't think you do!" Cassia said curtly.

Nola looked away, reaching out to grab Lincoln's hand for comfort. But she would not give up. Not until the Fae queen agreed to help her.

"Nola," Cassia said, modulating her tone, "Please follow me." She then led them to the other side of the field where her dragons had returned, placing her hands on Dergis and running her fingers gingerly down his dark, scaly skin.

Nola looked over as she felt Lincoln's hands brush up against her fingers. She smiled. His eyes averted from hers, growing wide as the other dragon stepped in his direction.

"Anaru," he said, looking into her eyes.

Nola watched Lincoln place his hand over the scar on his cheek.

The red-scaled dragon extended her wings and roared so loudly the ground beneath them shook like a thunderous storm. Her deep-black eyes blazed into his as if connecting with his soul.

Now, that is interesting, Nola thought.

"Fascinating," the queen said, shifting to Lincoln. "She remembers you well, pirate." Cassia smiled. "Anaru, surprisingly, is very fond of you. She wants you to ride."

"Ride a dragon?" he asked hastily. "I respectfully decline, Your Majesty." He took a step back. "I am no dragon rider."

Anaru let out another loud roar, causing Lincoln's hair to blow wildly in his face.

"Oh, she won't hurt you, pirate," the queen assured.

He narrowed his eyes as if annoyed by her comment. "My scar disagrees."

The queen chuckled. "That is quite interesting," she said to her dragon, then turned to Lincoln. "If you ride Anaru, she will respect you." She ran a smooth hand over the dragon's scales. "She was my brother's before he died. She's not had a rider since."

Lincoln shook his head. "I'm honored, Queen Cassia. Truly, I am. But I prefer to travel by water."

The dragon roared again, louder, and bowed her head. Nola felt her heartbeat pick up speed. Anaru was such a magnificent creature, and she was submitting to a pirate.

"If you have the opportunity to ride a dragon right now, Captain," Mazie said, who stood next to him, "you should! Go on, fly with her."

He raked his sweaty hand through his tousled hair.

"A dragon chooses its rider, Lincoln. And as odd as this situation is, she has chosen you," the queen said.

"I'll pass, for now," Lincoln said.

Queen Cassia laughed aloud as she climbed on top of her dragon. "Be courageous, pirate, or not even the sea can save you." Dergis extended his wings and took off into the sky, with Anaru following behind.

Chapter 29

A loud burst of laughter from the men above deck pulled Prince Elijah from his spell. It agitated him to no end. He would not be able to connect with his father with such deafening noise.

Lifting his hand, a black smoke drifted out through his fingertips and slithered slowly around the cabin. The dark magic crept under the door and down the hall, which led to the deck. Laughter broke off into screams. It brought a satisfying smile to his face before the silence loomed over him.

Ah, he thought, *there we go.*

Elijah was not stupid enough to kill the crew—he needed the sailors. However, they would be frozen until he had the information he needed. Also, his magic would be a warning to them. It took a lot of convincing for some of his father's men to turn on their kingdom. They were not easily persuaded to go against their king, so he had used his magic, possessing their minds into utter control.

A slight sway of the ship caused Elijah's heart to jump. He had not sailed the seas since he was a young lad.

Moreover, the ocean was laden with death and misery, all at the hands of the evil man he called Father. The voyage to seek out the siren, who loathed the King of Zemira as much as he did, was bittersweet. They should be allies, yet she would become his enemy in a few days' time.

If the siren had the ruby, that made her who he thought she was—the daughter of Maydean, Queen of the Undersea.

Elijah settled back on his pillow, closing his eyes, and clutched the Voleric pendant—it pulsated against his chest. The polished texture felt cool against his palm. He shut his eyes, feeling the rapid movement beneath his eyelids. His body suddenly felt weightless above the sheets, harnessing a tremendous amount of power to slip into his father's mind.

His growing anger was intoxicating. His father's spiteful, murderous behavior had made him a hard-hearted man. Finding the siren would help Elijah bring it all to an end.

"Hmmm!" he hummed as he watched the king's guard hustle to Mason's chambers.

"What are you up to, Father?" he said aloud; a dark, heavy pressure pulled at his forehead. He did not want to be snooping around his father's head longer than he needed. Going through the pain of venturing into Matthias's consciousness was draining.

Elijah watched as the king stepped up to Mason. Matthias no longer ignored the prince being inside his head.

Boy, have you come to watch? Elijah heard his father ask in his vile, warped mind.

The arrogant man felt no remorse for his actions. As much as Elijah hated to see Mason be tortured, it was inevitable.

The corners of his mouth turned up. *Mason was simply a pawn to keep you busy while I escaped on your ship,* the prince said to his father's mind. *Do whatever you wish to him, you dimwitted buffoon. I am days ahead of you.*

The prince winced, feeling his father struggle against his power.

Go ahead, try all you want, Elijah said, keeping his own thoughts hidden from the king.

As Elijah watched through the eyes of his father, Mason knelt on the floor with his arms bound behind his back. Two of Matthias's guards held him tight before the corrupt man. A few beads of sweat ran down Mason's forehead while his shoulders heaved.

The king lifted his fist, wrapped in brass knuckles, and came down hard against Mason's cheek. Blood drenched King Matthias's boot as Mason spat on the floor.

The wounded man attempted to stand and flee, but the two guards held him firmly by the arms, pulling him back down to his knees.

Elijah's face twisted in rage. He would not pretend he did not play a role in Mason being caught and abused. However, his plan to keep his father at bay for as long as necessary was working. Every man had their pain threshold, and he knew Mason would soon cave.

Matthias's lips curled into a sardonic grin. "I've been quite patient when it comes to you, Mason," he said. "I gave you the honor of Lord and head of my royal guard when you were barely eighteen. And now you betray me."

For the greater good, Elijah said to his father's mind. *Leave him alone.*

A dull ache pulsated at Elijah's temples, feeling as if, at any moment, the connection between their minds would break. Sweat pricked the back of his neck, soaking the sheet. Elijah had to fight the draining weakness in his body; it was his only chance.

Oh, my son, the king said to Elijah in his mind, *not until he tells me where you have fled to.*

"A siren!" Mason spat out. His eyes gleamed with defeat and dolefulness.

You little traitor! Elijah screamed in his mind, not caring if his father heard.

The prince felt his father's lips pull to the side in a gratifying grin as the traitor broke into tears, hanging his head low to the ground.

King Matthias stood straight. A rush of fury coursed through his body, so livid Elijah clutched the Voleric pendant and thought on releasing himself from his father's mind.

The prince could feel the king pretending to have complete control, but as he dug deeper into his father's consciousness, he scrambled his thoughts. Elijah held firmly to their connection, even if it meant crushing the king's mind until he no longer recognized himself.

"The Elven woman and her child caught that day at the market were released by the prince," Mason continued.

Elijah bared his own teeth.

Do not do it, Mason, Elijah said in his thoughts, though he knew Mason could not hear.

"He wants the siren; that's all I know," he continued. "He needed your ship," Mason stammered. "I did not mean to betray you, sir. I wanted to survive."

You have been a naughty boy, my son, the king said to Elijah's mind.

"Shameful, Mason," the king said to his guard as he stood tall, staring down at him, then signaled to his second in command. "Theodor?" he called.

Do not do it, Father, Elijah screamed to his thoughts. *He was only doing what he was ordered to do.*

He knew those words were not enough.

I used my powers on him, Father. He had no choice.

Elijah held little hope those last words would stop him from killing another one of his men who did not deserve it. But he had to try.

"Give him lashes until he passes out," King Matthias ordered. "Let him suffer for a few days; then sever his head from his body, won't you?"

"No!" Elijah screamed out loud that time, feeling a sudden rush of dizziness—the evil king was fighting against his power.

A few moments later, Matthias paced around to his bedroom mirror and looked back at his reflection. As the gleaming sparkle of the jewels on his crown shined bright, he ran his calloused fingers over the center emerald. A cynical smile flashed over his lips.

Elijah had no doubt his father considered him a bastard son. An accident which was never supposed to be. The look

Matthias gave Elijah as he stared back at him was clearly a warning.

"You believe yourself to be clever, boy?" his father said bitterly. "Bah! Even miles away, you cannot bring yourself to part from me. You believe you are strong enough to defeat me and take my crown?"

King Matthias took a step closer to the mirror, his forehead creasing and his eyes turning red.

"I'm coming for you, Elijah," Matthias said. "I will take the northern route through the raging storms in order to reach you in only a few days' time."

The threat turned the prince's blood ice cold.

Then, his eyes darkened before adding, ". . .And then my bloodline will end with you joining your brother at the bottom of the Portland Sea."

Chapter 30

The front of Nola's hair fell over her eyes as she leaned forward, dipping her toes into the lake. She swung her feet back and forth over the surface, barely caressing the water.

The charm of the fairy city had given her a sense of belonging. The Eastland Forest had magic, and Zemira did not. Nola needed magic. A few hundred fireflies lit up the early morning sky. It made the scene even more beautiful, peaceful.

This is better than I ever imagined, Nola thought.

All the creatures in the Eastland Forest were part of who she truly was. For a short while, Nola remembered all the fairy tales her father had read to her. The images she had made in her mind were nothing compared to what she was witnessing.

The bright colors and patterns of nature, dimly lit by the glow of dawn, were unlike anything she had ever seen. All the gorgeous landscapes Nola dreamed of as a child were real. She was surrounded by magic for the first time since she was born. Though Zemira would always have a place in her heart, it was the Eastland Forest that gave her life.

I am home, Nola thought as she took a deep breath, filling her lungs with crisp air.

Her eyes quickly darted to Lincoln as his fingers brushed up her spine. He dropped his hand, wrapping his fingers around hers.

They sat in silence for a few long minutes, not wanting to drown the beautiful sounds of the forest.

"Have you thought about what Cassia said?" Nola paused.

Lincoln raised a brow. "About riding her dragon?"

She nodded shyly.

There was no purpose in asking such a question, but it had loomed in her thoughts since the queen mentioned it. Those dragons were the ones she saw in her dreams—the connection was not a coincidence.

Hesitation shone in Lincoln's eyes. The dragon had scarred him, and Nola saw the fear in his features that he believed it would happen again.

"Aye," he said. "But then I thought that if I were to slip off that beast, I'd fall to my death. So, nay, I will not be riding a ferocious red dragon high into the clouds. It is literally the last thing I plan to do."

The temptation to snicker at his response itched at her. She shrugged instead.

"I think it would be quite the adventure," Nola said. "I could always speak with the dragon if you'd like. According to the queen, I can communicate with Anaru, as I am with you right now."

His lips pulled up. "I'd rather pretend to be a fearless pirate and hide the fact that I am afraid of heights."

Nola nudged him with her elbow teasingly. "You're not fearless," she said.

He chuckled. "Nah, I know I am not. At least not like Mazie. She has her flaws, but she takes on danger like it's the most natural thing to her," Lincoln replied.

"I guess you are right," Nola said. "Mazie *is* going to fight a giant."

"Aye," Lincoln said. "That is, if she finds the monstrous creature."

Nola and Lincoln stared at the moving trees while holding hands. It was the calmest moment they had had together since they met. Her hair blew up from the wind. She watched his eyes trace the curves of her neck while she ached to touch and hold him again. It was all she could think about since they met. Nola craved the taste of his lips and the gentle scent of his neck.

"How exactly do you catch a giant?" Nola asked innocently. She watched him withdraw his tongue to nestle back into his mouth.

"They like eating trolls," he answered. "The Fae had to round up a few to use as bait."

Her jaw dropped. "That's a bit barbaric."

"That's the Fae way, unfortunately."

A small frown crossed her features before she turned back to the forest on the other side of the lake. "Are you scared for her?" she asked.

A faint smile flickered on his pink lips, causing Lincoln's dimples to dip, hiding his tiny scar.

"Mazie?" he asked. "Nay. She is quite a barbarian; she is an incredible fighter. I not only trust she will survive, I trust she'll win."

Nola lowered her brow. "Oh, I've fought her, remember?"

Her laughter broke off as she pondered more about the memory. The one time she and Mazie bonded, it had turned a bit brutal at the end.

"Mazie told me the reason she doesn't trust me," she said. "She believes I will do to you what Sybil did."

The charming smile on his face faded. "Mazie doesn't like anyone, Nola. Don't overthink anything she says."

She arched a brow. "Well, she likes you."

"She tolerates me," he said. "There's a difference." He combed his hair with his fingers. "She thinks I'm a bastard."

Nola chuckled, suddenly feeling foolish for bringing Sybil up again. She cared for him deeply, but Lincoln had had far more experience than she did when it came to relationships.

There was an uncomfortable silence as his eyes still roamed over her face.

"Um," she began, trying to change the subject as quickly as possible. "I want to be able to control the change when I'm in the water," she said, fully knowing he would not understand. When his brows creased, she continued, "My tail, Lincoln. I want to be able to swim and not transition."

A small smile edged Lincoln's lips and he inched closer to her.

"You're afraid," he said.

She nodded. "I loved every part of my tail as I swam

away from Wentworth's ship. It felt invigorating. It was a part of me. But at the same time, what if I lose my human legs forever?"

Lincoln let out a long sigh, and the corners of his eyes crinkled. "Nola, they are not human legs. You are Fae. Think about that for a moment. A human is magicless. Your Fae body can do miraculous things. It all makes sense now. The precision when you fight. Your ability to see clearer than any of us. The ability to hear what we cannot." He gripped her hand again. "You are as magical as those fairies over there." Lincoln gestured to the city. "If you want your legs to turn back while submerged in the water, you can do it."

Nola's eyes were glossy.

You have more faith in me than I do, she thought, wanting to thank him, but she did not speak.

Instead, she glanced at the water ripples caused by the gentle wind coming through the trees.

The corner of her mouth quirked up for a moment before saying. "Come in the water with me." Her voice was a quiet whisper.

Nola's request caused a flirtatious grin upon Lincoln's lips.

"Shall I get naked?" he said, his alluring eyes teasing her.

She quickly drew her lower lip between her teeth, nudging him playfully with her elbow.

Then, with a hint of shyness in her tone, she said, "If I'm to be naked, then you shall too."

Nola laughed at her own response, watching his breath

agitate. Her cheeks gave her away when they flushed instantly.

Did I really say that? She asked herself.

Lincoln gave her a charming wink, sending an eager sensation between her legs. When his green eyes peered into hers, she could not turn away.

He reached out to trace his finger down the center of her cleavage. Then stopped.

Nola's nod was subtle before he continued to disrobe her, untying the string to her blouse. Her skin quivered from his tender touch—tiny tremors shook her legs.

She reached up to meet his hand, helping him undress her. Nola pulled her blouse over her shoulders and dropped it on the grass behind her. As she swallowed nervously, her chest heaved, letting out a breath before undoing the tie at her pants, wiggling herself out until she sat naked.

"Shall we?" she said.

After Lincoln undressed, the two lovers strolled hand by hand into the chilly lake. He appeared bedazzled as the water settled above her breasts.

The shallow water felt light against her skin. It was different, unlike the salty, grainy sensation from the sea.

"I already feel it," she said. "The muscles down my legs are fighting for the change."

Her confidence faded away before he said, "Will it away, Nola." His voice low and serious. "Choose not to change."

Nola squeezed her eyes shut, steadied her breath, and focused with all the strength she had. However, the pull continued bringing her legs together.

When she opened her eyes, she felt the burning sensation as if her legs had indeed changed.

Breathe, Nola. You can do this, she told herself.

Lincoln swam closer towards her and stopped once he stood inches from her face. He then placed his hands behind her neck. Nola stiffened. His other hand reached up to caress her lips with his thumb, leaning forward and giving her a few tender kisses.

"Come back to me," he said to her. "Come back to me, my love."

Fear spiraled inside her. "You're too close," she said, urging him to move back. "I might—"

"You won't hurt me," he said, "I'm not letting go. I trust you."

Nola felt safe with him, but she did not trust herself. All she could do was focus on the irises of his eyes. Their gaze would not falter. Her heart rate slowed and her mind was brought back to her tail, willing her body to transform again.

Lincoln's hand dropped to her waist, sliding across her hips, where the scales had formed. As his thumbs ran gingerly around her figure, her tail smoothed out, blending back into her delicate, soft skin.

Nola drew in a deep breath as the calming silence enveloped her senses. The tug between her legs was gone, her tail began to split, and the rough scales slowly went away.

As her body settled back to her human-like form, she felt his erection press up against her legs. His fingers trailed up to her breasts and slowly caressed her skin. Then, one of his hands slid down her navel and stopped in between her thighs.

Fear was quickly replaced by the lustful need she had for Lincoln holding her in the water.

Nola watched the animalistic craving reach his eyes, as he stared at the reflection of her naked body through the transparency of the water.

"Nola," he hummed in her ear, "you are stunning. No matter what form you are in. You're perfect."

She knew she was far from perfection, but hearing those words brought a tingling feeling between her legs. Nola looked heavenward as she roamed the tip of her fingers down Lincoln's sculpted chest, tracing the dips of his muscles. Though she felt abashed, she wanted all of him.

A satisfied smile shone across her face as she slowly wrapped her arms around Lincoln's shoulders. His lips crashed against hers as his toned arms tightened around her waist, sending a warm rush up her spine.

Nola released the kiss to get some air, but he quickly leaned forward, recapturing her mouth. He threaded his hands gently through her hair, carefully directing her neck to bend back, and hovered his lips near hers.

"Lincoln!" she said, nearly whispering from her shaky voice.

He released her hair and pressed his forehead to hers.

"Oh, how much I want to hear you whisper my name like that every single day for the rest of my life."

Nola wrapped her legs around his waist as he pulled her to his hips, keeping her secure so she would not fall back.

The moment was perfect.

Suddenly, an echoing bell rang out from a distance, causing the two to look over Nola's shoulder, followed by a tumultuous roar that shook the trees. The water swished around them.

"Horrible timing," he said, pulling her in for one more chaste kiss.

When their lips parted, she knitted her brows together. "What was that?" Nola asked.

His mouth curled up. "It seems as though they have found the giant."

Chapter 31

Nola scanned the noisy crowd of elves sitting not-so-patiently around the arena on the outskirts of the fairy village. She had not realized so many fairies and mystical creatures lived within the Eastland Forest until they were gathered in one place.

It is so odd, she thought.

In her mind, fairies were delicate creatures who lived in peace and harmony. What she saw instead was a vulgar, rowdy crowd of Fae, with their wings outstretched and cheering on for the spectacle to begin. The fact that they had an arena that had clearly seen better days made her wonder how often fights took place.

The flourishing woodlands surrounded them, caging them in and blocking the rays of the sun. The atmosphere was a bit chillier than it had been that morning.

Nola felt somewhat relieved that the rustic-built arena was slightly far from the village. If things went wrong, the giant was not so close to the city. The villagers had had enough destruction already.

Queen Cassia sat cross-legged on her throne while at

least a half-dozen Elven protectors lined themselves in a row behind her.

The Sybil Curse's crew sat among the Fae as onlookers, but they did not appear as pleased as the others. It seemed as if the fairies and elves had looked forward to the violence —as if Mazie was simply performing for them.

The queen insisted that Nola and Lincoln sit with her as her guests of honor.

This entire situation is uncivilized, Nola thought.

Lincoln, who still held her hand, turned, and after kissing her sweetly on the forehead, stepped back to take a seat. She smiled back at him; his adoring smile and disheveled, damp hair sent welcomed butterflies fluttering in her stomach.

"To be honest with you, Nola," Queen Cassia started, drawing her attention back to her as she sat down. "This is by far the most fun we've had in decades."

Her tone had a strange thrill behind it.

Nola, ignoring the odd comment, eyed the tents at the bottom of the arena until she spotted Mazie tying up her boot.

"Lincoln is confident this fight will not last long," she said, assuring the queen. "Mazie is a brilliant fighter."

"Fighting an enemy isn't only physical strength and power!" the queen said. "It's about honor and spiritual strength. Loyalty and selflessness," she gestured to her people with a wave of her finger. "Putting others before yourself, not below." She turned back to Nola and frowned. "Mazie is a skilled fighter, yes, but she is also arrogant and self-absorbed. She will always do things to benefit herself."

The hypocrisy oozing out from the queen's mouth irritated Nola. There was no doubt there was an unexplainable hollowness in Cassia's heart. One that would encourage her to put others at risk before herself. However, Nola desperately wanted to believe the Fae were a kindhearted race.

"You don't believe she can do this? Do you?" she asked the queen.

"No," she replied hastily, "I do not."

Nola looked at the crowd, waving her hand around the arena. "Then why all this?"

The queen's brows snapped together. "She tried to steal from me five years ago, Nola. I never punished her for what she had done."

Nola's jaw dropped.

It was quite a heartless act from a queen that Nola believed was on the side of helping others to bring peace. Cassia did not care if her friends died, and Nola was starting to notice it.

The duel is nothing more than entertainment, Nola thought. *All of it is.*

Lincoln was right about the Fae. The queen was so willing to sacrifice Wentworth and his crew all those years ago because they were dispensable to her.

"Nola?"

She looked up when she heard the queen say her name.

As Nola opened her mouth to respond, the queen placed a hand on her shoulder.

"If—and I say that mildly—*if* Mazie survives, I will not punish her for any previous crimes if she kills the giant.

And I might even consider fighting with you all," she said. "Let us hope you are right about your friend down there."

Nola looked over at Lincoln, drawing in a nervous breath as the queen stood.

"My people," Queen Cassia shouted to the crowd. "We have not gathered like this in quite some time, nor have we broken bread with pirates."

A subtle rumble of whispers rolled through the masses.

"Now it's time that pesky giant of ours finally meets her match."

The queen peered down at Mazie and winked.

Nola noticed a glint of savageness in Cassia's eyes.

She honestly believes Mazie is going to die, Nola thought.

"The time to bring infinite peace to our land has arrived, and Lincoln has picked his strongest warrior to make it happen." She pointed to Mazie at the center of the arena. "I present, Mazie 'Raven' Knight."

The crowd went wild.

Mazie's lips curled when she looked to her mates, then she pounded her fist into her palm, bent down, and picked up a long sword lying by her toes. She bounced on her heels in anticipation—or fear. Nola could not tell from where she sat.

Mazie had not battled a giant before, but the crew knew how desperately she wanted to free the pixie which the Fae had imprisoned in a cage like a pet. Nola had no doubt she would win.

The queen raised her hand to hush the crowd. When silence fell, she said, "Nola. Please stand."

Nola was not prepared to be part of the event and was

unsure what the queen wanted. She quickly turned to look at Lincoln with pleading eyes.

"Years ago, King Matthias attacked our land. He not only killed my brother, King Argon, but we lost a princess to the sea that night." She turned to face Nola. "Luckily, a fisherman found her and raised her among the humans. And now, twenty years later, she made her way back to us. The only real family she has left."

A frown creased Nola's forehead.

You're mistaken, Cassia, she thought silently. *Val and Duncan are my parents.*

Nola thought of them again. Her human parents were her real family, not the queen, nor any of her Fae descendants. It did not matter if they did not share the same blood.

Cassia would never understand what she had gone through and what her parents had sacrificed for her.

"My people. We will fight for Zemira and help reclaim the land we once lost," the queen added.

Why? Why now? Nola thought.

Moments before, the queen was still hesitant about helping her. She was confused but saying the wrong thing could change Cassia's decision.

"Thank you, Queen Cassia," Nola said. "This means everything to me."

The queen peered down. "I know, and you and I have much to discuss before we send our ships," she said, her features looking weary. "Zemira is a land I swore to never return to and wanted nothing to do with. I have sent spies all these years, only to protect ourselves. However, I agree.

It is time to start a war and finish Matthias once and for all."

The queen signaled to her guards at the far end of the arena; they began pulling back on a drawbridge and lowering it to the ground.

"Now," the queen said. "May the first of our battles begin."

Nola lowered her brow, turning to look at the queen's guards. "I don't understand; you've had the giant locked in a cage. Why not simply keep it in there?" she asked.

Queen Cassia smirked. "Oh, that cage isn't strong enough. That nuisance would be out within the hour," she said. "And besides, to kill a giant, you must rip its heart out."

Nola's color drained from her face.

Oh, Mazie, please be safe! Nola said to herself.

"We don't have the skill to do it. But Mazie believes she can," the queen said. "Either that or she will be the giant's lunch." Cassia snickered at her comment. "The trolls will be pleased about that."

The queen's waggish comment made Nola's jaw clench.

When she turned back to the pit, her eyes darted up as a large foot landed on the dry sand. The naked monster emerged from her cage but took a few steps back once she saw Nola and Cassia.

Though immensely tall, the giant's body was not broadly built. Her gangly, dingy-grey-colored figure hunched forward; her skin wrinkled like old leather. She tilted her head backward and inhaled, followed by a grimace as if disgusted by their scent.

Nola's eyes would not leave the beast. *I do not know what I was expecting, but it was not this.*

Mazie took her fist and pounded it to her chest. The corner of her lips quirked, and her eyes lit up in excitement.

"Over here, you dimwitted twat," she shouted, her voice held confidence and vigor, even though a heavy wave of nerves billowed in the pit of her stomach.

The giant turned her gaze away from the queen and over to Mazie. She hastily unsheathed her sword and widened her stance, ready for the giant to charge for her, expecting an immediate blow to the chest. Tauntingly, Mazie twirled her sword around and stopped, wielding the blade high above her head.

Queen Cassia stood tall. "May the fight between Beatrice and Raven begin!" she shouted to the crowd.

"That's right, you ugly piece of shit. Get over here!" Mazie shouted as Beatrice stomped once in her direction, shaking the ground. The giant jumped and landed next to Mazie on the platform.

The wooden boards split in two, tripping Mazie backward. She winced as a piece of the broken wood smacked her in the face. Then, she hurried back, keeping the sword wielded high above her head. Her right hand came up to wipe a small amount of blood dripping from her nose.

"Bitch!" Mazie cursed before jumping to her feet and charging for the giant. She swung her sword to the side, slicing through Beatrice's ankle. The creature roared in pain.

Mazie's proud moment dwindled when she heard gruff laughter from the crowd. It annoyed her. When she agreed to fight the giant, she had not expected the queen to make a performance out of it.

The giant was huge, but not as Mazie had imagined. She looked to be about twenty feet tall. Her copper hair was cropped short to her shoulders, ratted with leaves and twigs as if she had just awoken from sleeping on the forest's grounds.

Her fingernails were stained, and her skin appeared rough and covered in aging spots. Beatrice flashed her crooked, brown teeth at Mazie as she stomped forward again. Suddenly her face twisted from pain. She quickly looked down and saw a long laceration on her ankle.

The giant let out a piercing cry, then lifted her hand, backhanding Mazie so hard against the face she flew airborne towards the crowd of anxious onlookers. One of the fairies caught her but shoved her back into the arena.

"Oh, you got it coming, disgusting beast!" Mazie was ready to go right away once she planted her feet back on the ground. That time, she raced towards the giant, her sword out forward. The fear she had at the beginning was gone. The only emotion left was the determination to end that fight before she could get seriously injured.

Beatrice screamed and looked down as Mazie slid between the giant's legs, slicing the other ankle. The creature bent her knees, grabbing Mazie's hair with the tips of her fingers, and lifted her like a rag doll.

As the monstrous beast brought Mazie closer to her face, a low growl escaped her lips.

"Oh . . . bloody hell!" Mazie gagged as a foul smell flowed out of the giant's mouth.

Beatrice gripped her around the waist with her enormous and rough fingers and squeezed.

"Mazie!" she heard Kitten shout in the distance, as the rest of the crew growled and complained.

"I'm fine," Mazie shouted back, not wanting them to get involved. She knew they would if she was in real trouble.

Get it together, Mazie said to herself.

She was not going to lose to a giant known to have the intelligence of a woodland troll.

"Fucking monster." Mazie winced as the giant squeezed tighter, feeling one of her ribs crack. For a slight moment, her mind tried to leave her body as if blacking out from the pain—escaping the reality she might die.

The crowds' shouts were a mix of horror and excitement, and Mazie was unsure if they were cheering her on or hoping the giant would kill her.

"Come on, mate, you got this!" It was Lincoln's voice she heard that time.

Mazie quickly reached out and dug her nails into her enemy's nostrils, pulling her face closer to hers. She chomped down, digging her teeth into Beatrice's thick and repulsive skin.

A low squeal left the giant's mouth, then released Mazie to bring both her hands to her wart-covered face.

Time to die, you beast! Mazie sucked in a deep breath as an idea hit her.

She bolted again in the same direction as last time, climbed up the rows of seats, and pushed a few fairies out of her way. Mazie cared little about their safety as they stumbled down the steps. Then she jumped over the rail, landing outside the arena, and sprinted towards the forest.

Beatrice ran after her, breaking through the crowd, crushing the rows of seats in her path. The onlookers scurried away quickly as the giant followed Mazie, who had then disappeared behind the trees.

Once Mazie reached the clearing where she wanted the giant to follow her, she heard the stomping sound of the beast moving closer to her, but she blocked it out to focus.

Think, Mazie, think.

Turning on her heel, she latched on to the first branch, gripping her nails into the bark, and climbed up until she was taller than Beatrice.

Though Mazie felt fearless most of her life, her arrogance had put her into a situation where she could die.

The kind eyes of the queen may have fooled others, but not Mazie. It was apparent right away Cassia never expected her to win, and she would prove her wrong.

Beatrice reached her hands up in the air. For a moment, Mazie thought she was safe until the giant bounced off the ground to grab her. Her shoulders went rigid.

I am not going to die today, Mazie thought.

She pushed her heels off the tree and jumped towards the giant's head, landing between Beatrice's eyes, and gripping to a shaggy strand of hair. Mazie slid down, swung her feet out, and lunged towards the back of the giant's neck. Then, gripped her skin and held tight. The beast reached back to grab her just as Mazie took her sword and shoved it into her neck.

Beatrice screeched so loud, Mazie felt a buzzing sound pound in her ears.

Mazie gripped the hilt of the sword again and yanked it out, releasing her hold on the giant's hair, letting herself drop to the ground.

The sting at her ankle from the landing would have been much worse if it were not for the adrenaline running through her body. She was wise to believe the giant would not fight to the death. But, as the giant paused to regain some strength, Mazie's arm came back up with the sword wielded above her head, the giant's brows knitted together.

Mazie smirked.

"Let's finish this, you ugly hag!" She mustered one last insult before swinging herself up the tree again and jumped forward, driving her sword to the heart of the beast.

Mazie's eyes shot wide open, and a satisfied grin shone on her lips as the weapon sliced through the monster's chest. She watched the giant fall to her knees and over on her side. Beatrice's eyes glazed over, and her entire body went limp. Mazie, at that moment, jumped on her and clutched her sword. With a firm grip, she pushed down on the hilt, piercing through the beast's chest. She then reached in, moving her hand through the giant's rib cage as blood-soaked her hand and arm. When she felt the giant's beating heart, she smiled with relief.

It was over.

Bloody hell, I actually did it! Mazie thought, satisfaction running through her veins. *I won.*

Then she clutched to the heart, squeezing it between her fingers, and yanked it out of Beatrice's chest. The rancid, coppery scent of the giant's blood made her queasy.

Mazie held up a coconut-sized heart in her hand, high above her head, and jumped off the giant. Once on the ground, she turned on her heel proudly to head back to Queen Cassia.

As she walked out of the tree line holding the bloody organ, the *awes* and *gasps* from the crowd immediately satisfied Mazie.

She marched with a puffed-out chest towards the queen, and the corner of her mouth quirked up.

"Your Highness," Mazie said.

She dropped to one knee, letting the heart roll off her bloodied palm. It landed at Cassia's feet, red splashing on her dress.

The pirate looked up with a lopsided grin on her lips.

"I'd like my pixie now, please."

Chapter 32

Nola sat next to Lincoln, who rested against the castle's central courtyard's stone walls. The overgrown shrubs reached through the open windows—the gardens were filled with radiant colors, so bright it was hard for them to look at anything else. The walls stood tall with three pillars, two creating an arch over a tiny bridge that reached over a creek running across the city.

That courtyard was the only place they could have a quiet moment in the Eastland Forest—well, besides the Whispering Woodlands, a place where the trolls dwelled.

They needed to speak alone.

Nola sat in complete silence, reflecting on the recent events; she still felt reluctant about trusting the Fae. Especially after that morning's spectacle—a merciless, brutish battle between Mazie and the giant.

"Why do I have a feeling like we are being manipulated, Lincoln?" Nola asked. "The queen suddenly wanting to help us?" She turned away and watched the slow current of the creek. "What happened with Mazie—that is not the way my father spoke of the Fae; not what I imagined them to be like."

Lincoln wrapped his fingers over hers and ran his thumb gingerly over the top of her hand.

"I'm always cautious, my love. I do not trust easily. I, too, have suspicions about the Fae's willingness to help."

Nola was not convinced the Fae were on her side. When she arrived the morning after being stuck in the Marsh Wetlands, the fairies had bathed and dressed her but regarded Nola as a trespasser. However, once the queen learned who she was, a sudden shift in acceptance happened a little too quickly. Nola was still a stranger. The crown they laid upon her head meant something more than a long-lost princess coming home. She had not proven herself to them yet.

Queen Cassia had told her she was home.

Home.

This place will never be home, Nola thought. *Never.*

Especially after what I had just witnessed.

She could not become used to such a barbaric culture—one that found pleasure in watching humans and magical creatures die for sport. Nola did not want to kill anyone. War was inevitable to save Zemira, but she did not desire a bloodbath. Nola wished there was another way—there would be no celebrating the fallen.

Lincoln stretched his arm around her waist, holding her tight. The touch of his hands on her hips, blanketing her body into his, was inviting. Nola felt the heat of his breath in her hair as he nuzzled his nose near her ear.

"I will do whatever it takes to keep you safe," he

whispered, then caught her up in his stronghold, tightening his hands around her.

Oh, my, her thoughts mangled a bit in her mind. She did not even try to free herself from Lincoln's possessive hold. *This is all I needed.*

As he held her, Lincoln ran his fingers gently down the back of Nola's arms. His touch was sudden, seductive, and had taken her completely by surprise.

She let out a sigh.

"Okay, what was it you wanted to talk about?" Lincoln asked in her ear softly, withdrawing his hand from her hip.

"Did I say you could let go of me?" Nola said teasingly, feeling his lips part into a smile against her ear.

Lincoln's hand went back on her waist. His fingers inched around her hips and rested on her belly.

"Ever since the first moment we locked eyes," he said, "I have had this desire to protect you. I nearly lost my mind when Wentworth stole you from me."

When Nola turned to face him, his hands slacked from her waist and dropped to his side. "You make it sound as if I was doomed to fail," she said. "I may not be a warrior like Mazie or the elves, but I will fight for the people of Zemira. If that means sacrificing my life to do it, then so be it."

Lincoln lowered his brow, turning away from her.

"Do not say such things. The king's army is strong, yes, but—"

"I can't deny I am afraid, Lincoln, but I would die to save Zemira."

A moment of silence followed as she looked heavenward. Suddenly, a line appeared between her brows.

"As the Elven warriors risk their lives for the queen, I will do the same for my people. And for you." Nola reached up, running her hand down his broad chest. "Your brother's power frightens me, Lincoln. He was in my head. I couldn't escape him."

Lincoln winced at those words.

"I know," he said. "I know the magic my brother holds. Leave it up to me. I will protect you, my love. Not the other way around."

Nola tried to look away, but he lightly gripped her chin, guiding her gaze back to him.

"Can we fight for each other, then?" she said, placing her hand on his cheek.

Lincoln's nod was brief before pulling away. He then stood and held out his hand, helping her to her feet.

Placing both his hands on each side of her jaw, he planted a kiss upon her lips. The taste of his tongue and the sound of his moan against her lips made Nola's heart race, wanting every part of his body and mind.

Lincoln released the kiss and rested his forehead against hers for only a moment before she stepped back and watched the gloom in his eyes, wishing she could read his thoughts.

Suddenly, the wind picked up and the leaves rumbled; they both looked up as Anaru soared above them. The sound of her wings flapping got louder as she circled the courtyard and landed next to one of the stone fountains.

Lincoln staggered back, releasing Nola, and stared deep into the dragon's eyes, who watched them through the pillars.

Up until that moment, Nola had not realized there was an implicit connection between Lincoln and the dragon.

"Have you reconsidered what the queen said? About riding a dragon?" She gestured to the magnificent creature before them. "It is clear to me that Anaru has chosen you," she said, looking back to the animal.

They walked in silence towards the dragon with caution, but the magnificent creature seemed calm and welcoming. Nola slowly placed her hand on her scale-like neck, gliding her fingers along her body and feeling her rough skin against her palm.

"Ride, Lincoln."

He glanced at Anaru before turning back to Nola. "Not so much of a cold-hearted pirate, am I?"

She giggled. "Well, she did try to kill you once."

With tense shoulders, Lincoln finally moved towards the dragon. He joined the siren, placing his hand on the animal's scales as if finally allowing a bond to cross between them. "Try not to kill me, eh?"

Anaru lowered her head and closed her eyes, a sign of submission and respect.

Nola leaned forward, whispering into Anaru's ear. A bright yellow glow swirled within her eyes; a dragon's voice called into her ears with one loud, roaring cry.

Nola smiled. "I can understand her. I can sense her trust. You are safe."

Lincoln hesitantly gripped the creature's shoulder and pulled himself up onto her back. Wrapping his strong arms around her neck, he said, "Alright, you beautiful beast. Let us soar high above the clouds until it is the only place to exist—"

Anaru roared and jumped high, extending her wings and taking off towards the sky. Nola thought she had heard a muffled yelp from Lincoln, and she giggled to herself. She watched her handsome pirate disappear behind the pink-hued clouds on the dragon's back. Her whole face lit up.

A burst of distant laughter from the crew caught Nola's attention.

I better go see what they are getting themselves into, she thought.

As she walked back to the Fae palace, she saw Hill and Ardley mingling among the fairies by the shore. She started moving towards them, but her eyes caught Queen Cassia walking her way.

"Nola?" the queen said. Her Majesty's hand gestured towards the Whispering Woodlands. "Your crew will be held up for a while as my warriors teach them how to use our weapons. So, for now, how about you and I go for a stroll?"

Nola had heard the stories of the Woodlands. It was not a place safe for her or anyone, for that matter.

"Are you sure about walking through there?" she asked the queen.

She replied with a nod and said, "We will be fine as long as you stay close to me."

Nola followed Cassia on the narrow path leading to the Whispering Woodlands. As her feet dug into the grainy sand under her boots, the earth trembled, stopping her from moving.

"They know what you are, Nola," the queen said. "Though they do not welcome strangers, they will allow you to pass today."

"Who does not welcome me?" Nola asked.

"The forest," she answered. "It is as alive as we are, and it hasn't been happy lately, for the giant had been destroying it; we hadn't been doing much about it up until now. Hopefully, that has changed in our favor."

Nola looked up with the queen at the tall trees that grew close to one another, blocking out the sunlit sky.

"We need to stay on the path," Cassia said, ". . . and don't touch the lilacs. They may be beautiful to the eye, but the forest won't be too keen on a siren tainting their land."

Tainting? Nola repeated the queen's words in her mind.

"Am I that repulsive to everyone?" she asked.

"Not everyone," the queen said, then stepped deeper into the path, instructing Nola to follow closely behind.

Was the queen implying the forest has an intelligence of its own? Nola asked herself. *Great. What could go wrong?*

As they moved through the shrubs, a gentle whisper tickled against her skin. It sounded as if someone was standing right behind her, nuzzling up to her ear. Nola turned around, but no one was there. She could almost sense a spirit brushing up against her, grabbing her attention but not ready to reveal itself.

She heard a soft chuckle from the queen. "Ignore them."

"The trees?" Nola looked up again, and all she saw were branches connecting like interlinked arms covered in bright green leaves.

"Yes, Nola. Just stay on the path, and we'll be fine."

The trail was surrounded by lush greenery and delicate flowers covering each branch. It was a narrow and long path. Being exposed from behind made Nola feel unsafe. Any creature in the Woodlands could come up behind her at any moment.

A mild gust swooped through the trees. Nola placed her hand over her nose. "What is that rancid smell?" she asked once they reached a fork in the path. The scent spun her head as if she were in a daze. Then, Nola looked ahead, watching the queen turn left at the fork.

"That would be the trolls. But do not worry, they will only try to eat you if you walk onto their land," Cassia explained. "Stay on the trail."

Bile rose to her throat as it was becoming harder to breathe. "It's awful," Nola said. "It's making me ill."

"Yes, a troll's manure has been used as a weapon before to ward off their enemies. Try to breathe through your mouth."

Nola continued to follow the queen until she stopped abruptly and looked around as if she were lost.

"Oh, dear," the queen said, "not now." She rolled her silvery eyes as she turned to face Nola. "The trees are playing tricks on us. They *really* aren't fond of you being here."

"What now?" Nola asked. When the question left her lips, she looked up as the trees swayed, the ground trembled, and the bushes along the path shifted, moving the trail in a different direction.

A rush of adrenaline moved quickly through her body. "Are they—?"

"They're trying to get us lost. That's what they are doing," the queen said, irritated. "It doesn't matter how long I've been on this land; if I don't stay on the path, I won't be able to guide us back."

But the path is different now, Nola thought. *It looks nothing like it did before.*

Nola looked around again and said, "And if we get off the path to find our way, then the trolls—"

"Then they will eat us," the queen finished in a sinister tone. "Don't think because you're a siren, you can get us out of this either. The trolls from this land are resistant to your powers; they are deaf and blind. They will find us by tracking our scent or the vibration of our movements."

Nola's heartbeat picked up wildly, making her dizzy again. She was being hunted by a creature she had only read about in fairy tales. There was no weapon for her to defend herself, nor did she know what she was up against.

Why would the queen take me on a walk in such a dangerous place? Nola wondered.

The whispering came back but much louder that time. As the queen stepped on the new trail, the ground shifted again, creating three different paths.

This is getting ridiculous, Nola thought.

It was as if the forest could hear what she was thinking; the paths began to disappear before them, leaving the two women standing in the middle of nothing but a cluster of trees.

Nola looked up, watching the queen swallow as terror overtook her face. "Well, I think it's time we run."

They hurried through the forest. No path. No direction. Only the faint light from the sun shining ahead.

Nola heard heavy footsteps from behind, and as she turned to see how close they were, her foot caught on a root, and she flew forward, plummeting to the ground.

The queen had not realized Nola had fallen and continued sprinting through the forest.

I can feel you there, Nola said in her mind, wondering if whatever it was could hear her. No voices echoed back.

Nola rushed to her feet as a twig cracked behind her. When she turned, she was forced to look up, his height towering over her. It was not a troll. He was an elf—a gallant, Elven man. She had met several elves since she had arrived at the Eastland Forest, but none looked quite like him. His pointed ears stuck out through his long, midnight black hair, unlike the other elves, who all grew pearl-white hair. He also lacked the red and gold warrior attire—his all-black clothes pressed snug against his lean figure, with a sword at his hip.

Their eyes held each other captive before his gaze wandered leisurely down her figure. The elf's mouth drew into a thin line. As Nola parted her lips to speak, he turned abruptly, pulling the sword from his hip and thrusting it into a paunchy troll about to slam into him.

Though she instinctively took a hasty step back, her incoherent thoughts raced through her mind—she froze.

The Elven man bent forward, staring deep into her eyes. "Don't be a fool! Run, and never come back here!" he said, trying to grip her arm, but she moved back.

"Thank you," Nola said before racing towards the edge

of the forest. Once she reached the cliffs, finally out of harm's way, she found the queen resting against the rocks with her arms folded across her chest.

"Queen Cassia," she said, her breath hitched.

"You're alive. I thought I had lost you! I panicked when I turned around, and you were not behind me. The forest would not let me back in," she explained.

"It's okay. I am alive, at least. Someone rescued me."

The queen's silvery eyes widened. "Hm, I see you've met Aiden."

Chapter 33

As dusk drew near, Lincoln became unnerved. Sitting not-so-patiently at the edge of the dining bench, he looked up at his surroundings. He carefully watched Lyla, one of the fairy women from the city, serve supper for the Fae and elves.

Waiting was all he could do at that moment.

It had been a couple of hours after his flight with Anaru, and he and the crew had finally joined the Fae for supper. They had been getting used to their new weapons and learning how the two vastly different races could work together. They were all ready for battle, except for Nola.

According to Lyla, the queen had taken Nola on a stroll through the Whispering Woodlands. She refused to tell him why. Of course, that made him mad to no end, triggering an uneasy feeling deep in the pit of his stomach.

The dining table was on the shore, right outside the people's homes in an open field under the stars. Lights lined the trees, brightening up the woods. The moon beamed above them now—their brightest source of light.

Ardley leaned forward, and in a whisper, he asked, "What have they said?"

Lincoln looked over his shoulder, watching the fairy people going about their business. "They claim to know nothing! As if we are fools."

Mazie played with her knife. "They are the only fools into thinking we would not go looking for her," she said.

Hill reached out and stopped the knife from moving. "Are ye goin' to use that, mate?" he asked.

Mazie shrugged. "I'm nah opposed to killin' a fairy if that's what yer askin'," she answered, mimicking Hill's thick accent.

Perched on Boots's lap, Kitten wrapped her arms around his shoulders, leaning her head against his.

"It'd be a shame to start a war wit' the very people we need to fight the king," she said. "But somethin' tells me—"

"They be full of shit," Boots finished, a chuckle escaping his lips. "I'm not the intuitive type, hearties, but somethin' isn't right about Queen Cassia."

Despite the Fae's warning not to smoke on their land, Ardley sucked in a heavy puff from his pipe to calm his nerves. The smoke wafted in the air around his face.

Lincoln rolled his eyes when Lyla's bright lavender fairy wings fluttered past him before she joined them at the table.

"I'm sorry, Lincoln," she said. "I still have no word as to when the queen and princess will return from their journey to the Woodlands." She held up a little wooden bowl and poured a pinkish, hot liquid into each of the crew's mugs.

She is a terrible liar, Lincoln thought.

Lyla swallowed before adding, "I'm sure Princess Nola is

well." The fairy topped off Hill's mug and looked up. "Please, enjoy your tea." With a slight stutter in her words, she continued, "it w-will help you all relax—"

"Enough!" Lincoln shouted, slamming his hand on the table. Tea spilled from most of the mugs as adrenaline coursed through his body.

Lincoln's face reddened, his eyes burning with anger. He hastily jumped to his feet, dragging his hand across the table, knocking everything to the ground.

Mazie threw her legs over the bench and stepped back, her hand ready at her pistol.

Lincoln sucked in a heavy breath before he said, "I do not trust your queen any more than I trust my brother. They have been gone for over an hour since I returned with Anaru. She would have let me know before taking off into a troll-infested forest with a woman she does not trust." His jaw tightened. ". . . And I am to believe she's safe?"

Lyla's face scrunched up as her eyes scanned their dinnerware scattered around the grass.

"How dare you—" she started to shout, but Mazie shoved her nose in the fairy's face; her sword pointed at her long, thin neck. Lyla's periwinkle-toned eyes dimmed. However, Lincoln felt no empathy for the fear they had caused her. The fairy's jaw quivered.

"You heard the captain, you pathetic winged creature! Tell us where Nola is, or I will turn each and every one of you into dust." Mazie smiled at her threat.

Lyla jumped back and held up her hands. "Very well," she said, her voice stammering with each word she spoke. "The queen has taken her to our tree." A nervous smile reached the fairy's lips. "You are too late. You'll not reach her in time."

Lincoln's hands went into fists right before he lunged forward and shoved Lyla against a tree.

"Too late for what?" he asked, his fingers coming up to her throat.

The entire crew jumped to their feet as the queen's Elven protectors rushed to Lyla's aid. The fairies and elves had power, but not enough to defeat a handful of pirates with guns—bullets were faster than magic. All they could do was watch.

When Lincoln pressed his palm harder against Lyla's throat, she attempted to free herself. He tightened his grip, trapping her in place. She waved her hand at the protectors for them to stand down. One squeeze was all it would take to crush her bones and kill her.

The pirates held their weapons up, creating a barrier around their captain as the protectors held their own, awaiting Lyla's order.

"If you try to use your powers or fly away, I am going to cut off your wings," Lincoln said.

The moment his threat left his lips, he regretted it. He averted his eyes from hers, looking away for only a moment before turning back. "I find no pleasure in harming a lady, Lyla," Lincoln said, "but you are my enemy until you cooperate and tell me the truth. You have given me no choice."

Lyla's glimmering, light lavender hair fell over her fair-colored skin, hiding her eyes. Behind her undeniable beauty, she was just like the other fairies who hid their true selves. They may have saved him once as a child, but a lot had changed since he left that place.

Her wings flew out to her sides. They were as lucent as the most delicate veil. Lyla's energy, when frightened, was unlike anything Lincoln had witnessed. The vibration of her wings fluttering so wildly . . . it shook his very core.

Lincoln slammed his hand against the tree; pieces of bark fell over her shoulder and stung the skin of his knuckles.

"The . . . the tree forces the truth out of you," she said quickly; tears of fear glistened in her eyes.

Lincoln's gaze quickly turned to the sea as bellowing cries echoed in his ears. He could not even process what Lyla had just told him.

"What the bloody hell is that?" He had heard what she said, but a dark, harrowing sensation that whatever the noise was in the distance warned him it was a greater threat.

The crew turned their heads in the direction of the sea.

The fairy looked back to Lincoln. "A ship is approaching," she said.

Lincoln released his hold on Lyla. She immediately reached up to the skin around her throat as she gasped for air.

She nodded to the protectors to stand down as the pirates ran towards the shore.

Once they reached the water, Lincoln's eyes narrowed in on the ship docked one hundred feet from the Eastland Forest's coast. It was his father's ship, but it was not the king on the rower. It was Elijah.

"Bloody, fucking hell!" Lincoln cursed, pulling out his sword.

He was not ready to confront and fight his brother so soon, especially in a moment where his mind dreaded the fate of the woman he loved. She was still in the hands of a queen who had deceived them.

Lincoln's eyes locked in on his brother's, wondering how he had found them.

He glanced over to the ship, watching the kingdom guards standing on the vessel's deck, with their weapons ready. Elijah approached the shore on a small rower, unarmed. Lincoln knew his brother held dark magic at the tips of his fingers—weapons were not necessary. Lincoln looked over his shoulder at the crew.

"Stand back and wait for my signal," he said. "My brother is dangerous, and he will not hesitate to kill each one of us."

"Captain Lincoln, is it?" Elijah said as he climbed out of the tiny boat. "I've heard about you."

"Have you now?" Lincoln replied, taking one step back. His knuckles cracked around the hilt of his sword.

"Not all good, but they say you're a marvelous fighter," Elijah said. "It's a shame you've chosen such a pathetic profession. You'd be of great use to me."

Lincoln's eye gave off a twitch. "I'll take piracy over a corrupt kingdom any day, Elijah."

"*Prince* Elijah."

Lincoln bit his tongue, fighting the urge to tell his brother the truth. He had to, but he was unsure how Elijah would react or even if he would believe him.

Lincoln raised his sword as Elijah moved forward. "You can stop right there."

Elijah held up his hands. "I have no weapons, pirate. I am only here for the siren. That is all." Another foot moved forward. "Hand her over, and you may all head back to wherever you came from, safely."

Lincoln raised a brow. "What do you want with her?" he asked.

"My father sent me to retrieve the criminal who boarded your ship," the prince said. "She released two of the prisoners held in my father's dungeon. Now, she must pay for her crimes."

Lincoln huffed. "Well, isn't that a load of crock," he said. "What do you want with the ruby, Elijah?"

The prince's lips drew into a snarl.

"You will address me by Prince—"

"Do you not recognize your own brother?" The words slipped out.

Elijah's eyes grew wide as Lincoln's mouth set in a hard line. But, despite the kind of man Elijah had become, they were brothers, and they were best friends once.

Lincoln could see Elijah's muscles tighten from where he stood. "How dare you speak of my brother, pirate!"

"Look at me, little brother! Look me in my eyes," Lincoln said.

Silence loomed. The moment between the brothers stood still. The only sounds were the waves rolling through the sand and the sound of their steady breaths.

Elijah's brows furrowed, rocking his head from side to

side in disbelief. He raked his fingers through his well-kept hair. "It can't be," he said.

"Our father sent Mason to kill me out in the sea the night our mother died. But I survived," Lincoln explained. "I washed up here; the Fae healed me and sent me out to the sea to join Wentworth's crew."

"What . . . how . . . how do you know about Mason and what happened to my brother—?"

Though the truth stood right in front of him, Elijah continued to shake his head.

"It's me, Brother."

Elijah stepped in their direction, his mouth agape, and he peered into Lincoln's desperate eyes.

"Tristan?"

It had been two decades since Lincoln had spoken to his brother. For years, he traveled to Zemira, always hiding in the shadows, to see his brother grow into a man. But he had also watched him change.

Can I trust him enough not to attack me, as if we are enemies —strangers? Lincoln thought.

"Aye," Lincoln said.

"You became a pirate?" Elijah asked, looking over to the rest of the crew standing behind Lincoln.

". . . And you became our father," Lincoln said, watching Elijah's eyes darken. "You can change, Brother."

Elijah's nostrils flared. "You know nothing of what I've become," he said. "Father is a monster, and the only reason why I am even here is to stop him."

"Nay, you came here for Nola and the ruby, and I want to know why."

Elijah's lips twisted into a smile. "Justice. A plan is unfolding. You may have been my brother all those years ago, but I will not hesitate to end your life to get what I want."

Lincoln lowered his brow. "What? What could you possibly want that you don't already have at that palace?"

"Our mother!" Elijah shouted. "I want our mother back and it is the Kroneon that lies in a cave on Crotona that will help me save her."

As they walked along the cliffside, the queen shared a long, drawn-out story about how her protectors came to be and the role Aiden played in leading the Elven battalion.

Nola looked at her pointedly.

"So, you exiled an elf to the Woodlands for five years?" Nola asked the queen as they both leaned against the cliff's pebble stone wall. "That is quite a long time, Your Majesty."

"The punishment fits the crime, Nola. He refused an order when he became general of the battalion," Cassia said but did not elaborate further. "I am quite impressed he has been able to fight off those trolls for this long." She shrugged. "I thought he would have been dead already."

Nola blinked repeatedly. "But five years?" she asked, not even fathoming the cruelty of it all.

Queen Cassia nodded. "As I have said, the punishment was fair, believe me!"

Nola glared up into the queen's silvery eyes. "He saved me from a troll inside that forest," she said. "That does not sound like someone who deserves the kind of punishment you gave him."

The queen smirked. "Well, that was the first time Aiden's saved anyone, Nola. I was beginning to think there was no fixing him."

Cassia signaled with her head for Nola to follow her the remaining way down the cliffside. They entered a spacious yet empty field. The only piece of nature was a tall, black-barked tree standing at the center. The leaves were bright green, like the color of Lincoln's eyes—its beauty was hard to turn away from.

Nola could feel its powerful energy radiate out towards them. "What is so special about this tree?" she asked.

Queen Cassia placed her hand on the bark, but only for a moment. "It offers truth. For example, you stand here, with a great desire to wage war against a kingdom, but you are afraid, and you hide it quite well," she said, running her hands along the black bark. "It speaks to you, opening your mind to what you try to shield from others."

Nola looked at her quizzically. "I always believed the Fae to be an honest race. Why would you use this tree?"

Cassia smirked. "No one is honest, especially to themselves. This power allows us to find the truth when there is a crime. We don't even need a trial."

"So why am I here?" Nola asked.

The queen's brows quirked up. "Because I need a question answered that I do not believe you will give me the answer to."

Nola snickered. "And you think I am going to place my hand on that bark, willingly, and give you that answer?" she said; her tone sounded brave and courageous. However, she was anything but at that moment. "The Fae are not a bright race, either. Are they?"

I am going to regret that, Nola thought. A hint of fear, or maybe it was hatred, rushed through her veins.

No monstrous beast of the sea, swamp, or cowardly king had ever made her feel the way the queen did. She was threatening Nola to reveal her secrets. She was beginning to feel aggravated—feeling like she had no choice. There was no greater darkness than that.

The queen rolled her eyes. "I never said willingly."

Queen Cassia's wings came out from her back as she lifted her hand and moved it swiftly in the air. Nola flew forward closer to the tree until she planted both hands on it. The queen's strong power kept her hands to the bark.

"Stop!" Nola cried. "What are you doing?"

Cassia glided slowly over to Nola and grimaced. "When you were a baby, your father placed a ruby on your mother before the two of you went out to the sea."

Nola's stomach tightened, nerves making her nauseous. She had the ruby in the satchel placed under her shirt. All the queen had to do was reach up and get it. She pressed her lips together, willing herself to fight against the power flooding into her body.

"I believe you may know the whereabouts of that gem," the queen said.

Nola shook her head, finding the strength to shut her brain off so the words would not come. The power entered her mind, commanding her mouth to speak the truth. Her hair stood on end as fear swallowed her.

The queen scowled, looking frustrated. "The ruby, Nola. Where is it?"

Nola did open her mouth that time but only to ask, "What do you want with the ruby? What does it do?"

All Nola knew was, according to Elijah, it was a key to something called the Kroneon.

"Do you have it?" That time the queen shouted, her cheeks turning bright red.

"Yes, I have it!" The words came out before she could stop them.

Dammit! Nola cried in her thoughts. *Do not be a fool. Fight it.*

The queen smoothed out her hair and placed her hands behind her back, locking her fingers. "It's a key to a weapon, Nola—a weapon that belongs to the Fae. I only want to keep it safe from our enemies," she said. "Tell me where you have hidden it."

Nola shook her head, fighting the need to tell the truth. "What kind of weapon?" she asked the queen as beads of sweat trickled down her forehead. The heat from the magic made her feel faint.

The queen dropped her hands to her side as the features on her face grew hard.

"It is a shame you know nothing of your past." Cassia walked around the tree, resting her hand upon it, and looked Nola deep into her eyes. "When the ruby sits at the center of the compass, it activates its power." She pointed south. "The compass is hidden in a cave on Crotona Island. You can see the peak of the cliff from where we stand—at about an hour on a fast ship. You and I can go there together and get it. Unfortunately, I do not have the map anymore. But the ruby will help us find the compass, as the two powers will be drawn to each other."

Nola shook her head. "What power does the compass hold, Cassia?" she asked again, her body starting to shake. "What does it do?"

The queen's smile faded. "If you turn the key right, you move through time, into the future. Any *time* you want to go," she explained.

Nola's lips parted.

"If you turn it left," she said, "it will take you to your past."

Time travel, Nola said in her mind. *How is that possible*?

Nola mustered all the power she had and finally pried her fingers from the tree, then quickly stepped back.

It took her a few seconds to get her bearings. Nola held her stomach, taking a steady breath in. Her thoughts muddled as she remembered Elijah's words in the realm he had trapped her in.

Oh, to the Gods. That's it. Her thoughts dawned on her. *Prince Elijah is going back in time to kill King Matthias and save his mother.*

"The Kroneon helps you travel through time?" Lincoln said, his eyes growing wide from what his brother had just shared. "That's impossible."

Elijah's lips drew back in a snarl. "No, it's not. I need the siren, the key, and the compass to make that happen. And we will have our mother back."

Lincoln held out his sword, willing to do whatever it took to save the woman he loved. Going back in time, even to save his mother, could not happen. It would change everything.

"Elijah," Lincoln said. "Don't do this."

Ignoring his plea, Elijah continued to walk their way and lifted his hands.

Shit, he cursed in his mind.

"Run!" Lincoln shouted to his mates. They turned, bolting into the forest, right as black smoke left Elijah's fingers.

The black cloud rolled through the woods, blanketing everything in its path. They did not stop running, but the smoke was faster; it covered the trail, making it impossible to see.

Lincoln stopped when he could no longer hear his mates running behind him. The sudden shift in the air density felt like poison coming into his lungs—burning. The weirdly dense gas started suffocating him. His own mind drifted into a world his brother had created—a world where he no longer saw reality.

An out-of-place rumble pounded in his ears before falling into pitch-black darkness.

Nola's eyes grew wide and stepped back as she peered into the sky.

She looked up, watching the black cloud reach her. When the cloud stopped circling and took the shape of large fingers, it thrust forward, gripping hold of her waist.

"Nola!" the queen shouted her name, but her cries sounded like an echo in the distance.

The black smoke swirled around Nola faster and faster as if she was in the eye of a tornado. Then, the black cloud dissipated, taking her with it.

Chapter 34

Deep in the woods, Aiden slowly opened his eyes and looked up through the trees. A bunch of twigs and rocks pressed into his back. He sat up, still feeling queasy, and watched the black cloud disappear.

"What was that?" he said aloud.

"Aiden, you're up!" Cassia said, standing close to where he was. Her voice sounded out of breath as if she had run to his aid.

He reached for his sword, lifting it quickly in front of him. The queen stopped right as the sharp end pressed into her chest. She backed up.

"Stop, Aiden!" she said.

"I should kill you now." His ice-blue eyes burned with rage.

"I know you are not pleased with me—"

"Pleased?" he repeated. "I have been a prisoner in this—"

Cassia's hand came up, stopping him abruptly.

"I will free you from this place if you help me." Her words were quick.

He was not a fool to believe she would not do or say anything to keep him from killing her.

Aiden's dark, thin brows rose. "Free me?"

The queen nodded. "That power belongs to Prince Elijah. He's here, and he has taken Seraphina."

Recognition glowed in his eyes, and he took a step back, quickly remembering the girl he had saved from the troll moments before.

"Argon's child?" Aiden said. "I thought—?"

"She was dead? Yes. We all did. But she is alive and well. They call her Nola now." Cassia adjusted her dress, her wings folding back into her body. "She was raised by humans in Zemira. And now she's come to start a war."

Aiden's forehead furrowed. Not only did the two of them not trust each other, but he was always different than the rest of the battalion—and that, particularly, infuriated the queen.

There would be no forgiveness for his unjust imprisonment, but he decided to hear her out.

"Help you do what?" he asked sharply.

Years ago, Cassia wanted Aiden, son of Hagmar, to lead the Elven warriors in the battle with King Matthias.

Twenty years had passed since King Argon sent his father to hide the Kroneon on Crotona Island. Hagmar had barely made it back to the Eastland Forest alive. He had been badly wounded by the creatures living in that dreadful place and ended up dying in the queen's arms. Aiden remembered Cassia cared more about getting her map back than the lives of the elves King Argon had sent to their deaths.

Young Aiden had to watch his mother mourn for years before her own death. Then the queen dared to ask the same from him—only fifteen years later.

Five years before, Cassia's orders were clear. "Go to Crotona and retrieve the weapon, Aiden. Bring it back here, and it will guide us to find the key!"

Aiden would never forget those words. The queen's ambition was responsible for his defiance—disobedience that led to his exile.

Hagmar, his father, had lost his life protecting the Kroneon, and the queen had asked Aiden to get it back. His father would have died in vain. For that, he refused the queen, and she sent him to live alone in the woodlands, with the intention he would not survive.

What are you up to, Queen Cassia? Aiden asked in his mind. *To be so willing to let me go after all these years.*

Aiden looked up. Tiny specks of the black mist still floated through the trees. His brows drew together as he looked back at the queen.

"That compass your father worked so hard to protect is now in danger of being found by our enemies," she said.

And there it is, he thought. *The queen has not changed one bit.*

She stepped towards him, placing her hand hesitantly on his and rubbed gently over his smooth skin.

"I will release you if you gather the protectors and the rest of the battalion. Go to Crotona and retrieve the weapon before the prince and the siren do. But—" She swallowed. "You are to kill the siren and get the ruby before the two pieces unite."

Aiden's expression hardened. "You want me to kill the siren?"

The queen nodded. "You can do it, or I will. We were never supposed to be banished here, Aiden. The compass will allow me to go back to before we were sent to the Eastland Forest. My brother did not fight hard enough for us. He cowered to Matthias. That alone made him unfit to lead." She stepped closer, applying pressure to his fingers. "Your father died because of Argon."

Aiden stepped away from Cassia, wiggling his fingers away from hers—her touch made him sick.

"Why do you want to kill the siren?" he asked. "Seraphina is your niece."

"No, Aiden, she is my brother's bastard child. And if she lives, in all timelines, she is the next heir to the Fae. I cannot allow a half-breed to lead our people. And that weapon belongs to us."

With a brief tilt of his head, he asked, "If you go back in time, does that mean—"

"Your father will have never perished."

His pulse thrashed in his throat.

Could it be that simple? Aiden wondered.

He blamed Argon for sending his father to his death, but he hated the queen even more.

A slow smile reached his lips. "If you betray me, my queen, I will kill you."

The queen's wings came out again, brightly lit and ravishing.

"You are free," she said. "Prepare the ships for Crotona."

The two ships rocked against the waves as the storm rolled in. Aiden fixed his eyes to the one that once belonged to his father. The Elven warriors stood proudly on the deck, waiting for his command.

"Valkanon," he called. "Where are the queen's protectors?"

The Elven protectors would, no doubt, defend the queen. Still, most Elven warriors held loyalty to their own kind—not to the Fae, and especially not to Queen Cassia.

Hagmar would have never wanted his battalion to fight or harm innocent people. And Aiden thought no differently from his father.

What the queen asked Aiden to do was traitorous. It went against everything the sea folk, elves, and fairies agreed upon during the First Treaty. The treaty united the magical races to peace. Neither Aiden nor his loyal warriors would agree to such violence.

"Make sure the protectors are on the queen's ship, not ours," Aiden said. "Once a few miles from Crotona, our mission is to protect the siren, for she is the true heir to lead the Fae—Argon's first and only born child."

A swirl of nerves reached his stomach.

Valkanon smiled back at the newly appointed Elven general.

"You have our word," he said, giving Aiden a bow. "And, what about the pirates?"

"They have not awoken yet," Aiden replied. "Human

bodies are frail when it comes to magic. Elijah's power will make them sleep for hours."

"Should we wake them, then?" Valkanon asked, looking to the shoreline which led to the Sybil Curse. "We could use their skill in the sea."

Aiden shook his head. "No need to put them in the queen's path. Our mission is to find the siren and protect her. That is all. If the protectors attack our allies, then we will wield our weapons and put them down."

A cold feeling trailed up Aiden's spine. He was asking his men to go against what his father taught him as a child —never attack your own people. But the Elven protectors had lost their way, such as the queen.

Valkanon looked to the skies, watching Queen Cassia soaring the clouds above the ship, riding her dragon. He rushed to the boat, gathered up their weapons, and prepared the fleet for departure.

Chapter 35

A gentle breeze brought in the scent of the sea, while a cloudy haze created a misty dew upon Nola's cheeks. Her eyes shot open, looking up into the dark grey clouds above her. Her vision blurred as she turned her head, trying to make sense of her surroundings. Prince Elijah knelt beside her.

Nola could not remember what had happened in the last few hours. It was all a blur after the black smoke took her.

She felt the ship rock as they journeyed on the sea. Nola tried to sit up as she felt much more conscious than before. However, Elijah placed his hand upon her head, putting her to sleep again.

What felt like a few minutes later, she woke again and sat straight up. Her body stiffened when she saw Elijah so close to her.

"Easy, Nola," he said, as a flash of amusement crossed his features. "Your head will feel slightly dizzy for a while, but you will live."

His smile faded as he gingerly brushed Nola's damp

forehead with his fingers. Her brows furrowed at the unusually tender gesture.

"Now get up." His curt tone gave her heart a sudden jump.

Nola did not move. She brought her hands up and pressed her temples, trying to stop the pounding headache.

He is right, Nola thought. *Whatever he did to me scrambled up my head.*

Still ignoring the prince, Nola looked out to the mysterious island he had taken her—the black sand beach. Crotona.

She felt Elijah's hand at her elbow, helping lift her onto her feet. Then, he led her off his ship.

Once standing on the mossy, wet rock, Nola turned her gaze to the sea. About a mile out, a thick veil of fog encircled Crotona Island. She had not seen anything like it; it was such a strange phenomenon.

"What is that?" she asked.

"The fog?" he said. "Well, I do not doubt for one moment those pirates and the queen will be coming for you. It's simple magic, but it will buy us some time."

A line appeared between her brows. "You did that?" Nola asked.

She was all alone with him. Completely.

"Are your men joining us?" she asked, sitting down on the sand, leaning against a piece of driftwood.

Elijah shook his head. "I do not have the right to put men in danger when I can do something myself. So they will stay there off the shore, and you and I will go get the weapon."

Nola scrunched up her face and placed her hand against her hip, hiding the fact that she was looking for the satchel. To her relief, it was wrapped around her slim waist, keeping the ruby safe and hidden.

The sky was gloomy; only the moon reflected off the water, giving her a short moment of serene peace. The shore itself was wide open, minus a few overgrown palm trees leaning into each other. And other than the quiet whisper of the waves colliding with the sand, the atmosphere was nearly soundless. There was no buzzing from insects or chirps from birds within the trees. It was as if no life resided there.

Nola's eyes again looked back at Elijah's brooding features. His messy hair and dirt-stained clothes caught her a bit off guard, given how tidied-up he appeared the last time she saw him. However, even the darkness did not hide his beauty.

A large bag draped over his left shoulder, partially opened. At the tip, stuck out part of a bow.

My father's bow, she assumed. *The one he bargained for at the market for a meaningless conversation with me.*

Elijah's steely blue eyes gave her a piercing stare. It was a gaze that sent chills up her spine and would not break.

"It's going to get dark soon; we won't be able to see. We need to get moving. Get up!" the prince said again when she did not move. His hand reached out.

"You think this is the way, Elijah?" Nola's voice wavered, not acknowledging his hand. "What exactly do you think is going to happen here?" She got up on her own, not because he was ordering her to do so, but she felt an object press sharply into the bridge of her back. Nola looked down to see a seashell sticking through the fine, jet-black sand.

We are going to die here, she thought.

She looked over to the rocks lining the water coming to a steep, rocky path.

He sighed. "In and out, and then you can return to your pirate."

Elijah's words caused panic to clutch at her chest. "Lincoln—"

He held up a hand. "I know who he is," he said, "and no, I did not hurt him."

She swallowed.

He could be lying, she thought.

Nola glanced at him; Elijah's expression was entirely unreadable. His sullen eyes did not match the cynical grin across his lips.

He wants me to fear him, she thought.

"May I ask you something?" Nola said.

He nodded.

"How did you know about the ruby, or—"

"Key?" he interrupted.

Nola gave a brief nod. "What is it to you?"

"When a pirate does your dirty work, you have many eyes and ears out in the sea. Wentworth used to have a map before the famous Captain Lincoln stole it from him." He stepped closer to her, but she did not move back. "My birth mother's ancestors charmed the ruby. I'm connected to its power, and it is that power that will guide me to the weapon needed to activate it."

Elijah pointed to where the satchel was under her shirt. Nola's face blushed.

He knew where it was all this time, she thought.

"I felt the ruby that day at the marketplace, just as I feel it now. No map, only the power it holds calls me. And, well, it will ultimately guide me to the weapon."

Nola pressed her palm to the satchel, feeling the precious gem touching her skin. She knew it was only a matter of time before he forced it from her, but until then . . .

"Lincoln told me a story about the creatures on this island," Nola said. "You may be a fool, but I am not." She turned on her heel, heading back to the shore. "Have a nice journey up that cliff. I'm not going with you."

As she walked away, Nola felt his strong hand latch to her shirt, yanking her back. Flinging into his arms, he twirled her until she was facing him, then pushed her to the edge of the cliff, letting her body hang over the pointy rocks. His fingers quickly crawled under her shirt and ripped the satchel from her waist.

Elijah pocketed the satchel, his smile faint. "I still need you," he whispered to her ear as he pulled her towards him.

Nola shook her head, frustrated, but felt his finger under her chin, lifting it up to meet his eyes.

"The creatures on this island are preventing me from getting to the Kroneon," he explained, then sized her up. "Be more concerned about *why* I need you. The ruby is only a part of my plan."

"Oh, I have been asking myself that question over and

over again, but I'm certain you will only feed me lies." Her forehead crinkled as she raised a brow.

Elijah released her and stepped back, giving her space. "No. I have no reason to keep anything from you. I have you now."

He has nothing, she thought.

The prince reached out, gripping her arm and giving it a tight squeeze. Nola tried to wiggle from his hold, but he only increased the pressure until she winced.

"I get it," she said boldly. "You want to go back in time to change what happened to your mum," she said.

He stopped and looked up. "Then stop fighting me," he said, his tone brusque. The prince dragged her away from the water, forcing her to walk closer to the woods. Once they reached the forest which led to the cliff, he released her arm, leaning so close she felt his breath on her cheek. "I said stop fighting me. If you keep this up, we won't find shelter before whatever lurks in these woods finds us!"

"Oh, I plan to fight you every step of the way, Elijah," Nola said. "And just because I understand why you are doing it does not mean I agree with you." She watched as his face grew hard. "You cannot change the past. You have no idea what ramifications will occur. It could be catastrophic."

His nostrils flared. "I don't care." The prince caught her arm again. "This way."

He is unhinged or a damn fool if he believes I will help him, she thought.

Nola planted her feet. "What if we worked together?" she said, trying to talk him down enough to where he would not take her further into the island. "Now that the Fae have no intention of truly helping us, we could use your magic. Let us work together. Let's fight Matthias in *this* time."

Of course, that was a lie. Nola could never trust the prince.

His hand slacked around her elbow, dropping his arm to his side. "My mother would still be dead. The only way to get what I need is to stop him twenty years ago. I need that weapon, and I need the ruby to do it. I need *your* help to do it."

Nola's lips parted, feeling a tug of guilt. She understood Elijah's need to save the ones he loved, but not like that. And surely, she would not help a prince who would no doubt use that weapon in other means.

"Nola," he said, stepping closer to her. "I do not want to hurt you—"

"Then don't!" she shouted, choking on her words. "I have been kidnapped twice in the last few days. Chased by a wendigo—" she watched Elijah's brow rise in the darkness, "—almost killed by a Kraken, and the one queen, whom I had believed to want to help us, turned out to be no better than you." It was a bold move, but she stepped even closer until she almost touched his face. "Do not grab my arm again unless you want to see a side of me that I didn't know existed until a few days ago. The side which kills men like you," she added. "I can walk on my own."

His smile was faint, but it was evident her temper amused him. "Fine," he said, stepping back. "But I need you to use that siren call of yours to control the creatures on this land. We have to reach that cave without being torn to pieces." A small smile reached his lips. "I know who your mother was, Nola. I know what you can do."

And there it was. The reason the prince needed her.

Her stomach jumped. "I am barely able to control this magic of mine, Elijah."

He adjusted the bag on his shoulder and walked in front of her. "You controlled the mind of a Kraken," he said without turning around.

She struggled to catch up as he picked up the pace. "Why don't you use your own magic on whatever is here?"

Elijah stopped at the edge of the cliff and turned to her. "Are you always this sassy?"

Nola amused him, which, of course, irritated her.

"I'm serious! That black smoke of yours lifted me in the air. I zipped through space and time and ended aboard your ship."

He shrugged. "I am not that powerful when I do not know what I am up against," he said, "One siren call, and that's it, the path is cleared for us." Elijah flashed a charming smile.

Nola rolled her eyes as they continued traveling up the rocks. It felt as if they had been traveling for hours around the rocky cliffs.

"I need to rest, Elijah. Please."

The prince turned to her and nodded. "Here," he said, pulling the bag off his shoulder and reaching inside. He pulled out a costrel draped in black, embossed leather, and popped off the cork.

Nola reached out to take it while gesturing to the bag.

"Is that the bow my father sold you?" she asked, taking only a meager amount of water to quench her thirst.

Elijah rested his hand on the tip. "That it is. Here," he said, pulling it out of the bag and handing it to her. "I have no idea how to use it." He chuckled to himself.

Nola slowly wrapped her hands around the bow and looked up. "A bit bold of you to trust me with it."

"We can learn to trust each other. Aren't we *in* for the same cause? Or you can kill me with it now," he said.

Nola raised the bow and pulled an arrow back, aiming directly at him. A smile reached her lips.

"Your hands truly belong to a bow, don't they?" Elijah asked. His tone was oddly calm.

With slight hesitation, she lowered the bow. "Thank you."

Nola kept her eyes locked on the prince. She did not see herself killing Lincoln's brother. There had to be good inside him still. Could she save the prince from doing something he would regret after? Save him from becoming *his* father?

"So, this power of yours . . . you say you can feel the ruby? It somehow tells you where the other piece to the weapon is?" she asked.

"Yes. Sort of," he replied, stepping back. "I can't exactly *see* the cave, but I can feel a pull at my chest as if I'm tied to it. The closer we get to the location, the stronger the bond is."

Nola shook her head in disbelief. "I've had this ruby on me since I was a baby. How did you not feel it?"

Elijah shrugged. "I thought I felt it years ago, but then

the feeling went away." He looked at her. "My guess is you didn't spend too much time near the palace. And I never left it. I did not have the freedom you did."

Nola squeezed her eyes shut. Wealth and power were not everything. The look in his eyes was of loneliness and pain. She was blessed to have all that she did; parents who loved her, a home, friends, and a happy childhood. Their life may have been hard at times as they begged their neighbors for a decent barter in exchange for food. However, she had people who loved her; he did not. Prince Elijah lived in an extravagant castle but with a father who despised him.

Is this why he turned out the way he did? Nola wondered, watching his eyes dim. She felt pity for him.

The rock wall reached several feet above sea level; Nola did not feel safe that high above the ground. Crotona's vegetation was quite a mystery to her eyes. Black sand amidst a grove of leafy palm trees covered most of the damp land.

They were halfway up the mountain when the rain started to pour, creating even more of a muddy swamp. With each step, Nola slid further and further down. Her body was covered in mud as the rain poured harder, running down her eyes.

Nola gave a hasty glance over her shoulder, feeling as though they were being watched.

It was only getting darker.

"We can't go any further, Elijah! We need shelter."

Elijah pressed his hand into her back, trying to help her climb, but all they did was slide down. They slid further and further until they reached the spot right where they first started.

Nola focused on the sounds around her. The heavy breathing within the woods caused the hairs on her arms to stand straight. But aside from a bow and arrow, they had nothing. They were out in the open, amidst the darkness and the rain.

A fast movement between the trees caught Nola's eye.

"Elijah?" she called. His hand reached for her arm, pulling her behind him as she noticed an entity creeping in their direction.

"Alright, let's find shelter," he said, looking over her shoulder, her body stiffening.

"Oh, my—!"

He jumped forward, muffling her mouth with his hand to silence her.

"Shh," he said into her ear. Elijah slowly dropped his hand. "You might want to raise that bow," he said. "They're here."

Nola turned slowly when two red eyes looked back at her between the trees. She raised the bow, watching the creature move slowly out of the shadows. Its skin looked rough, almost grainy. The grotesque contorted features and its bony hairless limbs made Nola's hairs stand straight. The creature raised its hand, revealing dirty, unkempt nails which were sharp as blades. Much like the wendigo but not as pale. Not as lean. Despite the being's terrifying features, its form was more humanlike than a monster.

The arrow sprang from the bow, but Nola missed. Her hands would not stop shaking.

This is how I'm going to die, she thought. *I have to sing. It is the only weapon I've got left.*

She opened her mouth and sang, but when the creature kept moving, she stepped back. Panic clutched her throat.

"It's not working, Elijah. It's—"

"Are you doing it right?!" he shouted, the two of them backing up into a tree.

"Yes, I'm doing it right!"

"Get ready to run," he said. "Now!"

Nola felt Elijah's hand on her shoulder, yanking her away as the creature pounced across the grass, its claws missing her by an inch. The two darted through the forest, stumbling over every rock or twig on their path, but kept their pace.

"Use your magic, dammit!" Nola shouted.

Elijah gripped hold of Nola's hand to help her keep up, as he was running much faster than her.

He whipped around as they heard the growl from the creature coming closer to them. Elijah held his hands out, and Nola watched as his black smoke left his fingers and enveloped the beast. It screamed and cried, but it did not stop.

"It would be much easier if you could summon it to your will," he said, turning to her. "I can't use my powers to possess them, only slow it down. It isn't human."

"Elijah, I'm trying," she said. Nola sang again, louder that time, but the creature stomped towards them, its red eyes enraged. The creature's hand came out and slammed hard against Elijah's cheek, tossing him to the side as if he were weightless.

Nola stopped and stumbled back. She tried singing again, even louder, yet the savage beast would not stop.

The monster leapt towards her, straddling over her body, pinning her down and pressing its rough, dried-out legs against Nola's thighs and its hand into her chest. The other hand tried to gouge her eyes with its nails, but Nola shifted her body, the creature's hand landing in the dirt instead.

Nola cupped her hands over her ears to block out the piercing sound as Elijah used the jagged point of an arrow to stab the creature through the chest.

The lifeless beast collapsed against her body. Nola rushed to push it off her.

No! Nola thought in her mind. *It cannot be.*

"Elijah," she said, looking up. "I know why it wouldn't succumb to my power."

"Care to share your theory," he called out, still catching his breath while stepping quickly to her aid.

Nola jumped to her feet on her own. "Look above its navel," she said. His eyes darted to the creature, whose birthmark looked just like Nola's.

"You see it?" she said. "They are sirens, Elijah. I cannot control my own kind."

His eyes went wide. "Well," he said. "I did not see that coming."

She ran her hand nervously through her hair, dusting off some dry mud.

"We need to find shelter. Now," Elijah said. "We can't defeat them in the dark."

Nola had seen a small cave in the distance before they

were attacked. There was so much moisture in the terrain, they could barely walk through the muddy path.

The prince gestured to the cave. “That one,” he said.

She followed him closely, ducking under the arch and moving far away from the entry.

It was so dark inside she could not see a thing.

“I don’t know how safe we will be in here, but it’s better than out there,” Elijah said.

As they both sat on the cave’s floor, Nola wiped the mud off her cheeks and ran her hands down her shirt.

“It’s so cold,” she said, wrapping her arms around her waist.

She could not shake the thought that it was sirens roaming that island—sirens who had somehow evolved into something unrecognizable.

Nola placed her hand over her arm, rubbing against her smooth skin. Nothing had changed, but could it?

Could I become like—her? She swallowed, feeling a nervous lump in her throat.

Nola had been so afraid since she left Zemira. One dangerous, life-threatening encounter after another. She did not want to feel scared anymore. The need to fight for her kingdom consumed her, but her powers and training were not enough. No matter how untrustworthy and dangerous Elijah was, those creatures were worse. They had to work together. That—thing, wanted to kill her, and it would have.

“Elijah?” she called in the darkness.

“Yes, Nola,” his voice was not far from where she sat, but she still was not sure where in the cave he was.

She cleared her throat. "Aside from those hair-raising powers of yours, you seem nothing like I imagined."

She instantly regretted her words. The silence made her feel uncomfortable. Nola was thankful for the darkness, as she knew her cheeks had turned red.

"Anything else?" Nola heard him say.

Reclining her head back against the cave, she let out an exasperated breath.

"Do you promise to release me after I help you?" she asked.

Nola waited for his answer but was met with silence. Elijah would find the compass with or without her help; that she understood. It was about survival and getting back to the ship safely come morning. There was no way she could do it alone. Nola had no choice.

A sigh left the prince's lips as if tired of her being on edge around him.

"Yes," he said. "I give you my word."

She felt his fingers tug at her leg.

"Here." Elijah pulled at her pant leg. "We need to keep each other warm."

"What?" she said, realizing what he was suggesting.

"Without any ill intentions, Nola, I think we need to keep each other warm."

He wants to cuddle with me? "Are you mad?" she said.

She felt his hand drop.

"Then freeze to death," he said. She heard the rustling sound of Elijah opening his bag, removing a few items before he laid down.

She continued to shiver, rubbing her hands down her legs, still trying to catch her breath.

"I'm not going to bite, Nola," he said. "We will freeze to death if we do not warm each other. The temperature is going to drop, and we are drenched."

He is right, she told herself. *Dammit.*

Nola reached out, feeling the soft material he was wrapped in. The prince was well prepared before they came on the island, and she would be an idiot to refuse a blanket and warm body to keep her alive.

"Fine," she said stubbornly.

She moved quickly before she changed her mind. Though she could not see, she sensed Elijah's amusement as a quiet snicker left his lips before opening the blanket and cocooning her inside. His muscular arms wrapped around her and pulled her close against his chest.

"You know," he said. "It would be better if you took off those wet clothes—"

"Not a chance," Nola said, her voice stammering from the cold. "I'd rather freeze to death."

The breath of his quiet chuckle tickled the side of her cheek, and guilt wrapped her mind—confused and bothersome. She believed him to be cold-hearted. But was he?

He gave her a tight squeeze.

"Goodnight, Nola," Elijah said before closing his eyes.

Chapter 36

The sun had not fully risen, but enough light beamed above the horizon, allowing Nola to see through the trees. The morning had come quickly, though sleep was impossible. Despite the attempt to stay warm in Elijah's arms, her clothes remained damp throughout the night, and the ground's rocky surface caused her to shift every few minutes. The prince, however, slept soundly.

After she left the cave, she looked around. No sign of any of the sirens—well, whatever the sirens had become. Nola felt a strange disconnect within her body like she was becoming detached from herself. She shook her head, blaming the sleepless, cold night.

"Are you ready?" the prince asked as Nola walked back into the cave. There was a moment of silence as she stared blankly at the cave's surroundings, not understanding where they were exactly.

"What?" she asked, the sleepless night taking effect. Every step she took or word that left her mouth felt aimless.

Elijah's eyes softened. "Nola, are you okay?" he asked.

She felt his hand on her chin, but in an instant, he pulled back.

Nola blinked, their journey to the cave dawning on her. She wanted to run and flee to the sea in hopes Elijah did not stop her. Or try to change her mind.

She nodded hesitantly. "Yes. Let's get this over with," she said, turning on her heel to follow him.

There was an awkward silence between them. Elijah looked as if he, for a moment, questioned their purpose in that horrible place. But Nola knew it would not stop the prince, for he had waited twenty years to bring his mother back.

"This way," he said as he turned to a trail near the cliff. The rising sun had dried the mud, leaving it hard enough so they would not slip.

Once at the top, Nola heard a waterfall on the other side of a rock's peak. As they turned the corner, they both took a deep breath when they finally saw the cave's entrance. The atmosphere quieted around them aside from the water splashing into a gorgeous turquoise lake.

Crotona seemed like a different place when the sun was up in the sky. It gave them a sense of peace as they walked around the lake to enter the cavern. Elijah held out a hand for Nola to take, helping her down the stone-carved stairs. They traveled down the rock corridor before reaching a chamber with a gate—thankfully, unlocked.

"I can feel its power." He pointed to a room at the end of the third tunnel. "The Kroneon is in there."

Nola followed him, even when her mind told her to run in the opposite direction. Though, she felt it did not matter at that point; those creatures were still out there. She was in danger whether she was hiding inside that cave or running to the sea.

"Right here," Elijah said.

They entered a room with tall ceilings and a small opening to the sky. A ray of light shined into the cave, allowing them to see the space around them.

Nola's eyes immediately drew to the ancient petroglyphs covering the walls. Most of them were of the sea: the water, the sea folk, and—

"Is that?" Nola asked, running her finger over a drawing of a compass right beneath a sea craft. To the right was a woman, her hands outstretched, and carved stones surrounded her.

"The weapon was created by a sorceress," Elijah said. "My birth mother, Gal's, great-great-grandmother."

Nola turned to look at him. "What do you know about the weapon?" she asked.

A side smirk grew on Elijah's lips. "The Kroneon was created for the sea folk. It was meant to protect the Kingdom of the Undersea, not to create war."

She looked back, her gaze wandering slowly up the wall. "But that is exactly what it did," she said.

Nola felt the prince by her side, looking at the drawings with her. "Yes. Once all the races knew about it, they fought and killed to find it. Twenty years ago, the weapon was found by your birth father, and the Fae thought they could claim it. But it never belonged to the Fae. And it never will."

Elijah reached out and ran his finger over the

compass's drawing, then turned, facing an altar in the far-right corner of the room. There, at the center, was the compass.

Nola stared at Elijah, but then her eyes noticed other jewels and troves around them.

"What is all this?" she asked.

"These caves are ancient, Nola. Most have been here for centuries—a lot of what you see here is King Argon's treasure."

Large, open-lid chests in each corner, covered in sparkling jewels and gems of all colors and shapes, sparkled throughout the room.

Nola arched a brow. "This is a pirate's dream," she said. "Lincoln has been looking for this place for over a decade." Nola looked around again; a small temptation of taking a little bit here and there grew within her. But that was not the reason they were there.

They both sauntered over to the altar. Nola rested her palms on the surface, staring at the compass. Her eyebrows lifted, mesmerized by such a simple, ordinary device. It did not shine or radiate power, yet its use was as powerful as a raging storm.

"King Argon, from what my father has told me, had many treasure troves and kept them hidden here." He picked up the compass carefully. "The legend told that the monsters who lived on Crotona were here for one purpose; to protect his treasure, especially this."

Nola's lips drew into a hard line. "Argon decided to use my kind as slaves, Elijah," she said. "Trapping them here and giving them no choice but to evolve into monsters.

Luring them here under false pretense." Uneasiness stirred in her belly.

She did not know her birth father, but knowing that about him broke her heart.

Did he even love me? Or my mother? Nola wondered.

She reached forward and placed her hand on the compass while Elijah held it still. The bronze, rustic metal felt cool against her skin. It looked like any ancient compass she had seen in nautical literature. The only difference was a round hole on its front.

That must be for the key, Nola thought.

Prince Elijah's blue eyes settled on hers. "If you could see into the future, Nola," he said, "you could change it. If you could go back in time, you could right your wrongs."

He pointed at the round gap in the center of the weapon. Nola understood why.

With such an artifact, she could go back in time to meet her birth mother. Or even see the future of Zemira.

"May I?" she asked, holding out her hand. He nodded and placed it in her palm. Nola turned it around and on the back was an engraving. A shark eye symbol.

And there it is, she said in her mind—*the siren's mark.*

"Queen Cassia lied to me," Nola said, looking up. "I don't know why she wants this so badly, but she too will be coming for it."

At that point, Elijah's expression was hard to read. However, Nola had the feeling he already knew that about the queen.

Nola turned to the markings on the cave once more. She wanted to help him. But not the way he desired. She could not stop him; that was obvious. Elijah had both pieces to the weapon. The only thing Nola could do was try to change his mind.

Her fingers curled around the compass, keeping it safe and secure. The wisest choice, of course, was to run.

"If you do this, Elijah," she said, "I'm coming with you." Nola sucked in a breath and looked down at the compass, running her fingers over the smooth texture. "I know you've been searching for the Kroneon since you learned of its power." She hesitated but handed it back to him. "We can go together, and I'll let you look into your father's eyes and tell him what you must, but I won't let you kill him."

His mouth twisted into a smile, letting out a short, derisive laugh. "And you're going to stop me if I try?"

Nola shook her head. "I do not blame you for wanting to save your mother, Elijah. But I don't believe you will go through with it," she said. "And if you care at all about anyone but yourself, know that I would lose *my* family. Everything, and I mean everything, would change. Even you."

The prince gripped the compass, and a soft laugh left his lips. "You've thought about all this more than I have." Elijah placed his hand into his pocket and pulled the ruby out, placing it inside the keyhole, hearing a click.

They both watched the compass begin to glow.

"Right to go forward in time," Nola said, remembering what the queen had told her, "and left to go back."

The prince nodded as if he already knew what to do, then placed two fingers around the ruby and turned it left. The compass beamed like yellow pixie dust shimmering over its surface, brighter and brighter as the weapon activated. They shielded their eyes from the glow—marveled at its beauty.

The compass vibrated in his hand as he clutched tightly to it.

"Now what?" she asked and waited for his reply. Elijah only stared at the two pieces, his eyes drawing in as if he could not look away, even if he tried.

Nola gently placed her hand on his. "Elijah?" she called. "Elijah!"

The prince looked up quickly. "Sorry. Um, now, we join hands, and I think about the time and place where my heart desires to go."

Prince Elijah snapped his eyes shut and waited.

The compass grew warm, then hot, but they did not let go. Nola saw a light gleam as her hair whipped up into the air when a strong gust zipped through the cave.

Elijah was already looking around in the small, cramped space they were standing in when she opened her eyes. A cold sweat drenched her body as if the energy from the weapon had drained her.

"Where are we?" Nola asked, climbing to her feet.

Elijah placed the Kroneon in his pocket and walked through the corridor leading to the king's chambers.

"We're in the castle," he whispered.

"Well, then, *when* are we? Did it work?" she asked.

Elijah shrugged. "Guess we're about to find out," he said as they heard the king's guards shout from the other room. "Move back."

He placed his hand on Nola's chest, pushing her back

around the corner, and as she opened her mouth to speak, Elijah rushed his hand over her lips.

"Shh."

She nodded.

Footsteps grew louder as one of King Matthias's guards approached and stopped a few feet from the corner where they hid. The feeling of uncertainty crossed Nola's mind. She knew it was reckless to go back in time. Any wrong decision, any mistake, could alter their entire future. But then again, Elijah was not a man she trusted, and he could change his mind in an instant.

"I need to be alone," one of the men around the corner said.

Nola's eyes looked up. It was King Matthias's voice. His voice was much younger than how she remembered it from the times she saw him during Zemira's festivities.

Matthias almost sounded like Lincoln.

When a few guards stood at attention and saluted the king, Elijah pushed her further back.

"That's Mason," he said. "He'll kill us, thinking we are intruders."

"We *are* intruders." Nola focused her sight on the door ahead, trying to listen in to what was being said. The magic she held gave her the power to see and hear beyond what a human was capable of. It overwhelmed her.

"They're talking about the Fae. So many are talking at once! Ugh, I'm struggling to make sense of it," she said.

Elijah went to speak but closed his mouth as Mason entered a room a few doors down from where they stood.

"This way," Elijah whispered as Mason disappeared

behind the door. They hurried quickly across the hall to another door. "This was my room. We can hide in here until it's clear." He turned to Nola, giving her an intense stare. "We need to find my mother."

"Elijah! I don't think that's wise."

A young boy screamed down the hall, drawing Elijah's attention to the noise. Elijah froze as they watched the child run from another room and into the hallway.

He watched his young self collapse to his knees, placing his hands on his head. The boy tugged furiously at his hair while his eyes looked down at the floor. "That bastard. That bastard!"

Elijah stumbled back, and Nola gripped his arms as he slammed into her chest. "It's too late," he said. "We just received the news that my father poisoned our mother. It's too late, Nola." He placed his hand on his head, fighting back the tears. "It's too late—" He choked on the last words, no longer able to speak.

Watching the look on Elijah's face as the young boy learned of his mother's fate was beyond heartbreaking.

"Elijah," they heard another voice call out. "Elijah, what's happening?"

Young Elijah looked up at whom Nola assumed was Lincoln.

Lincoln! She said his name in her mind. *No . . . he was Tristan back then.*

"This is your fault, Tristan. Your fault. If you—"

"I didn't know. I didn't know!" little Tristan cried out.

Young Elijah jumped to his feet and leapt forward,

slamming his fists roughly against young Tristan's chest. He stumbled back, tripping over his feet.

"Stop, Elijah!" the older boy cried.

Young Elijah lifted his hand, grabbing little Tristan's shirt with his fist, but only hovered his hand above his brother's face. Still, he did not throw the punch. Just waited, with Tristan shielding his face from the blow which never came.

The young prince lowered his tightly clenched fist and backed up. "They won't let me see her," young Elijah said as tears welled in his eyes. "Not without Father's order."

Elijah held out his hand to help Tristan up.

"Then we need to ask him. He did this to our mother. He owes us a moment to say our goodbyes," Tristan said.

The young boys nodded to each other, then headed down the hallway to their father's chamber.

"I don't understand." Elijah turned to Nola. "Why didn't it work?"

She placed her hand on his shoulder and squeezed. "You went back where your *heart* desired."

He lowered his brows.

"Perhaps, Elijah, killing your father was never what your heart desired."

Elijah looked down at his feet and closed his eyes. For the first time, she saw real pain on his face. A tear left his eye and rolled down his cheek. Nola reached up to wipe it as he opened his eyes, but he gripped her wrist, stopping her. It was a rough touch, but he lowered his hand and stepped in her direction, pinning her against the wall. The way Elijah looked at her made her heart jump. But all he did was stare blankly into her eyes, then look over at his mother's room.

He released her but did not open the space between them. "I never told my mum that I loved her before she passed." Elijah ran his hand down his face. wiping away the few tears on his cheek. "In fact, I don't think I ever told her."

Nola sucked in a breath and moved to the side, no longer feeling trapped by his body in the corner. "Go, Elijah. Tell her now."

He shook his head. "We don't have time."

"What happens after this?" she asked.

"We're asking our father if we can see her, then he sends us off, allowing for our goodbyes. Mason takes us to her chambers, but she had already slipped away. Then, they take Tristan."

Nola placed her hand on his. "You may still have time. Tell her."

He nodded quickly and then rushed to her room.

A guard was standing in the corner, but they did not halt.

"Don't move!" the guard shouted, unsheathing his sword. Nola looked into the guard's eyes and began to sing. She sang until the guard dropped his sword and collapsed into a dreamless slumber.

Elijah stepped over the guard and entered his mother's room.

He quickly knelt by her bed, placing a hand on the woman's weak and frail arm.

"My queen," Elijah said. Her eyes were closed, but when

she looked up, they went wide. She did not flinch or move away, just stared up at him as her mouth gaped open.

"Elijah?" she whispered. "Elijah, my boy."

Nola let out a breath. Twenty years of aging, and she still knew her son.

"How?" the queen asked. "I do not understand. How is this possible?"

Elijah sat on the mattress next to her and gripped her hand. "I don't have much time, Mother. You're going to die, and I can't save you."

Queen Serena lifted her hand slowly and placed it on her son's cheek. "Oh, my child. What a handsome man you have become," she said, just seconds before white foam came dripping from her lips.

Elijah let out a hard sob, reaching up and wiping it away. Tears fell down his face. "I love you, Mother. I am sorry I never told you sooner. I love you."

The woman's smile was weak but pure. "You do not have to say the words for me to feel them, my son."

Nola could not hold back the tears at the sight of them.

"Protect your brother, Elijah. You must protect each other from that man, your father."

He nodded and opened his eyes to look at her one last time.

"Save Zemira. Save it for me. Save it for all of us," she whispered to his ear as he leaned on her weakened chest.

With those last words, her frail hand went limp, and she slipped away.

Nola tilted her head, narrowing in on her sense of hearing. "Elijah, they're coming."

The prince looked over at Nola, his cheeks pink, his eyes red from tears. He had no time to let his emotions run free. He had to watch his mother slip away. Nola had hoped coming back to his beloved mother's final moments was enough to give him peace.

She rushed to the bed. "Elijah, we need to leave. They are coming down the hall. Is there another way out?" she asked.

He nodded and wiped away his tears. "That way," he said, pointing to a bookshelf at the end of the room. "Every room in the castle has another way out."

They rushed to the shelf, removing a blue leather-bound book, and heard a click. Elijah pulled the door, opening it slightly, allowing them to squeeze through, and shut it right before young Tristan and Elijah entered the room.

Heading down the stairs from inside the secret tunnel, they heard the piercing cries of the queen's children, but they did not look back.

The tunnel led to a sewer entrance. Elijah wrapped his arms around Nola's waist and helped her up through a hole that led to the streets. She climbed out and quickly reached into the tunnel to help Elijah. They both looked around, looking for a place to hide. He pointed to a field in the distance.

"Over there," he said.

Nola followed him closely, and once they reached the grassy field, he pulled out the compass. They both held tightly together and closed their eyes, feeling the power, their thoughts going back to the present.

The bright flash of light burst around them, and when they opened their eyes again, they were safe and back in the cave.

But only for a moment.

A deep growl echoed inside the cave from behind them, the hair on Nola's skin standing straight. They spun around, and one of the siren creatures was crouched in the corner, its eyes blazing red.

Suddenly, it charged at them.

The siren creature leapt towards Nola, but she put her hands up, grabbing its head, and looking it into its bright red eyes.

For a second, the creature looked back as if it remembered what it once was. But that moment was cut short as Elijah pushed it away.

Coming back to her senses, Nola ran to her bow and arrow, picked it up, and swiftly positioned her shot. The moment the creature lunged at her again, she shot the arrow, aiming it into the siren creature's leg, only to slow it down. It screeched loudly, falling to its knees.

No more sirens will die today, she said in her mind.

"We must go, Nola. Now."

She felt Elijah's hand grab hers, and he took off quickly to the shore. With the daylight, they were able to see a faster route to the sand. They heard several feet running swiftly behind them.

"They're behind us, don't stop!" Nola shouted.

They spotted Elijah's ship, the crew already having a rower waiting for them. Once they reached the boat, they both turned, seeing a dozen sirens crouching low, not moving past the rocks.

Nola's heart hammered against her chest.

"What is happening?" she asked, watching the creatures staring silently.

"Sir," one of the men sitting on the small wooden raft said. "Your father's ship is drawing near. According to the spyglass, they are but a few miles from us. The two of you need to get on the ship, now!"

Elijah watched that man's eyes grow wide as he looked over his shoulder, seeing the horrendous creatures behind them.

The prince turned to the sea, watching three ships a couple miles out approaching Crotona.

"The fog is coming down, Nola. It is too late! My father is here." He turned back to her. "He has come to kill me, not you."

Nola's eyes could not leave the evolved sirens breathing heavily as if an imaginary barrier was pushing them back.

Her gaze finally broke from the creatures and looked at him. "Go, Elijah!" she said. "Take the weapon, and fight. I will be behind you shortly. I must save them." Nola placed her hand on his chest gingerly. "And then together, we will use our powers to destroy the weapon. It does not belong here in this world."

Elijah nodded slowly, taking the weapon and the ruby.

"When the war is over, I promise to destroy it. I give you my word," Elijah said.

Nola reached out and caught his hand. As his fingers

touched hers, she winced. Nola looked down, remembering the short but brutal night they had to spend together. Once she released his hand, she reached up to her long strands and tugged. A chunk from her hair pulled off her scalp so easily.

No! Nola thought, then peered over to the sirens again. The same was happening to her. Her mind clouded over, and for a moment, she forgot her name.

My name—

"Nola, what is happening?" Elijah asked. She heard the panic clutch his throat.

Nola, she repeated in her head.

"Go. I need to get the sirens in the water. This place makes you forget," she said. "They do not know who or what they are anymore."

A small desire to stay with the creatures crept into her mind.

This cannot happen to me. Not to any more of my kind.

"Go!" Nola said again. "Go, Elijah."

The prince reached out one more time and placed his hand on her cheek, running his fingers along her jaw. She felt the rough touch over her now-coarse skin.

"I'll see you out in the sea, Nola," he said before rushing to the rower to head to his ship.

Nola turned back to the sirens and called out.

"You do not belong here. You are sirens!" she shouted. A few heads tilted, but they only moved back as if afraid of the sea. Slowly she stepped back into the water. "Come, sirens. Follow me. Follow me into the water." Nola's throat pulled. Her eyes felt heavy. "Sirens. You. Are. Sirens!" She took another step back, the sea now touching her knees. "I am the child of Maydean, Queen of the Undersea. She would not want to see her people suffer like this! Follow me into the sea. Come home."

In that instant, one siren stepped forward, and the others slowly followed.

This will not be your fate, Nola said in her mind. *It is not your fate.*

As the ship moved west towards the king's army, a serene moment loomed around her—a split second of peace before the sirens charged towards the deep, blue waves.

Chapter 37

The Sybil Curse remained idle as they waited for Anaru to return—she was the crew's eyes until the fog cleared. Several hours had passed since the pirates awoke in the Eastland Forest after falling to Elijah's dark magic. The Fae's ships had already departed to Crotona to seek out the siren and the Kroneon. An unusually dense fog had completely enveloped the island upon their arrival, making it impossible for Lincoln and his crew to spot the other boats trying to reach the shore.

Their ship was not nearly as strong as the Fae's to withstand the storm that swept across the sea—they would have never made it safely to the island had they not departed when they did.

Mazie watched the grey, impenetrable fog along the surface of the water. The moisture in the air dampened her cheeks.

"We did the right thing by waiting, but I fear we are too late," Lincoln said to her.

Mazie knew Lincoln feared the creatures on Crotona

Island. But, even with a siren's power, the chance of Nola's survival was slight.

"What is all this?" Mazie asked Lincoln. The fog had closed them in, only allowing the ship to rock from side to side but not onward. "This fog is unlike anything I have ever seen out in the sea." She held up her arm. "I can barely see my own hand in front of my face."

"That's because it isn't real. This is magic," Lincoln replied. "If we can't see our enemy's ships, we are as good as dead."

The sound of Boots's newly patched-up peg leg hit the deck between Lincoln and Mazie. He folded his arms and stood still looking out with them.

"On the positive side," Boots said, "if we can't see them, they can't see us." He looked up to the sky. "At least we have a dragon on our side."

Boots is right, Mazie thought. *Having a dragon is our advantage against our enemies.*

Though they could not see Crotona, Mazie felt the mysterious power draw them in. Lincoln had shared with her memories of the black-colored sandy place—an island he said he would never return to.

Anaru had been flying above, guiding them in the right direction. Mazie feared even the dragon would have trouble seeing through the thick clouds.

The pirates felt the ship rock, and then when they looked up, Anaru stood perched on the edge of the railing, her heavy body lightly fracturing through the wood.

"What do you see?" Lincoln asked his dragon.

The dragon's wings stretched out, lifting herself from the rail. Lincoln tilted his head as if honing in on her thoughts.

"Anaru spots three ships coming from the west, and another, leaving Crotona," he said.

"And what of the Fae?" Mazie asked.

Lincoln turned back to her. "Two ships behind the Sybil Curse. I don't believe the Fae are our allies, Mazie."

"Five ships against the Sybil Curse," Mazie said to the haze, but the challenge appealed to her. She flashed a reassuring smile at Lincoln and his dragon, then turned to his crew.

"Be ready to fight once the fog clears," Lincoln said. "Let us not become shark bait today, eh, mates?"

Captain Lincoln's warning felt icy to the buccaneers. The moment they had been preparing for was there—though it terrified Mazie to the core. She did not expect they would survive.

All eyes looked up as an arrow shot through the fog, landing right at the center of the mast.

"They be shooting at us already?" Mazie said, aghast. "How can they see through all this—?"

A thunderous roar sounded through the clouds.

"Dergis," Lincoln said. "But they are shooting at us blindly."

The crew hit the deck, each finding a corner of the ship to hide in. Mazie turned to her pixie perched on her shoulder.

"To be honest, little pixie," Mazie said, breathing heavily as she used a water barrel as a barricade. "I'd rather face the ghost of my mother than not see my enemies coming from behind me." The pixie frowned at the pirate and shrugged her petite, pointy shoulders. "What about you?"

The little pixie folded her arms and leaned forward as if lost in thought.

"Not much of a talker, are you, little one?" Mazie stammered. Her voice sounded strange from the nerves clutching at her throat.

I haven't even given you a name yet, Mazie thought. *What do you name a pixie?*

The pixie had yet to speak to her—she wondered if she was mute. Since winning the pixie from the Fae queen, the communication between the two had been difficult. However, the bond was strong, and the pixie was growing to trust Mazie. The pixie's wings fluttered and she gave her a gentle smile before she looked back ahead, pointing forward with her tiny finger.

Mazie's stomach twisted in knots again as the fog finally cleared around them.

Here we go, she thought.

She unsheathed her sword and gave her pixie a nod, jumping to her feet. Right as she stood, three arrows shot across the deck, all coming from the closest ship belonging to the Fae. The other vessel seemed to be heading in a different direction.

Where are they going? Mazie asked herself as she watched a jet-black-haired elf, clad in fine, grey armor, raise his bow. However, the elf did not point his bow at the Sybil Curse—it was towards the protectors on the other Fae ship.

"Well," she said to her pixie. "Isn't that interesting." She held out her palm and the little creature stepped into her hand. Mazie's pulse jarred in her throat. "Let us fight like pirates and die like one too!"

She sprang across the deck.

"We are to attack the ship to the right," Mazie shouted, turning to Kitten. "I believe we have some Elven allies with us." She turned to the black-haired elf who had his bow still raised, and once their eyes locked, she gave him a nod, right before he shot his arrow at the queen's protectors.

"I'm going to go search for Nola," Lincoln said quickly. "Fend off the ships." He climbed onto Anaru's back and rose high into the sky, disappearing amidst the clouds.

Elijah dashed across the ship, picking up one of his men's swords from the deck as his father's three ships sailed closer to his. Using the black smoke leaving his hands, the cloud of magic wrapped him in a cocoon, carrying him across the sea towards his father. He landed at the center of the deck, wielding his sword above his head, and began fending off the royal guard.

Using his powers, he encircled the men, drawing them to their knees and sending them into a dream.

A slow clap sounded from behind him. When he turned, his father folded both arms across his chest, and a vicious grin flashed over his lips.

"I am impressed," King Matthias said. "I have not seen you use that kind of power since you were a young lad."

Elijah held out his sword. "That is because you were ashamed every time I tried, pretending my powers were a disgrace to you and our family. And when you needed to subjugate, you would force me to use my magic to accomplish your vile agendas."

The king ambled around Elijah, but with each step, the prince became even more anxious.

"Those powers *are* shameful, Elijah. You're a monster," Matthias gritted out. "Just like all the other Newick witches. A sorcerer is nothing but an abomination to our world." He straightened his back. "I did my best to be your father, but at times I could not bear to look at you."

Elijah glanced at the approaching ships. It was strange —the elves and the pirates were fighting each other.

The prince swallowed, turning back to his father and the other royal ships floating behind them, waiting for the king's orders.

"Oh, I assure you," Elijah said. "I have done plenty well without your help. You are nothing but a hypocrite who used the Newick gem for your own political needs." Elijah's nostrils flared, growling through his teeth. "You took everyone I loved away from me."

Matthias ran his fingers through his beard. "You were nothing but a tool for my ideals. But you were not even useful! Who would want a complete failure for a child?" he taunted.

Elijah felt frozen in thought. The hatred he had for the king ran deep, but those words made him feel as if his heart had been ripped out.

The king snorted. "Enough of this banter. Use your sword, boy. Fight like a man." Matthias's eyes narrowed as he unsheathed his own sword. "Prove to me I didn't raise a coward."

The use of magic would have ended the duel in moments, but the power from the emerald on the king's crown would shield him against the prince's magic.

Elijah gripped the hilt of his sword hard, not caring about the pain. He leapt forward, swinging the blade quickly at his father. The king scampered back, holding his sword up high, blocking the hit.

"I beg you, Father. Do not do this! End this madness and let the world regain magic! You will kill the kingdom!"

The king jumped forward, slicing across Elijah's chest, but only grazing across his shirt, cutting the skin beneath.

The prince winced as his skin burned from the wound.

Matthias's face scrunched up, wielding his sword above his head, right as a cannon fired from a close range. Elijah slashed his sword at his father, as the king was momentarily distracted by the noise. His crown fell off his head and onto the deck.

"Fire!" Mazie shouted, lighting the cannon pointing towards Queen Cassia's protectors.

Mazie looked up as Queen Cassia directed her dragon to the pirates, commanding Dergis to release a blaze of fire upon the Sybil Curse. Mazie searched for Lincoln and Anaru, but all she heard was the dragon's roar from a distance, hoping he was safe.

The pirates quickly took cover, looking up again as the

queen disappeared back into the clouds. Mazie could no longer see Cassia, but they had caused damage to the Fae's ship from the cannonball.

Ardley held the spyglass to his eye, counting the Elven warriors who fought with the black-haired elf. "Eight elves fight with us," he said. "Not sure why they are helping, but it seems as though we share a common enemy. The queen's protectors outnumber us, though."

"Fire off the cannon, Kitten!" Boots said.

Kitten pointed the cannon again while Boots loaded and lit the barrel.

"Fire!" Hill shouted. Another cannonball flew across the air, hitting the queen's ship again, rending the vessel unable to move or return fire.

Mazie looked to the clouds, trying to locate Lincoln again, but he and Anaru had disappeared from their view.

"Alright, little pixie," she said, turning back to her palm.

The pixie's wings fluttered so fast Mazie could barely see them.

"I need your help now," Mazie said. "It is the reason I freed you from the Fae. I need to get to the sky." She pointed to the clouds. "Up."

The pixie frowned, placing her hand back on her chest, then, mimicking Mazie, pointed up to the sky.

"You want to fly?" the pixie said in a tiny voice. Mazie's lips grew into a wide smile.

"You speak?" she asked, feeling elated. It would make things a bit easier between her and the pixie.

The tiny creature nodded again and fluttered above

Mazie, holding out her hands. Speckles of pixie dust sprinkled from her fingers.

The colorful particles of pink dust clouded the space between Mazie and the pixie, tickling her nose.

Mazie looked down, watching her feet lift in the air. She felt her body tilt forward, so she raised her hands out to her side to steady herself.

"I'm going to fall," she said. Though nervous about being so high up, a smile tugged at the corner of her lips. "I'm flying." She looked down again, the ship becoming smaller as she glided higher in the air. "I'm actually flying." For a moment, Mazie's heart remembered her sister. Now she would fly for them both and for those lost to the king's atrocities. "Thank you, little one. Let us get everyone else up here."

The pixie bowed her head and zipped to the right, heading towards the rest of the crew, releasing the remaining dust from her palm, and watched as it landed on Kitten, Boots, Ardley, and Hill.

Mazie wielded her sword as the crew's eyes grew wide, watching their bodies float into the air. Nerves pulled at her chest. She would fight and fight like hell.

"Avast ye, hearties," Mazie shouted through the sound of the cannons. "Look at your enemies. Fight for our lives and for the freedom of Zemira. Let us rid this world of that bilge-sucking bastard of a king. We must win freedom in the sea, and if we fall to the depths of the ocean, may our bodies feed the fish, and our souls fly high to the clouds!"

Ardley flew to the mast, raising the Jolly Roger.

"For the captain!" Boots cried, lifting his sword in the air, pointing the tip of the blade at the sky.

"For the Sybil Curse!" Kitten hollered.

Hill smiled widely, raising his sword above his head, pointing to Lincoln and Anaru, who glided gracefully above the ship.

"Ahoy, mates!" Hill said. "Let us fly!"

The crown was within Elijah's reach. Both the prince and his father dashed for it. Elijah's fingers reached for the stones, wrestling his father until the metal of the crown broke. When his fingers met the emerald, he ripped it from the crown.

King Matthias's eyes darkened in horror as Elijah slammed the gem hard against the deck. Tiny shards from the crystal pierced into his skin as the emerald shattered under his palm.

"No!" the king shouted, right as a green glow of power flashed through the sky and over the seas. The gem's extinguishing power lit brightly around them. The energy moved quickly, covering the Portland Sea and all that lay in its path. Instantly, the sight of magic was restored across the kingdom.

Elijah shifted his body, his elbow crashing into his father's nose. The prince jumped to his feet, picked up his sword, and pointed it at the king's bloodied face.

Matthias looked up. "What have you done?" the king bellowed.

"What I should have done years ago," Elijah replied.

"You will pay for this." King Matthias's voice sounded breathless, as the energy released from the destroyed gem had taken all his strength.

"And now, you shall meet the same fate, Father."

The prince took a slight step back as his father clambered to his feet, holding his own sword outstretched. Right as Elijah jumped forward, a large, red dragon wing came out and knocked the king back. That time, he struck his head against the side of the railing and rolled to the side. A low groan left his lips, but he did not move.

Elijah turned as Lincoln held his sword up to his brother's throat.

"Where is she?" Lincoln asked.

Elijah swallowed. "I don't have her, Brother. She stayed on the island."

"What?" Lincoln said. "She stayed? Elijah, she will die there."

The prince quickly shook his head, reaching into his pocket. "Here," he said, handing Lincoln the Kroneon, with the ruby inside. "Out of good faith, Brother. I do not want to kill you. I did not change anything from the past. I could not. You were right." He placed his sword into the sheath and held up his hands. "We can fight our father together."

Chapter 38

Lincoln looked to where the king had fallen, but he was not there. They both turned as they heard a shot ring out.

"No!" Lincoln cried, pressing on Elijah's shoulders as he collapsed forward into his arms. "Elijah," he said, shaking his brother, who felt limp in his arms. Elijah's fingers dug into Lincoln's skin as they both fell to the deck.

"Hand me the damn Kroneon, pirate," King Matthias said, holding a pistol at level with Lincoln's chest. When Lincoln did not move, the king repeated. "Hand me the weapon!" Matthias's nostrils flared.

Lincoln looked down at his brother. The bullet had grazed the side of his waist—his stomach still rose and fell. He was alive but bleeding badly.

The king staggered when Lincoln looked up to meet his gaze.

"Wha—?" the king said, but his words stopped in his

throat, clearly recognizing his child's eyes. "Tristan, is that you?"

Lincoln slowly lowered Elijah to the deck and rose to his feet, holding out his sword. The magic hovering over the ship was fading as the prince's strength weakened. The king's guard slowly opened their eyes and began to stand up.

A look of heartbreak and disgust flashed over Lincoln's features. "Matthias, you have let this nightmare go on for too long. You are no king!" he said before looking up, right as Anaru swooped down, breathing fire at the Zemiran King.

Matthias shielded his face with his arm, the blaze of fire scorching the skin at his elbow. He screamed and ripped the sleeve of his tunic from his arm. The sails of the ship quickly became engulfed in flames.

Suddenly, the boisterous band of pirates approached Matthias's ship from the clouds.

"Fight, buccaneers of the Portland Sea!" Mazie shouted. "Protect the Sybil Curse! Protect the captain!"

Lincoln's eyes grew wide as they came down, soaring through the air.

They are . . . flying? He thought. *How?*

The noise of the buccaneers dwindled out into a faint sound of music in the sea. Lincoln recognized the sound immediately.

"Cover your ears!" he shouted to his crew.

Lincoln began searching the skies for Anaru, while Mazie, Kitten, and the rest of the Sybil Curse's crew peered down, watching a swarm of sirens move beneath the turquoise surface.

"They are headin' towards the king's ships," Kitten yelled as they all covered their ears.

Then, all at once, the sirens emerged from the water, jumping high onto the deck. The savage women clung to each of the royal guards. Without warning, they sank their teeth into men's flesh, and their claws dug into their arms. One by one, the sea creatures threw the guards off the deck and into the water.

The Elven protectors shot their arrows at the sirens as they swam towards their ship, but they were too quick and missed. Dozens of sirens jumped out of the water and onto Cassia's vessel. The queen's protectors cried in agony as the sirens' sharp fangs pierced their necks.

Lincoln's eyes drew back to his father, who still held a pistol at his head, his arm badly scorched from dragon flame.

"Go ahead, Father, try killing me again!" Lincoln shouted right as Nola sprang from the sea, her human legs forming a split second before she hit the deck. Two of the king's guards shielded the path, protecting the king, but Nola lunged forward, her fists plunging into their chests and ripping out their hearts. As the men fell to the deck, she looked ahead at the king, dropping the bloodied, still-beating hearts to the floor. Anaru's fire had spread across the ship and was growing to a fierce inferno behind Matthias.

She breathed heavily as the king's eyes widened. He

stepped back, his hand shaking with the pistol aimed at her chest.

Nola's skin was red, rough. Her teeth resembled jagged knives, her claws soaked in blood and flesh. Her crystal white eyes blazed with anger as she saw Elijah. The prince was lying on the floor near the railing of the ship, covering his wounds.

Nola stomped forward, swiping her claws at Matthias's throat. The king fired four shots, hearing a click on the fifth attempt. He dropped his weapon and moved back, witnessing what he had done.

Nola glanced down at the bullet holes in her stomach. Lincoln watched in horror as blood ran down her belly—her hands covering the wounds before falling to her knees.

Lincoln rushed to her and lifted her into his arms. Burning pieces of the ship's mast began to rain down around them.

"Oh, my love," he said, tightening his grip around her shoulders to pull her closer into his chest. "You will not die today." Lincoln released her and reached into his pocket. He stood straight looking at his wicked father, took out the compass, and turned the key. Matthias let out a scream and lunged towards the captain. A flash of light surrounded Lincoln, forcing the king back. Lincoln watched as the yellow dust of the compass's magic spilled around him. All he could think of was going back to save Nola from his father.

Time began to flow backward.

He stood back on the ship, watching as Nola came out of the water. That time, however, he knew exactly what was going to happen. He picked up his sword and moved quickly.

Nola stood before two guards protecting King Matthias. She reached outward and tore their hearts out.

As Matthias lifted his pistol at Nola, Lincoln brought his sword forth, slicing through the king's neck. Nola's eyes went round as the king's head rolled down to the stern of the ship, while Lincoln clung to his bloodied sword.

Nola and Lincoln looked at each other—time stopped between them.

Chapter 39

Nola wanted to run to him, but they both looked to where Elijah had fallen. He was trying to stand, blood still pooling under him.

"Elijah!" Lincoln shouted, hurrying to help his brother lie back down on the deck. "Stay still before you hurt yourself even more!" Lincoln laughed out of relief, putting his hand out to prevent his brother from standing.

They both looked up as the Elven warriors stepped onto the ship. A few ran to suppress the flames that were spreading to the deck of the ship. Lincoln held up his sword, but Aiden put his hands out, a flask in his right hand.

"Our water," Aiden said, looking down at Elijah.

Lincoln nodded.

The elf quickly knelt beside the prince and held the flask to his lips. "Drink."

Elijah drank from the water. The flow of blood stopped, and the wound began to close.

"What about the protectors?" Lincoln asked.

Aiden looked over his shoulder at the ship. "The sirens killed them all. All but the queen." He peered through the clouds, searching the sky until he spotted Dergis. Then, raised his bow to the dragon and released the arrow. A loud roar pierced their ears as Dergis fell to the sea. The queen extended her fairy wings to keep herself from falling into the water and landed on the ship.

A bright lavender hue bounded off Queen Cassia's body as her powers grew with her rage.

"I should have known you would betray me, Aiden," Cassia said, looking up at the warriors who stood behind him. "All of you." Her voice was laced with hatred.

Nola's skin had smoothed out, and her light bronze skin had returned, but though she was not in her siren form, the beast inside her screamed to attack.

"And you," the queen said, turning to Nola. "I should have searched a little harder for you the night your mother perished."

Nola's fists tightened.

"My brother was a fool to send the key away," Cassia continued. "It was too late for the compass, as Hagmar was already in Crotona before I sent my men to kill you and your mother and bring back the key."

What? Nola thought, reeling from the truth.

Nola's blood boiled. "You . . . *you* killed my mother?"

Nola watched Lincoln move back, ushering the crew to the bow of the ship.

"You were supposed to die with her, the ruby retrieved and returned to us. Unfortunately, by then, she had already sent you away to be found by the humans. Though, at the time, we believed you were already dead and the key lost to the sea."

Nola felt her body temperature rise again. A rush of rage charged through her body.

Where are you? Nola said in her thoughts. *I summon you.*

A luster of power grew at the queen's fingertips. The twinkling particles were so bright it was nearly blinding. The crew and the elves had to shield their eyes to block out the light.

"Now, it is I who will change the past to what it was always meant to be," the queen said. "That weapon will take me to the day King Matthias banished our kind from Zemira. I will destroy all those who did not defend our race. The king and his men will fall, the humans will submit to my will. My brother will have never met Maydean, and you will never have been born. Then I will be Queen of Zemira and the Fae." Cassia stepped forward, her powers growing brighter. "Where is the weapon, Nola? It belongs to me."

Nola closed her eyes, whispering quietly to herself again. She felt the ship rock and listened intently to the lapping of the waves against the wooden sides.

There you are, come to me and unleash your wrath upon my enemy, she called in her thoughts, feeling the creature's movements beneath the ship.

The queen lifted her hands out, her eyes glowing purplish as her wings flapped out.

A crash through the waves drew her attention to the sea.

"Oh, to the Gods, what is that?!" the queen shouted, right as a Kraken reached out one of his tentacles and wrapped itself around her legs, breaking through her power.

"Nola!" Cassia screamed, pounding her fists against the

creature. It lifted the defenseless queen by the foot, then yanked her violently off the ship. The Fae queen landed in the water while the Kraken swam slowly towards her. The gigantic beast squeezed her body until her bones crumbled beneath its tentacles, then dragged her into the depths of the Portland Sea.

Nola let out a breath of relief and turned to the men standing behind her.

"You're incredible," Lincoln said, running to her again and drawing her up in his arms. He planted a kiss upon her lips.

She felt breathless as he released the kiss.

"Let us get some dry clothes on you, my love," he said before concern crossed his features. "Nola, what is wrong?"

Nola's eyes were somber. She loved the man before her. However, she knew the next moments would be of heartbreak and pain. Unfortunately, the future no longer held the two of them sailing together.

Lincoln turned to his crew, watching Mazie and the other buccaneers settle on the deck.

"Lincoln," Nola said, drawing his attention back to her. "I need to tell you something. It cannot wait."

He placed a hand on her cheek. "What is it, love?"

How can I tell him? Nola thought as she lowered her head to the ground, avoiding his eyes. *How can I tell him what happened on that island?*

"Nola," Lincoln said. "Tell me."

Her eyes stung as they flooded with tears. "The monsters on Crotona were sirens, Lincoln."

Nola watched his face go blank.

"When I was there," she continued, her voice stammering, "Elijah had to kill a siren to protect me."

He let out a breath of relief and gripped her elbows, pulling her in. "Oh, my beautiful siren. You two did what you had to do to survive."

She shook her head as more tears fell. "After the sirens followed me into the water, I was able to speak with them; they finally came back to reality—back to their true selves, but—"

"Nola, what is it?" Lincoln asked. "You are scaring me."

Nola let out a hard sob. Lincoln's charming touch had made her feel worse.

"They knew the siren we killed. They mourned for her." She ran her hand through her hair. "Lincoln, the siren Elijah killed was Sybil."

Her cheeks reddened with shame and guilt.

Nola instantly felt Lincoln's hands slack from her elbows before he stepped back from her. She had to tell him everything, no matter how painful it was. The man she loved with all her heart had lost a piece of his soul to Sybil.

"They told me that Sybil came to that island to find the treasure for you as a wedding gift," she continued, "but the island took hold of her as it did with the others. She forgot who and what she was. They all did when the magic from the awful place warped their minds." Nola wiped the tears rolling down her face. "I am so sorry," her voice cracked. "Lincoln, I—"

The captain held up a hand to cut her off and staggered back. "Anaru!" he shouted against the wind. "Anaru, take me back to the Sybil Curse." He looked up. "Anaru!" he called again.

The beautiful dragon descended to the ship. Lincoln climbed on her back and held on to her long neck as she took off.

Chapter 40

King Elijah set in place a new reign, mending his father's wrongs. The rebels who led the resistance disbanded when the threat to the kingdom died with Matthias. The Fae found themselves living again amongst the humans in Zemira, brokering peace with the kingdom. Their power filled the soil with life, bringing fresh, healthy crops once again to the land.

The new king stood at his official coronation, smiling back at his people. He promised the Zemirans a safer, more peaceful world. Not a world where they would fear as if that day could be their last.

Lincoln entered the Grand Royal Hall, watching Nola lean against the wall as if trying to stay hidden. When their eyes met, her cheeks flushed, but all she did was turn and rush in the opposite direction, exiting through the back gate.

Bloody hell, woman.

"Nola, stop running from me, dammit!" Lincoln shouted. "Get back here so we can talk."

She stopped abruptly at the edge of the courtyard's

fountain and turned. When Lincoln looked into her pain-filled eyes, it broke his heart. He was foolish to have left her the way he did. In no way did he blame Nola and Elijah for defending themselves from what they believed to be a deadly monster. Sybil had become a mindless creature who would have killed her.

At the time, he could not process what she had told him. He left in haste and regretted the moment he jumped on Anaru's back. Lincoln left her standing there, wondering if she would ever see him again. Then, he had watched her sail with the Elven warriors back to Zemira without him. The Sybil Curse's crew kept their space, leaving him alone in his chambers as guilt clutched to him until he could barely breathe.

She was the love of his life, and he had let her go.

Nola wore a beautiful, long, teal dress down to her ankles—it flowed freely in the gentle breeze behind her. Her hair was styled into a braid resting over her right shoulder. The smell of flowers came up with the wind, and Lincoln's eyes shone with desire and need as he breathed in her scent. She had to have noticed how much he cared.

"You look nice in a dress, by the way," he said, a playful smile on his lips.

"What are you doing here, Lincoln?" Nola asked. "I thought you would be on your next adventure."

He snickered. "Aye, 'tis not the adventure that I want at the moment."

"Lincoln—"

"You did what you had to do to survive, Nola." He reached out and touched her arm but pulled back when her shoulders stiffened. "I do not blame you for one moment for what happened with Sybil."

Nola's brows pulled together.

"Nola, there you are," Nola's father interrupted from the garden's gate.

Lincoln stood straight and smiled back at her father, happy to finally meet her family, though he was not done making it right with Nola.

"Father, um, this is Lincoln," she said. "The captain of the Sybil Curse whom I told you about."

"Ah yes. Nola has been telling her mum and I 'bout you and all the adventures you went on," Duncan said, with a wide grin that met his eyes. "I cannot thank you enough, lad. For saving my little girl."

I would save her a thousand times again, Lincoln said to himself.

"Very nice to meet you, Duncan. However, it was Nola who saved us," Lincoln said. "Saved . . . me."

Lincoln hoped the hidden meaning of his words did not go unnoticed by her. Nola had not only saved Zemira and those on the ship that day. What she did not know was how she saved his heart from loss. She freed him from years of pain and mourning, though he was a fool to make her believe otherwise. Nola rescued his heart.

A small smile reached Nola's lips. "Where's Mother?" she asked.

"Oh, she's taking quite the interest in the elves and fairies. Now that the king is dead, and the power he used on the people is broken. There is magic again for all of us to see. 'Tis a glorious day, my child."

Nola nodded, running her hand down her father's arm. "Alright. The king has requested to speak with me after the coronation. I will meet you and mum after at the tavern for a drink?"

Duncan straightened his back before landing a kiss on his daughter's cheek.

With one nod and a knowing smile, Duncan stepped aside and left her alone again with Lincoln.

They watched her father walk back into the castle before Lincoln's hand came around to Nola's cheek and moved her gaze back to him.

"My love, please come aboard our ship again. I cannot stand letting you go."

Nola nibbled on her bottom lip while he wondered if his unrelenting forgiveness would be enough.

Lincoln leaned forward, planting a tender kiss upon her forehead. His lips lingered before he asked one more time.

"Is there anything I can say to you for you to change your mind?"

Lincoln watched as Nola tried to hide her pout by turning away. However, a flash of pain and guilt, which he did not want her to feel, shone on her features.

"My parents need me, Lincoln. I don't belong under the sea any more than I belong on your ship."

Lincoln squeezed her hands. "Nay, you know that isn't true."

"I've already given up the crown to rule the undersea. It belongs with Queen Ara."

". . . 'Tis not the undersea where you belong," Lincoln said. "You're a pirate, Nola."

She tried to step back, but he reached out, taking her arm and pulling her into his chest, planting a passionate kiss upon her lips. Nola tried to wiggle away, but he held her tighter against him.

"Lincoln," she said as he released the kiss. "We can't."

So, so stubborn, he thought.

He reached into his pocket and pulled out a bandana, handing it to Nola before releasing her.

"At least take this," Lincoln said as she caught her breath.

Nola raised a brow. "You're giving me a handkerchief?" she asked.

Lincoln placed the cloth in her palm and closed her fingers around it. "A gift," he said. "It was my very first bandana when I was initiated as a pirate. I had a little something sewn on it by the town's seamstress."

She opened her palm. "I can't take this."

Oh, bloody woman. Take the damn gift.

He stepped back. "It's yours, Nola. Stop being so stubborn and take it."

If she would not accept his plea to go with him on the ship, then he would leave her with a part of him. Just so she would always have something to remember him by.

Nola gave him a side smirk and closed her fist, clutching to the old piece of cloth.

"Tell the crew I said thank you, especially to Mazie. I want them to know how much I grew to love each and every one of them," she said. "You are all my family, Lincoln."

He nodded. "I love you, Nola. I will love you until I go down with my ship."

Nola's eyes glistened. "And I love you, Lincoln. I always will."

Lincoln dropped one more kiss upon her forehead before stepping back and turning to the gates leading back to the harbor.

There was a moment of emptiness in Nola's heart as she watched him walk away.

It is for the best, she thought. *Isn't it*? She questioned herself with every step Lincoln took.

A few minutes later, as Nola entered the Grand Royal Hall, she saw King Elijah sitting on his throne. Most of the crowd had dispersed after the ceremony. It was the first time she had seen him with a king's crown upon his head.

Nola curtsied. "Your Highness," she said. "You wanted to speak with me?"

"Elijah," he said. "Call me Elijah, Nola. We are friends."

He stood and gestured to the throne next to him—the one suited for his future queen. "Sit, please."

She sat, adjusting her long dress to get comfortable.

"When do you leave?" Elijah asked her.

"There's a colony near the far eastern sea. The merfolk need help to rebuild. They were one of the first to fall after my birth mother died," she explained. "And then I plan to return to Zemira to take care of my parents."

Elijah flashed a beautiful smile. "I see," he said.

Then he held his hand out until she placed hers in his palm. He gave her fingers a gentle squeeze. "The people of

Zemira will be taken care of, Nola. Ara has promised to help the siren folk rebuild, and Aiden now leads the Fae and Elven battalion." He released her hand. "And your parents will never go hungry again."

She raised a brow. "Thank you, Elijah, but—"

"You're a fighter! You do not belong *here*, just as my brother does not."

He is as persistent as Lincoln, she thought.

Elijah chuckled as if he had read her thoughts. "It was a compliment, Nola. You are *better* than this place. You know where you belong, and you know *who* you belong with."

King Elijah stretched to his side and grabbed a black velvet sack. He reached inside, pulling out the Kroneon.

"Elijah—"

"It's yours," he said, handing her the weapon carefully.

She shook her head in disbelief. "I thought you destroyed it," she said, then frowned. "You were supposed to destroy it."

The corners of his charming eyes crinkled. He leaned back, watching Nola run her thumbs over the compass. "And miss the shock and horror on your face?"

Nola rolled her eyes.

"It is not mine to destroy," Elijah said. "The compass belongs to the sirens. It is yours." He paused, giving a throaty laugh. "Yours and *theirs*," he added, his eyes looking out the window that faced the docks.

The hairs on her arms stood straight. She wanted nothing more than to sail the seas with the crew. She loved Lincoln with all her heart. But how could she abandon her people?

"You are overthinking this, Nola. Trust that Ara, Aiden, and I will keep the people safe—land, sky, and sea."

Nola lifted the bandana Lincoln gave her to wipe the tears rolling down her face. Then, when she looked closely, she saw the embroidered design on the side. She unfolded it, laying the cloth flat on her lap. A white pirate skull stared back at her, and under it was stitched lettering.

"What is it?" Elijah asked.

Nola closed her eyes, recounting the moment Lincoln told her he would come up with a pirate name for her. He had.

The king leaned forward, reading the words on the cloth.

"He gave me my pirate name." She looked up. "Finola, Queen D'Sea."

Elijah leaned back against his throne. "My brother will never admit his born legacy of being the rightful King of Zemira. But you, Nola. You will always be *his* queen, whether you are sworn into that position or not."

After folding the cloth into a triangle, she placed it against her forehead, tied it off in the back, and turned to Elijah.

"How do I look?" she asked. The bells chimed from the royal court, drawing their attention to the doors. "Ah, you are officially the King of Zemira," she said.

He gestured to the bandana with his finger. "And you are a pirate of the Portland Sea."

The only way Nola could move forward was to accept the painful memories of her past and forgive herself. Yes, she would forever live with what she had done, but it also had changed her. Nola was a girl who had a dream of fighting for her family. A goal her father helped her achieve by teaching her to put others before herself. She took a risk on a pirate ship and found she was more than a human—more than a siren and more than a fairy. She was a friend, a daughter, a lover, and though her heart still struggled to accept what others thought of it, she was also a pirate.

Elijah escorted Nola to the gates before kissing her on each side of her tanned face.

"Can a pirate ask for one more favor?" she asked, realizing what her words meant as they left her lips.

"Anything for you," he said.

She bit her bottom lip before asking, "Rename the Portland Sea," she said.

His brows knitted together. "Can I do that?" he asked.

"Your father once did. It belongs to Zemira, as we are all *one* people again."

He nodded. "Then what do we call it?"

She exhaled; a gentle smile touched her lips.

"The Sea of Zemira."

Captain Lincoln placed both hands on the railing of his old, creaking ship.

Mazie staggered to him, already buzzed from her drink. "I am ready to get back to our adventures," she said, looking up to him. "Aren't you?"

Lincoln chuckled. "What? These last two weeks haven't been adventurous enough?"

Mazie threw back her mug. "I miss the days when I didn't wake up feeling like I could take my last breath any minute."

Lincoln reached out and took her drink. "Oh, come on, Mazie. Isn't that what being a pirate is all about?"

She chuckled. "As long as I have my mates by my side."

Captain Lincoln threw back the drink, tasting the sweet rum on his tongue. "Aye," he said, handing it back. "All but one."

Before Mazie opened her mouth to speak words of comfort, Hill's shoe stomped across the deck their way.

"Did you get our water, Hill?" Mazie asked jokingly.

She and Lincoln threw their heads back, laughing at her joke.

"Cheers, mate," she said, lifting her chin. "To the best battle we have ever fought."

The crew felt the ship move forward, pulling away from the shore as Kitten turned the helm north. Ardley puffed out his smoke from his pipe into the air.

The wind suddenly picked up as Anaru broke through the clouds. The dragon circled the ship, for the crew had become a part of her—they were family.

"Where to, Captain?" Kitten asked. "North, south? Anywhere ye want to go."

"Wherever it is you're going," the crew heard the familiar voice, "may I join you?"

Nola wore the bandana Lincoln had given her, tight black pants slick against her long legs and a maroon shirt showing off the curves of her body. She pulled out her bow and quiver of arrows and jumped from the ship's edge and onto the deck.

The smile on Lincoln's lips was so big, his charming dimples dipped. He ran straight to her but stopped short as Nola pulled out the Kroneon with the ruby within.

"What—" Mazie started, running to Nola, but Nola handed it to her.

"King Elijah gave it to us," she said. "It belongs on this ship. It belongs to us."

Lincoln shook his head. "It's too dangerous to turn back time, Nola," he said. "We cannot change the past. Remember?"

Kitten reached out, only to run her fingers over the rustic metal. "We can always go into the future, even for just a glimpse?" she asked.

Mazie nodded. "Well, let's give it a go then," she said, but Hill reached out, taking it from her hands.

"Alright, what do I do?" he asked eagerly.

Lincoln shifted slightly, nervous to see an artifact so fragile in Hill's hands.

"Easy, mate," he warned. "That thing almost got us killed, remember?"

Hill waved his hand in the air. "Bah, just press down, eh?" he asked.

Nola looked over her shoulder. "It doesn't press down," she said. "It turns right or left."

Hill gave Nola a quizzical look. "No, it presses down. Look."

"No!" the crew shouted quickly as Hill pressed the ruby into the compass.

It lit up, warming his fingers, but he held tight to the compass, looking straight ahead. A flash of light seemed to split the very air in twain, revealing a dark pathway.

"What the bloody hell is that?" Ardley asked.

"Blimey!" Boots said, watching Hill's hand tremble so badly Nola had to reach out and take the Kroneon from him.

Nola let out a heavy sigh. "The Kroneon. It does not only move forward or back in time. It *opens* time," she said, turning to Lincoln, whose eyes were wide from shock.

"A portal," Lincoln said. "Bloody hell."

"Well," Mazie interrupted. "Not *when* do we want to go, mates. But, where?"

Lincoln's breath caught in his throat; he could barely breathe.

Boots stomped his peg leg on the deck and straightened his hat. "Are you ready for our next adventure, Kitten?" She bumped her curvy hip against his side and gave him a wink. "A secret portal into another dimension," he said.

Kitten wrapped her arms around his neck. "Anywhere wit' ye, m'love."

Lincoln gripped Nola's waist and pulled her into his chest. He ran his hand down her neck gently and brushed his lips against hers.

"You decided to become a pirate, eh? My Queen D'Sea," he asked, biting his bottom lip.

Nola brushed her fingers over his lips. "It took a bit of convincing from your brother." The smile on her lips was small. "I've also said my goodbyes to my parents," she added, "for they, too, know where my heart lies."

Lincoln closed his fingers over hers and tenderly caressed her lips with his. Then, slowly, he ran his hands to the back of her neck, tousling under her hair, loosening her braid.

"I'm ready for the adventure, Captain," she said boldly into his ear. "To sail wherever the Sea of Zemira takes us."

Lincoln's jade eyes gleamed as she pressed her body into his.

"I do like the sound of that name," he whispered.

Then he turned around, looking straight into the black hole. "Ahoy, mates." Lincoln held out his sword and pointed to the portal, keeping his other arm wrapped around his love. "Say goodbye to the Sea of Zemira, for today, we sail into a new world. A new danger." He turned to Nola. "A new adventure."

"Ahoy!" they chanted together. "Ahoy to the Sea of Zemira!"

The story of the siren girl and her ruthless pirate lived on. The Sybil Curse's journey through the roaring seas was filled with magic beyond their imagination. Not a battle, conflict, nor a different world could break their everlasting bond.

The Kroneon took the ship to new worlds and new voyages along with that mighty, fierce, and exceptionally brave crew of pirates.

ACKNOWLEDGMENTS

Thank you to my incredibly talented friend, Laura Morales.

Not only did you put your heart into editing this story, but you have been the most amazing friend and cheerleader throughout this journey. I feel blessed to have met you and know that our friendship will only grow from here.

Thank you to my hardworking proofreader, Courtney Caccavallo. To my beta readers who read this story before formatting. You are all a part of this journey with me.

To my husband, who had to spend many days of listening to me talk like a pirate and sing sea shanties to get in the mindset. Love you with all my heart!

ABOUT THE AUTHOR

D.L. Blade grew up in California and studied at the California Healing Arts College, going on to work as a massage therapist for thirteen years. D.L. now lives in Colorado, where she worked as a real estate agent before deciding to concentrate on her family and writing.

D.L. always loved writing, concentrating on poetry, rather than prose when she was younger. That changed, however, when she had a dream one night and decided to write a book about it. In her spare time, D.L. enjoys a wide variety of hobbies, including reading, writing, attending rock concerts, and spending time outdoors with her family, camping, and going on outings.

In the future, D.L. hopes she can continue to write exciting novels that will captivate her readers and bring them into the worlds she creates with her imagination.

CPSIA information can be obtained
at www.ICGtesting.com
Printed in the USA
LVHW021205240921
698652LV00010B/507